About the Author

After twenty years working in IT for a Financial Services Company in London, Andrew Salter moved back to the West Country, where he now spends his time hiking the Dorset – Devon borderland and the local coastline. He developed *Island on Fire* from an original film screenplay that was probably too ambitious and costly for a first-time writer. His other interests include military history, cricket, football and music.

Island on Fire

Andrew Salter

Island on Fire

Olympia Publishers
London

www.olympiapublishers.com
OLYMPIA PAPERBACK EDITION

A CIP catalogue record for this title is
available from the British Library.

ISBN: 978-1-80439-333-8

This is a work of fiction.
Names, characters, places and incidents originate from the writer's
imagination. Any resemblance to actual persons, living or dead, is
purely coincidental.

First Published in 2023

Olympia Publishers
Tallis House
2 Tallis Street
London
EC4Y 0AB

Printed in Great Britain

Dedication

For Ben.

Chapter 1

Who knew how long the fire had been burning. Weeks, months, maybe even since the first day of the war. Mortimer was lucky; he had a window with a grandstand view. He slept during the day to get the full benefit of the glowing orange fireball at night, mesmerised like a Stone Age man watching the lightning burn the forest down. You take your pleasures where you can in solitary confinement; twenty-one hours a day in the cell, thirty minutes to wash, two hours' exercise in the yard, thirty minutes for lunch in the canteen. All other meals served at home.

Sheerness Maximum Security Prison stood on a flat grey uninhabited strip of land off the Kent coast, accessible only at low tide. A soap factory stood half a mile away inland to the south, hit mistakenly by two Reagan Mk 1 missiles, according to the government. One missile could be a mistake, but two? The factory was left to burn out on its own. But the fire refused to die.

The US knew what it really was – a bio-chemical weapons development facility. It was built close enough to the continent for scientific and military personnel of the Homeland to come and go as they pleased on their quest to develop a fatal knockout weapon without the mutually assured destruction of nuclear Armageddon. Weapons wanted by both sides, weapons feared by both sides; the ultimate soap, the ultimate cleansing force.

The sun rose an hour ago. Mortimer did not hear the steel door open or the footsteps approach his bed but he did feel the blast of cold water strike his face. It might as well have been a blowtorch. Eyes still shut, he banged his head into the wall before the recoil bounced him off the narrow bed onto the floor face down, a few inches from the tip of a leather boot. Mortimer opened his eyes.

"Fucking spastic," spat Callaghan.

The prison officer withdrew his boot slowly and put the plastic bottle that served as a blowtorch back into his pocket. Mortimer looked up at Callaghan, the overseer's gut tucked into his black tunic like a sack of blancmange. Over fifty, closer to five foot than six, with eyes and mouth far too small for a hairless head the size and shape of a miniature gravestone, Callaghan was where he wanted to be. Too old to be called up for the frontline but he still got to hide behind a uniform and see a man's face next to his boot. Cracking heads in Sheerness was a lot easier than fighting US marines street by street in the north.

In a fair contest, it would be no contest. Mortimer, six feet two and a half, lean, forty-one and an occasional martial arts practitioner in his past. Even after the rigours of eighteen months' solitary at Sheerness, Mortimer fancied his chances with Callaghan.

"Get up."

Mortimer lifted himself to his feet.

"Move."

Mortimer walked past Callaghan through the open cell door and stopped to attention without looking at the two prison guards stood either side.

Mortimer knew this was the day he had been waiting for since his conviction for murder. He was ready for it and he would give them nothing.

Mortimer felt the gaze of the taller guard on his left, at least a few inches taller than him. What was he staring at? What did he want to see? Tears, a broken man or maybe just a curiosity at wanting to know how a man acts when he knows he will be dead in fifteen minutes. Later, he even might reflect where he would finish in the league table of self-respect and stoical dignity when faced with the ultimate test. Mortimer did not twitch or turn his head. His eyes were a long way from this place. This was all the spectators would get.

"Cuffs." The guard on the left now spoke.

Mortimer held out his wrists in front of his face and the guard on the left obliged.

Callaghan clicked briskly past the three men and continued down the corridor.

"Move." The taller guard spoke again.

Mortimer set off before the guards at an urgent pace, each pace a little bit wider and a little bit quicker than the last one, forcing them to keep up, to stretch their legs in an unacceptable display of disrespect. The tall guard reached him first and swung his truncheon hard against the back of Mortimer's knees, which sent him sprawling onto the concrete floor.

"He don't stand up too good any more," sneered the tall guard.

The shorter guard, no more than twenty-one, grinned like an idiot.

After a few more corridors and no more fuss, Mortimer emerged into a walled courtyard. On one side stood a handful of dark-grey-uniformed officers from the prison and a government representative in civilian clothes. No sign of the governor. Well, what did Mortimer expect at seven thirty a.m.? All that exercise had made Mortimer sweat. His heavy cotton navy-blue jump-suit stuck to the backs of his legs, his buttocks and the inside of his crotch. As usual, the synthetic paper underwear had disintegrated before the end of the month. Another two days and he would have got a new set. Forget about a new prison jump-suit: That's another ninety-two days away.

Mortimer stopped to take in the gallows stood at the other end of the courtyard. He swung his head back to look up to the sky: grey and overcast. He would not even get to see the sun for the last time.

The tall guard gently, even mildly respectfully, tapped Mortimer on the back of his leg to nudge him forward. He looked down at the tapped leg and saw the end of a coiled chain lying at his feet that must have been missed by the morning watch. Mortimer dropped down, grabbed the chain and swung the end of it around the ankles of the tall guard. The guard raised his baton over Mortimer but missed his chance as he fell backwards, chain pulled tight around his ankles. The young guard froze. Callaghan pulled out his pistol and Mortimer raised his hands in the air. Both looked down at the guard awkwardly trying to unravel his lanky legs.

"You don't stand up too well." Mortimer could not help himself.

An utterly pointless outburst of defiance and Mortimer knew it. But what could they do, shoot him? And it gave his audience and Callaghan something to remember. Especially Callaghan, his incompetence plainly visible to his superiors.

Callaghan tried to contain his anger but his crimson face gave it away. He raised his pistol and jabbed it towards the gallows.

"Move," he growled, the voice hoarse so as not to draw any more attention.

Mortimer advanced towards the gallows then moved slowly and heavily up the three steps to heaven. His executioner, a man

12

in his mid-fifties with hair the same colour as the morning sky, in a matching uniform, waited on the platform. He stood by the noose, holding an electronic tablet reader. It flashed a mugshot of Mortimer and displayed his personal details. The grey man started, "Are you William Alexander Mortimer, age forty-one, born fifth November 1991?"

"I cannot disagree... unfortunately," Mortimer replied. The grey man jabbed his finger at the screen twice.

"Please confirm your number."

Mortimer sighed. "743851."

One more jab at the screen. "Good," said the grey man.

"That's a lotta prisoners," said Mortimer.

The grey man looked up but avoided Mortimer's eyes. "Would you turn around and step backwards, please."

Mortimer turned to stare at the dignitaries, and after a few seconds he nodded at them. They stared back but no-one returned the gesture. He then stepped back and planted his feet into two footprints cast in a metal base directly under the noose.

"Please ensure that you are standing in the foot-holes provided," said the hangman, stood now at Mortimer's right-hand side. He pressed the red button that protruded from the right-hand strut and the noose lowered itself soundlessly a few centimetres above Mortimer's head.

Mortimer stared upwards at the whitish-grey clouded sky. So, what were the best bits and what were the worst: Probably playing football on sodden pitches and cricket under blazing blue skies. For a few seconds, Mortimer was there again.

Roaming the fields, the woods and countryside around his Dorset village. Just like now, you were on your own. And then sex, especially when he got good at it in his late twenties as the frequency and variety multiplied at a decent rate. And sex was like sport back then: You got yourself into decent shape, strode onto the pitch, engaged the opponent, took your opportunities and got it. But Mortimer was not thinking of the raw physical act but the girls, the faces. Some he should have tried harder with, others he probably spent too much time on. Where were they all now? Shame they were not standing next to the dignitaries now, tearfully waving goodbye.

All of these physical distractions had prevented him from planning for a higher purpose. Could he have achieved more and done better? Become the sort of person who runs a prison or a country or at least ascended into the middle management levels of a medium-sized private bank? Never. These people had always been a plague on his life: Authority figures, management control freaks; at best a tedious and unnecessary never-ending presence, at worst prepared to kill you for defending your own wife and son. Hard to say whether it was all worth it; marriage, family, then this. Maybe Mortimer should have thought about it beforehand, but he had stopped walking in the countryside a long time ago. At least if he were a Christian, Mortimer knew he would meet his son again very soon. But he was not a Christian and had no plans to change his beliefs because he was about to die. Any God worth their name would see through such cowardice and insincerity. You knew you were going to die since day one and now you are actually going to croak, you come crying to me. No. Mortimer was not going to apologise to anyone or ask for the key to eternal paradise. God would judge him anyway and that was all fine. There was nothing more to say.

For a split-second Mortimer felt proud of himself. He was not a coward or a hypocrite after all and he even felt dry between his legs.

Then the light was switched off. The grey man had nimbly

14

dropped a black nylon hood over his head. Still enough air to breathe but pitch black. Welcome to death. He felt the noose tighten around his neck, the grey man careful to position it into exactly the right position for a quick snap. You cannot ask for more than that.

"This will make it easier. Nice 'n' quick," he said quietly.

Suddenly there was a crackling sound near his ear, like a radio being tuned erratically. It was the ear piece worn by the hangman. The executioner dropped his hands from Mortimer's neck.

"Now... But... Yes, straight away, sir." The hangman sounded harassed as he spoke into the microphone concealed within his collar.

A second of silence then the man's hands were back around his neck again, no longer careful but yanking and tugging anxiously like a child encountering an overwrapped present on Christmas morning.

He pulled the noose up over Mortimer's face, which clamped the cheap nylon bag tight in his open mouth. Mortimer grunted then shook his head wildly to loosen the hood. Now it was caught on his nose as the hangman tried to pull it off. He said there would be no mistakes.

"Cut him down." One of the uniformed dignitaries ran up to the gallows with both prison guards in tow.

"Cut the rope, you idiot," he shouted.

Callaghan had not joined the commotion but stood in front of the dignitaries, quietly fuming at this outcome.

No need – Mortimer had twisted his head back, enough to allow the hangman to peel off the noose and hood. Everything now seemed a lot brighter. Mortimer squinted at the whiteness of the sky and then slumped to his knees.

The officer who wanted to save Mortimer now stared at him, hands on hips. Mortimer looked up at him. "Looks like I am in Hell."

"You will be," smiled the officer.

The rest of the audience started to leave through a door at the side of the courtyard.

The officer spoke again. "The governor has reprieved you. The Shield Brigade needs new recruits. You are to be transferred to Enfield barracks at six p.m. today."

He then turned around and paced back towards the dignitaries.

Mortimer jumped off the platform, ignored the bemused Callaghan and walked back to the doorway he had passed through five minutes earlier. For the first time today, Mortimer did not know what to do. He had planned and prepared to die, not to live.

Callaghan, the taller guard and the novice followed Mortimer through the doorway.

"Christ, what chance have we got at the front... really scraping the barrel of shit." Callaghan was not going to hold back even if the now formerly condemned man was about to join the Shield.

"Of course, he will probably get shot for cowardice. Shame, would have been a lot quicker if we'd finished the job."

The streak of piss grunted a stupid animal sound in appreciation.

They reached the cell door, where Mortimer stopped. Still laughing at his own joke, Callaghan did not see Mortimer swing round and throw his fist low into his paunch. The bully folded in half and sank to his knees. The novice grabbed Mortimer around the shoulders without any conviction. A sharp elbow to the chest sent the spindly sidekick sprawling against the wall. But Callaghan was up again. Head down, he rammed into the side of Mortimer, knocking him onto the floor. The bull then tripped on Mortimer's ankle and fell face down, smothering Mortimer's chest and arms. Both guards grabbed their commanding officer and pulled him off Mortimer, who still managed to plant his knee into his undercarriage. This pointless resistance led to more than a few well-placed kicks to his ribcage before he was also dragged to his feet. The novice then opened the cell door and his senior colleagues hurled Mortimer by his shoulders onto the cell floor and slammed the door shut.

As his right shoulder careered into the leg of the metal bed frame, a stab of pain then the electrical sensation of an awakened nerve told him it really was true. He was alive.

Chapter 2

Enfield barracks had been erected in Theobalds Park, not far from Winston Churchill Way, just off the A10 in north London. The government had requisitioned the wide-open greenspace for military use a few days after the US army landed in Scotland and Wales. More specifically, it was used by the Shield Brigade, the armed wing of the Shield Movement, to assemble and organise new recruits. These were not normal recruits but ex-convicts forcibly conscripted from the prisons of the United Kingdom and the Homeland Europe. Each barracks housed up to one thousand two hundred men across twenty wooden huts, each containing enough bunks for sixty men.

Mortimer was far-away in a better place when the morning sirens wailed. All the excitement of his last day at Sheerness followed by a four-hour journey in the back of a military lorry to Enfield had drained him. He had arrived at ten p.m., accepted the offer of a half-loaf of bread and a slab of processed meat that might have been pork then happily followed the guard to his bunk in Hut Eight. It was a shock to suddenly share his sleeping arrangements with others but he soon fell into the best sleep he had had for what seemed a very long time.

His fellow conscripts roused themselves from their bunks with conviction, as if someone had pressed a button in each of them. The double doors of the barracks opened automatically and the sirens got louder. Mortimer opened one eye, rolled over and watched the men filing and jogging out through the open doorway. Hundreds of prisoners, in the same blue boilersuit garb as Mortimer, now congregated in the prison square, lining up in columns just as they did every morning at six thirty a.m. Eventually, Mortimer slipped out of his bunk and followed the stragglers out of the hut and joined the back row. The siren stopped.

Over a thousand men stood in stiff silence on the main square of Enfield barracks ready for roll call. The square was in fact a rectangle surrounded by six watch towers each manned by armed guards. And there was no call at roll call. The drone hovered above the men, slowly and silently counting each man. After a minute or so, the siren started again but now let out three intermittent blasts deeper than the alarm call. All conscripts were present and correct.

Then a clear, calm and soothing female voice spoke over the camp intercom, the sort of automated voice used pre-war to inform and re-assure passengers at railways stations of an impending service delay or cancellation.

"Your camp commander will address you in five seconds... Your camp commander will address you in four seconds..." The voice counted down. "Your camp commander will address you in three seconds... Your camp commander will address you in two seconds... Your camp commander will now address you."

On cue, the barrack commander in the black tunic and trousers of the Shield Brigade appeared on the balcony protruding from the concrete administration building high above the square. The middle-aged man then began to read from an electronic tablet in hand.

"The following convicted men are required for Shield combat operations. Four... Five... Two... Two..." Pause. "Seven... Six... Six... Two..." No names, just numbers. Anyone convicted of murder or man-slaughter was an automatic pick for the frontline.

Next to Mortimer stood Vukovic, a Serbian mafia enforcer, who had carved out a successful career maiming and murdering any rivals to the Red Star gang. Unfortunately, this all came to an abrupt end in 2032 when their friends in the Metropolitan Police were found passing the gang confidential information in return for bribes. Eliminating rival gangs suited everyone: monopolies are loved by governments and criminals alike. It keeps everything simple and predictable and the same people in charge. But it all got out of hand when the local MP, a rising government minister, Gerald Parkinson, wanted a cut as well. Not content to hide the cash in an offshore bank account like any other self-respecting representative of the people, he had to set up a children's charity. This certainly brought him more exposure than he had hoped, particularly when news broke that the charity imported children from all over the world to serve the Very Important Paedophile class that proliferated in elite political circles.

This was manna to the growing political fortunes of the Shield movement. Everything they said about elected governments was true: hypocritical, corrupt and criminal as well as harbouring a nest of filthy perverts. But of course this did not prevent them from doing a deal with their enemy. In return for their support in the House, the government handed over control of internal security matters, known sentimentally as the Home Office, to the Shield.

"Eight... Eight... One... Six... Three... Two." The numbers went on like a sort of dead man's bingo. No-one on the square even twitched. After about a hundred numbers, "Seven... Four... Three... Eight... Five... One," Mortimer dropped his head to his chest and sighed with deep satisfaction. He wanted to punch the air this time rather than a guard. He really was getting out. The Serb, Vukovic, stared at Mortimer.

"We're off to war. Looking forward to it," hissed the Serb to Mortimer in that slightly mannered breathy tone common to the English accent of East Europeans.

Mortimer turned to his new comrade in arms and immediately recognised the red star tattooed under Vukovic's chin. The bold tattoo indicated a man of status, a man who was protected and could not be touched, a man who had probably spent most of his life urinating in the milk of human kindness. At Sheerness he always avoided the gang members, which, being a condemned man in solitary confinement was easy. But not any more; Mortimer knew he was amongst scum now, real scum of the earth, a lot worse than petty-minded uniformed thugs like Callaghan. Mortimer may have been convicted for murder, but a one-off reaction to defend his family from peril did not make him a career psychopath.

Vukovic stared back at the anonymous Mortimer and wondered what his crimes were and whether he was a man worthy of his respect.

"It's okay to kill for the Shield… that's why they want us. Tell me, what is your weapon?" On he mumbled in his mocking mock-English.

Mortimer stared at the ground. "A full belly…" he said. The Serb threw his head back and laughed.

"Six… Four… Four… Three… One… Twenty-two." It was the last number. The commander looked up from the handheld tablet and paused. "All numbers not called must return to their barracks. Numbers called remain standing."

The uncalled immediately broke from the lines and scurried

back to their barracks.

Whilst Mortimer pondered how to avoid any communication with the Serbian psychopath without causing offence, two green military transport lorries swung through the large double gate at the far end of the square and pulled up under the balcony.

A detachment of about twenty black-uniformed Shield soldiers armed with sub-machine guns jumped out from the back of each lorry. The only soldier without a sub-machine gun at the ready stepped out in front of his men. He was the officer in charge. He unnecessarily raised his right arm to get the attention of the conscripts.

"You must all report to the train station about a mile away... my guards will escort you." The guards fanned out to the left, leaving a clear path to the gates. Mortimer was not going to wait. Without a second glance at the guns, he strode towards the exit. He might have been last out of the barracks but he was not going to be last out of the square.

It was an easy walk along a recently laid tarmac track that ran all the way up to a railway buffer. No one tried to make a run for it into the countryside around them; the surrounding fields made it an effective killing ground for the escort. A line of eight steel freight wagons waited on the railway tracks, their slide doors open and ready for the human cargo to climb aboard. Emblazoned on each door about the height of your average man was the insignia of the Shield: an upside-down silver teardrop with a tapered end on a black field. But there were no tears in the Shield; it was meant to be the classic twelfth-century Norman kite shaped shield in the hands of twenty-first-century design. Mortimer was first aboard his wagon and claimed the far right-hand corner as his seat for the journey.

Chapter 3

Two hours later, the line of steel wagons clanked and juddered into London Bridge station. The doors opened and the Shield recruits jumped out onto an empty platform. Mortimer was happy to be the last man out again.

"Would passengers please make their way to the barriers…" It was that soothing female voice again. But there were no barriers, just a long line of thirty or so grey-uniformed Shield Police, probably the reservists, given the number of middle-aged men and women in their ranks. The rather casual slung-down-at-their side, arms-not-at-the-ready way they held their semi-automatic weapons marked them out for this kind of duty. A couple of guards stood at the opposite end of the platform to deter any wild optimists with plans to see the sights. No-one would get far if they tried to make a break for it. Sensors were sewn into the padding of their prison wear, which meant every camera and patrol drone would identify you in minutes. So what looked like a crack detachment of industrial cleaners shuffled towards the line of guards, who parted to form a gauntlet to funnel each man towards the station exit. Behind the line of guards, a few bored-looking, arms-crossed-over-their-chests black-uniformed officers watched the procession.

Mortimer felt strangely upbeat that morning even though he was back again in a railway station where all his troubles had started. The journey had been no more cramped and uncomfortable than he remembered as a commuter and his fellow passengers were not that much worse than the plugged-in zombies he used to share his mornings with on the 7.22 a.m. from Strawberry Hill.

Outside the station, the conscripts were split into smaller groups of twenty and then packed into Aardvarks waiting on the side of the road. Aardvarks were the black-armoured personnel carriers used by the Shield to police civilian areas as well as move men at the front.

They were on their way for registration and screening at Shield House. Shield House used to be the London University Administration building, the imposing art deco monolith in Bloomsbury, central London. In the unfortunate event of a German invasion in the last century, this same building would have become the UK headquarters of the black-uniformed mid-twentieth-century European death cult known as the SS.

Heavy traffic slowed the vehicle holding Mortimer along Shaftesbury Avenue. Private vehicles, with their own armed escorts if they were bankers or businessmen friendly to the regime, competed with the cabs and buses carrying workers in and out of the White Zone.

The White Zone was the inner security ring that stretched from Hammersmith in the west to Greenwich in the east and from Streatham in the south to Hampstead in the north. Armed checkpoints were stationed at all the main routes into the White Zone.

A large BMW had ground to a halt in the road due to bullet holes in both rear tyres. SecuriState, the outsourced private security group who had replaced the old Metropolitan Police, would be charging the BMW occupants for the use of their bullets. But this was the least of the car occupants' worries; two men and one woman who could have been of South Asian or

South European origin were stretched over the bonnet with their arms and legs tightly bound. As the Aardvark slowed past, two SecuriState men carried the largest of their three captives from each end like a badly wrapped carpet and slid him into their van. Mortimer drifted off and missed the rest of the journey.

The glowing white fortress that was Shield House sent out the right message: the Shield is big and you are small. The central courtyard was enclosed on four sides by tall rectangular concrete blocks dotted with small windows on the upper floors that had once been centres of learning for the students of London University. The windows from the third floor down had been completely bricked up.

The doors of each Aardvark swung open and the guards waiting outside shouted in unison, "Out, out." They had done this sort of thing before. Mortimer, next to the door, fell out first, followed by the others. But these were not the reserved reservists of London Bridge station but a far more zealous unit of the Shield Security force. Once the parked Aardvarks were emptied, the commanding officer came forward and threw out his right arm like a traffic cop. He pointed at a large open doorway in the far wall away from the parked Aardvarks. The entrance was high enough and wide enough to swallow a line of well-behaved Indian elephants.

"Single file, gentlemen. And then through the doors... Now..." the officer shouted. His men spread out behind him, not really in any formation but with sub-machine guns at the ready.

The man in front was too slow and forced Mortimer to drag his right foot in a slightly exaggerated limp so as not to stumble on the back of his heels. Even before he entered, Mortimer could see the flickering, almost strobing white light and hear the recorded sound of warfare. Inside, the line of recruits veered around to the left and entered a long wide corridor with a low suspended ceiling, no more than a few feet above their heads. The light came from a widescreen film playing along the entire length of the corridor walls. It was footage from the frontline: Shield troops attacked burning buildings, shoved their guns into the shoulders of forlorn-looking US POWs and smiled at the camera; the silver shield on a black banner fluttered from the top of a tall Victorian building still standing, unlike its surrounds in a northern city. These images of Shield conquest were accompanied by the sound of exploding shells and cheering voices, the usual cacophony of victory.

On top of all this entertainment, the female voice issued instructions.

"Keep moving towards the light. Your future is the future of the Shield. Your loyalty is your honour. Keep moving towards the light." Again and again.

The ceiling angled downwards and the corridor narrowed as the slow moving single file of recruits got closer to the four bright white strip-lights shining from above. Mortimer, like everyone else, raised his forearm to protect his eyes. The film show now was no longer really visible but the sound and flickering still contributed to the all-round sense of disorientation.

Mortimer almost walked into the same man again but he suddenly disappeared into an unseen doorway to his right. Mortimer lifted his head up, still covered by his forearm, to see a line of doors on both sides, each guarded by a single black uniform wearing a dark visor. This building served as a student halls of residence before the war.

Mortimer was looking in the other direction when an extended arm yanked him through the doorway into a side room. Out of the blinding white light and inside a dimly lit rectangular box of a room, Mortimer found himself stood in front of two black uniforms. The door closed automatically behind him. The arm had come from the bulkier, broader, motionless one, still with his visor down. The other man was shorter, without a helmet and with a single silver Shield flash on his epaulette. This and the fact he was sat down behind a trestle table showed who was in charge. The man at the desk looked up from his electronic tablet and said nothing.

The TV screen behind his head came alive instead. A bald head with dark eyes and an eye patch over the left eye spoke. "I am Commissioner Hendrick, head of Shield Security. And I welcome you. As a condemned man, you have many unique qualities. And now your fearless character and uncluttered conscience is to be harnessed for a new order fighting side by side with comrades from the Homeland against the enemy on our island. We demand only loyalty and obedience." The head and the voice disappeared and the screen switched off.

For a few seconds, Mortimer stood there thinking. Did everyone get the same message? Were all the men transported today murderers due to be executed? Or was the message tailored for him, a man who was not a murderer?

"Strip, 743851," said the officer. Mortimer was impressed; at Sheerness, the goons got his number wrong regularly. But first time right, that was good. It must be the new order of things. The walls were bare and grey, the uniforms were bare and black and his number was correct. The Shield liked to pride itself on its austerity and efficiency, no unnecessary fripperies to distract it from a higher purpose.

Mortimer unpeeled his sweaty blue prison uniform and threw it to the floor. The officer nodded to Mortimer's right. The naked Mortimer walked into an alcove where there was a toilet

27

in the floor opposite, a shower head above him and a small sink on the wall that could just about fit a pair of adult hands. No space spared. A warm blast of water sprayed him head to toe from above for about twenty seconds, followed by thick globules of soft cream that landed on his head and upper body. Mortimer rubbed the cream over his shaven scalp and into his sweaty, stinking body. Hung on the inside wall was a small rubber towel, like the sort he had used when he went swimming at his sports club many years ago. Once finished, he stepped back in front of the desk to find grey underwear, a folded black tunic and baggy grey moleskin trousers rounded off with military-issue black leather boots.

Mortimer noticed that the man behind the desk seemed more interested in him now; it must have been the protruding eyeballs. The leering officer broke the awkward silence.

"Well, don't just stand there, get dressed."

The same officer was really quite happy for Mortimer to stand there naked all day. Mortimer wanted to ask if the summer wardrobe would be different but thought better of it.

He did as he was told and the officer started again with eyes lowered.

"So, 743851... Everyone keeps their number here."

He glanced down at the tablet.

"Murder... as expected. But with moral justification, it says here. A little old-fashioned," the officer condescended.

"I'm an old-fashioned kind of guy," replied Mortimer.

"Why weren't you just given a long sentence?"

"Well. The man who tried to kill my family was never charged. Someone high-up in the police wanted him off, so I told the judge that when I got out I would track down and kill the piece of shit and the corrupt son-of-a-bitch who set him free,"

Mortimer explained.

"Ah, I understand now… The Shield is your last chance. In return, we expect absolute loyalty at all times. You have been assigned to combat training."

"Where's that?"

"The Ardennes in Belgium, for twelve weeks. Then the frontline."

Chapter 4

Dr Martha Franshell was not a believer but she did believe in science. This was exactly what she was doing that evening, sat at the kitchen table of an unmarried couple in a once prosperous middle-class neighbourhood in Boston, USA.

The black couple, in their mid-thirties, were desperate for a child. Not just any child but the right sort of child, a model that could integrate socially from their first day of schooling to their last without any possibility of deviant behaviour, as measured by the Federal Board of Social Ethics. Successful socialisation would legally entitle the parents to a job with the government or with one of the major corporations. Failure would mean a life of poverty and insecurity in the shanty towns outside the city with the rest of the underclass. The female was pregnant, twelve weeks gone, long enough for Franshell to assess their possible child's future chances. The possible parents knew that what they were doing was illegal but they would only get a heavy fine at worst. The Child Building laws were like the old vice laws: the supplier always got treated worse than the consumer. Franshell would be lucky to get a life sentence.

Franshell sat opposite the couple and tapped into a flat-screen device in her right hand. She needed to retrieve the possible child's profile data for the meeting. The couple stared at their stork, a little disconcerted by her paramilitary dress sense: a thick grey tunic with large pockets on each side, black combat trousers and trainers with reinforced metal toecaps.

"I work for Jemson Hardware. I'm an engineer, and Sylvia works in retail," said the man, a little overweight and a little under six foot but still with a good head of hair.

"In the warehouse actually, a picker controller..." Sylvia said quietly.

Pete and Sylvia both spent their working lives checking that the machines did as they were told. If they were lucky, their child would at least be able to check the people who checked the machines.

"We got to know his chances. We cannot afford a difficult child... he's got to have more than us..." said the man.

"My grandfather, Walt, ran a printing business in Des Moines. Hopefully he's got the entrepreneurial gene." Sylvia smiled sheepishly at her man and placed her hand on his.

"Yes, but entrepreneurial can mean criminal as well," retorted the man.

In her early thirties, with golden brown skin and dark brown eyes, with high cheekbones and long black hair falling over her shoulders, slightly under six feet, Franshell was built more like an athlete than a top-ranking geneticist. She could pass as latino, but it was the Choctaw blood from her grandmother that made her distinct.

"Like Grandpa Walt, he is a boy. Right... let's look at the test results..." She tapped into her screen to retrieve the report then started to read the highlights.

"Brown-eyed, brown hair. He will grow to five foot eleven inches, six foot possibly. Twenty-three per cent chance of anti-social tendencies, seventy per cent chance of above-average intelligence. Actually, there's a correlation between intelligence and anti-social behaviour..."

"No-one in our families has ever been to prison..." Sylvia

stared at her mate with a question mark in her eyes.

"The doctor ain't saying that. We got to keep an open mind," responded Pete, trying to keep his wife calm.

"Well, all the men on my side are over six foot. I've brought some photos." Sylvia bent down and fumbled in her handbag under the table. She pulled out and unfolded a flat-screen device in black leather and placed it on the table between them. It showed her about five years earlier stood next to two taller men. All three of them were smiling at the camera.

Dr Franshell glanced over at the photo then sighed

"Excuse me, but holiday snaps tell me nothing. This is a scientific process."

Sylvia's eyes slid to the tablet. It had been a lovely day, the day she had met her two brothers and their families for a weekend's camping in the Green Mountains in Vermont. The taller of the two brothers had been in the US Marines but was now dead, killed fighting in the UK a few months ago.

She thought she had got over this tragedy, but she had never overcome her deep insecurity on meeting another woman whom she considered prettier or more intelligent than her. And Franshell won on both counts.

"What's wrong with a family photo?" Sylvia raised her voice.

"You heard her…" said Pete. "This is nothing to do with science."

"I bet you have got some on your screen," Sylvia continued.

Franshell looked up from her screen. "I can promise you, hand on heart, I do not have any family photos on this device or any other screen that I own." Pause.

Sylvia picked up the flat-screen device on the table and returned it to her handbag.

"Someone will be in touch within the next twenty-four hours with the date, time and address. Then you have a further forty-eight hours to either accept or decline the proposed treatment. If you do not respond, all communication will cease," Franshell clarified in a quiet monotone.

She stood up, packed the screen device into her ruck-sack and lifted it onto her shoulder. "Now I must go."

Pete and Sylvia stood up. Pete extended his hand. "May I thank you for coming?"

"My pleasure," replied Franshell.

"You're not a normal woman. Why do you do this?" said Sylvia.

"Because someone has to…" Franshell was bored now. She knew she had been in the house too long. She eyed Pete's hand and for a second considered whether to accept it. She always preferred to minimise words and actions and general flummery when meeting a new couple. For personal safety reasons she did not want to leave any impression.

"I've got to go now."

At that moment, the room fell into complete darkness. The spotlights in the kitchen ceiling switched off as did all the lights in the flat. Sylvia screamed. Franshell spun around and launched herself at the back door a few yards away that led out into the garden. She grabbed the door handle but was thrown back by two policemen forcing it the other way.

"Vice and Virtue. On your knees," shouted the balaclava wrapped head in the kitchen doorway. He then raised a long handled torch above his head that could equally serve as a baton to emphasise the point. Next to him stood another policeman with the barrel of his semi-automatic rifle trained on the three immoralists in the kitchen, the thin red infrared beam moving between their faces. Each policeman wore a blue tunic and trousers with the initials V-V in large, shiny black letters across his back. The torch-holder wore a balaclava rather than a helmet because he was the officer in charge of the unit.

Vice and Virtue, formally known as the Committee for the Promotion of Virtue and Prevention of Vice, had been introduced by the Constitutional Theocratic movement to enforce the moral code of the new Republic. Any activities that intervened in the creation of human life other than basic medical assistance at the birth, such as gene therapy or abortion, were deemed to be morally wrong and therefore illegal.

The religious police division were called the 'Black and Blues' not just for the styling of the uniform but also because that was how you would often end up if you met them.

The two improbable parents dropped to their knees in fear. Even though the infrared beam made her squint, Franshell stood there in disrespect. From behind, one of the back-door entrants jabbed her hard under the ribs with his right fist. Franshell retched in pain and could not stop herself folding to the ground. Her assailant then yanked her right arm and her left arm back behind her head. She yelped but did not resist. The other policeman grabbed her outstretched wrists and wrapped them together with a tight plastic green cord. He gave a final tug to check her bindings before the infrared red beam withdrew from her face. Franshell bowed her head, closed her eyes and breathed deeply to slow everything down.

Sylvia sobbed quietly, still on her knees. She would now be tagged and monitored by her nearest federal medical centre. She would have to have the child as God intended without any artificial intermediation. She would also probably lose her job. Pete bowed his head and kept his arms behind his back and quietly stared at the kitchen floor.

The four policemen ignored the couple. They had only come for Dr Martha Franshell, a leading light of the Life Underground and on the most-wanted list for over six months. Officially declared a terrorist organisation, the LU supplied illegal abortion drugs or provided gene-based therapies to modify an unborn child. As well as being one of the technicians within the movement, Franshell exposed herself to greater risk by meeting and advising clients like Peter and Sylvia.

The torch-holder in charge spoke. "Dr Martha Franshell," he barked. "I am arresting you for acts of moral terrorism under the New Constitutional Code."

The United States of America was now governed by the word of God. Any human activity that contradicted the literal truth of the Bible, or, those carefully selected passages of the good book that could be used to stamp on the face of individual freedom were now illegal. And what Dr Franshell had been doing went way beyond wearing a short skirt in church on Sunday, she was an enemy of the state.

Chapter 5

St Genevieve Federal Correction Centre was situated on the outskirts of Boston, a five-storey concrete box surrounded by a barbed-wire fence and armed guards. It used to be a regional head office for a long-gone publishing company but was now committed to obtaining information rather than providing it. This was a holding pen for those guilty of serious crimes, where the federal authorities would decide whether to publicly try you or move you quietly inland without trial to a penal colony.

Warden Hughes, the manager of this information retrieval facility, stared through the one-way window at the prostrate figure of Dr Franshell. She was laid out on a low wooden table a little longer and a lot wider than her. Hughes was a bespectacled, stout, well-built man in his late fifties with a bald head, a thick pointy beard and a medium-sized beer belly. His beard was generous enough to make it look like he had his head on upside down.

It had been a few years he had witnessed an Interrogation. He had stepped out of the ring once his career moved into middle management. But even from behind the screen, Hughes could smell the musty, airless chamber on the other side. It brought back many happy memories of doing God's work, although he was never as bad as some of them. Breaking a man physically and mentally was a lot more rewarding than report writing, planning budgets, and managing staff as well as all the political bullshit in his role. But the job promotion and extra salary had improved his more than reasonable pension, which would mean many happy years sailing his yacht off the New England coast.

And today was a first for Hughes in his years in the Federal Correction Service and something that he could not miss: the first woman to be interrogated in his facility. As interrogators, females could be zealous, frequently over-zealous and were actually reprimanded more than the men for not following procedure. There would be no female interrogators today and Hughes was there to ensure compliance to all relevant safety procedures.

Franshell lay quiet and motionless, face up and stiff with fear. Her arms and legs were tied and buckled to the low wooden table in the shape of a cross. Her prison-issue orange jumpsuit was pulled down to her waist, exposing her top half, covered only by a thin white t-shirt. The table was no higher than twelve inches off the floor, supported on four stout and stumpy legs. It was the sort of table you would expect to rest a cup of coffee on whilst flicking through a glossy interior design magazine rather than re-enact the religious inquisition of the sixteenth century.

A plastic bucket of water full to the brim, a piece of blue cloth the same size as a tea towel and a roll of cellophane had been left on the cell floor behind Franshell's head.

The cell was lit by a bright white strip light along the full length of the low hanging ceiling. The two men responsible for persuading Franshell of the benefits of co-operation with the federal authorities stood either side of her. Jake, the shorter of the two, with a blond crewcut, in his early thirties, handed a small rubber-encased flat-screen device to his assistant.

"Make your mark, Scooter." Jake smiled, as he really did believe Scooter could not write. Scooter had been rolling up his sleeves very slowly in the preceding ten minutes. His white nylon button-down shirt was too tight for his large frame. But now he had finished, the sleeves were tightly bound above the elbow and he was ready.

Scooter stabbed his finger against the handcuff icon on the screen and handed it back to Jake almost in one motion. Jake sniggered, took the device and completed the interrogation record on screen.

Scooter loomed and leered over Franshell. "Well. You're very quiet... first time in years, I'll bet."

He hailed from a small farm a few miles south of Montgomery in Alabama, where quiet women were appreciated.

"Why, that's fine by me, sinner. I do like a woman who respects a man by keeping her mouth shut." His words slowed to become more deliberate to emphasise his deeply held complex philosophical beliefs.

Franshell met his eyes.

"I don't think we have much in common." She spoke curtly but could not hide her Southern accent. Scooter grinned at the accent, a wide stupid monkey face if ever there was one.

"Oh, I think we do... You're from..."

"You cousins or something? Quit this bullshit. Let's get on with it."

Jake had finished with the electronic reader now.

Jake Canning was from Buffalo, New York State, degree-educated and brimming with aspiration to join the senior ranks of the domestic security service in Washington away from the hicks and crackers like Scooter. He understood their importance as the foot-soldiers of the Christian States revolution, the militias who bravely stormed federal government buildings across Texas and the South before the army stepped in to take control. And the regime loved to eulogise these true patriots and their backwoods lifestyle on TV. But all that God, girls and guns redneck porn just kept them poor and stupid.

"Right then, Jakey Jakey… Let's see Miss Wet T-shirt."

Jake carefully placed the folded towel over Franshell's eyes, and with his left hand pressed it firmly against her forehead. When the lights went out, Franshell started to breathe heavily. She knew she had to get her breathing right, slowly and deeply to relax as much as possible to lower her pulse and reduce the oxygen required for the coming assault. Scooter stared at her chest heaving gently and was surprised. It was the only part of her body moving. He expected her to start twisting and writhing about now or at least try to kick out the leg straps like they usually did. As per procedure, Scooter extended his left forearm over her midriff until he could hold the other side of the table. This ensured the victim's body did not over-convulse on the table and remained under control. But his right hand did not make it. En route, as not per procedure he tugged her t-shirt downwards. He loomed even closer as the stretched material emphasised Franshell's small, firm breasts, typical of an athletic build. Her hard nipples pushed upwards but thankfully still under her t-shirt. Franshell took deeper, longer breaths.

"Pretty. Very pretty, like puppy dogs' ears," leered Scooter.

Jake raised the plastic bucket of water behind Franshell's head. "You got her?"

"Nice and tight, sir."

Franshell breathed in hard and exhaled harder than before to clear her body of as much oxygen as possible. Jake tipped up the end of the bucket to release a steady stream of freezing water onto the clothed face. Franshell thought she had prepared for this but nothing can stop your body going into shock. She shuddered long and hard as the tremor ran though her arms and legs, shaking her hands and feet in the clasps. But she still held her breath. The water flooded her nose and poured through her sinus channels. She tried to close every orifice but this only made her feel her conscious was shutting down.

But there was a light. The cloth over her left eye had thinned to let in a glimmer from the strip light. She concentrated on it as hard as she could and still held her breath. She wanted to draw in air deep into her lungs. But that was the beginning of the end. The dam would burst, the water would rush in and she would lose control. They would then stop, give her a few breaths and start again. But the mind would be broken, ready only to lose control again in even less time than before. And it would be repeated again until the spirit disappeared as well. But she had to breathe. As another heavy cold wave swept over her, she exhaled as slowly as she could through her nose for a few seconds then stopped, knowing it would come again. Another cold shock, then another few seconds to breathe out.

Suddenly the cloth was ripped off her face and Scooter released his arm. Franshell heaved her head forward then emptied her lungs frantically before sucking in great gasps of air. Her t-shirt was soaked. Scooter still smiled the same bug-eyed smile of a man watching a porn video who had not yet finished himself.

"Okay… twenty seconds." Jake spoke behind Franshell.

But it was no more than ten seconds when Jake pulled her head back and the cloth went back on again.

This time, the cold wave filled and chilled her whole head. She could tell her sinuses were probably full because the drowning sensation was not getting any worse. Franshell restarted the intermittent breathing technique she had learnt from the LU. For a split-second she thought she was getting used to it. But she wasn't really. The freezing pressure moved through her body like a high-speed virus. She wanted the water to stop, the cloth taken off, get off the table and shake her head. Then, Scooter tugged hard on her t-shirt. He also found it hard to control himself. He rested his right-hand palm on her breast. Uncle Luther was back. The pig-ignorant, lustful redneck back home in Sunny Pines mobile home park. Her body fell limp and lifeless, her breathing tightened but control was there just like all those years ago at bedtime.

Then the waterfall stopped and the cloth was unstuck with such force that it jerked her head to the left. She furiously gasped and gulped for air. Scooter could not help himself. "What a pretty little mouth."

"You can let go now."

Jake swivelled his eyes to the right. He tried to divert Scooter to the brown-uniformed man standing inside the doorway opposite them. Captain O'Reilly was the official Federal Interrogator Witness, in charge of Jake and Scooter.

"How many rounds?" He walked towards the table. Jake stepped back and Scooter returned from his lustful trance.

"Only two. Twenty seconds and twenty-five seconds... It's her first time, sir." Scooter sniggered.

"Okay. Let's untie her and get her over to the wall." A bare wooden chair stood a few paces in from the far wall, directly under a white semi-circle fixed on the ceiling. The light was switched off.

From behind the screen, Hughes applauded as the two torturers raised her off the table. He was impressed. The woman had shown greater strength and dignity than most men. And she had left a clean table.

Each interrogator took one of her shoulders and walked her limp frame to the chair like a piece of furniture that might collapse at any moment. She was sat down and her arms tied to the back of each leg.

Warden Hughes eyed her soaked hair hanging limply down her back, as if she had just got out of the sea. This made him think of the only woman in his life, the *Liquid Lady*, his thirty-seven-foot Sunseeker swaying in the breeze off the New England coast. The sky was blue and he was gently manoeuvring her across the Nantucket Sound in the early afternoon. And he was a long way away from all this degradation and cruelty.

Franshell threw her head back, stretched out her legs and slumped in the chair as best she could. She breathed heavily out of shock rather than out of necessity. And she found it hard to empty her mind of Uncle Luther. She had not thought about him since the day after her seventeenth birthday when she had set light to his trailer with him sleeping inside.

Jake and Scooter left the cell without a second glance at O'Reilly. When she opened her eyes, O'Reilly was standing opposite her, arms crossed.

"Dr Franshell. The last of the East Coast heretics." He smiled at Franshell. "You do know what happened to the others."

"You killed them," replied Franshell.

O'Reilly smiled. "The FBI are smart guys."

"So why not me?"

O'Reilly's smiled turned down and his arms pushed out at his sides.

"I ask the questions here, bitch."

Even in her state, Franshell could not resist a slight smile that quickly disappeared. The smile of someone who knows they have annoyed an inferior being but does not want to let on; O'Reilly had lost control of the situation already. She bet he was a full-on red-blooded fundamentalist.

"Play ball and you'll be cleaning the toilets in a federal

penitentiary out West. Else you'll join your friends." O'Reilly now circled around the seated Franshell. "We need the names and contacts of the Californian chapter, the leading heretics working out of San Francisco. You're in constant contact. We've broken your encryption." He completed the circle.

"No-one's talked. No-one, have they?" Franshell was thinking a lot faster than her slow, breathy drawl.

"You want to go under again, do you?" He jabbed his index finger at Franshell.

"A few had... accidents. Brake failure, hit and run, disappeared, but no-one's talked." Franshell coughed. As her throat cleared, so did her mind.

"That's why I'm here."

"Look, you rationalist bitch, I have given you something, very dear to you." Hughes gripped the ends of the arms of the chair and leant over Franshell. She could feel his warm, stale breath on her face.

"A choice."

Franshell knew that California was still under a State of Emergency, a hotbed of rationalist resistance to the new Christian order and she also knew the names of the leading scientists and doctors working for the LU in San Francisco.

Franshell pulled her legs back and twisted her spine into the depth of the wooden chair, which forced her back and shoulders up. She felt more comfortable facing O'Reilly upright.

"So, who are the doctors in San Francisco? Who is Mendel? Is he the main man?"

O'Reilly pulled back a few feet and put his hands on his hips.

"An Austrian monk who discovered the laws of genetic inheritance in the nineteenth century by observing the characteristics of pea plants..." started Franshell.

"Don't be blowing me smoke, bitch…"

"You mean like being born of a virgin." Franshell could not help herself.

O'Reilly opened his mouth but nothing came out. For a second, he could not believe what he had heard. His face then loosened into a smile. "You're going back to Scooter."

"A grown man named after an infant's toy. I'm impressed," Franshell replied.

O'Reilly glared at Franshell, not knowing what to say. He consoled himself with the knowledge that next time the treatment would be increased to thirty seconds. He turned around and marched towards the cell door, slamming it hard as he left. Two guards then entered and untied Franshell from the chair. They stood back to let her stand up. She saw that the door was open, so she walked slowly towards the exit. They took her back to her own private cell, a six-feet-by-six-feet-by-six feet concrete cubicle with a perspex window in the ceiling, a single folded blanket on the floor and a half-filled bucket of cold water in the corner.

It was late and Warden Hughes was tired and wanted to go home. Certainly too tired to listen to Lieutenant Major Greengrass of the Military Intelligence Corps of the United States Army. Just as he was locking his desk that evening, a small convoy of one jeep and two lorries arrived at the gate. The guard at the gate had put Lieutenant-Major Greengrass through to Hughes, who had to meet him immediately to discuss a highly urgent and confidential matter that could only be conveyed in the quiet and solitude of his office.

"So how far have you taken Dr Franshell?" asked Greengrass.

"All the way. She's a girl who goes all the way." Hughes smiled. Greengrass did not.

"She's tough, still standing. We're not the FBI here," Hughes admitted.

Hughes stared at Greengrass, a black man at least a decade younger in a senior intelligence role, probably from Los Angeles given his lack of obvious accent and confident manner.

"Let me give you some background. As you know, Dr Franshell is a leading scientist in the field of human DNA," started Greengrass.

"She has valuable scientific knowledge that could change the course of the war in Europe. I cannot give you the specifics, but I am talking about biological weapons. So the army needs her."

"What about all the other doctors and scientists and college professors in the Underground?"

"Franshell was younger than the others and not tied down to a regular home and family. That's why it took such a long time for Vice and Virtue to bring her in," Greengrass continued.

"So why don't you go to the FBI and borrow some of them?" He knew it was pointless asking a military intelligence officer questions, but the warden wanted to remind Greengrass who ran the joint.

"I am under orders to remove Franshell from the facility tonight."

"She's a political case. My hands are tied." Hughes shrugged his shoulders.

"They've cut the domestic security budget again, I hear. You can't be happy with the new bonus scheme. Handling political cases doesn't add up like it used to." Pause. "And boats are expensive, especially anything over fifty foot."

Hughes could not help the shit-eating grin that spread over the bottom half of his face.

"Ah. Well, like every patriot, I do want to see victory."

"I have the paperwork all completed. We have set up the bank account in the Bahamas. You'll be sent the codes," Greengrass reassured Warden Hughes.

"All sounds fine to me."

Greengrass stood up. "Now, which cell?"

Two green-uniformed soldiers of the US Military Intelligence Corps lifted a bound and gagged Dr Franshell into the back of the lorry and lowered her very gently onto the floor like a vintage Persian rug. Franshell started to shiver and shake, her nerves were all over the place, not helped by the sharp night air. But she was relieved to be out of the cell and on the move, even with a chemically cleaned towel wrapped around her mouth. If they intended to execute her and dump her body in the middle of the night, it would be Vice and Virtue or some plain-clothes security organisation like the FBI but not the US Army. She closed her eyes and curled up into a cold adult foetus. It was a ten-hour drive to Blackstone Airbase, Fort Pickett, Virginia, and Dr Franshell would get her first night's sleep in seventy-two hours.

Chapter 6

16 months later…

The huge TV screens at the square-sided plinth of Nelson's Column played the latest news from the front to civilians and anyone else who wandered past Trafalgar Square. The smooth, professional female voice could have being selling a line of expensive household cleaning agents.

"Although outnumbered by the enemy, Shield volunteer brigades counter-attacked heroically against US marines holding the suburbs of Derby. Over four hundred prisoners were taken and the invaders were put to flight. At Derby. Remember the name. Victory to the Shield."

An image of Shield fighters sat with arms aloft on a burnt-out *US Pretraeus* Mk2 tank was frozen on the screen. A few passers-by stopped and stared. The beaming warriors, huddled together like a triumphant football team, seemed larger than life, which of course was the intention of the image. Those civilians who did not want to feel small and insignificant kept on moving, heads down, across the square.

"These men have brought peace to our island and forced the US invaders to sign a truce." And so the selling rolled on.

Lines of dejected US prisoners of war waited by the roadside as camouflaged *Tiger* Mk4 tanks careered past them. Then, a close-up of a bare-chested Shield hero; the camera honed onto his tattooed torso: a large black skull topped by a raven in flight

47

with "Odin Awaits" embossed underneath. The son of Odin also held a symbol of his victory: a wooden flag with a red lion, rampant with the words "The Red Lion" above and the word "open" below. At last, the pubs could open again! Next up was a line of five Shield soldiers stood to attention; the camera slowly panned across their faces in close-up.

"These men have defended the Homeland and kept you free." The viewer was moved on from a sense of their own inadequacy to an inner glow of gratitude and relief that these men existed to protect them.

Mortimer was stood at the end of the line. Fresh from his battle and clad in the green-brown mottled baggy camouflage of the Shield Brigade, his face was blackened from the dirt and smoke of close combat in the streets of Derby. A Shield general, evidently not fresh from the frontline given his clean pressed black dress uniform, fixed the Oak Cross onto Mortimer's chest. The Oak Cross was the highest award in the Shield for valour on the battlefield.

Mortimer's face was frozen for two seconds before the gratitude of a nation was made flesh on the big screen. Somewhere deep inside the English countryside, white, black and brown-skinned families cheered and waved from a green hill-top. The sky was blue and the sun was golden. Then the camera found an attractive light-brown-skinned teenage girl. The colour of her skin seemed to be a combination of everyone else on the hill. She stepped forward and picked a clump of wildflowers from the ground. She smiled, prompting a close-up and then threw the blue and red and yellow flowers high into the blue sky. The flowers were of course dead now, like many of the Shield cut down at Derby. But this was not really the point.

"Everyone everywhere thanks the Shield. A safe home in

their country for every English man, woman and child."

Mortimer rocked back in his chair opposite Senior Intelligence Officer Downton in the cramped office ten floors up. Things had changed a lot since his first visit, so much so that the Shield Security Service had invited him back to their London HQ to assist them with his newly acquired battlefield skills. Mortimer wanted to enjoy this moment.

Security Intelligence Officer Downton had spent the war fighting the internal enemies of the Shield from his desk: anti-social elements on the streets as well as those in the government who still opposed the Shield takeover of the functions of the State. Few things make a secret policeman feel more uneasy than a decorated frontline fighter who has proved himself unlike the deskbound bureaucrat. Nevertheless, four years at Cambridge University before a fast track into the inner sanctum brought comfort to Downton that he had been selected to bring some credibility to the new order by dint of his brain and birth. Just as nature had selected him.

Downton stared at Mortimer and pondered how a man in his early forties could have survived the brutal fighting in the northern cities, the cauldron at Derby, let alone be decorated. Over three quarters of prison recruits had been killed or seriously injured, as you would expect from frontline cannon fodder. And now he faced one of the few survivors, a battlefield hero, a symbol of the movement no less, more than ten years older than him.

"You know, the war continues on the Home Front. Against enemies some would say are as dangerous as the Americans. A different type of enemy."

"Oh, really…"

"Some of the eastern urban areas of the White Zone are becoming no-go areas for the police. Law and order have completely broken down here. Criminal syndicates are running whole communities. They organise food banks, black market prescription drugs, even healthcare for those residents who work for them."

"You mean like governments used to."

"The discredited parliamentary system fell because it was weak, corrupt and unable to provide basic security for its citizens. The new regime will not fail, I assure you."

For a thin, willowy figure, Downton carried slightly too much in the cheeks and under the chin for a man not yet thirty. As he listened to him, Mortimer was reminded of a certain type of senior manager at the bank: the round, pasty face, pale skin, the non-existent jawline, the unkempt blond fringe and the delicate hands all finished off with an accent born to rule. From a good school and a good family, always in the best jobs irrespective of personal integrity or intellectual ability. Governments come, governments go but the same people are always in charge, doing the same thing.

"So, these gangs give them work as well."

"Oh yes. Stealing financial assets from the banks as well as sabotaging the state infrastructure. Some of our biggest corporate partners have been under attack. Millions of Euros have been stolen."

"They must be getting well trained." Mortimer nodded in appreciation of the achievements of the criminal gangs.

"Large-scale criminal hacking operations have been set up. And they need to be eliminated."

"What about the Yanks? They could be behind it," enquired Mortimer.

"We have not found any link and it is perfectly possible that Washington is behind this. But there are protocols in the Truce that protect international business from the conflict. As we know, the banks operate here and in America. So I cannot see any motive there." Pause.

"But anyway, this is why we need you, Mortimer. Not many men in their forties could perform in a combat situation. The Oak Cross… very impressive!" Downton grinned.

And he really gave himself away. Just like the good old days saying yes, sir, no, sir to the Portfolio Managers. The world had not changed at all: that timid, self-conscious smile, a very slight condescending nod of well done and if you were very lucky a mumble of gratitude. Certainly no effusion of body language or beaming smile that could make you look like a village idiot or even a decent human being. Always tepid and understated that showed you they knew your place and you knew their place. But he wanted some fun with the young lord of the new order.

"It's amazing what a man can do with a little self-realisation."

"Self-realisation?" Downton was confused.

"When you know you're probably gonna die, and there is no-one to get you out and you're on your own, really clears the mind." His left eyebrow arched. "You know what I mean?"

Mortimer's grin was so wide it could have consumed three courses of ordure. Downton stared at Mortimer for a few seconds, not needing to answer. But he did. His type could not help it.

"I can't say I do." Downton slowly spat out the words at Mortimer.

Mortimer wanted to burst out laughing but the fun was over. He had gone far enough. Or else Downton would have the last laugh, as they always did.

"But you are still a convicted criminal, a murderer who has found redemption in the Shield. You need the Shield." Pause. "And I need men like you in the Shield to set an example. Proven loyal fighters who can show the police brigade." Downton sighed. "How to deal with our enemies effectively. Some of the police brigades are not reliable…"

"Don't worry. You're preaching to the converted," interrupted Mortimer.

"Those elements not wanted by SecuriState were drafted into the Shield. A lot of them are incompetent on street level, and their leadership is weak and possibly corrupt."

If Mortimer had learnt one thing in Sheerness it was that many inmates were guilty of working for the wrong criminal gang, the wrong family, the wrong organisation, the one not in partnership with their local police force.

"For now, we have to do our best with what we've got. But in time, they will be reformed and cleansed like every other institution and individual on the island." Then he paused.

Mortimer wondered if Downton actually believed what he just said. Did senior apparatchiks of corporations actually believe their own propaganda or are they simply careerists who crank it out to create a wall of bullshit to impress the minions? In his experience, the intelligent ones always tended towards bullshit whilst the stupid ones actually believed it.

And for a split-second, Downton wondered why he had said that. Mortimer and others like him could never be reformed.

"Just remember, Mortimer, where you came from. You could always go back there. You owe the Shield everything." Pause.

"It does occur to me sometimes that I got out of one prison and straight into another."

Downton rocked back in his chair and widened his eyes at

the sound of such impertinence.

"But maybe it's tough doing God's work," Mortimer continued.

Downton threw his head back and bellowed with laughter. "Ha ha. Very good."

The head then bounced forward, nodding vigorously like it was on a cord being pulled by a bored three-year-old. "Indeed it is," he spluttered.

To the right of Mortimer, the TV screen on the wall flickered alive with a photograph of the same bald head and eye patch who gave the introduction speech at the recruitment fair. This time it was set against a white Shield symbol in a black field.

"Ah, my reminder. Commissioner Hendrick..." Downton turned to Mortimer.

"You are staying in Barracks Twelve. Your orders will be sent through."

Mortimer stood up, straightened his body and saluted Downton slightly too stiffly.

Chapter 7

It was a long time since Mortimer had last not worn a uniform. He laid out each item of clothing on his bed: a dark-green sweater, a navy-blue sweater, two white shirts, two black t-shirts, two pairs of grey polyester jeans and a medium-length black leather jacket, all provided free of charge by the Shield. The Shield even had their smart-but-casual look for the off-duty warrior. Mortimer placed each item of clothing in the cupboard, the shirts and trousers on separate hangers, the sweaters and t-shirts folded neatly on the inside shelves, the underwear rolled up on a lower shelf. After his fourth attempt, Mortimer closed the cupboard door, satisfied now that everything was where it should be. A free bed and a free cupboard in a free room for a free man with a river view from the Hammersmith barracks.

Mortimer lay down on his bed, arms behind his head and pondered his new life as an indentured enforcer for the Shield. That was as good as it was going to get until the inevitable bullet, the blackout and then nothing. The noose was never far away from Mortimer's thoughts. He had been very lucky so far.

"Hey… hey… you seen this… she's good. Only a few streets away." His Shield comrade stood in the open doorway holding an electronic tablet.

"A new brothel has opened round the corner. Got your ID ready." The shaven-headed warrior flashed a shiny white grin at Mortimer, expecting an affirmative reaction. For any Shield fighter, whores were free as long as you showed your ID at the door.

Mortimer stared at the man. "Where?"

"Half a mile over the bridge. Check the menu." He proffered the tablet to Mortimer.

"Lot better than the street meat we had up north."

Mortimer took the tablet off him and flicked through images of naked women. Number thirty-two was available this afternoon, enjoyed pottery and spoke five different languages. Mortimer lingered on her outstretched naked body, wondering how she found the time and resources to buy the clay and maintain a potter's wheel in a brothel. Number thirty-three... He dropped the tablet.

"Hey, man..." complained the shiny white grin.

"Sorry."

Fortunately, the tablet fell onto his bed mattress and no damage was done. Mortimer quickly retrieved the tablet and re-opened the screen on to number thirty-three. She was a lot slimmer than in the last few years of their marriage. In fact, she had lost weight, toned up to emphasise her natural curves and looked like the woman he had once fallen in love with. Liberated from the monopoly of monogamy, market forces always improved the product, and she was no exception. She was also sexually active, something else that was different from the last few years of their marriage.

"Yeah, this one looks like a real whore, one hundred and fifty per cent slag."

And where did that come from? From that swamp deep inside where he tried to bury all the bad memories, but now and again spat them out for him to swallow all over again.

"There's more than one..." said the shiny white teeth at the door.

"I'm coming with you." Mortimer stood up and handed the tablet back.

Mortimer and the shaven-headed Hardwick stood outside the front door of the three-storey red-brick townhouse. Once the haven for a banker's bonus or for a middle-class family seeking a comfortable life in the city, the house was making money again.

A security guard in a shabby, faded black tunic and trousers with pistol in hand approached from the side of the house.

"Hey, Dredge…" Hardwick extended his hand to greet the even larger shaven-headed man.

Mortimer and Hardwick reached for their pockets as Dredge mumbled, "ID." He pulled a pen from his pocket and ran it along the bar code strip on the back of each ID card.

Dredge then marched up to the front door, forced up the single bar handle and yanked the door towards him like he was trying to pull it off its hinges. The reinforced steel door required a man of similar size and dimensions to open it. Dredge opened the door just wide enough to let Hardwick and Mortimer squeeze through into the hallway. The door slammed shut behind them. The hallway was long and dreary with no natural or electric light. The grey-washed walls, broken only by a few closed doorways and the utter lack of decoration, gave no clue to the business undertaken there. Nothing of any consequence ever happened in the hallway: it was the waiting room.

"We got to wait for the manager," Hardwick explained.

Then on cue, from the first doorway on the left emerged a small, balding man in rimless glasses in his late fifties.

"Great to see you, Joe." Hardwick low-fived the extended palms.

"Two of you today… your friend is new. Is he the voyeur for

twenty-four…?" enquired Jo.

"No… no… he'll be here Wednesday," Hardwick replied.

"Popular place… I am here for number thirty-three." Mortimer was getting impatient.

"She's waiting for an appointment," replied the manager.

"I'll wait."

Joe turned to Hardwick.

"Oh, the uniforms for Dolls… can you bring 'em tomorrow? Dress uniforms, yeah. Nice and shiny black." Then he smiled at Mortimer.

"Fucking in black uniforms. Big bucks on the live stream."

"They're coming… I promise," said Hardwick.

"Is thirty-three a film star as well?" Mortimer had to ask.

"Jesus, no. The girls in the films are young. Real tight young things for our Shield studs. Not grannies like thirty-three," beamed the manager.

"Bet you need a real Shield man though," asked Hardwick.

"No… we've got proper actors."

Mortimer had had enough. He made for the open doorway and spotted the staircase to his left. Upstairs were more doors and more rooms.

"Hey, hey, I'll give you another number. Thirty-three ain't ready yet," shouted the manager from the bottom of the stairs.

On the landing, Mortimer stopped to scan five closed doors. He walked to the furthest door along the corridor, opened it and marched into the middle of the room.

A hard-cheek-boned brunette with pale skin and warm hazel eyes sat on the bed. She was slimmer than her image in the catalogue. She looked up at him. Her eyes widened and almost leapt out as it sunk in. "Bill…"

"Well done, Karen, you remember."

"I am Candy, not Karen. Throw him out." She turned to the manager, who now stood in the open doorway.

"I can get you banned. You won't be allowed back."

Mortimer ignored him. "You've landed on your feet, or is it your back?"

"You bastard. I lost everything," Candy hissed.

"Leaving me to rot in prison I can take, but not telling me where my son is buried..." This was all too much for Karen as tears started to roll down her cheeks.

"You were going to die. I couldn't..." Then her voice faded out.

"You have to leave; this is the final warning." The manager stepped forward between the ex-couple.

"Tell me."

"Teddington. Teddington Cemetery." She spluttered it out.

Mortimer moved his eyes away from Candy to the floor. That made sense, because they all lived together once in Strawberry Hill, a small suburb enclosed between Teddington and Twickenham in South West London. Mortimer's anger turned to relief as he realised that Tom was buried nearby, not in the village in Derbyshire where Karen was from and where she had gone back to live after his conviction. A screw-up in the prison bureaucracy meant he never attended the funeral. He reckoned it was because the funeral took place back in Karen's home village and it was too much trouble for them to take him up north and back. Maybe Karen had returned to London because her village was near the frontline and only the residents of the local church cemetery felt safe there.

Mortimer turned to the manager. "I'm going."

In front of the door, he caught a framed photo of Tom, a year or so before he died, next to a smiling Karen. Meanwhile, Karen sobbed and sobbed into her hands.

"Candy… Candy… please, Mr Golitsyn won't want to see you like this."

The manager almost sounded sympathetic. Not Mortimer though, who grabbed the photo frame and put it in his pocket and stormed out without even a backwards glance. To him, Karen had died years ago, and Candy was someone else who had somehow got hold of a photograph of his son.

After his arrival at Sheerness, Karen had never bothered to visit him. Except for one letter telling Mortimer she was leaving London to live with her parents and that her lawyers would be serving him divorce papers, she never made contact with him again. They had been together for twelve years before the assault, and their marriage had gotten to the point where they were tired of each other. A young child and long working hours for both of them had taken its toll. Mortimer and Karen knew things were not right any longer but neither had found the time to ask why.

Like most men with a hard luck story and a truckload of grief to handle, Mortimer fell into a trough of despair and self-pity. Thoughts of suicide were inevitably the main course on the inner contemplation menu for the first few months in solitary confinement. And the guards made it very clear to him that suicide was an option worth his consideration. Maybe it was their antagonism, the long hours alone in his cell or being allowed to distract himself from himself in the prison library every second weekend that recast Mortimer. But after about a year, all the inner pain and "woe is me" stuff drained out of him and left nothing behind. Raw and unmediated as he could ever be, he could now go back to basics. He wanted to live but on his terms.

An elegant, tanned man in his early sixties, dressed in an expensive suit, stood at the bottom of the stairs. Mortimer pushed past the waiting Golitsyn, who was happy to look the other way.

Near the front door, the large figure of Dredge swung a cricket bat one-handed into the right-hand corner of the wall. The hard crack of wood against plaster stopped Mortimer in his tracks. Dredge turned around and kicked a dead rat across the floor.

"I get seven Euros for each one. There's a whole family in here. I know it."

The security guard smiled, the shy embarrassed smile of a man who knew he did not impress anyone. The dead rat reminded Mortimer of a local newspaper headline from years ago when they had local newspapers: "More vermin than people in London." How could they ever tell the difference? Mortimer smiled inside at his joke.

Dredge pushed the front door open, and Mortimer stepped outside. He pulled the photo frame from his pocket then opened the rear clip and gently slid out the photo. He tossed the frame into a bin standing a few yards from the doorway. Without a second thought, he then tore off the picture of Karen, screwed it up and tossed that into the bin as well. Fortunately, the photograph had been printed on cheap paper that tore quickly and easily, almost like newspaper, and left Tom undamaged.

He then carefully folded Tom in half, opened his military-issue nylon wallet and slipped the photograph behind his ID card before putting it back into his top pocket.

Chapter 8

It was late afternoon when Mortimer walked into the deserted Teddington Cemetery in South West London. He paused between the tall stone pillars at the entrance to scan the graves either side of the road that led to the Victorian gothic chapel in the middle of the plot. The graves stretched out as far as he could see. At least a couple of hundred graves lay on each side in front of the chapel and probably a few hundred more were behind the chapel.

An unkempt and overweight man in his mid-fifties appeared from behind a tree close by to his left. He carried a spade and headed straight towards Mortimer.

As he got closer, Mortimer raised his hand and called out. "Hi. I'm looking for a grave."

The gravedigger stopped a few metres in front of Mortimer. His baggy and worn green sweatshirt carried the logo of Richmond Borough Council.

"You've made a good start."

"2037." Mortimer got to the point.

"A good year for dying, your own headstone. Not in one of the pits."

"Burial pits?" queried Mortimer.

"Over near the railway embankment, hundreds were buried after the firestorm in Kingston. The Homeland thanks you for your sacrifice but no gravestone." The gravedigger smiled, amused at his own cynicism.

"Adult or child?"

"Child."

"That's easy – against the wall at the back." He then raised his arm and pointed to the back of the cemetery. "Straight on."

"Much obliged."

Mortimer walked along the road, curved around the chapel then once he saw the tall brick wall, broke into a jog. He stepped off the road then zig-zagged around the graves until he reached the wall. His heart pounded hard; a sense of stress and anticipation coursed through his veins.

The graves here were smaller and decorated with photographs of young children or teenagers, the inscriptions more sentimental and more revealing of loss than anything found on the adult graves; testament to the inherent un-fairness of life. Mortimer tried not to dwell on the tragedy of others; the twelve-year-old girl released into eternal paradise after a life of illness, the five-year-old who died because fate had better plans. For a moment he forgot about his own tragedy; other children's graves have that affect.

Then he fell upon a stone angel, head bowed and wings raised up over the headstone. "Here lies Tom Mortimer, beloved son, in our hearts forever" said the inscription. The words read like a command to shut down and Mortimer duly did. His rational thinking part vacated the premises. This cleared the way for his feelings to have a rare day out. The rage rose from the pit of his stomach then swelled up through his chest and limbs, intent on tearing its way out into the open air. Maybe it was the injustice of missing his son's funeral, and only today, years later, discovering the location of his grave or maybe, the simple hard truth that he failed to protect Tom and that is why he lay dead in the ground. Whatever the reason, it all came together for Mortimer, standing at his son's grave. But just as the beast was ready to blow, it stopped, the anger choked in his windpipe. It could not get out. Then the nothingness in his mind released itself and started to recover its usual place. That calmness that helped him face the walls of Sheerness and then the might of the US military enveloped him from top to toe. But this time it was so much better. It was like floating in a warm, flat sea.

Mortimer exhaled deeply and dropped to his knees. He ran his arm over the top of the headstone and re-read the words. He liked the clarity and economy of the epitaph and appreciated the absence of any allusion to Tom's tragic death or whine against fate. It said it all. It also reminded Mortimer why he once loved Karen.

Now settled in front of the angel, Mortimer told his son that he had become a killer of men, which was not something he was proud of, but that was his job now. That Tom was in a place of peace where there was no killing and that if he ever reached that place, he would change and become the father he remembered.

Mortimer felt exhausted when he at last stood up. He lifted his eyes to the wall behind the grave. There he spotted a small round plastic black cap about three inches in diameter embedded in one of the red bricks. He recognised it from his time at the frontline; a "stick on the wall" camera frequently used by troops in house clearance operations. Even here Tom could not be left in peace.

So he walked around the grave, knelt down, not caring whether it was on or not, picked up a loose half-brick lying in the ground and slammed it into the monitoring device. The camera crumpled on impact and fell out of the wall. Mortimer then picked up what looked like a large dead cockroach with wires for legs and slung it over the wall.

He then stepped back to the grave, bowed his head and stared down at the statue of the angel and his son. Alone again.

Mortimer looked around him and reckoned he was the only sober man in the back of the Aardvark armed-personnel carrier. He was also the only man in the trademark mottled camouflage fatigues of the Shield Brigade amongst the eleven grey-uniformed Interior Ministry policemen. They were a motley crew of young and middle-aged men, more physically resilient than the prison guards at Sheerness but certainly not mentally fit enough for frontline combat.

Next to Mortimer, a young policeman swigged from a flask handed him by an older man.

"Cheap shit." He spat out the economically priced vodka onto the floor next to Mortimer's boot.

"Not sweet enough for you, eh," slurred the older man opposite him.

Head slumped forward, eyes closed, Mortimer saw nothing. He was unsuccessfully trying to micro-sleep, a few minutes of deep slumber to give him the edge later. The pointless automated announcement did not help.

"Internal security is the new frontline and you men are the chosen instrument of enforcement. Every man must do his duty. Forward today and tomorrow."

Mortimer thought this a rather half-hearted rallying call, compared to the promise of Valhalla on the real frontline. In the last months of the war, a cult of Odin had been unofficially encouraged, everything from free tattoos to questionably historic films of Viking derring-do streamed to every Shield fighter. Anyway, it turned the thoughts of some of the drinkers in the back of the Aardvark.

"You gonna show us… war hero." The young vodka-drinker

turned to Mortimer.

"Heh?"

Mortimer did not move.

"Sleepy head." The man slapped his knee. Mortimer opened his eyes.

"We're gonna have some fun today, yeah?"

Mortimer opened his eyes and glared at the man. Not discouraged, the young man raised his bare forearm to show the words "Long Live Death" tattooed in gothic text followed by the inevitable skull.

"What do y' think?" The young drinker smiled. Pause.

"Probably more than you," replied Mortimer. The older man opposite laughed out loud and took a swig from his can.

Before he could re-arrange his mouth, a loud explosion swung the vehicle sharply to the right, throwing the men on top of each other. The rocket-propelled grenade had skimmed the top of Mortimer's lead Aardvark before exploding in the adjacent block of flats. A second explosion at the rear of the convoy sent the eighth and last of the Aardvarks careering off the road. The local residents' welcoming party was now in full swing.

The lead vehicle, followed by two others, swerved off the road into an empty disused parking area that lay in the centre of an L-shaped block of derelict flats. The other five Aardvarks accelerated deeper into the estate.

Each Aardvark slammed to a halt in front of the blocks before grey-uniformed men poured out of the back. Most men ran for cover into the open doorways using grenades to clear their path. The really drunk ones fired aimlessly and pointlessly into the road that ran around the block. Molotov cocktails launched from the flats on the opposite side harmlessly exploded in the road. Harmless, that is, if you were not as drunk as a lord.

The older man in Mortimer's vehicle, who had enjoyed the joke moments earlier and quite probably more sloshed than anyone else, stumbled into the road and fired off a volley of rounds in the direction of the Molotov cocktails.

The Molotov cocktail rain suddenly stopped and the policeman raised his gun triumphantly at the men still under cover.

"Forward," he screamed, still with a stupid laugh in his eyes.

Mortimer and the rest of his unit took up position, crouched down on the ground near the open doorways. Mortimer bellowed, "Stay here."

The old man still had his arms aloft as the Molotov cocktail exploded on his head and engulfed him in flames. The blood-curdling scream only lasted a few seconds before he fell to the ground, a black shadow shrivelling in the flames. The policemen froze and stared at their comrade burning to death.

Mortimer turned to his unit.

"Two lessons, gentlemen: the bullet-proof vest provides no support if you catch fire. Secondly, alcohol is an inflammable substance. Now up we go."

The nine men followed Mortimer through the open double-doorway, a few yards inside the entrance hall and then up the staircase onto the first-floor concourse.

A long empty corridor dotted with closed doors stretched all the way to a window on the other side of the floor. On either side of this central corridor ran two more, the view of each obscured from the stairs.

Mortimer turned to his men and raised his finger across his pursed lips.

He then dropped to his haunches, followed a second later by his now very nervous unit and all listened to the silence. This was broken by a door slamming above them and a sudden shriek of glee as if someone was struggling to contain their excitement. The door slammed again. Although the sound was muffled and distant enough to be a few floors above them Mortimer guessed that the locals must be coming down the stairs. He also felt heads starting to twitch around him. He raised his finger to his mouth again to calm his men.

Effective close-quarters combat in high-rise buildings was always about not getting ambushed and then finding your enemy before he found you, not occupying dead floor space. The policemen to a man looked nervously at Mortimer, utterly reliant on his lead.

He raised his right-hand palm with five fingers spread and then jabbed in the direction of the corner of the right-hand corridor about twenty feet away. Five men, including the young vodka drinker then crawled in slightly self-conscious, trying-to-remember-their-training way, over the hard floor and around the corner. Another door slammed and a loud cackling laugh came from above the stairs. Then, the clack of moving feet on stairs above, as if the group were expanding as well as getting closer to Mortimer and his unit. But the cheap, thin plastic tiles on the stairs gave their position away.

Mortimer stood up and led the remaining four men towards the corner of the left-hand corridor. Seconds later, the local community stopped at the top of the second-floor stairway. A young girl with purple hair, no more than fifteen years old, gingerly walked down a few steps until she passed the ceiling of the first floor, then knelt down and craned her head into the empty space to scan the now empty concourse.

She smiled and then called back to her gang. "Hey… empty."

The young man at the front threw her a semi-automatic rifle, which she caught easily.

The rainbow coalition of old and young, white and black, male and female then processed down the stairs. Each clenched a weapon; a few had semi-automatic rifles; some had pistols; the others had improvised metal staves and axes. A civilian militia had taken up arms to defend their property, their land from a State that had given up on them decades ago. These communities had no choice but to take control of their lives. So the new-style crime organisations moved in, more like corporations than traditional crime gangs who, unlike the real corporations, were keen to employ people and communities in a way that had not been legitimately done for decades and decades. But like those companies, they could have trained their staff better.

The teenage girl led the way down onto the concourse. She turned her head from left to right and saw no-one and heard nothing. The rest of the people's army shuffled onto the concourse.

Behind the right-hand corner, Mortimer pulled the pin from the grenade, counted to three and rolled it towards the girl. The force of the explosion dismembered the girl and the two men next to her instantly. From both corners, the policemen stepped out and formed a straight line of fire.

Disorientated from the grenade blast and the smoke filling up the concourse, the locals stood no chance against the raking fire of the sub-machine guns. The fifteen or so strong community action group were cut down straight away.

Mortimer watched from the corner the falling bodies. Once convinced that all the assailants were dead or down, he raised his arm to cease fire. He then stepped through the bloody mess and onto the stairs, followed by his unit, up to the next floor. At the top of the stairs, Mortimer threw a smoke grenade onto the second-floor concourse. Once the area was filled with the swirling purple mist, he continued up to the third floor, again empty and another smoke grenade and then up to the fourth. Voices from the floor above brought them to a halt. They could hear an argument between an older man and his younger subordinates: they had not correctly packed the Molotov cocktails or something. The younger voice had a gun, which was good enough for him.

Not speaking, Mortimer signalled to his men to follow him onto the fifth floor. Just as Mortimer dropped his arm, a door at the far end of the central corridor creaked open. A white-haired old man in a cardigan and torn trousers appeared at the open doorway. Head down, he shuffled into the corridor towards the policemen. Probably over eighty, using a stick to move, he was only interested in the few feet in front of him. Each man in the unit stared as if mesmerised at the advancing man of advanced years. They did not know what to do. This was too much for the youngest policeman, who stood up with a smile on his face and pointed his machine gun at the old man. Mortimer jumped up and wrenched the machine gun out of the young man's hand and knocked him off balance to the floor. The prostrate fighter grunted and reddened with anger but knew he was in no position to take on Mortimer.

The old man did not look up but slowly arced his way around the staring policemen, then turned left into a new corridor.

Mortimer watched the old man on his way to be sure. Then he hissed at his men.

"We go up. We hit from behind. Weapons ready."

The men stood up quickly, adjusted their sub-machine guns and followed Mortimer up the last flight of steps.

The fifth and final level was an open concourse without any corridors or obstacles except for a line of thick concrete pillars to support the roof that ran from the stairs to the balcony at the far end. The balcony provided great views of the estate and would have been ideal for a rooftop restaurant maybe once upon a time. A line of about a dozen or so locals, young and older, men and women, looked out over the waist-high barrier to the battle ground below. A couple of plastic crates of Molotov cocktails lay behind them, undisturbed. A few leant over and casually pointed their assault rifles at the road below without using them as intended; others clasped a weapon to their side and simply seemed to be enjoying the view. More like spectators than combatants, possibly a little confused by the chaos unfolding five floors below them but distracted enough to not bother to turn around. Maybe they thought the gunfire from the floors below was their own side; maybe they had not heard the gunfire at all from outside on the balcony. But they were not ready for Mortimer and his men.

Two policemen darted behind the nearest pillar to the stairs and then two more took cover behind the next pillar. And so on. Mortimer crawled between the pillars then launched a hand grenade at the balcony.

The explosion, followed by a rain of shrapnel, took down at least three in the middle. Seconds later, the remaining locals fell in a heap before they could make a move, each body riddled with machine gun bullets.

After a short silence of realisation, the young policeman nearest to Mortimer punched the air.

"Yessssss." Then the others started to cheer, a spontaneous, from the bottom of the gut, brute exhalation of sound that was victory and relief in equal measure. Not one casualty in their unit and they had done what they had to do. Only Mortimer did not celebrate. He wandered over to the balcony, stepped over the dead bodies and leant over the barrier to survey the scene below.

Chapter 9

A single-file line of captured men, women and children shambled along the road, flanked on both sides by police guns. Mortimer wondered if he should have given the locals on his floor a chance to surrender. But it was too late now; the milk had been spilt. Too bad for them that he had been hammered and bent into shape by the Shield Brigade in frontline combat. Taking prisoners or making yourself one always came a distant second in battle. As he turned around, he kicked a soft object with his right boot. A battered paperback book lay on the floor. Mortimer stared at it for a few seconds: *Robinson Crusoe* by Daniel Defoe. It had been a long time since Mortimer had seen a book let alone read one. Strange to think that one of his enemy that day, the criminal underclass, read classic eighteenth-century literature. He bent down, picked up the book and squeezed it into his top pocket, curling the curled page ends back even more.

The radio in his collar crackled and a clipped voice spoke. "Mortimer, report your status."

Mortimer spat back quickly, "Position terminated. No prisoners."

"Very good, Mortimer. Please bring your unit down to the square." The voice sounded impressed. And so was Mortimer, once he realised who it was. This was the voice of Commissioner Hendrick, the head of Shield Security Service. His commander-in-chief, the man on the TV screen who had personally recruited him.

The central square of the ghetto was not a square but a one-hundred-metre-by-fifty-metre rectangle of tarmac in the middle of six housing blocks crisscrossed with walking paths. It seemed to shrink as it filled up with a steady stream of captives, prodded forward at gunpoint by jeering Shield police auxiliaries. Each unit had its own mini-parade of prisoners cheered on by the other units who had already dumped their human booty. The square itself was full of misery: local men, women and children of all ages milled around in shock or huddled together for safety or simply sat down exhausted and cried.

Only Mortimer's unit did not join the party. They slumped on the ground at the southwest corner of the square, coming down from their killing spree. An air of disappointment lingered in the group that they could not show off their victims because they were all dead. Mortimer ignored his men and the square and instead opened the book that he had pocketed in the flats. He knew who would complain first.

Hungover and drained, the young drinker from the Aardvark broke the silence.

"We got nothing to show off. We killed them all."

"That's because we did our job properly," shot back Mortimer without raising his eyes from the page.

The young man then spotted a weakness in Mortimer, the book, evidence of a man who could not be a real warrior, someone who did not really fight on the frontline.

"A book, old man." The sneer in his voice was clear and present. "Why... you reading?"

Mortimer smiled. "Well, Mr Fletcher, if I read enough, maybe I'll find out why one day."

Fletcher pulled his face back, confused, then looked at the others for approval. But no one else joined in.

"We only liquidated those who wanted to kill us. There are innocent civilians out there. We don't kill non-combatants." Mortimer looked up.

He shut the book and his son fell out. He had pressed the photograph in the book earlier to keep it in good condition. Like the photo, reading a book reminded him of a previous life long gone. At least he had something to hold and see that was not the square or the drunken rabble under his command.

Fletcher now knew what to say. "It's got pictures, then."

"Yeah, but that won't help you." The other policemen laughed.

Slighted, the young drinker threw up his arms in the direction of the square. "That's where we should be, at the fucking circus."

By now, the mini-parades had finished. About two hundred or so civilians had been herded into the square. And the entertainment continued. They were now running, shambling, or limping if infirm, in a clockwise circle whilst policemen shouted orders and cajoled them to keep moving. If anyone fell over, old or young, a policeman ran over and kicked the person until they got up and re-joined the circle. Other uniforms lounged at the side, laughing at the spectacle or sleeping off their hangovers.

Then their commander arrived. He always liked to arrive on foot whenever engaged in field operations. Three black-uniformed men approached at a brisk pace from the opposite side of the square to Mortimer's unit. Commissioner Hendrick was flanked by his two bodyguards. Without breaking stride, the three men in black passed through the police lines, as if they were invisible, and halted in front of the miserable scene. The braying from the grey lines fell to silence; those policemen in the square stopped their bullying and immediately stood to attention. And the circle slowed as the captives became aware of the authority of the black uniforms. Hendrick turned to his right-hand bodyguard and nodded. He pulled out his pistol and fired it into the air.

It was the eye-patch that gave him away. According to Shield propaganda, the eye-patch originated from a piece of shrapnel that removed his left eye at the siege of Stoke. Everyone could see that Hendrick was a real warrior.

Hendrick was one of the three heads of Shield Security, specifically responsible for domestic security and policing in London and the area designated as the Demilitarised Zone (DMZ). The other two heads were responsible for political security and foreign security. Each head of security reported directly to the seven-man Shield Junta that effectively ran the government in London. In the finest traditions of organisational divide and rule, the responsibilities of the security heads sometimes overlapped, resulting in distrust and antagonism between the different branches, which ensured that none of them ever got too big for their boots. The Shield Junta were the leaders of the Shield Movement, a mixture of professional zealots; politicians and ex-corporate bosses and bankers who were bored of money-making and wanted to rescue the nation in its hour of need. For all the dreams of the ideologues of a new but really very, very old order, it was the corporates who had made the Shield powerful at Westminster and in the City of London, the two institutions that used to control the United Kingdom.

Hendrick was an ex-naval intelligence officer who had been forced to resign his position once his extra-curricular political affiliations became evident to his bosses. He used his professional knowledge to serve a higher purpose, so he took a leading role in the Shield Security Service. Hard, cold intelligence is rarely combined with a lack of material or sexual corruption but Hendrick broke the mould. Commissioner Hendrick saw himself as a Knight of the New Order; the austere, idealistic warrior who embodied the highest values of the Shield. His time had come. He even proved himself in combat and led his own Special Security units on the frontline against the US invaders. This of course made life difficult for those who could not maintain such high standards. He was as widely feared within the ranks of the Shield as within the civilian population.

No longer cajoled or beaten, the unfortunates in the square dropped to the tarmac in relief. Not one of them looked up at Hendrick, except for an eight-year-old boy who sat nearby with his mother. The mother, in her early thirties, sobbed whilst clasping a baby in her arms. Maybe it was her crying or the staring eyes of her son that caught his attention but he moved closer and crouched down next to her. He inspected the family in the same way a slightly annoyed doctor might view a problematic patient. His eyes darted around the thin, scruffy woman and her baby then onto her son. But there were no tears in the eyes of the eight-year-old boy, only blazing hatred directed in deep breaths towards the man in black.

"So, did you shoot at my men?" The woman brushed her cheek and straightened her neck.

"No. Sir."

Hendrick moved his eyes to the boy. "I meant your son." Pause.

"I believe your son is a brave boy. He has honest eyes."

The mother instantly threw her arms around her boy, wiping the hate away. Hendrick stood up and turned to the surrounding policemen. His voice was no longer quiet and tender.

"You are a rabble. A drunken, incompetent rabble." He

barked in a loud voice so everyone could hear. No policeman moved a hair.

"And you need to learn. We are honoured to have a highly decorated Shield man here today." Pause.

"Brigade Leader Mortimer, please show yourself." The bark got louder.

Mortimer had watched it all from the sides and as commanded he slowly raised himself to his feet. He had an uneasy feeling about what would come next. All of his brigade turned and stared at him.

"Go on, show us a magic trick," said the young drinker.

Mortimer walked the short distance into the square and passed through the police units until he reached a respectful distance from Hendrick. All eyes were on Mortimer. He clipped his heels to attention. "Sir, Brigade Leader Mortimer."

There were no salutes, military or roman in the Shield. It prided itself in an egalitarian ethos between the ranks; each man of the Shield was special.

"Mr Mortimer, please set an example. I want you to execute this terrorist."

All this was said in a very matter-of-fact tone, as if he were asking someone to dispose of a piece of litter. Hendrick then pointed to the eight-year-old boy. The mother started to shriek in a high-pitched wail. She grabbed her son and pulled him under her wing. The boy remained silent but started to tremble; his head nodded in small, jerky movements as if powered by a low-voltage electric shock. Mortimer did not move.

"Excuse me, sir, but I kill only combatants. They carry weapons, like me and you."

The commissioner raised his one working eye to the sky to allow the disobedience to sink in.

"Bring me the boy." He turned to one of his bodyguards.

The mother threw herself at the black uniform, who elbowed her aside hard in the face. She held her face, screaming, with blood pouring from her nose mixing with the tears. The obedient silence from the staring policemen only seemed to amplify her pain. It was one thing to take part in an act of loosely controlled collective violence against well-armed criminal scum and then humiliate the survivors. But to coolly murder a single child on your own like this would take a lot more than another crate of beer. Even more shocking was the fact that the perpetrator had not raised his bloodlust in the morning assault and was sober. In fact, Commissioner Hendrick had come straight from breakfast.

The black-uniformed bodyguard forced the eight-year-old to his knees between Mortimer and Hendrick. Hendrick took a pistol from his holster and pushed it into Mortimer's palm.

"Now do your duty as a Shield man."

Mortimer pointed the end of the barrel downwards against the hard corner of the boy's skull.

The boy wanted to look at his killer so he raised his eyes to Mortimer. His forehead gently pushed the barrel back and forced Mortimer's arm to retract slightly. There was no defiance in his eyes now, just resignation. The calmness in his face unsettled his would-be executioner. This was the response of someone far older, an adult at least. But the eight-year-old had seen his father shot down in cold blood earlier, and now it was his turn and soon he would see his father again. His father would be proud of him, especially as he had shot the grey-uniformed murderer with the pistol given to him by his father.

"You're no older than Tom. Eight or nine, maybe." Mortimer could see the gates of Sheerness and the cell that would be waiting for him.

"I have given you an order. Execute this criminal," snapped Hendrick.

Mortimer turned to Hendrick and threw the pistol to the ground.

"I'm not a murderer."

Hendrick's eyes bulged in shock then narrowed sharply in their sockets.

"Arrest this man... Now."

Both bodyguards lunged at each shoulder-blade and forced Mortimer down onto his knees. One of them pointed a pistol into Mortimer's skull. A low murmur of confusion reverberated around the watching throng of Shield policemen.

"You," said Hendrick to the boy. "Stand up... now."

The boy stood up slowly, his head bowed to the ground.

Hendrick turned to the stunned crowd and boomed, "I assure you this man will be... an example."

Mortimer had been here before.

Chapter 10

By seven p.m., the office floor had switched to the bank's own local solar supply to offset the effect of the power cuts. The dimmed ceiling lights only deepened the glow from Mortimer's everlasting monitor screen. That evening, Mortimer was the last person on the floor. This was the first time ever that Mortimer was the last to leave. Whilst his colleagues usually worked late, he always chose to leave as early as possible, preferably by five forty-five p.m. This meant he could go to the gym or the swimming pool or get home at a decent time. Occasionally he would even sidle off to the cinema rather than work late. But that night was different. Everyone else in the office had left early to avoid the Shield Movement rally in Trafalgar Square. Last time the Shield came out in force, so did their opponents, which led to rioting, tear-gas exchanges and frightened bank employees.

Mortimer reckoned the Underground would be overcrowded, full of their supporters arriving for a big night out, especially as the government had agreed to pay for their tickets. And so he decided to work late for once. Three floors up in St James, Mortimer could not see Trafalgar Square or hear the speakers but he heard the distant cheering of the crowd, sometimes rising to high excitement then falling quiet before rumbling louder again during the speeches.

Mortimer stood up in his chair ready to leave, but his screen did not want him to go so soon. An urgent squelch and a white box outlined in lilac appeared across the middle of the screen, containing a message in bold black Gothic script. "You are required to attend a meeting at ten a.m. tomorrow in the Gold room." The giveaway was the gentle lilac border. It was the house style of Human Resources. Mortimer had expected this for weeks, ever since the announcement of imminent restructuring.

He clicked away the message, picked up his jacket and made for the lift. Over ten years' service should probably earn him about six months' redundancy. Maybe someone from the seventh floor would drop by and see him still here, the only one working late. But it was too late now for Mortimer.

He had never used his cubicle, a personal living space with single bed, shower and basin provided by the bank for every staff member for late-hours working. The more hours spent in your cubicle, the higher the bonus and the higher your prospects, possibly even as high as the seventh floor. But his key had never entered a cubicle slot, so nothing would be recorded and so zero would appear on his Cubicle Usage chart at the HR meeting tomorrow. Which is probably why they wanted to get rid of him. Well, fuck 'em.

The lift doors opened and Mortimer stepped in and pressed the green G button. He knew he could give his family a better life away from the bank, London, the overcrowded South East. Sell up and go west, live in the countryside next to the sea. But he would have to persuade his wife Karen to leave behind the current level of wealth and security afforded by a nice terraced house just about big enough for the three of them in a nice part of South West London. That's if you could call a large mortgage a form of security and wealth. Especially in these times with an even larger pile of debt called the global economy going to hell in a handcart.

Millions now faced the same problem of plummeting living

standards as the early twenty-first-century debt bubble finally burst. And now the piper had to be paid. The only thing the government could do was to cling onto power as best as it could with the help of its friends in the media and big business. Clinging onto power without ideas or principles was about the only competence left in democratically elected politicians. But then, from this social and economic chaos came the Shield Movement, a popular nationalist movement that went far beyond the nostalgic imperial clichés of the Brexit movement decades earlier. It wanted a new society based on a pre-industrial localised Britain, where communities and classes would co-operate to work together for the benefit of all. Well, that was the line!

The Shield Movement were pushing the government into closer ties with the Homeland Organisation, their ideological masters, who now ran what used to be called the European Union. As national governments across the continent collapsed, electorates fell under the spell of their own local Shield Movements with their promise of a new and secure future based on the best of the past. Differences of gender, class, race and religion no longer mattered in the new Europe, the homeland of civilisation, which had brought together so many different races and tribes thousands of years earlier in the Dark Ages. And would do so again. But of course, there had to be an enemy. And that was the United States of America with its warped and hypocritical values of individual sovereignty and Christian superstition. Whose hollow and failed economic model no longer created enough wealth for enough people. And so, when the money ran out, so did the freedom and democracy.

Back came the Christian fundamentalists, the new face of the old world, backed by the most powerful military on the planet. The Shield wanted to join the Homeland and, like the rest of

Europe, withdraw from NATO. Some people reckoned this might lead to war. So if things got bad then Mortimer and his family would certainly be better off in the countryside. Maybe even as far as Cornwall. For Tom's sake at least.

The doors opened on the ground floor. The taller one giggled and then raised her hand apologetically over her mouth. Even though she carried an unopened bottle of champagne, she had already been drinking. The shorter one, who also clutched an unopened bottle of champagne, just smirked at Mortimer. Although both were appropriately under-dressed for a night out, theirs would be a night in at the expense of the bank. Each girl was no more than twenty years old, but they headed for the seventh floor as quickly as they could.

Mortimer strolled out of the bank's offices onto St James, where armed police stood at regular intervals up and down the pavement on both sides of the road. Mortimer sensed an atmosphere in the air so he decided to walk to Waterloo station. He dropped down to the Mall, which was empty except for more armed police, then as he reached Admiralty Arch, he saw the back of the throng stretched beyond Nelson's Column and onto the road. They could not see the preachers but they could hear the defiant words.

"Comrades, the Shield is committed to the defence of these islands from those who would threaten our European home."

Uninterested in the show, Mortimer put his head down and twisted and turned through the rapt throng.

"We are the weapon that will defend these islands. We are right and we will fight," continued the speaker.

The bodies around him cheered and clapped as Mortimer ploughed on, avoiding any raised arms. He passed the

Underground entrance and pushed on into the open spaces of Whitehall. About twenty metres away stood a line of black-suited and booted riot police. Water cannon vehicles were parked at the roadside, ready and waiting for action. Interestingly, the lines of police faced down Whitehall as did another thicker black line further up. They seemed to be there to protect the crowd although there were no signs of any counter-demonstrations.

Un-accosted Mortimer entered an empty Northumberland Avenue. Five minutes later, he crossed the footbridge over the River Thames then down the steps and across to Waterloo station for his commute home.

As expected, the station concourse was crowded more than usual that evening. Mortimer knew the drill: head down, shoulders forward, elbows taut and look for any space however temporary to open his way through the throng.

As usual he made for platform seventeen. But tonight, a red cross flashed on the front of each barrier onto the platform except for one, where a long queue had formed. Two SecuriState policemen were checking each commuter before letting them pass onto the platform. The Shield had warned the government of a possible terrorist attack on their supporters, so the private police force reciprocated by checking the identity of each commuter on and off the platforms.

Mortimer joined the back of the queue and watched the large TV screens on the wall above: buildings burned; mainly young male civilians ran and threw objects at uniformed men, who wielded batons and fought the civilians.

"The Interior Ministry announced today that the army will be stationed across the north to support civil authorities in Manchester, Sheffield, Hull and Middlesbrough."

Mortimer looked at his watch. It was 7.41 p.m. and his train left in less than ten minutes. In front of him stood a young, smartly dressed female office worker, plugged into her music, handbag slung around her shoulder. Bored and mildly annoyed at the wait, she did not see the young man of similar age slam into her side. She toppled sideways off balance; her knees folded as if she were going to fall. The young man instantly stretched his arm around her shoulder and hauled her back up in time whilst his other arm extended deep into her shoulder bag, all in a single motion.

"Oh… sorry, babe. I'm really sorry. You okay?" He opened his eyes wide and tensed the ends of his mouth to gain her sympathy. Her eyes met this face of sorrow and sympathy, oblivious to the bag invasion.

It was clear to Mortimer that he had done this before. He lunged forward and grabbed the shoulder of the wandering arm. The arm retracted from the bag like Mortimer had pressed a button. Although puffed up in a thick nylon anorak, Mortimer felt a sinewy shoulder that held a wiry frame together at least four or five inches shorter than him. He then levered the younger man off the female, careful not to push him over in a way that might justify a reaction. The assailant stumbled backwards then gathered himself.

Mortimer spoke first. "Excuse me."

"Hey, what ya doing?" He jabbed his index finger at Mortimer, angered and humiliated by the intervention.

"I saw your arm in her bag, so piss off." Mortimer got to the point.

"What y'talking about?"

The female, still plugged in, swung her head from Mortimer to the young man and back. A portly SecuriState policeman in a bright-yellow high-visibility jacket stepped in between the scruffy tightly zipped padded anorak that could conceal a weapon versus a smart suit and a fifteen, even twenty, year age difference.

"Identity card," he barked at the young man.

"Hey, man, he… hit…"

"Get out of here. Now. Or we will take you out of here."

The young man's mouth shaped into a slow sneer, the sneer of a man who had done it before and probably practised in front of the mirror at home. He then flounced off past his female victim towards the queue at the next barrier.

The train eventually left ten minutes late. Mortimer got a window seat, which meant he could rest his head easily and doze for the thirty-three-minute journey into the suburbs of South West London. Nearly a decade of the same journey day and night meant he always woke up in time. Sometimes Mortimer would only jolt himself awake as the train stopped at the platform. But he always made the doors before they closed.

Chapter 11

It was past eight-thirty and only a handful of commuters walked out of Strawberry Hill station with Mortimer. Three young males in their early twenties hung back on the platform and waited for the regulars to file out of the exit. The station lighting was low and Mortimer was tired, so he did not see the young man he had confronted at Waterloo now joined by two taller men. Mortimer walked past the Railway Arms and continued straight onto the T-junction. Left again and eight houses down he pushed open his black wrought-iron front gate. Halfway up the garden path, he remembered from his morning run the orange lilies for sale in buckets outside the shop at the bottom of the street. And the shop was always open late.

Five more minutes would not make a difference, but a bunch of lilies would. Mortimer put his front-door key back into his pocket and walked briskly out of his gate towards the lit shop-front.

Mortimer returned, clutching a bouquet of six orange lilies in his right hand. He did not see that his front gate was open wide. But he made sure he closed it behind him. And the front door was slightly ajar. Without considering why, he pushed the door open. The moment he knew why, it was too late. The fist from the sneering mugger at Waterloo caught his cheekbone and sent Mortimer sprawling backwards through the doorway onto the garden path. Before he could right himself, the largest gang member moved out of the shadows in the front garden, clasped both of Mortimer's shoulders and drove him back into the house. This made him drop the flowers and realise what was happening.

The homeowner threw his crown back, butting back hard into his assailant's nose, which exploded in blood. This loosened his heavy embrace and allowed Mortimer to fire both elbows into the pit of the thug's paunch. The attacker retched and fully let go of Mortimer. The homeowner saw three five-litre plastic water bottles just inside the front door. He had been planning for the coming war. Luckily for him, Karen had not brought them in yet. The assailant shook his head then pulled out a thin seven-inch blade. Mortimer swooped down and grabbed the plastic ring lid and swung the heavy five-litre bottle upwards through a semi-circle into his advancing enemy's temple. The lump now fell backwards through the doorway and landed face up on the garden path. Stunned by the blow, he was unable to move. Next to his head lay a broken paving slab. Mortimer reached down and without pause for breath or reflection dropped the hard triangle slab, edge down, into his fallen attacker's face.

"Bill... Bill..." Karen called from inside the house.

Mortimer stormed back into the house and turned right into the lounge. And there he froze. The man from Waterloo held Karen around the neck with a knife pointed at the side of her throat.

The third member of the gang, slightly taller but unmistakeably the brother of the leader, stood next to Tom, Mortimer's eight-year-old son. He pointed his pistol barrel to the boy's ear. The boy was stiff with fear, his eyes closed and the rest of his face clenched tight. The brother looked at the doorway, waiting for the dead man. Tears streamed down Karen's face.

"Bill."

But Mortimer just stood there a few feet inside the room, not wanting to move forward or back.

"Hey, Sphinx, Sphinx… where are you, man?" The man from Waterloo called for his dead sidekick.

Mortimer said nothing.

"This is the police. Put down your weapons." Everyone looked up at the ceiling. The deep robotic voice came from the police helicopter that circled above the house. The electric-blue beam of the searchlight fell through the crack in the middle of the closed curtains.

"Where the fuck is Sphinx?"

"Drop the gun… please… drop the gun…" Mortimer drawled slowly at the brother.

"What the fuck? Where's Sphinx?"

"Kill the boy, Ram," ordered the man from Waterloo.

Karen screamed. Mortimer felt his breath sucked out of him.

The first armed policeman through the doorway bundled Mortimer against the wall. But Ram pulled the trigger, and the lights went out for eight-year-old Tommy. The second armed policeman shot Ram between the eyes.

He then gave the leader a chance.

"Let her go."

SecuriState arrived late but that did not matter to the justice system, because everything had been captured by the street cameras: the home invasion, the homeowner fighting back and the homeowner killing the invader.

Seven days later, Mortimer re-entered Kingston Courtroom Number Eleven to receive his verdict. The jury had already left the courtroom as the judge started to speak.

"William Alexander Mortimer, this court finds you guilty of murder. A man died on your property by your hand. Have you anything to say?" The judge was a slight figure, hunched forward in his black robes of authority.

"Fuck you, you're no better than the scum who entered my house."

Mortimer stood ramrod straight, as tall as he could in the dock. He could look down on the court physically as well as morally.

The judge raised his voice.

"According to the Public Safety Acts of 2031, the cameras are able to provide all the necessary protection. You knew the police would arrive very quickly. Self-defence is illegal and not a matter of private choice."

"And what about my son? Where was his protection?" Mortimer replied.

"The police are not and cannot expect to be perfect. The world is imperfect."

Mortimer silently seethed at the man in black.

"So, this court will now pass sentence. For the crime of murder, albeit under extreme provocation, William Alexander Mortimer is sentenced to twenty years in prison."

"Excuse me, I've got something to say." Mortimer interrupted.

The explosion from the rocket-propelled grenade rocked the square and sent civilians and brigades running for cover into the surrounding blocks. Fortune favoured those least exposed to the flying fragments and Hendrick's bodyguards gave him that. Mortimer instinctively rolled to the ground, sliding up to the now dead eight-year-old boy. Blood gushed from the side of his forehead where a flying slab of tarmac had entered his skull. The Shield bodyguard with the pistol writhed and moaned on the ground from a piece of shrapnel wedged in his chest. Mortimer recognised his noises: it was the sound of a man unable to believe such physical pain was possible. But he had also done his job and saved his boss, who lay still underneath him, face down, trying to make himself one with the tarmac.

The other bodyguard shook himself to his feet like a man who had just drunk the bar dry. He fumbled for his pistol but the concussion in his head and out there in the open meant he did not stand a chance. A Molotov cocktail exploded at his feet and set his bottom half on fire. He loosed off a few bullets in the direction it had come from before the flames brought him down to his knees. Mortimer watched the man flap his arms hysterically to extinguish the fire until they could flap no more.

Another homemade device exploded nearby and immediately belched black smoke over the centre of the square. The nasty chemical fumes quickly filled his nose and throat but Mortimer still got to his feet. Smoke was your friend in these situations, even if it made your eyes stream and stomach retch. He rode the black shroud off to the southern side of the square and streamed into the nearest open doorway. It was the pedestrian entrance to the old multi-storey carpark.

Inside, wounded policemen were strewn around the parking bays. Those who were still fit enough clustered around the doorways and fired back at the local hostiles in the opposite buildings.

Mortimer turned back and looked out at the burning square. Where was Hendrick? He had disappeared. Typical, men like him always survived; they did not die easily, like the mass of ordinary, clueless idiots around him.

Mortimer returned to his senses thanks to a stinging thump on the side of his head. An empty vodka bottle fell at his feet. He spied the young drinker from his brigade lying about six feet away. He grinned the grin of a helpless fool who could not stand up. He clutched his midriff with his non-drinking arm to staunch the flow of blood.

"Got a drink, mate?" said his subordinate.

Mortimer sighed and said nothing.

He fumbled in his pocket and threw the man his flask, probably not enough to satisfy the young drinker but it would ease the pain.

Mortimer had to leave this desperate place now. A set of double doors marked with "Exit" in red letters at the far end of the parking bays seemed his obvious destination. No-one followed him into the long, empty corridor. He broke into an easy trot and felt himself unwind a little as the sound of gunfire got further away. Or as much as any man can who knew he would be running forever. His open show of disobedience to Commissioner Hendrick would at least earn him a permanent return to Sheerness if he was lucky or else a quick bullet in the neck and an unmarked grave. But for the first time today he was on his own in this grey concrete sanctuary and it felt good. The longer the locals resisted the better his chances of escape. And maybe Hendrick was even dead.

He swung around the corner at the far end and only avoided the open door in his path by careering awkwardly into the adjacent wall. His left shoulder took the brunt of the collision. It was the door of a maintenance cupboard; brown boilersuits hung from rails with the word "Energy" stitched in red letters across the back. These outfits were used by visiting contractors from the energy companies to identify and protect them on the estate. According to the government, all supplies of gas, electricity and water into areas controlled by criminal gangs had been officially disabled but even in these times you could not stop market forces.

Mortimer pulled off his Shield tunic and dropped it into the corner of the cupboard. He then grabbed what looked to be the largest of the three outfits off the rail, unzipped and stepped inside it. His damage-free shoulder twisted easily into the right arm but he grimaced as he forced his painful left shoulder into its arm. He then rubbed the lump on his thigh to check that the pistol was still pocketed in his grey police trousers under his new brown uniform.

At the bottom of the corridor, Mortimer pushed through another set of double doors into the daylight of late afternoon. Gunfire still reverberated from the other side of the building. The fugitive dashed into the grassy waste ground that lay ahead then stopped at a single-lane road that ran along the perimeter of the estate. Today it was unsurprisingly quiet and traffic-less. Across the tarmac was an empty gravel area that may have been a carpark once. It stretched a short distance then suddenly disappeared into the tall grey blocks of the city in the far distance. Mortimer picked up the pace again towards the steep drop at the far end of the gravel. He stumbled down the bank onto the verge of another road, this time wider, and it went somewhere. A large Enfield green road sign towered over Mortimer a few feet away. It pointed drivers to places in Kent, which meant the opposite way was London. No traffic again, he legged it across to the other side into the welcoming screen of thick fir trees. The cover soon ran out and Mortimer emerged into the layby of a service station. It was the truck-stop, large enough for a fleet of twenty or thirty vehicles, but today only a single articulated lorry was parked tidily at the side of the curb. Printed on its black curtain in six-foot-high letters was the word "Albion".

Mortimer recognised the Albion convoys from his days at

the front, supplying food, equipment and weapons to the soldiers as well as transporting prisoners of war into captivity. According to the BBC, Albion was a voluntary aid organisation provided by the people of Europe to assist a country devastated by foreign invasion. Now it brought supplies to the civilian population, anything from bread to pets' toys. All the necessities and trivialities required by a country in chaos. But this was not a benevolent aid scheme at all; this was a highly profitable monopoly run by wealthy corporate funders of the Shield Movement for the benefit of every man, woman and child in the single European home.

Chapter 12

The lorry faced towards London just as Mortimer required. He strode towards the driver's cab and waited outside on the curb. The driver would be fast asleep or relaxed and resting, not expecting a fugitive to be knocking on his window. Mortimer counted the seconds before the driver appeared upright in his front seat. Eleven, nearly twelve but probably shaken reluctantly out of his R and R. A long, greasy black mane half-hiding a stubbled face with a pair of dark glasses resting on his nose wound down the window.

"Yes, squire...?"

Mortimer cleared his throat.

"Sorry to disturb you, but I was wondering if you were going into the city?"

"Sure. Get in t'other side."

Mortimer walked around the front of the lorry and climbed in through the open door. He hauled himself up into the passenger seat and closed the door. The driver was dressed in a blue denim jacket and trousers lightly flared at the bottom, finished off by a pair of patterned cowboy boots. Under his jacket he wore a black t-shirt.

"Hi, I'm Roger." The name and dress of a throwback to an earlier age when people were happy to talk to people they did not know.

"I'm Bill."

"You caught me at the right time. Just about to leave."

As Roger pressed the ignition button under the steering wheel, Mortimer heard a low, barely audible voice from the radio that the driver had probably turned down seconds before he got in the cab. Roger leant forward and switched off the radio.

"Don't let me interrupt," interrupted Mortimer.

"No, that's okay. Prefer to listen to a real person."

Eyes back on the road, Roger pulled off the layby and onto the A road. Mortimer looked ahead and then into the rear view mirror; still no other traffic in either direction.

"London… yeah. Whereabouts?" enquired Roger.

"As close to the centre as possible," replied Mortimer.

"So, what happened? Did you get left behind out there? Not a good place to be left."

"Yeah. I was in a water team on the estate and all hell broke loose. Police and troops everywhere. Obviously a raid or something. I was out of there; God knows where the others are."

Roger said nothing but stared blankly at the road ahead. Mortimer closed his eyes. A few minutes sleep now would help him later when he really needed to be alert. But of course, Mortimer's brain did not follow orders easily. Why the urgency to leave? And then to switch off the radio so quickly in his own lorry. Roger was in decent physical condition; within the long dark locks and denim suit hung a strong, wiry frame around six foot tall, somewhere in his early forties, like Mortimer. The t-shirt puffed up only very lightly around his stomach. Hung behind him was the flag of the Confederacy, the original rebel flag. Mortimer reckoned Roger was probably a man who wanted to look back to better times. Mortimer lay back, stretched himself out and closed his eyes. But he could not sleep; the adrenaline was still racing and he felt he should take the initiative and fill up the silence on his terms as best he could. He gave it no more than five minutes.

"You're part of the aid convoy?"

"That's what they call us. Yep, heading into the underground depots just north of Regent's Park, at the cricket ground."

"That's near where I'm going." Mortimer sounded relieved.

"Yeah, good." Roger turned and smiled.

From the side of his eye, Mortimer caught the cot that Roger had been relaxing in twenty minutes ago. An unfolded and unmarked large field-green tarpaulin sheet lay on the bed. Mortimer recognised it as the standard military-issue groundsheet provided to any Homeland soldier. Roger kept his eyes on the road, at a steady speed of sixty miles an hour on the A2 towards London.

"So why are you going to Lords? The cricket's been cancelled." Roger broke the silence.

"I live round there." That's all Mortimer could say.

"Nice place to live. Bet not many plumbers live inside the White Zone." Roger turned to Mortimer.

"Well, it pays better than driving a lorry." Mortimer could not help himself.

"I'd rather be a lorry driver than a man on the run," fired back Roger. Mortimer could see that the traffic was building up now as they got closer to London.

Vehicles pulled on and off the A2 in both directions. It occurred to him that he would rather be in an articulated lorry swerving out of control into cars than in a car swerving out of control into an articulated lorry. But there was a seat in between that would give Roger enough time and space to fight Mortimer off.

"I heard on the radio. You shot a Shield officer on the estate and then buggered off. Respect, man."

Roger took his right arm off the steering wheel and raised his palm towards Mortimer. "Total fucking respect, man. The Shield are the biggest cunts around, and you got a big one there."

"You sure about that?" Mortimer growled back.

"Plumbers do not wear Shield-issue leather boots, Mr Mortimer."

Roger felt confident in both assertions.

"You're all over the police networks. That's what I was listening to."

"Obviously it's my lucky day." And Mortimer meant it.

"Sure is. Albion trucks don't stop at roadblocks. We'll be in town before dark." About half a mile ahead, red warning lights flashed on and off from a roadside camera tower. A police checkpoint; they were getting closer to the city.

"Fuck the Shield, man. I have had enough of these gangsters. This country's gone and those bastards are moving in with all their bullshit about a new home. They're as corrupt as fuck, man."

Roger paused before delivering his withering coup de grâce. "Cunts."

"You'll get a reward if you hand me in," replied Mortimer.

"They might own the politicians but they don't own me."

Mortimer smiled and looked out of the window, not quite believing his ears, given the fine examples of human nature he had witnessed only a few hours ago.

"And I tell you, I wish there were more of us fighting back like the UKP."

Mortimer ignored this last point. The UKP had been Yank collaborators and deserved everything they got.

"Tell me. Did you fight in the north?" asked Mortimer.

"I was in the army, not the Shield. Transport, drove trucks. I saw the atrocities committed by those bastards, against our own as well as the Yanks."

"There were collaborators, you know, and war is war."

Mortimer did not know why he suddenly started to defend the Shield war record, given that he was forcibly conscripted on pain of death.

"But they're the worst. I'm telling you."

The traffic started to slow as they got closer to the police checkpoint. The driver flicked the indicator before pulling into the outside lane that would take them past the checkpoint. The lorry slowed to no more than ten miles per hour as it passed the armed policemen waiting in the left-hand lane.

"This is as fast as I can go, I'm afraid."

After fifty metres or so the lorry swung back into the inside lane.

"So where do you plan to go?"

"I haven't planned anything," shot back Mortimer.

The sun was getting lower in the early evening sky and the city was lighting up all around him.

"You'll be on TV soon, the renegade policeman."

Mortimer knew that his Shield mugshot would be beamed from all the street screens in central London, accompanied by a voice-over declaiming him as a terrorist and a threat to public safety. Whatever that was supposed to mean, the message was clear. Mortimer knew he had to get indoors for the night, somewhere out of the reach of the security forces. Curfew at ten p.m. would give him about four hours to go to ground once he reached the city centre. If he was still on the streets at curfew, he would be back in solitary in Sheerness by dawn if he was lucky.

"I hope you've not got a family, for their sake," said Roger.

"Don't worry, I'm on my own."

But that was not true. There was still Leah. She would be a fully grown mature yellow Labrador now. The last time Mortimer saw her, she was a six-month-old puppy that he had bought for Tom for his eighth birthday. And Leah lived with Terry, the only mate who had ever visited him at Sheerness. Unable to cope after Tom's death, Karen got rid of Leah by giving her to Terry. Terry lived in Maida Vale, not a million miles from St John's Wood.

"Man, I wish I could help you, but I gotta be back at the depot," Roger went on.

"I know where I can go." Mortimer wanted to put Roger out of his misery. "A mate of mine lives a few miles away."

The driver turned to Mortimer, his eyes widened, wanting to ask the question. Pause.

"It wouldn't be fair on you or your family."

Roger looked hurt, offended at the lack of trust shown in him by the man whose life he may have saved. But he also understood that too much information could be a bad thing. Anyway, their journey would end soon, and Mortimer was on his own and he could do nothing more to help him.

The articulated lorry crossed over the river at Vauxhall Bridge and made its way towards Hyde Park.

As it slowed onto the roundabout, Mortimer faced himself, unsmiling, from a hundred-by-hundred-feet television screen in the middle of the circle. The word "Deserter" flashed in black letters above his unsmiling, newly shaven head. The image was taken from his Shield ID. A completely shaven head does not flatter a man of forty plus; it makes him look like a man who has still not come to terms with the world, who is stuck in a rut, maybe, or stuck in an institution where you probably have to wear a uniform to match the haircut. In other words, William Alexander Mortimer. As Mortimer smiled to himself, Roger noticed the silver Shield insignia on the black collar. He sighed.

"You're wearing a Shield uniform. I thought you were just a conscript copper who had had enough."

"No; I was a Shield brigade leader who fought and killed on the Mercian front." Pause. "Please drop me at the top of the Edgware Road, by Regent's Park."

Roger sighed again and switched back to concentrating on the roundabout exit. Mortimer looked out of his window into the gathering twilight and yawned. At least the brown overalls had done the trick so far.

A minute or so later, the lorry pulled over abruptly and stopped in front of the entrance to a black-and-grey Brutalist office tower block. It had been built in the last century but strangely it did not feel out of place or out of time. Mortimer turned to Roger with his hand outstretched.

"Thanks, mate."

Roger stared at him for a few seconds then accepted his hand. "My pleasure."

His tone was as dull and flat as a Lincolnshire beach in the middle of winter. Mortimer opened the passenger door of the cab and jumped onto the curb. He had no time to explain himself to a man whose ideals could not be reconciled with the reality of the last hour or so. Mortimer turned to raise his arm, but Roger was only interested in the rush-hour traffic in his rear-view mirror. The gap only gave him a few seconds but foot to the pedal, he pulled the articulated lorry away from the curb. Mortimer stood there waving, feeling very, very grateful to Roger.

Chapter 13

Although the rush hour had started, the pavement was not crowded. London was never that crowded any more. Head down, Mortimer set off, passing by a large branch of the German supermarket chain Werners before he came off the main drag at his first opportunity. He turned down a nondescript road lined by modern blocks of flats then swung first left onto Sussex Gardens, a tree-lined avenue of wealthy townhouses and most importantly, no cameras. For people who could pay, cameras were an unnecessary infringement of their freedom to do what they liked. With the tree cover as well, this was a good place for Mortimer to be. Although he did notice after a minute or so that he was the only person on either side of the street. A few house lights were switched on, but many were still dark and only Mortimer was outside, walking as fast as he could to Maida Vale.

When he reached the junction of Praed Street and London Street, he stopped to take his bearings and caught sight of the large edifice that was Paddington station. He could never board a train even if he wanted to. You needed identification to buy a ticket, so that meant a long weekend in the West Country was out of the question. But then he heard loud cheering, triumphant-sounding male voices, as if football fans were inside the station. Football, alas, had been halted due to the war and who knew when it would start again. First one appeared, then three, ten, fifteen – more than fifty black-uniformed Shield militiamen strode up the slope that fed the cavernous station entrance-exit.

The Shield Security Militia was the elite guard unit responsible for domestic security as well as internal security of the Shield. They managed the police units as well as any private sub-contractors like SecuriState. The Militia were the muscle of the movement.

It was the victory rally in Hyde Park to celebrate the repulsion of the US invaders. Thousands of regime loyalists, as well as these thugs, would soon be swarming through central London. The black mass reached the top of the slope and then broke into two to avoid the traffic. A small minority of very arrogant or simply very drunk militiamen walked between the cars. The cars slowed to a crawl to allow the defenders of the faith their right of way. One section sprawled onto Mortimer's side of the street and marched towards him. As they got closer, Mortimer could see the smiling, beaming faces of young women.

Black uniforms always looked good, as every nasty bunch of control freaks on a mission has understood for centuries, but they always look better on females: the tighter, more stylish tunic with the trousers cut off just under the knees folded into tall leather boots, albeit flat-heeled for obvious reasons. For a few seconds, Mortimer forgot he was now a fugitive but that he was a decorated war hero who fought for these fine young men and women. They would look up to him as a role model, a bad man made good by the Shield, awestruck and jealous in equal parts by his valour on the Mercian Front. And the stories he could tell the young women that would make his age disappear in front of their very eyes.

It was only when the advance guard were a few metres away that reality shook him out of his fantasy. One ambitious, sharp-eyed opportunist and he would be in a cell again. Mortimer could not draw attention to himself, so he walked slowly away from the station, letting the mob catch up with him. As they waltzed past, he dropped his head and turned to stare through a shop window full of boxes of supposedly organic vegetables. The prices were exorbitant. He thought about retreating inside the doorway of the health food store, but his movement might turn a black head. He was good at retreating; he could tell the lovelies about Derby, where he saved his men. After a few minutes of wondering who could afford the fare on offer and concluding that it would be the usual suspects; the elite, their well-paid wing of their service class in the banks and government, the mob had passed by and Mortimer could move on. He followed them from a distance up Praed Street and then took the first left.

The pavements were empty again on a much quieter residential street. He passed a few blocks of flats then noticed two policemen stood at the first turn-off under the dim light of a street camera. These were not the grey-uniformed Shield cops but the private plods of SecuriState. Their uniforms were bigger and baggier than the greys and so were the men and women inside them. They seemed to be chatting idly, but Mortimer realised they had been stationed there on purpose. Security in the capital would be tight tonight because of the Peace Rally, which might provide an opportunity for what the government would call a "terrorist" attack.

Halfway between him and the coppers stood a double-doored entrance to a bar with the word "Crusader" flashing in blue neon lights above. Mortimer looked down at the pavement, hunched forward until he reached the blue light then shoved through the doors as if he were a local. He swerved around the tables, not looking at any of the drinkers and stopped at the bar.

Next to him, three older men, probably in their late fifties, chatted quietly, more interested in what the other had to say and the whisky in their glasses than the TV screen on the opposite wall. The fifty-inch screen belted out the usual propaganda: happy, smiling soldiers of the Homeland, grim-faced US prisoners of war and cheering civilians. The volume had been turned down but it would not be long before the inevitable news flash would appear.

It struck Mortimer that these ruddy-faced, greying whisky enthusiasts were proper, civilised drinkers able to hold strong liquor early in the evening without making fools of themselves. Each man was well-built, with a hard, weathered, lived-outdoors face, probably builders or maybe trackmen from Paddington who had finished their shift. And probably a damn sight more useful in a house-to-house combat operation than his colleagues on the estate.

"Drink?" the young man behind the bar enquired.

Mortimer noticed the St George's logo on the beer tap in front of him.

"Yeah, pint of Fuller's, please."

It had been a long time since Mortimer had tasted decent bitter. As the bartender filled up the glass with the foaming brown liquid, the nearest and largest of the three whisky drinkers moved towards the doorway in the right-hand corner marked "Gents". His full glass of malt whisky stood a few inches from Mortimer's elbow. Mortimer felt the space open up next to him and the glare of two men stood the other side of the whisky group. Both men were dressed in black leather jackets and loose-fitting black jeans. He realised these were men on a mission. He turned back to the barman.

"And a box of matches, please."

"Five Euros altogether."

The bartender placed the full pint on the bar-top and a box

of matches without a second glance at the fugitive. Mortimer pushed the five Euros into his open palm. Mortimer picked up the glass, head down, and lifted the glass to his lips, sipped then took the glass away and stared at the bottom longingly and breathed deeply. The men in leather moved from their spot. Mortimer supped again, to give them their chance to say hello.

"Game over, buddy."

As expected, the few seconds of bliss came to an end, and also as expected, it was the short one who opened his mouth first. He was chubby as well, with grease-stiffened blond-grey hair like a badly fitted hairpiece on his solid round head. The other one was a few inches taller than Mortimer, with a long, angular face. The tall one wore an earpiece and held up a phone screen with "Wanted, 90,000 Euros" flashing in red on the same photo displayed earlier on the TV screen at Hyde Park.

The short man spoke again. "You're a wanted man, Mortimer."

"Really? Who wants me?"

"The Shield Security Service."

The short man smiled triumphantly as if the devil himself would fear the Shield Security Service.

"Or maybe two bounty hunters," said Mortimer.

A licensed bounty hunter could legally carry a weapon as well as get instant access to real-time electronic feeds from the government crime database. This put them on a par with any policemen, certainly SecuriState, who were only left to tidy up: check the identity of the body, fill out forms and transfer the reward money into the required bank account after the bounty hunters had done their dirty work. SecuriState controlled the licensing of bounty hunters that provided them with a healthy revenue stream and also removed any liability for errors such as the death of or injury to an innocent civilian. Corporate unaccountability was one of the few things not lost from the early years of the twenty-first century.

"Shit. Other trackers are out." The tall man spoke.

His device flashed "75,000 Euros". The short man looked down at his screen. Mortimer leaned back against the wooden bar rail and pushed his right arm out to steady himself and touched a full whisky glass. Without looking around, he curled his fingers around the cylinder and drew it into his palm. He waited for the short man to look up then threw the brown sticky liquid into his fat face.

Doused in a fine single malt, the short man moaned and raised his fingers to wipe his eyes. When they opened again, he saw a matchbox in Mortimer's left hand and a single unstruck match in his right.

The tall man pushed his hand inside his jacket.

"Put it away. Or your boyfriend will need a new face."

The tall man dropped his hand. The three whisky drinkers saw the commotion and retreated away from the bar into an interested semi-circle around Mortimer and the bounty hunters. The hand-held device bleeped. Mortimer's price had dropped again; "60,000 Euros" flashed in red.

Head down, Mortimer charged straight through the growing circle of onlookers towards the open doorway in the far corner. The word "Gents" was painted in large golden letters on the wall above. He surged through the exit onto a steep wooden staircase beyond, no more than twenty-five steps in height. Two steps covered for each one of his, he reached the landing. Walled ahead, he swung right, the only way he could go and charged up a longer flight of stairs. The effort required to raise his knees made him curse the second set of stairs, somewhat ungratefully, considering they delayed the return of the whisky drinker who had left Mortimer his weapon. The stairs finished at a heavy mahogany door marked with a large G symbol.

He pushed the door open, slipped inside then slammed it shut. He groped around for the light switch and illuminated a far more impressive pub privy than he had expected. A traditional shiny white ceramic stand-up urinal, wide enough for at least four adult males, stood against the side wall, with two toilet cubicles against the opposite wall. Fixed between the cubicles were two shiny white ceramic basins with thick chrome taps. All very compact, in the limited space available. The floor was stylishly tiled with black-and-white squares on a solid-grade laminate. Everything was encased in a spotless, gleaming white-tiled chamber. And most importantly, it was empty, as indicated by the gap at the bottom of the cubicles.

But Mortimer noticed that there was something missing amidst the above-average sanitary ware. The window. An extractor fan whirred away a few inches below the ceiling above the urinals, but no other ventilation point existed.

Mortimer heard the bounty hunters on the stairs. Three black metal bolt latches were fixed to the door, one at the top, one in the middle and one six inches off the floor. He pulled each barrel across to lock the heavy mahogany door.

The two bounty hunters reached the toilet door but rather than force the door open got distracted by a tall, long-haired figure in a long black leather coat climbing the stairs towards them.

"Surprise, surprise," muttered the taller man sarcastically.

Not all bounty hunters worked in groups. Most did because it gave them extra firepower and greater resources, but there were always the lone wolves. This one came from Paris. The

Frenchman stopped on the final stair in front of his fellow professionals.

"I have spoken to the manager. Two things. There's no window in there and this place is Albanian-owned."

The short man smirked when he heard the heavy accent, nodded at the Frenchman and turned back to the door.

"You're going nowhere, Mortimer. There's no window. You're trapped," he bellowed triumphantly.

"I suspect he has worked that out," said the Frenchman slowly and quietly like he was talking to a small child.

On the other side of the door, Mortimer heard and said nothing. There was nothing meaningful to say. They were right. A few seconds later, the Frenchman spoke again but this time to Mortimer.

"But that's okay, dude. We can wait."

The short bounty hunter was not sure. "I'm not hanging around in this dump. Let's go through the door."

"It's okay, Mal. I've registered him. Any damage and we pay. You know who owns this bar," the taller of the duo explained.

The fat jowly face fell into a sigh. "I fucking hate them. But we can't have trouble from the Albanians and still work round here."

Meanwhile, Mortimer stared at the white walls and ceiling, all sealed in white ceramic with the pipework running over the tiles rather than inside the wall. Obviously, the owner did not want to have to rip up the tiles every time there was a leak, or maybe it was for artistic purposes. Anyway, there was no way through without a pickaxe or at the very least a small-handled axe. But the two thick plastic water pipes that supplied the cubicles and the sinks gave him an idea: The chamber was small and watertight, and he could flood it.

Mortimer entered the nearest cubicle, stood on the toilet seat and grabbed the plastic water pipe with both arms and yanked it downwards. The pipe loosened and the collar cracked. Mortimer pulled harder and the pipe slipped out of the collar completely. Cold water streamed over his head and down his neck. He jumped down quickly and left the water pouring down the wall onto the floor.

"Hey, no hurry in there. It's great you brought us to a restaurant." The short man had realised he could claim a meal back on expenses. The taller bounty hunter laughed.

Mortimer now realised he had not checked the door. It had been fitted to comply with fire regulations so in theory nothing could get between the door and its frame, not even light. But he could see what might have been only a few millimetres of gap between the floor and the bottom edge of the door. Fortunately, two whitewash towels hung side by side above the handle. He lifted one of the towels off its hook and dropped to his knees in slow motion.

On the other side of the door, a young, attractive Columbian waitress was busy taking the food order and distracting the three hunters. The height of her skirt and the depth of her top meant the three bounty hunters would never have heard Mortimer even if he shouted his order.

He rolled up the towel lengthways as tight as he could and jammed it into the gap. The chamber was now ready.

The three bounty hunters agreed that three burgers between them would be enough. Anything else would slow them down, especially salad.

Mortimer lifted himself onto the rim of the sink furthest from the door and pulled hard on the plastic water pipe against the wall. Same as before: the pipe sagged and then loosened at the collar. One more tug and the pipe flew out of the collar, spewing water onto the floor. The sound of the water pouring onto the now saturated floor startled Mortimer. High-pressure fast-flowing water was exactly what he needed but not to be heard outside.

The Frenchman rapped hard on the door and called out. "Come on, my friend. Do you want to order as well? The menu is very good."

Mortimer violently pushed the broken end of the pipe against the wall to force the water to run down the wall rather than arc into the air then splash noisily onto the floor. The sound of the water instantly quietened to what could be a trickle from a tap. Mortimer dropped down to the floor. The water now filled the floor and was rising over his ankles, well protected in his Shield-issue leather boots. This was a new bathroom, installed quickly and cheaply and rather fortunately for him, the water pressure was higher than required for a relatively small public karzi.

Mortimer now wondered why the bounty hunters did not force the door. He knew the police would not be interested for a day or so. The licence allowed bounty hunters forty-eight hours to bring him in without interference from the authorities. Maybe they really did want to eat first.

As the water reached his knees, Mortimer realised the brown maintenance uniform would give him away back out on the streets. But he could not change until he got out of the Crusader. And then he would be a mess, soaked right through, trailing water down the street and quite a sight even at night-time. The uniform had to be saved from the water.

He perched himself on the double sink unit, unzipped himself from the neck down to his groin and twisted his arms out of the maintenance-man outfit. The flapping flared trouser ends made it easy for him to pull his legs out. He then took off his battle-dress tunic, trousers and boots. He retrieved the battered paperback from the long side-pocket of his tunic, letting the photograph slide into his fingers. It was still there. This reminded him of the boy on the estate earlier. Was Tom as brave as that boy? Mortimer slammed the book shut with the photo inside and laid it over his uniform before rolling it into a tight bundle. He then entered the nearest cubicle and placed his most precious possessions on top of the cistern. They would be out of the water there and he would wrap them around his neck when the time came to exit. His sweaty body easily re-entered the brown overalls. He then dropped himself slowly into the water, which now reached his waist.

"You know we got here first. So it's only fair we get a larger share," said the short bounty hunter.

"You know where you can stick your bullshit poetry," the Frenchman shot back. "Two minutes after you but I still registered him in time, so it's a fair split."

"But there's two of us and one of you. So a third each is fair."

The short man looked at his tall sidekick, who shrugged his shoulders.

"We're two different crews. So it's gotta be fifty-fifty. Check the code." The Frenchman was getting annoyed now.

The attractive Colombian waitress then re-appeared on the stairs with three burgers and chips and three beers, compliments of the house.

"The manager said he would call the owner, Mr Kyriax. He will send someone to take the door off for you."

"Great news. When will they be here?" The short man lit up.

"In an hour… he said," replied the girl.

"That's okay. We can wait," assured the Frenchman.

The waitress smiled at him and held it for a few seconds, raising the possibility in his mind. But the Frenchman was not interested and looked away. This was work, his work, his livelihood, lucrative work that could easily be screwed up.

"Great piece of meat." The tall English bounty hunter smiled at the waitress. His short partner giggled, almost choking on a mouthful of medium-rare cooked meat.

"Allo, allo, my friend. We are still here… soon the door will be opened… Yeah." The Frenchman rapped hard on the door.

"You know, he's got to be up to something."

"A shit. A long shit. That's all he can do in there," said the tall Englishman.

"Thank you," interjected the shorter one, disturbed by the image whilst filling his face.

The Frenchman picked up the burger from the plate and held it a few inches from his mouth.

"He is too quiet."

"Let's enjoy the food… and wait. It's that fucking nutter, Kyriax. You ever come across his men?"

Mortimer stood on the toilet seat in the cubicle nearest to the door to keep as much of himself out of the water as possible. Thanks to that water pressure, the water was above his midriff now. His precious bundle now sat on top of the cistern.

The water was cold and carried a grey-brown film on the surface from the grease and dirt on the toilet floor. This blurred the white walls under the surface and seemed to darken the chamber. Mortimer felt the chill rise through his body at about the same speed as the water rose. It was not as cold as the English Channel but certainly chilly enough to make a man impatient to get out. Mortimer craned his neck and stared up at the ceiling two feet or so above him, where the white strip light still shone brightly. Give it another foot or so until the water was above his shoulders.

Outside, the bounty hunters enjoyed more beer on the house. It would be good publicity for the bar.

"Hey, you've spilt your beer." The short man stared down at the damp patch on the carpet that ran up to the mahogany door. The cheap red cord overlay was a shade darker than before.

"No, I didn't," replied his taller colleague.

The Frenchman crouched down and ran his palms over the carpet. It was saturated all around the door.

"Hey…" He looked up at the door.

The water now lapped his chin; the time had come. Mortimer sank under the flat, greasy water, threw out his arms and took three strokes to reach the door. The ceiling light still worked, which meant he could see the two submerged bolts. He reached down and flicked the bolt open with his left hand. First time, it slid out of the latch, any resistance neutered by the water. Then he held his breath and dived down and pulled the latch open at the bottom of the door. He rose to the surface and stroked his way back to the cubicle, grabbed his precious roll from the cistern and raised it in both hands above his head. It brushed the ceiling as he kicked his legs to get back to the door. The filthy water lapped into his mouth, making Mortimer cough and splutter loudly.

First the wet carpet and then the rattle of the latches: the hunters knew something was happening on the other side of the door. The short bounty hunter pummelled the door with his right fist. "Hey, Shield man, we're coming for you. Open the door."

The taller man stood behind his partner on the postage stamp of a landing. The Frenchman dropped to his haunches on the top step of the stairs. He stared at the damp patch, deep in thought.

"I don't think you should ask him to do that."

With the clothes roll pushed against the wall above the door frame, Mortimer pulled the bolt from the top latch. The hammering and the voice from outside got louder. "Open up, buddy."

Mortimer put his head into the corner of the door and shouted through the crack. "Open the door, I'm coming out."

"Don't…" the Frenchman shouted.

But the short bounty hunter wanted his man. He did not have to pull very hard, as the water surged through the gap, forcing the door wide open. The corner of the hard dark wood crashed against the side of the bounty hunter's skull, dealing him a terminal blow.

The pressure of the wave knocked his taller colleague backwards over the Frenchman, spinning him down the stairs. The Frenchman toppled backwards as the wave rolled over him and left him gasping for air, prostrate on his back. Mortimer was sucked out feet first with his clothes roll stuffed into the top of his brown maintenance uniform under his neck. He ploughed into the face of the Frenchman, who blacked out under the force of Mortimer's size elevens.

The fugitive came to a halt on top of the taller hunter now laid flat out on the landing halfway up. Repeated blows to his head from the wall and the edges of the steep stairs left him too disorientated to even raise his arms. Mortimer jammed his knees into the man's stomach to lever himself to his feet. The fallen bounty hunter man retched pathetically and then gurgled, water rising around his head.

"Mal, hey, Mal…"

Mortimer slammed his right foot into his jabbering maw to send him into silence.

The wave of water had now slowed to a continuous gush, but

this still made the steep carpeted stairs treacherous. With outstretched palms held firm against both walls to stabilise his descent, Mortimer managed to reach the ground still upright. Five or six drinkers gathered in a large puddle of water and gaped at the oncoming Mortimer. At the last second, they stepped back to let the charging bull through and out of the Crusader. The policemen were now gone, so with the clothes roll clasped to his chest, he pumped his knees as hard as possible in the heavy sodden overalls to run as fast as he could away from the bar.

Chapter 14

Like a rat, Mortimer knew his best chance was to be inside a dark and empty building with easy access to a canal. The quickest and safest way to Maida Vale was via the Paddington canal. He could reach the canal via the derelict St Mary's Hospital only a few streets away from Praed Street. Terry had told him about the derelict hospital and the canal in his letters to him in prison. It was where he walked Leah. Burkair Healthcare International, contracted to the NHS, had closed St Mary's in 2034 as part of the emergency measures to stave off national bankruptcy. Of course, like all the other measures, it failed.

Mortimer swung first left, where the SecuriState plods had been standing earlier, to get off the main drag. Disused and unlit commercial buildings greeted him on either side of the road. He stopped for a few seconds to survey the road ahead. The lack of people and any street furniture at all sent a shiver of warmth though his cold, sodden body. Further down, a few lights were on in the aging blocks of flats, but the pavements were empty. He turned into the nearest carless carpark and made for the corner of the red brick building. According to the sign above the glass entrance, a distributor of electronic surveillance equipment used to own the building.

Around the corner, and the cloying darkness made him instinctively drop the clothes roll to the ground and rip his zip down as low as it would go. Mortimer then yanked his arms out of their holes and peeled his legs out of the maintenance uniform for the last time. He realised his feet were dry, bone dry. These boots were good. The Shield always had the best: the best guns, the best food and the best leather boots with their rubber lining that kept his feet dry even under water. The Shield giveth. The Shield taketh away.

The camouflage fatigues were cold and damp but against his body they felt like a heated linen suit after the brown wetsuit. Mortimer's body began to feel itself again. He rolled up the soaked overalls and threw them under a bush next to the perimeter wall. From his top pocket he took out a small electronic flat-screen device that automatically flashed his position on the local street-map as soon as it touched his palm.

St Mary's Hospital was only a street away now. Mortimer returned to the roadside and jogged past more old commercial buildings that had been converted into flats. The lights were on, but the street was still empty. He crossed over the junction at the end of the road and headed towards the river. The silence from the skies above reassured Mortimer. By now, helicopters should be tracking him. Maybe it was the Peace Rally and the potential of a real terrorist threat that gave Mortimer his chance.

A lone dog walker, probably returning from the river, approached Mortimer, who now slowed to a purposeful walk. The large shadow of the derelict hospital building loomed into view. He continued past where the entrance hall had been and swerved down the side road used for human and non-human deliveries. The tarmac quickly fell apart into a broken track that took him down to the canal. No cameras, no streetlights. He relaxed in his own loneliness. According to his palm, Maida Vale was due west along the canal path.

Mortimer thought of his village in Dorset where he grew up. There was no street lighting at night. Incomers had always wanted to install streetlights because they thought it would make the streets safer. But the locals knew different, that street-lights attracted trouble and crime because they lit the way for people outside of the community. Of course, street lighting and cameras were introduced. The incomers had their way, as money always does. And, of course, crime and anti-social behaviour increased. Mortimer had not been back to his village since his mother died ten years ago. Maybe he would go back there someday.

He passed under the Westway Bridge, then another ten minutes before he crossed over the canal at Little Venice. Here the streetlights were switched on as you would expect. He strode through the expensive but short residential streets of white classical stucco houses. From his memory of drinking with Terry in the local pubs, he knew he was close to his destination. He turned into Shirland Road and pulled up his camouflage hood again. In front of him at the junction with Sutherland Avenue stood a black metal post, thicker and taller than a normal lamp post with a red light flashing atop. This meant that it was less than thirty minutes to curfew. When curfew started, it would stop flashing. The skies overhead were still silent, as were the streets. There was nothing to do except walk past it. Mortimer knew that many of these cameras filmed but were not actively monitored before curfew, especially in the areas where the management class of the government and the banks and the corporations resided. A few steps later and the camera spoke through the familiar comforting robotic feminine voice, the same as the one in Trafalgar Square.

"You are now entering Police Zone Eleven, be vigilant, be safe at all times. Curfew starts in twenty minutes. I repeat…"

Sutherland Avenue was busier than the other streets and all those still out were in a hurry, certainly not in the mood to stop a

Shield man. Mortimer could now feel less conspicuous in his brisk walk-jog. He continued along the avenue until the second right turn came into view. He crossed over and entered Thorngate Road. The housing stock was a little more modest here but still a nice place to live. And as Terry pointed out in his letters, there were no cameras down his street.

Then it dawned on Mortimer, he had not heard from Terry since his departure from Sheerness. Maybe Terry had moved; maybe he had died. Mortimer felt cold again, not from any lingering dampness but from fear. Fear of having nowhere to go in curfew.

Mortimer looked around him and could not see any cameras. He started to run, forty-two, forty-four. He ran faster. Fifty-four, fifty-six, fifty-eight. Some houses were lit. Some were dark. Number seventy. He stopped outside the house where he hoped Terry Arliss lived. Mortimer's best mate from university days, a solicitor who worked for one of the largest banks in Europe, VolkHut AG, originally German but now a European-wide enterprise co-owned by a consortium of Russian energy, German manufacturing and English technology oligarchs. VolkHut AG now owned and financed large parts of the bankrupt British state, and it was Terry who spent long hours drawing up the contracts that handed over the functions of the government to the recommended partner companies of VolkHut AG at a very generous price to the taxpayer. SecuriState were a partner of VolkHut AG.

No light downstairs. Mortimer rapped his knuckles hard against the front door. No answer. Mortimer checked his watch: five minutes to curfew. Within ten minutes, police helicopters would be overhead, infra-red cameras filming and monitoring every movement on the ground. He had to get inside, even if it

119

meant breaking in, even if Terry did not live there any more.

He shoulder-barged the front door, which slipped easily off the long broken latch. But as he pushed into the dark hallway, the bark from Leah stopped him. She stood upright on all fours a few metres in front of him, fully grown now, with the deep, throaty bark of a big dog.

"Hey, Leah... good girl."

But she continued to bark louder, to the point that her front legs lifted off the ground in the strain for volume. She did not growl though, and her hackles were down, which was good enough for Mortimer to say hello. And this meant Terry must still live here.

"It's me, Leah... good girl."

He moved towards his second lost child and carefully swept his arm around the side of her body to avoid her large jaw and stroked the back of her head and neck. You never knew; she might still be resentful at him leaving the family home. Luckily for her, on that fateful evening, the dog walker's car had broken down earlier so she never made it home that night. But Leah responded by yelping excitedly and swinging her head back and forth, affectionately demanding more caresses.

Did she remember him or was she just a useless guard dog?

Mortimer eyed the artificial light shining through an open door on the landing above. He closed the front door behind him and made for the stairs. Leah wagged her tail from side to side.

After the day he had had, Mortimer felt quite happy to disturb Terry unannounced. He skipped up the stairs and almost in the same motion he knocked on the door, pushed it open and stepped into the bedroom. Hunched on the floor, back to Mortimer, clad only in a t-shirt, with trousers wrapped tightly around his ankles, was Terry, thrusting hard into a rubber doll.

"Lights on, Terry? Not like you."

His laughter burst out immediately, as much out of relief at seeing his old mate again as catching him in flagrante.

"Bill, mate… Jesus Christ." Terry glowed a deep pink-red like any man caught having energetic sex with an inanimate object. He stood up and pulled up his trousers. Terry was a thick-set figure, shorter but broader than Mortimer but also the same age.

"What the fuck are you doing here?"

"Sorry, mate… sorry to disturb you." He lowered his convulsions to a broken snigger and nodded at the rubber lovely spread-eagled on the floor.

"But it's great to see you," Mortimer said.

"I don't know if I want to see you. You were on TV about half an hour ago."

"You've heard…"

"Why here?"

"Where else? You're my only chance, mate." Pause. "I will go early tomorrow. I promise. I just need to stay tonight."

"Do they know me? Am I on your file?"

"No. I did not report you when I went inside. And you never put the address on your letters, as I asked."

Terry shook his head. "You're back to square one, aren't you. You bit the hand that fed you."

"Unlike Leah, thank god." She now stood in the doorway, still wagging her tail.

"Come here, girl." Terry beckoned her in.

"It's all a bit more complicated than that…"

Mortimer paused himself. He did not want to explain why he had refused an order to execute a boy, or why the boy reminded him of his son.

121

"Come on. Let's get something to eat." Terry smiled.

Being a single man meant that Terry had had enough time on his hands over the years to become a competent if not adventurous cook. Mortimer appreciated this fact as the last mouthful of lamb casserole fell down the back of his throat.

"The best food I've had for years, mate."

"What do you get in the Shield?"

"High-energy snacks and fizzy drinks. Designed to keep you going but never a pleasure. Unlike decent fresh food like this."

"You won't starve in London if you know where to get it."

Both men sat at the kitchen table at the back of the house. Even though it was dark outside, Mortimer studied the back garden, partially lit from the kitchen through the window. Fir trees, seven to eight feet high, lined the three sides and stood in front of an even taller wooden fence.

"What's at the bottom of the garden behind the fence?"

"An alleyway; runs down to the lock-up garages and takes you out onto the main road. Different from the one you came up."

"Garage, eh… I could do with a car."

"And where are you gonna go? The Reservations…"

"I haven't made any plans," scoffed Mortimer.

"A home in the country. That's what it says on TV all the time. They're moving thousands of civilians out of the towns where all the fighting was, where you were in the Midlands and the North. Still a fucking mess up there. I've heard some horrible stories."

"Still better than London for me." Mortimer stared at the bottom of the garden, thinking of the garage and the car parked there.

Terry passed Mortimer a rolled-up cigarette and then

commenced to roll another one. Mortimer put one end in his mouth, took the lighter from the edge of the table, lit the cigarette and drew hard.

"Inside Sheerness, you'd get ten lashes at the post for one of these. They said smoking was bad for us. Cunts."

"So what are you going to do?" Terry now reached for the lighter.

"Into the DMZ and then north to the coast and a port, maybe. A port always gives a man options."

Mortimer inhaled the tobacco and relaxed back in his chair. Terry now had the TV remote control in his hand. He pointed it at the dark flat-screen embedded in the wall behind Mortimer's head. The screen lit up. Before a clear image could settle, Terry changed channels. He did not want the news on.

Mortimer craned his neck around and stared at the TV screen. A chimpanzee that had been dyed royal blue from the neck down and yellow from the neck up stood on a stage in front of a laughing studio audience. The chimpanzee closed his eyes, threw his head back and swung it round and round manically to avoid the gaze of his taunters.

"*Pets Got Talent...* It's great... Belgian TV," said Terry in a flat monotone. "It's either this shit or the news."

"Let's stick to the chimp," said Mortimer.

"Y'know, Bill, you'd think you'd learnt your lesson. They gave you a chance..."

"Truth is, I got out of one prison and found myself in another... this whole country. There's nothing left for me here."

"You're always gonna be on the run, you know that." Terry flicked the ash from his roll-up onto his empty plate.

"Problem is, mate, if you make the right decision in a wrong world, you're always on the run." Pause. "But running ain't gonna get me far." Mortimer shrugged.

Terry sighed. "Well, take my car."

"Really...?" Mortimer blinked then coughed up the smoke in his lungs at this unexpected offer.

"Yeah, it's all ready for a man who has to leave quickly. I hacked into the DVLA database at work and got it registered on special government business. No drone will pick it up and you'll be waved through." Terry sounded very confident.

"And you can get another one."

"No problem."

"Thanks, mate."

Mortimer did not know what else to say. He thought a hug and a kiss followed by tears of gratitude may not be acceptable from one grown man to another. But that's what he felt.

"I do owe you something. For giving me her."

Terry turned and smiled softly towards his snoring Labrador.

"Yeah, I noticed your girlfriend in the bedroom was blond as well."

Chapter 15

Terry always rose early, at six a.m. If you live on your own, it is very easy to follow a routine and that was his. He walked past the open lounge door, ignored Mortimer and entered the kitchen. Mortimer was still lost in a deep knockout sleep, head arched back on the arm of the settee and chest rising and falling with each breath. Terry always made a cup of tea before he opened the curtains in the lounge. This morning he made two cups of tea.

He then entered the lounge but did not wake Mortimer and went straight for the curtains. Two cups of tea were enough break with convention for one morning. Terry pushed open the curtains with both arms and craned his neck forward to look out and check the street in the usual order, first north then south. But this time he did not look south; an Aardvark was parked at the far north end of the street. Five SecuriState men, each armed with a semi-automatic rifle, stood chatting next to the vehicle. The officer in charge stood away from his men, talking into his collar, keeping his station up to date with the lack of progress so far on the house-to-house searches.

"Wakey, wakey, hands off snakey," Terry shouted.

"Bit rich coming from you." Standing behind Terry, Mortimer was dressed and ready.

"How many houses away?"

"Twenty, twenty-five or so on both sides," replied Terry.

"Shit…" Mortimer nodded towards the southern end of the street where another Aardvark reversed into position to block any incoming or outgoing traffic.

"But I can't hear a helicopter."

"Upstairs then," Mortimer barked.

"I need to use the roof."

Terry swung out of the lounge, followed by Mortimer, up the stairs, turned left on the landing past his bedroom then down to the end of the corridor. Up the spiral staircase they pounded and through the open door into the loft. Both men stopped by the solitary single bed that sat under the skylight. The opening to the sky was certainly wide enough to swallow either of them. Leah brushed past Mortimer, who could not help himself bending down and stroking her golden mane.

"You look after him, girl."

Terry brought out a set of keys from his pocket: his car key fob and the old-fashioned garage key. Mortimer jumped onto the bed and pulled down the skylight bar, letting the window fall open.

"Five houses down." Terry raised his arm and pointed southwards.

"Down there you'll find an alleyway. Follow it round and there're a load of garages." He handed Mortimer the keys.

"Number ten. There're supplies in the back."

"Cheers, mate."

Mortimer wanted to say a bit more to Terry, whom he had not seen for years, who now put his own life in danger to save his. But time did not allow anything more than a knowing nod.

"Good luck. Remember to write."

The fugitive grabbed the corners of the opening with both arms, pulled his upper body up though the gap with as much effort as he could muster then dropped himself slowly, face down, flat onto the roof. Mortimer twisted his body around to free his legs then slammed the skylight shut.

Fortunately, the skylight faced the back gardens and not the street. The weathered and uneven tiles gave Mortimer enough purchase to cling onto, stretched out on the down slope of the roof. He heard voices from the street, voices of intent and urgency. He reckoned the police were probably only four or five houses away. They would be entering each house, checking each room then questioning the residents in a cursory fashion. Nothing gained so onto the next house. The cameras must have caught him somewhere, probably on Sutherland Avenue. One of the benefits of the economic collapse was the limits it imposed on the surveillance possibilities of the State. Cameras still only monitored movement at ground level.

The terrace roofs were a symmetrical line of upside-down Vs, each house separated by a one-foot-high brick wall to delineate their boundary.

Mortimer re-pointed himself in a ninety-degree arc, raised himself onto his haunches and scurried, legs bent towards the low brick wall. Careful to keep his head under the peak of the roof, he stepped lightly across the second roof and over the next barrier. Mortimer still heard the voices of the police in the street, who seemed to be keeping pace with him.

He reached the end of the fifth house and came to a halt. Just as Terry had said, the alleyway separated this house from the next. But he would have to go through the back garden; the drop from the roof to the alleyway was too high to avoid at least a couple of broken ankles. Not particularly difficult as long as the occupants were still asleep. He sat down on the roof, facing the back garden, and slid himself down to the edge. He caught his feet in the guttering to stop his momentum from throwing him over the end. He looked down to a rather tasteful natural-stone patio that ran right up to a wooden fence next to the alleyway. A patio meant a patio window and a dining room with maybe a family starting the day underneath him. Again, too high for him to jump without damaging himself. He would have to shin down the pipe. Fortunately, it ran down the side of the wall that was wide enough to completely cover his dangling body from anyone in the kitchen.

Mortimer turned over onto his belly, unhooked his feet from the guttering and dropped them over the edge. He caught the downpipe between his heels and slid his weight down, his midriff protected from the sharp slate edges by the padded felt lining of his tunic. Somehow, he forced his waist and stomach over the roof guttering without bringing the whole thing down. Then he pressed his palms onto the last roof tile and jammed his knees into the wall to steady himself as he lowered his face below the guttering. First his chin then the skin on his bigger-than-average nose scraped against the sharp plastic edge. Once his scalp was below the lip of the pipe, he edged down slowly for a few more inches then pulled up his knees and fired his body off the wall onto the patio below. The drop now was no more than ten feet. Mortimer landed on his ankles as intended and rolled away onto the grass at the side of the wooden fence.

But there was a large rectangular window on the side wall that faced the fence, probably the kitchen window. Mortimer wanted to know what was happening inside. If anyone was up and about that would make things tricky but would not be the worst-case scenario. That would be policemen inside the house already and about to enter the garden.

The window was closed, and Mortimer could not hear a sound. He waited a few more seconds and still he heard nothing. It would save a lot of time and risk if he always assumed the worst and just got on with it. The horizontal beam halfway up the five- to six-foot dark-creosoted wood fence would make it easy for him to do that. Mortimer stood up as if he owned the property and put his left foot on the beam and swung his right side over the fence. He slid down the other side onto the gravel-mud path. Without looking back to the street, he launched himself, head down, in the opposite direction as fast as he could.

He soon entered a gauntlet of lime trees whose branches flicked and caressed his face from either side. A few more yards, the path curved right around a sharp corner then bent left and Mortimer found another line of garden fences, broken up at irregular intervals by the backs of garden sheds and more trees. Openings between the trees that could make him visible from a kitchen window did not distract or slow Mortimer. He kept going as fast as he could. From his Shield training, he knew that the fleeing ninja always cleared his mind of any image of his pursuer, as this would only draw their gaze. Another corner and Mortimer stumbled as a man of forty would running full pelt. His left shoulder bounced him off a tree trunk but without bringing him to the ground. Ahead of him lay a thicker line of trees that obscured the view from the houses on both sides, finished off at the bottom with an arch of drooping branches. He surged on through the leaves and onto the tarmac. Mortimer was out in the open again. In front of him stood a line of twelve garages as Terry had said, each closed with a light-blue door. Behind the garages were the windowless sides of semi-detached houses, two rows running away into the distance.

Number ten. Mortimer stabbed the key into the lock and turned it to the right then pushed his weight forward. The garage door growled and loosened itself reluctantly. The bottom tilted upwards and the top disappeared inside. As promised, a black BMW sat in the gloom. Mortimer squeezed between the breeze-block wall and the car on the driver's side, clicked the key fob and the door opened just enough to let him in. He could not miss the green lump on the back seat. He reached over and pulled the tarpaulin cover back.

As promised, packets of dried food: apples, nuts, cartons of long-life milk, a few loaves of bread, jars of jam and sealed strips of dried meat, probably beef. And a large bag of dog food. But most importantly, a semi-automatic rifle lay in the foot-well of the back seat with five clips strewn around it. Mortimer settled into the driver's seat; large square panels of soft, smooth, grey leather, not too much stitching or fussy design and easy to wipe clean. He wanted to pull down the garage and lock himself in till Christmas.

He wondered if the police had reached Terry's house yet. He would be okay. He would show them his identity card, they would run a check and find who he worked for. That should be enough to prevent any further intrusion. VolkHut AG was a leading commercial partner of the Shield.

The car started first time. Mortimer reversed out of the garage and turned away from the path towards the road. He pulled into another residential street, thankfully not the one he had come from. If Mortimer wanted, he could enter his destination into the driving console, fall asleep and let the car take him there automatically. But this was the frontline again and Mortimer knew that over-reliance on technology often got a man killed. And any car trying to find the fastest way out of North West London would be easily identified and intercepted.

He switched the car to manual to give him something to concentrate on, something to distract him from the more urgent need to plan his route out of London. Anyway, he always struggled to concentrate behind the wheel when you still had to drive cars. Driving never required such a high degree of concentration that it absorbed you, but it could never be a background low-level-of-attention activity like watching TV whilst flicking through your messages. It required an intermediate level of attention, a naught-but-summit experience that never stimulated and generally bored Mortimer. But today, he would concentrate his every waking second on the road, knowing that his life and everything he knew depended on it.

At the end of the street, he turned onto a main thoroughfare busy with other vehicles. The early-morning traffic was building up nicely. Only a few streets then he reached the Westway, the start of his route out of the metropolis. Before it reached the over-policed and over-watched M40, the BMW veered off northwards through the quiet suburban streets of Ruislip, past the common and onto the open parkland of Denham Country Park. Mortimer knew these roads well from his days navigating the outer reaches of North West London and Buckinghamshire in the noble cause of club cricket. The traffic thinned out considerably here as he expected, though you would think in these times more people might seek out this green solace away from the hysteria of the city. Then, under the M25, the BMW sailed along the tree-lined Denham Lane into the B roads of Buckinghamshire.

The government invented regular news stories of carjacking on the quieter roads and lanes in and out of London to discourage drivers from not taking the motorways or main arterial routes. The country roads into the Chilterns were known to be particularly dangerous according to the BBC, which of course really meant that this rugged landscape was beyond the reach of reliable surveillance cameras. It was not the country air or the serene green landscape of rolling hills and sudden woodland that made Mortimer feel like he was breathing for the first time but the fact that he was out of the lair of the beast. He would be happy to drive around this landscape forever.

Chapter 16

As per the terms of the Truce, the London Government had agreed to remove any military forces or installations to the west of a line that split the country from Southampton on the southern coast up to the Peak District in the north and across to Liverpool on the coast. This measure protected the US military forces based in Wales from any sudden attack by Homeland forces. The London Government gave de facto authority to enter the (DMZ) to the Shield, who planned to rebuild and regenerate this area, much of it devastated by the war, through a return to traditional rural values. A refugee resettlement scheme known as The Reservations was the centrepiece of this policy.

Mortimer knew he had to cross the M40 motorway for the Demilitarised Zone (DMZ), which started ten miles west of Oxford. The BMW left the cover of the Chiltern Hills and dropped down towards the motorway where a line of thick concrete bollards, two deep, blocked a lane at the side of the road. Mortimer stopped just beyond what he recognised as anti-tank barriers and looked back down the lane. He saw the motorway underpass a short distance away. The authorities really did not want you going off the beaten track. He was only a few miles from the underpass that would take him into open country away from London and the Shield. But unless he wanted to ditch the car and go on foot, he would have to risk it on the M40. And anyway, the BMW was a damn sight more comfortable than yomping across the countryside. The time for that would come, but for now the car gave him speed and distance.

He followed the road still left open to him and passed along a pretty avenue of trees, planted there to suck up the sound of the motorway. He soon joined a long, slow snake of vehicles on the inside lane of the M40 grinding their way towards the northern horizon. Cones ran down the centre of the middle lane. In the outside lane, the traffic moved freely at speed; military transport vehicles carrying tanks and artillery back from the front as well as civilian-looking but probably government vehicles or their corporate friends. The outside lane was clearly forbidden to everyone else. No signs were necessary. By now, this was obvious to the civilian population.

Mortimer noticed the dial dropping to fifteen, fourteen, then twelve, ten miles an hour. He had time to think. He would have to take the next exit road, even though he really wanted to get closer to Oxford before he left the motorway to get as far away from London as possible. He dropped his eyes to the petrol dial. The tank was half-full, but Mortimer saw that as half-empty. One day, when everything was gone, only the roads would be left. Our stone circles for aliens to discover, to navigate, to dig up and then wonder why. Mortimer quickly left his fantasy about aliens landing on pristine grey strips in a wasteland as the large black people carrier in front slowed suddenly. It was not a vehicle to crash into. The protruding metal body armour bolted to the side panels and the grilled windows radiated nothing but threat. The giant cockroach had been built for battle. Mortimer instinctively opened the glove compartment and relaxed; the Glock said hello.

For the first time, Mortimer noticed the civilians wandering along the edge of the hard shoulder towards him, some on their own, some clustered in small groups, probably families, but all looked exhausted. They carried their only belongings in suitcases or old rucksacks. The luckier ones pushed shopping trolleys rammed full to the brim. The refugees from the north were walking south for sanctuary or a new home in the countryside. In places, the column of misery bulged into the adjacent fields. Those who were victims of chemical weapon blasts were conspicuous by their bandaged eyes and stumbling reliance on a friend or family member to lead them by hand. No-one waved or smiled, so they would never be shown on TV in Trafalgar Square.

Mortimer had not seen the cockroach come to a halt. Just in time, he jammed down hard on the brake pedal, stopping the car inches from the three thick metal bars that ran across the hatch.

But he did not have time to swerve away from the cricket bat that crashed through the passenger windscreen. A young man fumbled for the door handle. Mortimer grabbed the pistol from under his seat, nestled it in his midriff and pressed the button to open the door. The door opened, the cricketer lunged forward but was not fast enough. Mortimer shot the man in the head, who fell backwards to the ground. The cricket bat dropped into the foot-well. Then Mortimer heard and felt the thud of a heavy weight landing on the roof directly above the driver. The batsman's younger obese associate had clambered onto the car. Mortimer instinctively slithered into the passenger's seat but could not help leaving his ankles hooked between the handbrake and the gear stick. Upright on his hind legs, the slob grunted before he thrust the metal stave straight through the driver's roof, piercing the spot on the leather seat where Mortimer's groin had lain a few seconds earlier. He had given Mortimer his position. Mortimer fired once then twice though the roof of the car. The first missed but the second bullet entered the man's neck. The large body slammed down onto the windscreen, floundered onto the bonnet then rolled off onto the tarmac on the passenger side. Led by an outstretched pistol, Mortimer got out of the car.

There were no more attackers but there was an audience from the roadside. Some of the closest walkers stopped and stared blankly at the bodies for a bit but said nothing. Mortimer reckoned their death was a deterrent to any other violent opportunists. For a moment he wondered if the attackers had come from the cockroach or the roadside. He looked up to see that the cockroach was now twenty or thirty yards away in the distance. The traffic in the outside lane continued to flow freely as if nothing had happened.

"Have you finished…?" It was the driver in the car behind, leaning out of his window. Mortimer turned and stared at the man, quietly taken aback by the gentleness of his intervention.

"Come on. The traffic's moving again now."

He was a more attentive driver than Mortimer, more aware of road hazards and had stopped at least six, seven yards behind. The large grey unmarked van was probably carrying important goods. Although mildly annoyed, the driver's calm acceptance of the violence meant he was either a criminal or worked for the State. Mortimer guessed the former, given that he wanted Mortimer to move on. He was probably a smuggler moving black-market medical supplies between London and the north.

Mortimer raised his arm to acknowledge the smuggler and climbed back into the front seat. As he accelerated into the gap in the traffic, black smoke rose from buildings on his side of the road not far away. The motorway service station was in flames. More and more refugees spilt over into the fields, walking away from the burning shops and fast-food outlets. It must have been the fire and the refugees wandering onto the roadside that had slowed the traffic. But now past the hazard, the traffic sped up like there was nothing to see. Soon he was over forty miles per hour, then fifty. Mortimer started to feel the tension from the cricketer's attack ebb away. Killing in close combat, not just in self-defence, was always first and foremost an act to preserve your own life. The relief at the continuation of your own existence always outweighed any moral doubts. Immediately after battle, the senior officer gave each man a strong downer to eradicate the stress that had flooded their nervous systems and to start the inner after-party. That memory was good enough for Mortimer; the straight arm on the steering wheel slackened to a soft V shape, the foot on the pedal lightened and most importantly, his chest loosened.

For a few minutes, he allowed the gap between him and the car in front to widen. At the roadside, a blue motorway sign showed a slip road to Ibstone and Christmas Common one mile ahead. Then behind it, another road sign. Amber letters flashed on a black background: "Roadblock Ahead – Please Slow". In the distance Mortimer could make out a tall metal gantry with towers on either side of the road. It was a Shield roadblock.

Mortimer left the motorway at the slip road and headed downhill towards a roundabout. Left to go west and again into the rolling cover of the Chiltern Hills that stretched into Oxfordshire. He did not use the sat nav in the car to avoid surveillance. The directions were simple: avoid main roads to Oxford, Reading, High Wycombe or any major towns. Stick to the country lanes and narrow roads and follow the afternoon sun now beginning to sink in the cloudless blue sky as best he could. A few miles on and Mortimer remained the solitary car on the grey strip winding its way through the green mosaic of woodland and pasture. During the war, US forces had never pushed this far south, so the countryside here had escaped the damage and destruction to the land wrought up north. But Mortimer still saw no evidence of humanity. The occasional farm or clutch of houses on the side of the road all seemed empty. But the countryside often seemed like that. Alone in the middle of nowhere, Mortimer felt he was on home ground.

For no good reason other than memory and custom he slowed to thirty as instructed by the road sign on entering the hamlet of Christmas Common. Again, the village seemed devoid of any human life. Getting out of London really was like Christmas.

Thick woodland started again outside of the village on his side of the road all the way up to the horizon. The road then disappeared as it dropped down into a valley before it curved upwards towards a sharp bend to the left. As the BMW entered the valley, Mortimer caught sight of the parked Aardvark at the other end. Four Shield policemen were manoeuvring the tripod and barrel of a heavy machine gun in the middle of the road whilst other policemen milled around the vehicle, doing nothing in particular. Mortimer lost sight of them as the road dropped down. He braked hard; there must have been cameras at the side of the motorway; the incident with the young marauders must have been picked up. Too late now to ponder how and why they knew he was here. He had to get off the road. The targeting capabilities of the heavy machine gun meant that even the average copper should not miss a large object speeding towards them in an almost straight line.

Still there was no helicopter and that was a good sign. Mortimer slowed again, almost coming to a halt before the twist in the road that would take him higher again. The heavy machine gun would now be assembled, loaded and readied for him. At least it was the police and not a Shield combat unit. They would not have allowed him such a pleasant country drive.

Looming high above him on his left, thick woodland strode across the top of the ridge. A single large field lay between the road and the treeline. The lower section inclined gently uphill then the higher, shorter section rose steeply to the woods. Even a rabbit crossing the field could be seen from the sharp bend to the left. But the field was his only chance. If he turned around, there would be another detachment waiting for him and anyway, he had to go west. And there it was, a gap in the hedgerow and an open six-bar gate inviting him in.

He stopped and reversed the car to get a decent run up. He pressed hard on the accelerator and hit the field at thirty miles an hour. Thankfully the ground was dry. But the lookout propped up in the hedge shouted and gesticulated at the BMW. The car bumped up and down on the uneven ground but still made its way up the gentler lower section of the field. Two policemen, now perched on the roof of the Aardvark, drew their weapons. The first bullet entered the rear of the car and lodged in the back seat. The second missed the car completely. The third bullet skimmed and scratched the bonnet. Mortimer ploughed on towards the treeline. As the field steepened, the car lost speed and power. Six or seven policemen stormed into the field from the side, firing rounds from their semi-automatic rifles in the direction of the car. A bullet punctured the rear right tyre then another pierced the front right.

The car juddered and shook as the uphill climb took its toll on the axle. Mortimer turned the steering wheel on full lock to the right to swing the car back on itself to expose the passenger side to the incoming fire. He opened the driver's door and threw himself into the hard ground of the hill. More bullets slammed into the stationary car and passed over the bonnet as the men in grey got closer. The fugitive was only about fifty yards from a barbed-wire fence and the trees. Then from the trees the yellow-red flash of a muzzle; bullets were coming from there as well. Police reinforcements, thought Mortimer. And there he was, a static target fixed to the car in full view, unable to escape. He pressed his head into the grass and wished it would swallow him up. Another muzzle flash from the woods then another from the previous spot. But no bullets were coming close. Even by police standards one should have hit him or at least the car. He rolled himself around the back of the car, expecting his pursuers from the Aardvark to appear very soon. But the nearest policeman was lying face down, motionless on the ground, less than shouting distance away. Another policeman was slumped nearby, holding his arm from a bullet wound. Two more lay dead just beyond their wounded colleague.

The other policemen had retreated into the Aardvark that now wobbled and growled its way into the bottom of the field. Then a loud whooshing sound came from the woods. A rocket-propelled grenade exploded in the ground a few metres from the Aardvark. Another whoosh from the woods and the second grenade slammed into the petrol tank, engulfing the front half of the vehicle in flames. Two policemen tore out of the back in opposite directions but were picked off easily by the marksmen in the trees.

After about a minute of silence, the wounded man in grey trapped on the slope slowly stood up and raised his arms aloft. Mortimer did likewise. A camouflaged man emerged from the trees into the field and waved Mortimer and the policeman towards him. Mortimer cleared his mind, put one foot in front of the other and walked up the slope. Keener to reach his captor than Mortimer, the policeman, clasping his bleeding forearm, jogged past Mortimer and fell to his knees in front of the camouflaged man. Mortimer stopped behind the man in grey but remained on his feet. Another armed man dressed in a black boilersuit with bullet-proof padding across his chest and wearing a gas mask came out of the woods. He reminded Mortimer of some of the heavy-metal bands he had liked as a kid. Mortimer wanted to laugh but the raised barrel of Mr Slipknot made sure he kept it inside his head. Then out of the trees came a horse bearing a tall man, probably in his early fifties, whose legs were a little too long for the horse.

The horse followed the camouflaged man and Mr Slipknot up to their captives. The tall man on the horse was obviously in charge. He raised his arm and pointed at Mortimer.

"You, man on the run, you want to fight for freedom?"

"Well, two flat tyres and a broken axle. Why not," replied Mortimer.

Other camouflaged fighters then poured out of the trees into the field. Each man took an arm of a dead policeman and started to haul their carcasses uphill back towards the woods.

"Who are you?" Mortimer asked.

A loud explosion behind them distributed what remained of the burning Aardvark into smaller parts all over the bottom of the field.

"I'm Harper. Welcome to the UKP," replied the man who was far too big for his horse.

Chapter 17

Harper led his men, their new recruit and their solitary prisoner on horseback along a single-track path deeper into the woods. No one talked, but the partisans were relaxed after the ambush, knowing they were safely under cover. Hands tied and bound together, the captured policeman walked at the front of the column. If he tried to make a run for it, each partisan could take it in turns to cut him down. Mortimer walked freely at the back.

The track entered a clearing dominated by a steep, rocky outcrop at least forty feet high. Harper raised his right arm to halt the column. Each fighter broke away and made for the green rock wall, to sit or slump against it or just to take comfort from being close to something that had existed for millennia. Mortimer stared at his former enemies. He wondered if any of them had fought with the Yanks at Derby. The now dismounted leader of the band walked over to him. Harper was a bear of a man, taller than Mortimer, with broader shoulders, a thicker trunk and a large head that could have been cut from the rock wall. Atop was a thin layer of black-streaked grey hair but still long enough at the front to give him a fringe he could sweep back. Mortimer could see why he was in charge.

"This is our cover until dark. If we hear helicopters, we get inside the cave."

"There is a way in?" Mortimer asked

"A disused mineshaft lies under all that. Medieval or something but enough room for every man and Shiloh." Pause.

"The horse." Harper nodded. "And then what?"

"When it's dark we'll move again. Another six, seven miles then a couple of helicopters will pick us up and take us back home west."

"The Yanks?"

"Yep, all the way beyond the DMZ."

"The US military zone." Mortimer raised his eyebrows. Pause.

"And your horse?"

"Shiloh stays at a friendly farm round here. We have our supporters everywhere, Shield man."

The Truce had decreed that the US army could occupy all land to the west of the Brecon Beacons and Shropshire hills. From there, US forces covertly armed and supplied the UK Partisans, the largest anti-government resistance movement in the DMZ. Of course, officially, the US government denied providing logistical support for the rebels and, officially, the London regime accepted their word.

"I think I'd better sleep on that." Mortimer yawned. "It's been a long day." The thought of confronting his old enemy again on top of everything else that day was too much for Mortimer. His brain and body wanted to shut down and leave this world. Harper nodded at Mortimer.

"I bet it has. Go find a spot over there."

It was pitch black when Mortimer jolted himself awake. He had slept well in those few hours but his shoulders and back finally rebelled against the cold, damp floor of the woodland. The cloud cover blocked the light of the moon and the stars. It was a perfect night to be outside for the men of the United Kingdom Partisans.

Except for the guards posted a few hundred yards away on

perimeter duty around the clearing, the men huddled close to the outcrop. Some had started fires to keep warm. Mortimer saw Harper in conference with one of his fighters, his second-in-command, Conroy, at the other end of the rock, next to the entrance to the old mine. Mortimer stood up, swigged from his canteen and walked over to them.

Harper spotted him before he got close.

"Well, fellow terrorist. We could do with a man versed in the ways of the Shield."

"Long time since I had a decent job offer."

"I am not sure we can offer the same incentives as the Shield Triskel battalion."

"It was the high mortality rate," smiled Mortimer.

"You must wake up a disappointed man." Conroy snorted with amusement.

"Some days."

"We do take all sorts," Conroy interjected.

"Including ex-policemen?" Mortimer looked across to the man in grey, sat against the rock wall, wrists loosed and sucking from a sachet full of liquid. Probably a US army-issue energy drink to keep him going.

"He was given a choice. He wanted to live," explained Conroy.

"Anyone willing to fight the scum of Europe who would foul and trammel this beautiful land."

Mortimer was impressed. Not since he had read Shakespeare at school had he ever heard anyone use the word "trammel". A fine English word that sounded as old as oak. But Harper had not finished.

"Rich, poor, strong, weak, clever, stupid, pikeys, chavs, spivs, posh cunts, yids, wogs, benders. Even ladies and turncoats." Many of these words were not much younger than "trammel" to Mortimer's ears.

"Excuse me; I assure you, Mr Harper is not prejudiced against any minority," Conroy interrupted.

"My diversity policy is second to none. I fucking hate every gender, colour and creed equally without favour, fear or prejudice," Harper growled.

Mortimer smiled; a man you might be able to rely on. No-one used that language any more, even in the lower ranks of the Shield. The age and honesty of Harper's sentiments belonged to a place like this: dark and forgotten in an old English forest that had probably seen it all.

Behind him, a commotion had started. Two or three fighters were running headlong into a wall of about ten to fifteen fighters, each trying to ram his way through. Others were content to laugh and cheer. The fighters had overdosed on their US army-issue energy drinks.

"Ah, British Bulldog. I used to be a schoolteacher, you know... still am."

Harper's voice softened as he watched his children play.

"It's great for morale."

"But we'll need to move again soon to get back for dawn." Conroy wanted to keep his boss on track.

Mortimer raised his eyebrows. "How far is it?"

"Too close." Harper sighed.

"Well, you'd never survive out here alone." Harper eyed Mortimer a little suspiciously for a moment but kept his thoughts to himself.

His concentration was suddenly broken by a loud scream of pain signed off with the word "Cunt" at the top of his voice from an unfortunate victim of the melee, who then repaid his discomfort with gales of laughter.

"It's a very dangerous game to play in the dark," said Conroy.

Harper sucked in his cheeks and turned back to Mortimer.

"Before the war, I was an average man in an average job. But now it's all different. And it will always be different."

Mortimer understood exactly what Harper meant. Like him, he was a civil man for a civil war. But unlike him, Harper knew he did not have a hope in hell. But he was having a ball.

"So it's all safe out here. I thought the Shield were in control?" Mortimer enquired.

"Bullshit. They have the towns, their garrisons in these reservations. But no-one's in control. And you won't see any Shield patrols at night." Pause. "They're too scared of the cannibals." Harper smiled.

"Cannibals." Mortimer was unsure if he had heard him correctly.

"Even though they taste like shit." Conroy laughed and slapped Mortimer on the shoulder, enjoying the bemused look on his face.

"The DMZ is a very dangerous place, Mr Mortimer. There is no rule of law, no civil authority, just ruined towns and ruined people trying to survive," Harper continued to re-assure Mortimer.

"Well, thank god I have a tour guide."

Chapter 18

Away from the mainland, in one of the most thinly populated areas of the United Kingdom, the Western Isles of Scotland had always been used for secret military research and development, from the release of anthrax in Gruinard Bay during the Second World War to early missile test sites after the war.

So in response to the bio-terrorist attack in Frankfurt in 2031 that killed over seven hundred people, a disused mental hospital built into the cliffs of Castle Bay Barra on South Uist seemed the ideal site to develop the latest generation of biological weapons. The government had left the gothic grey granite Victorian exterior but converted the interior into a high-tech science facility. Dug deep into the rockface to provide the required secure storage facilities, it also provided living quarters for up to one hundred military and scientific personnel. When US paratroopers landed on the west coast in the early days of the war, the-state-of-the-art facility had only been open for nine months. Although the British army had successfully evacuated the scientists and other key personnel, they had neglected to activate the insurance policy planted in the deepest shaft in the rocks: a high-explosive bunker bomb. Or maybe it just failed to explode.

Dr Franshell rubbed her eyes and stared up from her desk at the flat TV screen on the wall. Pairs of white lines, some straight, others squiggly, all with two-digit numbers underneath them streamed across the black screen. She scanned the screen from left to right and then right to left just to check that she had not missed any detail of the karyotype, which was easy to do when you came to the end of another twelve-hour day.

Since she had arrived at the facility two weeks ago, Franshell had worked long hours. Not just too impress her would-be liberators from Boston but to avoid unnecessary contact with colleagues and minimise any prying questions. Vice and Virtue were everywhere, their spies watching and listening. Like a powerful virus, they could easily infect the staff of a military scientific community on a remote Scottish island. It was easier to trust no-one.

To her great relief she mainly worked alone, to extend her research that she had undertaken with the Newbold Project before it was closed down by the regime fundamentalists. Thankfully for Franshell, the military took a more pragmatic view of her skills.

For her, the scientific method was everything: observe, question, hypothesise and test to identify the truth. Content to refuel spiritually day and night in the laboratory, hard rational thought had always been her saviour from her earliest days back home in the trailer in Monroe in Louisiana.

Martha Franshell was raised by her maternal aunt and uncle after her mother had died from a drug overdose a few months after she was born. Aunt Tonya worked in Kmart for minimum wage and Uncle Pete worked in the local Conagra Foods processing plant for little more. Both worked long hours and showed no interest in her schooling, assuming that she would follow in the family tradition of low expectations, low grades and low self-esteem. But the solitude of the trailer and few material distractions gave Franshell the opportunity to think and to work things out. It was clear to her by the age of fourteen that the only way out of her predicament was by reading and learning. People who were in control of their lives were educated; those who were trapped and desperate and worst of all dependent upon others were not educated. Franshell wanted to be educated. Hours of online study introduced her to the subjects of human biology and psychology, which taught her why some people functioned better than others and were not trapped and dependent on others. This process only deepened the gulf between Martha and her guardians.

One relative who did openly express his kind of love for little Martha was Uncle Luther. He worked as a part-time preacher in a local Baptist church in between bouts of drunkenness in the trailer next door. He first showed his strange sort of love for her at bath time, when she was no more than five or six years old. Always on hand to help look after her when the principal carers were at work, his affection continued well into her teenage years, in fact, until exactly one day before her sixteenth birthday.

She awoke early that momentous day, just after three a.m. She climbed out of her bedroom window, crawled under her trailer and retrieved a box of safety matches, a half-full five-litre petrol can, and a length of plastic tubing. On that moonless night, Martha approached the open window of Luther's trailer, inserted the plastic tube and poured the petrol through the tube onto his kitchen floor. By the time she had emptied the can, the trailer had been flooded with petrol. Deep in a drunken sleep, Luther did not even reach the door before the flames consumed him. By the time Luther's screams woke the site, Martha was already back in her bed, very satisfied at the birthday present she had given herself: a righteous act of vengeance that made the world a better place.

But Luther had taught her one valuable life lesson: men cannot control themselves when in the company of a nubile young female. This matter of fact enabled her to pay for her college fees, working in the late-night bars of Baltimore.

A voice from the TV screen on the wall started: "According to the Newbold Project, the existence of an extra Y chromosome in young males born with the XYY karyotype predetermines a set of behaviours that create the conditions for criminal activity. These include an extreme oppositional stance to accepted cultural norms and an irrational sense of independence."

"Excuse me, Martha, may I interrupt?" It was the head of the Advanced Biological Weapons research team.

Franshell moved to the screen and touched it lightly with the tips of her fingers to instantly freeze the voice on the wall.

"Of course, Dr Carter."

"You look tired. You really need to sleep more." He smirked; fifty-five but with a mop of messy grey hair that made him still feel attractive. But a smirk on a loose-chinned middle-aged face looks more like a leer to a woman under fifty.

"I have a lot to do. My research is crucial to the war effort." She stood ramrod rigid, as close to the screen as possible.

"Indeed, you are most valuable. So valuable that I have arranged a meeting with the CIA. They want you to compare notes with their own weapons scientists on Anglesey. Their program is very important to the authorities. They may even take over the army program here."

The word "CIA" froze Franshell from head to toe but the self-evident bullshit that followed brought her back to her senses. The CIA did not build or develop weapons; they were the nasty weapon.

"Really…"

"They'll be here the day after tomorrow. Okay?" continued Dr Carter.

"I have just finished the genome sequencing with Goodlass."

"Goodlass, good, good. The CIA will be pleased." Pause. "Well, be seeing you."

Dr Carter turned and left the room. Franshell eyed the back of Dr Carter until he was down the hallway, round the corner and out of sight. The open-plan layout of the laboratories meant that there were no doors, no barriers and no privacy, just interconnecting workspaces and hallways bathed in the deepest bright white light.

So, Anglesey would be her final destination on these islands before the inevitable detention for life in the mid-west gulag. Without looking down, Franshell opened the drawer under her desk and felt around the corners until she found a plastic tablet container. Her small, agile fingers shook it. Three tablets rattled inside. She then pulled her arm out of the drawer and dropped the tablet container in the right-hand pocket of her grey nylon tunic. Now she would be ready to go to sleep.

Franshell returned to her quarters, a narrow cubicle just wide enough to fit a single bed, a bedside table with a lamp and three drawers. On top of the bedside table lay a bible and a packet of tissues.

Next morning, Franshell rose early and donned her grey robe and sandals that were obligatory for entry into the underground swimming pool. With morning prayers at six thirty a.m., the pool would probably be empty except for the morning hymns. No Wesleyan dirge but upbeat morning risers.

Today, Franshell entered the water as *What a Friend we Have in Jesus* belted through the PA by the Mississippi Mass choir. She wore a single lycra black bodysuit that stretched from her hooded head cap to the waist then split at her crotch into shorts to the knees. Modesty rules forbade female staff from showing any exposed flesh between the neck and the knees if using the swimming pool in mixed company.

Up and down she pumped her arms and kicked her legs at about the same speed for thirty lengths. This was her treat for the day, especially if she was alone. She could go for longer but she did not need to; she was fully awake and ready. Franshell climbed out of the swimming pool at the side, put on her robe and sauntered into the locker room, dripping water. Surrounded by lockers on three sides and a shower area, she bowed her head, closed her eyes and rolled back the stiff lycra hood over her crown. Her unravelled hair fell over her face, covering her vision, but she still felt a sticky gaze upon her. Dr Carter appeared from behind the line of lockers, also wearing a grey regulation swimming robe.

"You missed morning prayers again, Martha."

Franshell ignored him and moved to locker number seventy-two, where she kept a spare set of white lab overalls. She entered her security code on the keypad. The locker door swung open. He walked towards her and stopped within touching distance.

"Here, let me help you."

He draped his towel around her shoulders, letting his fingers clamp tightly onto the taut flesh either side of her neck.

"You know, I can make your life easier."

Franshell started to rifle through her lab pockets, looking for nothing in particular.

"My shoulders don't think so."

"Maybe my hands are a little hard."

The empty pockets provided nothing and Franshell had had enough. She spun around to face her invader. Dr Carter jolted backwards as his hands slipped off her lycra shoulders.

"You have no fucking clue, have you?"

She then moved her right-hand thumb and index finger to the zip of her black bodysuit just below her neck and pulled the zip down quickly all the way to her crotch. She then slipped her right arm and then her left arm out of the bodysuit, letting the top half flop down below her back. Only her thighs remained covered. Carter's eyes bulged from their sockets. His head moved up and down as thousands of years of genetic programming took over.

After a few seconds, Franshell spoke. "Now your turn."

Dr Carter dug his thumbs into the knot that held his grey regulation swimming robe belt together. The belt loosened, the robe fell open and both fell to the floor. The naked Carter then looked Franshell square in the eye and smiled. It had been a long time. He tilted his head to the right slightly, his eyeballs blinked excitedly and his mouth flopped open but no noise came out.

"Good. Now that we're both naked, or in my case, almost, we can be honest."

She realised he was probably not listening to every word.

"It's not that you want to fuck me. I can accept that. It's that you think I'm weak and helpless. You reckon you can force me to do whatever you want because you know that my life, liberty and happiness is in danger from the CIA. True?"

Carter closed his mouth into the smuggest of grins and straightened up.

"You need me. You do…" He smiled then reached over and cupped her right-hand breast.

" I can protect you."

"So, I am right."

"If I wanted to, I could keep you here for a very long time at just the flick of a key. You don't have to go to Anglesey…"

His palm kneaded her breast flesh like an excited baker playing with a new consistency of dough. Not a step forward nor a step back, Franshell felt nothing except vindication.

"Good. A naked woman always gets the truth from a man."

Then from the Public Address, a strong mid-western male voice rang out.

"That's it, folks, for today. Praise the Lord will be with you at the same time tomorrow."

Franshell turned around and grabbed her spare white overalls from the locker. Carter's arm dropped limply to his side. She moved quickly to the bench, leaving Carter to leer as she pulled off the rest of the lycra, dried herself efficiently and slipped quickly into her scientist's outfit. She then faced the mirror to comb and straighten her long, damp hair.

"So… what about it? My cubicle. Tonight."

She stared at his reflection in the mirror without turning around.

"Just book the fucking helicopter, you filthy little creep."

Chapter 19

Next morning, Franshell found Elvis in the canteen just before nine a.m. He had left Anglesey just after dawn, like he did every few weeks, to fly staff between CIA headquarters and the island. He was a corpulent fellow who spent most of his time sat down and always enjoyed breakfast as well as lunch and dinner and anything he could eat in between meals. Elvis Shaw was to be her cab driver to perdition.

But not today. He stood frowning at the selection of fruit, nuts, cereals, pulses and yoghurts all laid out under the transparent counter window. The battle between his hunger and natural antipathy to any food not fried, boiled or mashed raged inside him. Even the bread had nuts in it, large, smooth shapes that reminded him of broken cockroach shells. The slimmer figures employed at the facility glided around the large frame to help themselves, as if he were a misplaced pillar.

Franshell could not miss the lumpen figure in a faded baseball cap, with a helicopter patch on the right shoulder of his blue uniform.

"Not hungry?"

"Not any more. No proper food here. Bacon, grits, pancakes..." The disappointment was obvious.

"The treats come later. They believe this will make us perform better. A healthy body is a healthy mind."

"Bullshit." He turned to face Franshell. She smiled and Shaw forgot his hunger for a second.

"You just got here?"

"Yeah, flew in early, ma'am. We've come to pick up a scientist or someone." Shaw returned the smile.

Although he was a large man, Franshell's eyes settled on the white V&V logo in three-inch letters sewn onto the front of his baseball cap. And stood so close, the pilot could not help but follow her eyes.

"I am a helicopter pilot now. This is old. I am not with them any more. Much easier life flying helicopters than being a cop."

"Well, hi, pleased to meet you. I am Dr Franshell, your passenger." She pulled at her fringe then swept it back before she extended her hand as well as the ends of her smile.

"Oh wow. Elvis Shaw, at your service, ma'am." Both of his mitts clasped her hand and squeezed tightly.

"We are meeting out front, I believe. I've got my gear ready, so I could…" Her eyes widened and focused on the narrow blue eyes of the pilot. "…talk to the chef and pick up some bacon rolls or sausages."

"That would be wonderful, ma'am. Thank you very much. You see, I haven't eaten today."

An hour later, Dave Windows, the escorting CIA officer, closed the door behind him and eyed his watch. Everything was running to schedule. He was surprised that Dr Carter had signed the transfer authorisation without complaint, considering her value to the weapons development program. Maybe Dr Carter was a Christian and hated heretics even if they were doing God's work. He looked across the tarmac landing strip to a drab concrete shelter where Dr Franshell waited inside. He knew she was there because there was an armed guard standing by the door. Purpose-built decades ago, the ugliness of the worn prefabricated concrete was exacerbated by the picturesque purple-and-green mountains sweeping around the north of the airstrip.

Windows swung his head around in the air to check nothing was about to land and then strode across the airport runway. It was a short, narrow runway that could only accommodate light aircraft and helicopters. Other than their helicopter, no other aircraft stood on the tarmac.

As he got closer to the double entrance, he heard Franshell laughing. He raised his pace and ignored the salute of the guard to find pilot Shaw leaning against the only window, chewing on a half French stick overflowing with layers of bacon. Opposite him, Dr Franshell sat cross-legged on a bench.

"Y'know, I think you're right… absolutely spot on… Martha."

Shaw tried to speak between mouthfuls whilst gazing at her. Such an overload of the senses meant he did not see the CIA officer in the doorway.

"Sorry to interrupt, folks. Hey, Shaw, can I see you outside?"

Windows ignored Franshell and stepped outside onto the tarmac. The morning sun sparkled on the becalmed dark blue sea that reflected the cloudless sky. The occasional seagull circled and cawed overhead, hoping for a full stomach like pilot Shaw.

Shaw arrived, rubbing the grease from his roll onto the sides of his trousers.

"Sure is a beautiful day, sir."

"I told you not to fraternise with her." Pause. "She's under watch, you know that."

"She was being friendly. Hell, you would, sir."

Windows sighed. "I don't think so." He maintained his clipped impatient tone.

"Are we ready to go?"

"Yep, fuelled up and ready, sir."

"Good. Let's go." Elvis Shaw started to make his way to the helicopter parked on the runway.

"By the way, where did you get that food? From the canteen, I hope?"

"Yeah." Pause.

For a second, Shaw was baffled. Maybe Windows wanted a bacon roll as well.

"From the canteen. Definitely, sir."

Windows re-entered the shelter. Franshell was up and ready. She clutched a small rucksack containing everything she owned: washing and sanitary items, a half-litre bottle of water, a rolled-up green US army-issue nylon tracksuit and a penknife she had stolen from the lab.

"Dr Franshell, I have come to escort you to the helicopter."

"Yep. I'm ready. How long before we take off?" she asked.

"As long as it takes you to climb aboard," shrugged Windows.

Franshell moved out of the shelter towards the helicopter, followed by Windows. She calculated that the tablets required another forty-five minutes or so to take effect. As soon as she handed over the three half French sticks outside the canteen, Shaw tore into them like a Labrador whose breakfast was five minutes late. He had finished the first one before they even reached the tarmac of the airstrip. He was a big man and required a lot of bacon and really appreciated the generosity of Dr Franshell.

The Black Hawk 20 climbed high in the sky, sweeping over the Scottish coastline. Windows sat next to Shaw in the front, doing his best to ignore Franshell and his pilot. He was going home for leave in a few days, which meant long days on the beach at Fort Lauderdale with his wife, Jean, and their two young daughters. After nine months non-stop in North Wales, thank god he lived in Florida. Anyway, they were on their way now and after a stop-off at the US army base in Shrewsbury, where he had to register Franshell's entry into the Southern Occupation Zone, they should reach Anglesey just after lunch. Pilot Shaw sat upright and silent in the pilot's seat, concentrating hard on the clouds ahead.

Franshell sat strapped in directly behind the wide frame of the pilot. With the light of the windscreen almost completely blocked from view, it was like sitting behind a large wardrobe. Since take-off, without looking down or moving her top half, her right arm autonomously fumbled under the seat. She knew she could go lower. Eventually her hand settled on a plastic button under the back right corner of her seat. She pressed it once and the seat lowered itself slowly until it came to a halt. Now she was completely in the shadow of Shaw, where she wanted to be. Franshell then lay back in her seat and closed her eyes. Sleep, or at least the impression of sleep, always kept any unwanted intrusion at bay.

"Fuck…" screamed Windows. "You fat fuck…"

Shaw had passed out, his hands slumped to his side off the throttle and control stick and his chin on his chest. Franshell had been waiting for the alarm for about twenty minutes. The helicopter was accelerating to the ground in full descent.

"Wake up…" screamed Windows.

The back end then tipped upwards and the helicopter started to nosedive. But without a pilot at the controls, the autorotation suddenly kicked in to slow the descent as much as it could. The rotor blades revolved free of any engine control, though this would only delay the inevitable.

Franshell hunkered down into her leg-well, pulled her knees up to her chest and nestled behind the thick, meaty overhang of Elvis's shoulders that draped over the low-backed pilot's chair like curtains.

Windows swung his head around.

"What are you doing?"

Even though Franshell was scared, she could not help a sly smirk.

"You fucking bitch... you did this."

The RPM of the main rotor suddenly dropped; the blades fell quiet. Windows shook the control stick. But without rotor support there was no chance to glide. The back end lurched upwards, sending the helicopter into a spiral downwards to the ground. Thrown face first against the windscreen, Windows sucked in air frantically. Franshell curled herself up as small as she could behind the fleshy airless bag.

Windows eventually unstuck his face, only to get a panoramic view of the pine trees advancing towards him. The rotor blades scythed through the thin branches at the top to slow the descent. Franshell closed her eyes, breathed in deeply and sucked in the sweat of the shirt of the unconscious pilot. Once the windscreen shattered, the branches entered the cockpit like a synchronised spear attack on the helpless Windows. First his sides were pierced before a thicker branch ran right through his neck and out the other side. Even his screams could not waken Shaw, who was skewered in silence. The now collapsed wide girth of Shaw protected Franshell from the deadly incoming attack from the trees.

With the ground in sight, the front passenger door swung open and Windows spun out of the helicopter. The now almost certainly dead Shaw was then thrown against the windscreen, with Franshell clamped behind as the helicopter jolted to a halt.

A thick lower branch had entered the open door at forty-five degrees and smashed through the ceiling, impaling the helicopter against a pine tree. Franshell opened her eyes and unpeeled her face from the back of the sticky bleeding bulk. A lifetime diet of bacon, burgers and fries had saved her life. And she was pleased, in a perverse sort of way, that Shaw had been unconscious during the crash. He did not deserve that death but nor did she deserve to be on that helicopter.

The helicopter started to creak and sway; the branch would not hold the helicopter for long. Franshell pulled herself up and slid towards the open doorway, swung her legs out and looked down at the forest floor below. It was safe to jump. She dropped to the ground and yelped as her recently coiled knees, too stiff to open easily, collapsed on impact. She gritted her teeth and stood up, only to hear the branch that had intervened so fortuitously creaking under the weight of the Black Hawk. She half-ran half-stumbled into the nearby undergrowth of ferns.

"You fucking… bitch…"

Windows lay there in the ferns in front of her, struggling to rasp the words from his mouth. Both of his legs were bleeding below the knees from the impact of hitting the ground. Somehow he still lived, even with a branch through his neck.

Franshell sighed and then pulled out the plastic container that held the tablets she had put in the bacon roll to render Shaw unconscious. She tossed the tablet container at Windows.

"You're going to hell." A hoarse, slow whisper but still spoken like a true believer.

"And you'll be waiting for me."

She stepped over the gurgling and spitting Windows onto a

strip of dark earth that led out of the undergrowth into a clearing, pine needles strewn across the brown earth floor. A crescent of pine trees curved around her fifty or sixty feet way. She looked upwards, the sky still blue and all around. She wanted to run, to get away from the helicopter and Windows. She would think about her location, her predicament and her future later. Just run into the woods; she was alive.

The adrenaline rose up inside and her thighs, knees and arms responded. She dashed out of the clearing, past the pines and brushed though the waist-high ferns. She picked up her feet to avoid the roots and dents in the earth. Exhilaration washed through her mind as she then realised that no-one knew where she was now. Not the US army, not the CIA, not the prison authorities and certainly not what remained of her family. She was alone in the best sense of the word. Not the loneliness of lying awake at night in her cell or in the trailer as a child. This was as free as she would probably ever get, out here in the English forests.

Franshell crashed through another clearing and wall of ferns and came to a halt at the side of a single-lane sandy track that stretched as far as the eye could see in both directions. Boggy grassland covered the other side that then gave way to more pine trees. She dropped down onto the track. No electronic device to guide her; maybe she should go back and put Windows out of his misery then ransack his pockets for anything useful. Too late now. At least she had a water bottle, but that would not last forever. Right seemed to take her back to the helicopter and where she did not want to be. So it had to be left.

For the next hour or so she ran, walked, jogged and rested then walked and jogged again. The woods were empty of all life, it seemed, except herself and her thoughts. Franshell knew she had to leave the US-occupied zone and head for enemy territory. The Shield was the enemy of the US government and therefore her friend. And she could offer them her services, to build biological weapons for them. But how could she be sure she would not be repatriated, given the Truce? And the route of the helicopter would have been logged and recorded; the exact location of the downing would have flashed on monitor screens in Anglesey. If she was still in the US zone, drones and rescue aircraft would soon be out to pursue her. Although, back home there were constant rumours of resistance movements holding out in heavily forested states like Washington and Idaho, so maybe she had a chance.

Around mid-afternoon, Franshell reached a fork in the track. One leg thinned out and seemed to disappear altogether amongst the pine trees in the distance; the other leg twisted around a bend about fifty metres ahead and kept its shape. She swigged from her water bottle, careful not to take more than a single gulp then made for the bend. Head down and heavy-legged now, she wanted to stop and rest properly for an hour at least, but that was out of the question. At least all those lengths in the swimming pool to avoid her colleagues were now paying off.

But the automated voice from the loud speaker did stop her on the track. It came from further up on the other side of the bend. The accent struck her straight way, an English accent, a cheerful, clipped and polished English female voice in the woodland. Franshell broke into a stiff-legged jog. This was the Shield zone.

"Keep moving. Follow the road home. Keep safe. Keep moving forward to the Reservation and be safe. The Shield welcomes you to your new home."

Franshell instinctively slowed as she rounded the bend and dived into a clump of young dwarf conifers. A bit of caution was

162

still a good idea, even if your enemy's enemy was probably your friend. The track veered downwards almost ninety degrees to the right, joining what looked like a wider track at the bottom of the slope. Parked at the intersection was a military personnel carrier and what seemed to be the source of the female voice. All around the vehicle swarmed a large crowd of civilians. Many carried suitcases; a few pushed shopping trolleys full of their most precious possessions, including young children and pets. Armed men in black uniforms funnelled the crowds along the track. On each right arm was a grey-silver arm-band with the black Shield emblem. Their guns were mostly drooped downwards to the ground, as if the uniforms were present to protect the civilians rather than cajole them.

Franshell looked up to the sky one last time. Nothing. And then she stepped out of the trees and skipped down a short, steep bank onto the track. She walked a few steps unseen then stopped and raised her arms in the air to surrender. The nearest Shield guard slouched against the door of the Aardvark and stared down at a small screen-based device strapped to his forearm.

"Hey."

It still took him a few more seconds to drag his eyes away from the distraction.

"I wish to claim political asylum." Franshell smiled.

"Keep moving. Follow the road home. Keep safe. Keep moving forward and be safe," the female voice continued.

Chapter 20

Camp Ajax was tucked away in a large field at the bottom of a valley fenced in by trees on both sides and steep hills in the distance. Before the war it had provided four football pitches, three rugby pitches and a cricket pitch for the recreational sportsmen and women of Ludlow in the county of Shropshire. The US army used the area as one of its forward military bases, able to respond rapidly to any deterioration in the security situation along the border of the De-militarized Zone. Rows of long single-storey prefabricated steel storage units, about double the length of a trailer home, provided the living quarters of the Twenty-sixth Air Infantry regiment and local friends.

Heavy rain had been falling for the last twenty-four hours, hard, driving, vertical rain that hammered into the ground and bounced back up again. Vast puddles lay all over the camp. The ground turned from green grass to a mud-bath as the garrison continued with their daily duties, undeterred by the weather. This included the true believers of the Twenty-sixth. Next to the helicopter landing spot, visible to everyone in Ajax, almost one hundred soldiers knelt on both knees, heads bowed, in rows of ten before their chaplain in the driving rain. With one arm pointed upwards, eyes closed, the saturated man in black led the morning prayers in front of a giant Christian cross. Plain and without any decoration, a steel pole slightly thicker than that used to carry a flag, stood upright about forty feet high with a vertical steel bar crossing at the perpendicular three quarters of the way up.

The cross was the first thing that caught Mortimer's eye, high up in the approaching transport helicopter. Unlike the twenty or so partisans lain around him, Mortimer was wide awake.

When the first helicopter touched the ground, the fighters inside roused themselves quickly and easily, as if this were a regular routine. Which it was, since the Truce. Men and women who fought and collaborated with the US military forces during the war were now required for covert surveillance and sabotage activities in the DMZ.

Each partisan dropped down the ramp, head ducked and body hunched to avoid the still spinning propellers as much as the torrential rain before splashing their way over to the living units at the side of the camp. Mortimer was last off but did not follow the others. He could not help but be impressed at the sight of his former enemy at prayer, fully exposed to the tears of God now drenching the earth. He really was witnessing true devotion and belief. Harper followed his men out of the second helicopter and noticed Mortimer standing there on his own, getting soaked. He walked over.

"Impressed?"

"Jesus Christ…"

"Oh yes, there's lots of him about here."

"It's true; they are fucking fundamentalists."

"You must have seen this at Stoke."

"The prisoners used to pray a bit, but only if they knew they were going to die."

"Well, that's why they are praying today."

Harper heard the incoming US army officer squelch up to them, who had reluctantly left his dry desk to greet his guests. The smiling Englishman stretched out his hand but the

165

American's stayed firmly jammed in his pockets.

"Goddam fucking weather; it never stops."

"You should buy an umbrella, Captain." Harper smiled.

"Is this the traitor you found?"

Mortimer did not respond but still fixed his gaze on the rows of silent praying men.

"You looked awed, my friend. Each man handpicked from the most Christian families in the United States of America. Pure men without taint or corruption. God's own warriors."

It was the turn of the captain to smile now.

"If that were true, I really would be awed."

The captain frowned. "Get inside now and dry off. Major General Colquoun does not want your man dripping all over his office." He then turned on a sixpence and set off as quickly as he could back to his desk.

"Come on, Mr Mortimer, let's get inside." Mortimer followed Harper towards the nearest hut.

Major General Colquoun stood in front of the mirror, combing back what was left of his hair at the sides. Tall, lean, with a long thin face and a hook nose and deep eyes, he had the appearance of a vulture, albeit one with a tidy appearance. Colquoun had had a long career in Military Intelligence, an experience that made him an ideal ground commander for the truce, when both sides would be watching and waiting. And this man Mortimer was a stroke of luck for him; he had turned up at exactly the right time. Get this right and Washington would be grateful, and he would be on his way home off this miserable rock in the North Atlantic. After a final check of his fingernails, splayed out like the arms of a starfish, he was ready.

"Sir… we are ready."

Major Daines, the de-facto commander of Ajax, called from the meeting room next door. Colquoun fastened the top button of his tunic and strode out of his private bathroom into his office.

Major Daines and the be-suited Reverend O'Donald of the CIA sat at each corner of Colquoun's mahogany-wood desk. In front of them stood Mortimer, who stared ahead, at ease with his new surrounds but resigned to his fate, whatever that would be. He would not be here if they wanted to dispose of him immediately. Colquoun approached his seat briskly, rubbing his hands together in that manner that says, I am ready for business.

"Okay. Take off your shirt please, Mr Mortimer."

Mortimer waited for Colquoun to sit down and then pulled the green t-shirt out of his belt and over his head. Daines and O'Donald both stared at him, motionless. Mortimer revealed a thin, wiry, muscular frame worn down by the hardship of prison and then military service.

"Turn around, please," continued Colquoun, "and raise your arms above your head."

Colquoun leaned forward and squinted at Mortimer's back, as if looking for a secret inscription.

"No tattoos… I thought every Shield man was decorated with his own story of valour. Looks very impressive on a dead body."

"No pagan marks," O'Donald remarked.

"It ain't my style." Mortimer opened his mouth at last.

"Good. And nor is killing civilians." Colquoun smiled at Mortimer, half-expecting a flicker of gratitude for his compliment. But nothing came back.

"This is Major Daines and Reverend O'Donald of the CIA. We're all very interested to talk to you."

Colquoun pointed to each man.

"Remind me, Mr Daines. I'm not a detail man."

"Three Europa Stars for frontline action, including Oak Cross First Class with cluster at the Cannock Kessel."

Daines spoke without referring to notes.

"And stopped our advance on the Mercian Front, which led to a stalemate and the Truce," Colquoun interrupted.

"And then disillusionment... No, no, it does begin with a "d"; disobedience. Or maybe disaffection. And now you're on the run with nowhere to go. You know we can send you back. Don't you?"

"Get to the point."

Shocked at Mortimer's terse response, Daines pulled a shocked face. But Colquoun kept him busy.

"Mr Daines, the mission, please."

"Yesterday morning, a US military aircraft was shot down in the De-militarized Zone not far from the Truce line. On board was Dr Martha Franshell, a key scientist in our weapons program. Her body was never recovered. We know that the Shield have got her," Daines continued.

"You sure she's still alive?" enquired Mortimer.

"She will be when they know what she has to offer. And put it like this: she is not the type to stand up to torture. She is an intellectual, not a military combatant... and a woman."

"Put simply, Dr Franshell's capture jeopardises the entire US mission to reconvert these islands." O'Donald broke his silence.

"Anyone got a tissue? I'm all welling up..." Mortimer could not help himself.

"Ideally, we need Franshell back to complete her work. But that is... almost an impossible task, shall we say. So you must terminate, with extreme prejudice."

Colquoun always felt good after saying that; it drew a line

under the plan, the ultimate statement of intent. And he had heard it in his favourite films.

"You mean, I gotta kill her in cold blood," Mortimer retorted. Colquoun pursed his lips and nodded abruptly.

"She is close. We have her chipped and we know approximately where she is. Mr Daines." Then Daines started.

"We got a signal near Reservation Twenty-Seven, north-east of Hereford. About thirty to forty miles the other side of the line. Then we lost contact, which means that the Shield have neutralised her surveillance chip. Our intelligence tells us this Reservation may be cover for covert Shield military activity."

Colquoun took over. "And we cannot use overt military force without breaching the terms of the Truce, which is where you come in, Mr Mortimer."

"Can I have a look at her?"

Daines reached down into his briefcase and passed over an enlarged photograph of Franshell to Mortimer; a standard issue ID photograph taken just before she arrived in Scotland. The hair was short and spiky, her prison-issue crop was growing out and her stern gaze and sullen mouth made her look quaintly fashionable from an older bygone era, like a female member of a punk rock band from the last century. But Mortimer liked what he saw.

"To all intents and purposes, her current circumstances make her an enemy of the Constitution and the US people," Colquoun continued.

"And you, Mortimer, you will be pardoned for your previous crimes against God and the US army and be granted free passage to the USA. You will be saved and not just in this life. God loves the sinner." O'Donald provided the ideological angle again.

"What about Canada? It's more English, I hear," Mortimer

replied.

"Of course, we will need evidence. In the back of her forearm, a two-centimetre bio-rod was implanted when she arrived in Scotland. It only becomes visible after the body dies; it will push up to the surface of the skin a few minutes after termination. Like a large mole. It carries her unique identity code and will validate her moment of death," Daines explained.

"Well, I don't know where Reservation Twenty-seven, Twenty-eight or Twenty-nine is."

"That's where your new friends in the UKP come in. You'll be left close enough to find Reservation Twenty-seven. And our man inside will be waiting for you."

"How do I make contact?"

"He will make contact with you. He's got your image."

"Oh, you've really thought of everything." Mortimer smiled at Daines.

"It's very simple. Just bring back her biochip as evidence." Colquoun clarified the objective.

"I might not be able to wait around for your wonderful technology to work. If I can't get that, what about her head in a bag?" Mortimer smirked.

Colquoun's face tightened in disgust at the very thought of Franshell's head perched on his desk.

"That would be different. We would have to validate the DNA, but it would prove her identity, sir," Daines interjected.

"Savages... a country gone backwards," Colquoun thought aloud.

"Now, if you don't mind, I need some sleep."

"That's a very good idea, Mr Mortimer. I daresay you must be exhausted."

Mortimer nodded his assent to Colquoun, turned around and

walked out of his office. Down the corridor and towards the double exit doors at the other end, he completely missed Harper, sat in an alcove halfway down. Harper glanced up at Mortimer but said nothing. He would hear soon enough.

"Can we trust Mortimer?" asked Daines.

Colquoun rubbed his hands together as was his habit and lay back in his chair.

"His record, his escape from London, reaching the rebs, shows the man has talent and a little bit of luck. But he knows one day that luck will run out. We are his last hope, gentlemen. Let's use that." Pause.

"Now, Mr Daines, please could you call in Harper."

"Praise be the Lord," uttered O'Donald.

"Amen." Colquoun smiled.

Mortimer had always struggled with sleep from when he could remember. If he went to bed too early, like before midnight, he always awoke in the middle of the night then tossed and turned, in and out of a very light sleep, until morning. There were a few years at home with Karen when he thought he was beginning to master sleep; not too early, not too late, before an undisrupted night. But the long hours on the train and at the bank were as relentless as his married man's sex life was not. So he ended up staying up too late again, trying to stimulate himself at the end of the day, not wanting to go to bed until he had done something worthwhile or interesting. Prison had sent his poor sleep management into a spiral. Nearly all day, every day in his cell meant he had become a ghost of himself, his sleep often a conveyor belt of mild hallucinations from his past and from a mind that could not shut down.

The Shield used the tried-and-tested military method of managing sleep patterns through pharmacology. Substances like Modafinil enhanced your mood, alertness and cognitive powers for seventy-five hours, before a guaranteed six hours of total shutdown followed by another wide-awake seventy-five hours. Maybe this was why Mortimer survived the front line, because for the first time in his life, his sleep was successfully managed. The drugs gave him optimal performance in an environment where that was the required minimum to live.

Mortimer had the lower bunk nearest to the entrance of the living unit. The upper bunk was empty. All the other bunks were full of sleeping partisans, relieved to be under the warm sheets of the United States Army. They were alive and comfortable and tomorrow was another day. Mortimer stared upwards at the lines of metal springs about ten inches apart and probably no more than three foot wide. But he was not counting or measuring like he used to do in his cell. He was thinking about his day with the Yanks. Although he had killed US soldiers at the Cannock Kessel, he did it to survive, not because he hated them. He never really believed the Shield propaganda, that the US forces were religious terrorists, Christian fundamentalists who had perverted religion to establish a theocracy to first enslave their own people and then Europe. Mortimer had seen the prisoners praying, desperate men who wanted a drop of solace and comfort before the inevitable. But also, he had never taken the organised religion bit seriously; Christianity, Islam and Judaism were just another opportunity for liars, conmen and ego-maniacs to control people and hopefully make a large profit. Not very different from the international banking system really. But if the CIA was run by creeps like O'Donald, talking like some sixteenth-century conquistador, the lunatics really were in charge of the asylum.

What was happening in the USA was an old story. A very old story. And the Shield may have a point.

But the scientist must have something special for all this attention. Colquoun was very keen to see her die; he really did not want her back. The love of God obviously did not extend to everyone. Mortimer could not sleep; he was too wired and his brain was in overdrive again.

"I must protest at being sent in again so soon." Harper did not agree with Colquoun's plan.

"May I remind you that you are under the jurisdiction of the US military and you are expected to serve the US military." Colquoun leant back stiffly in his chair.

"My men are not rested. It's too dangerous." Harper seethed from the other side of Colquoun's desk.

"It really is very simple. Who feeds you? Who equips you, Harper?" Daines smirked at Harper.

"Don't piss down my back and tell me it's raining," Harper spat out at Daines. If nothing else, it removed the smirk.

"I think your men would think differently after baptism," O'Donald interjected.

Harper stared at O'Donald and told himself to say nothing. Words like "superstitious mumbo-jumbo" would not just endanger Harper but would certainly see all the partisans ejected from the base. He exhaled deeply instead.

"So to recap, we will land you north of Monmouth in the woods about six miles from the border. There is a Shield communications post there, on an old industrial estate or something. They've only just set up. Hit them at dusk, put on a show, remind them who the UKP are and then get out. And leave Mortimer behind."

"Why can't you send Mortimer in alone?"

"The Shield are building up their surveillance of the Truce line. They know we fly you in and out. They'll just think this is a smash-and-grab by the partisans. We do not have time to wait for Mr Mortimer to go across miles of country. We need him as close as possible to the target. You know the area and can get him close…"

"It's a pleasure to be of assistance." The sound of grinding teeth almost muffled Harper's words.

Colquoun smiled. "Get back to the drop-zone and you'll all be tucked up in bed for sunrise."

Chapter 21

The British Army, supported by the Shield Militia, had fought the US Army to a standstill along the Welsh Marches. The Truce borderline had been determined by the steepest hills, gorges and valleys of South Shropshire and Herefordshire. A natural defence line for centuries had become more natural since the magnitude-eight earthquake that hit Bishop's Castle in 2032 fractured and cracked the rolling landscape.

From the two hundred men and women UKP fighters based at Camp Ajax, Harper picked who he thought were his best seventy-five. Each partisan was expected to take part in every third excursion behind Shield lines. These excursions involved sabotage operations against government command-and-control centres, ambushes against military convoys and the occasional bomb attacks on Shield political offices. Very rarely did the Central Division of the UKP commit to a full frontal attack on a military base, given their superior weaponry and readiness to call in air support. But the creation of the Reservations in the western reaches of the DMZ brought the Shield forces closer to the UKP.

Harper's most effective fighters were not just the youngest and the fittest but also those with a bone to pick who had lost family members to Shield atrocities. Then there were the head-bangers, the outsiders who wanted to live the warrior life, enjoying every moment that the collapse of western civilisation could offer. Most of these types ended up in the Shield but circumstances conspired to drive some into the UKP.

It would be another hour or so before it got dark enough to cross the Truce line, so the men and women of the Central division hunkered down at the bottom of a wooded gorge. Once the grey cloudy sky turned dark blue-black, the column of fighters would move northwards to enter the DMZ. Harper seemed to be dozing against a tree but no doubt with one eye open. Mortimer thought it wise to keep physically close to Harper to avoid any unnecessary conversations or questions from the ranks. He lay on the ground nearby, cleaning the barrel of an M16 assault rifle, the standard-issue semi-automatic weapon of the US Army. Stretched around were all the other fighters. Some slept, some drank their alcohol rations, a few had disappeared into the woods together to find mutual satisfaction. Other than the occasional mumbled exchange, there was little chatter. Harper started.

"So, the Yanks have provided you with the best." Mortimer stood up, holding the weapon.

"Uhh… I do hope so." Harper scowled from the tree.

"It ain't gonna be straightforward later. You know you are strictly excluded from combat."

"I guessed so." Mortimer opened the muzzle and eyeballed the chamber.

"I have allocated two guides for you. They know the territory and will get you in range of the Reservation."

"That's very generous of you. I'll leave a tip."

Harper rubbed his eyes and moved towards Mortimer.

"These are for you." He pulled out a pair of night vision goggles and tossed them to Mortimer, who caught them with one hand.

"As you're not fighting, you can be my observer."

Harper then walked on past Mortimer towards a large rock in the ground with a flattened top. He gazed at it for a second, deemed it suitable and then lifted his large frame onto the podium. Hands on hips, he took up the stance of a leader and surveyed his fighters.

Two were missing.

"Where are Holgate and Kenyon?" Heads turned as Harper called out, loud enough to send any badgers emerging nearby for their evening reverie scurrying back to their burrows.

"Here we are."

A woman, no more than twenty-one, with shaven blond hair, stepped out of the woods on the other side of the gorge with a taller bearded darker man in tow. He had two M16s strung over each shoulder whilst the girl was weapon-less.

"Sorry, sir," the bearded man apologised.

"I won't ask you if you have checked your weapon." The girl turned crimson and the bearded man smirked. The rest of the Central division were now sufficiently roused and ready to listen to their commander.

"Okay... listen... the Shield are expanding westwards. They're coming here. Some of you may have heard of the Reservations; they're used to house refugees and civilians in the DMZ. I call them Labour Camps... Well, three clicks over the line is a Shield outpost. No more than thirty or forty combatants, according to Yank intelligence."

Instantly, a number of partisans started to whistle and jeer.

"I know. I will say it again... Yank intelligence." Others burst into mock applause.

"So, just like the training exercise at Brockley Green... Two groups: United and City. It's an old industrial estate with a cluster of office blocks near the entrance and large warehouses at the back. The Yanks want the Shield base shut down; they think the warehouse may become a Komm Uni Kayshun facility." Harper spat out the words like he was back performing in front of his class of curious but sarcastic fourteen-year-olds.

"Oooh… oooh." Many of the partisans enjoyed Harper's little soliloquy but not as much as Harper.

"Now music. I enjoy a wide palette of sound, as you know, but easy listening is out. We have too many casualties. Metal, hardcore, disco, you can even kill to reggae, it's a rhythm thing. But no lounge. I've told you before, it's too fucking slow…"

"What about musicals?" a tall female fighter called out two rows back from the front of the audience.

"Fuck off, Kerry," Harper retorted. Cue gales of laughter from all sides.

"If you want to die, Kerry, that's up to you. But I would prefer you stayed alive. If I had my way, you'd all listen to Elgar." Harper waited a few seconds for the laughter to subside.

"Our objective is simple: burn it to the ground and get out quickly."

The partisans at the front start to cheer and punch the air.

"Let's send the black-shirted vermin to hell."

More partisans at the back of the group started to whoop and clap.

Mortimer was impressed. Humour and straight-talking was rarely used to lead men or women into combat. It certainly did not exist in the officer class of the Shield forces from his experience and given what he saw at Ajax was probably absent from the US army. God bless Harper.

"We have a few hours before we move out." Pause. "So let's be safe tonight, and may your God go with you." Harper then jumped down off the rock.

This final injection of thoughts of the deity left his audience to consider their own mortality. Arms and voices dropped but Harper had done his job.

The industrial estate lay a few miles north of Ross-on-Wye. Like many towns in the Marches, it had changed hands during the war and suffered a level of physical destruction and civilian casualties not seen since the chaotic and turbulent reign of King Stephen in the twelfth century. When Shield forces drove the US Army back into Wales for the last time, a few hundred civilians took refuge in the ruins of the nearby Goodrich castle. The Shield said they were US-backed guerrillas so brought up heavy artillery to flatten the ruins, killing or burying alive every man, woman or child under the Norman brickwork.

Minutes before dawn, the men and women of the Central division of the UKP were in position around the Shield base. Two columns of rectangular warehouse buildings, side by side, lined up behind two three-storey office blocks that stood either side of the road in and out at the front. A nine-foot barbed-wire fence surrounded these buildings and marked the perimeter of the base. Given it was peace time and that the Shield did not want to draw attention to themselves, the base had not been fortified to their normal standards. Stationed inside were the Shield personnel, a mixture of communications corps and militia men. Their purpose was to monitor human activity along the truce line by planting miniature monitoring devices such as infrared cameras and body-heat readers in the fields, hedgerows and woodlands.

A solitary black-uniformed guard sat on the ground against the wall, haunches raised, with his weapon balanced over his knees. It was not clear in the darkness if he was asleep or awake. But he was not taking much notice of the movement less than one hundred metres in front of him.

Mortimer stared through the night vision goggles from a small copse of trees behind the ex-carpark that lay in front of the barbed wire. The tree had splintered down the middle from age or some other shock, leaving a perfect V for frontal observation.

"The cities and towns, well, what's left of them, are watched, stored, processed twenty-four-seven. They want to do the same to the countryside. But it costs a lot to keep the hackers out."

He took the glasses down and turned around to make his point.

"You know, the Yanks used to embed cartoons in their worms. They couldn't be bothered to crash the network but would give the police *Bugs Bunny* to watch. Kept them awake, I s'pose."

"Really… I am impressed." Harper craned his neck forward.

"Shows how shite the technology is."

"Okay…" Harper mumbled into a thick plastic communications strap around his wrist.

"United at the front. Full cavalry charge. Then City, come in from the back after everyone's out of bed. City, are you there?"

"Yep. The scans showed no cameras or heat tracers. So we've cracked the fence…" a young female voice crackled in Harper's ear.

"Good… thirty seconds, United… Thirty seconds. Bobby Charlton to kick off."

United strung themselves out in the copse that curved around the decayed and cracked tarmac of the carpark. No-one spoke. The only movements were the rocket-ropelled grenade (RPG) and mortar teams quietly unfolding their equipment and laying out the shells. Each man and woman of United was silently focused on the health of the solitary Shield guard and one of their oldest comrades; Bobby, their fifty-five-year-old sniper. He pushed the barrel of his rifle through the leaves, careful to not extend it out the other side, and locked onto the possibly snoozing or maybe just plain bored guard. A second later, his chest exploded and he was now permanently asleep. Thirty to forty United fighters emerged from the copse en masse, sprinting over the waste ground, led by the falling mortars. The first mortar shells exploded in the central area between the warehouses. United reached the barbed-wire fence then lay down, knelt down or squatted down, weapons at the ready. The warehouse double doors at the front were thrown open and black-uniformed fighters streamed out to face a fusillade from the grey-green UKP line. Of the first twenty Shield black-shirts out, about half were killed instantly. Most of the others were badly wounded.

Harper and Mortimer moved onto the broken tarmac of the carpark, watching the battle.

Harper shouted into his watch, "Range forward, thirty metres." A few seconds later, the mortars hit the warehouses at the back.

The initial killing spree spurred United on through the entrance and past the office buildings. But a group of Shield fighters started to fire down from the second floor of the office building on the left-hand side. Some of the United fighters fell to the ground; others veered off towards the two nearest warehouses to take cover against the side, out of view of the office block. The chained-up doors prevented the partisans from getting inside, but fortunately there were no Shield fighters inside the warehouses.

"Where's the RPG? Jesus Christ, we need the Lord."

Harper railed into his wrist. "Get me the Lord."

A few seconds and the Lord appeared. Six foot ten inches tall and probably only a few inches less across, or it seemed like that in full battle camouflage, the UKP fighter strode out from the corner of the warehouse into the open with an RPG readied on his shoulder. His comrades from both warehouses lay down covering gunfire to force the black-shirts on the second floor back inside. The man-mountain dropped to his knees and the warhead left his shoulder.

Harper spat into his watch, "The wrath of the Lord is coming... The Lord. The Lord."

The second floor exploded into a bright amber fireball. All the enemy fighters in the tower were down. The Lord then got back to his feet and legged it back towards the side wall of the warehouse and cover. More Shield emerged from the centre of the industrial estate and their quarters at the back.

Harper could see United fall back again to the warehouses. "Move, City, move."

With the barbed-wire fence split open, the thirty-strong City section poured into the industrial estate. They launched grenades and sprayed gunfire into the rear of the Shield fighters holding up United. With United snipers now firing from the undamaged office block and ambushed by City from behind, the Shield resistance quickly died down. It was brought to an explosive end by the Lord, who fired his RPG at the final cluster of Shield defenders. The battle was done.

Mortimer was impressed.

"Well, that was good. But tell me, why is he called the Lord?"

"Didn't you see? He walked out there, a hulk of a man, in the open. And not a scratch on him. That's what he does. And you know he is a convert; he believes in all that Yank Christian bullshit. He must be getting protection."

"Faith is a wonderful thing. But his luck will run out."

"Yep… one day." Harper sighed but quickly returned to his wrist.

"Now burn every building and get out. I repeat: burn everything to the ground…" Harper then looked up.

"Come on. You need to meet your escort."

Chapter 22

Mortimer Forest ran along the March, an ancient hunting ground for both animals and men a thousand years ago but now a relatively secure route for partisans crossing into the DMZ. The hilly terrain, covered in a thick coniferous layer, made it difficult but not impossible for the Shield to monitor movements on the forest floor.

Even so, Mortimer and his one-man and one-woman escort did not take any risks. Drones and helicopters would be out after the destruction of the Shield communications facility earlier that day. They hiked northwards, avoided clearings, glades or any openings to the sky and used only paths not lit by the late afternoon sun. But the ground here had been intermittently invaded by thigh-high ferns, which made it slow-going through the undergrowth.

Doug, a short, thin, ginger-haired man with a pinched face, in his late thirties, led the way, with Mortimer behind him and Tennant at the back.

"Y'know, if they have not found Harper, the helicopters will turn north."

Mortimer made the point again, for a second time in the last thirty minutes. After the dawn assault, Harper had taken his brigade eastwards into the DMZ, thinking the Shield would expect him to move southwest back towards the border.

"Oh really." This time Doug replied.

"Yep, and we could find ourselves in the open again. We

need to stop and camp round here until nightfall."

Doug stopped and turned around.

"What's up, Shield? Can't you hack early mornings with the partisans? I wanna keep going."

Mortimer slowed down, but Tennant stomped past both of them, head down, before delivering her opinion.

"Sooner we leave you, renegade, the better."

"The lady does have a point." Doug sneered again.

"I am the customer here and the customer is always right. So if I want to stop, we will stop."

Doug sighed and shrugged his shoulders and walked on.

"We can pick up the pace again at night," Mortimer continued.

Doug pulled up and swung his head around.

"You're fucking joking, man. That's when they come out."

Tennant watched from under a thick oak branch ahead. She sniggered, loud enough to distract Mortimer. "What you talking about?"

"The fucking cannibals, man. Gangs of them looking for food," Doug replied.

"Jesus Christ, Doug."

Tennant caught Mortimer's perplexed stare.

"Supposedly, some civilian survivors turned to cannibalism during the fighting, but we've never met any... have we, Doug?" Tennant craned her head forward towards Doug, eyes widened in disbelief.

"They live on the deserted farms near the border. Like Morden farmhouse. We went up there on patrol. What about the skeletons? They'd been skinned; they were fresh."

"What is a fresh skeleton, Doug?"

Doug looked confused; he had nothing more to say.

A loud screech that tailed off into a roar suddenly rose from the dense green silence all around, loud enough to unmistakeably belong to something feral, a large feline or wild cat but it seemed too far way to be an immediate danger. Each head spun around but no one could determine the direction of the sound.

"What the fuck, man, fuck?" Doug swung around.

"Calm down, man. We've come across the odd lion before, even a jaguar once. Probably released from a local zoo. They won't come near us."

"You're a great tour guide. Now I know why Harper sent you." Mortimer smiled at Tennant.

"Bet you're still wondering about Doug, though."

Doug had dropped to his haunches and stared in the direction where he thought the roar came from, as if expecting an imminent attack. But there was nothing out there.

"And who knows how to use the tech? Bitch."

Doug jerked himself back to his feet and slapped the hard plastic casing of the electronic compass on his left forearm. As well as giving you a bearing, it provided a detailed topographical map of the landscape.

"Yeah, an all-round genius. I forgot." Tennant then shrugged her shoulders.

"Bet yours is still in your bag, in its wrapping." Doug re-checked the direction on his arm then trudged past Tennant along the narrow path into another domain of ferns.

"Dick," Tennant muttered to herself.

Another hour of tramping through woodland and as Mortimer predicted, the helicopters arrived. Two German Wolf attack helicopters circled above, one close by and visible from the ground on the eastern side of the woodland, the other a few miles to the west, skirting the ground between the trees and the border areas. The sound of their hunters forced the trio deeper into the canopy.

The whirring rotor blades got louder as the eastern helicopter hovered directly overhead. But wary of attack from heavy machine gun fire or a rocket-propelled grenade from the ground, it was careful not to drop below one thousand feet. The three travellers instinctively fanned out and dropped to their knees in the ferns.

"We will be out of here on the scarp soon. There's no cover there." Tennant broke the silence.

"No good being out in the open. Let's move again at dark." Mortimer looked across at Doug, who was silently staring at his forearm. The sound of the whirring blades dropped as the Wolf banked away and swung southwards. The ginger-headed partisan raised himself up and stomped off away from the others.

"Over there. Across the track, through the trees." Doug called the way.

Mortimer and Tennant watched for a moment then got up and followed the man who knew how to use the compass, over the path through a thick patch of elders and creepers before a tall dark shadow emerged behind the trees. The shadow was the gable end wall of a ruined stone cottage. The sloping roof had collapsed centuries ago but both ends were more or less intact, joined by the ruined stonework of the original walls. Although the daylight was falling now, it seemed a lot darker and safer here from prying eyes in the sky. Mortimer nodded at Doug in appreciation. Doug ignored this gesture and took out his bedroll from his pack and dropped to his knees.

"Time for beddy-byes."

"Yep, we'll move out after midnight," Tennant agreed.

"It's been a long day." Mortimer was pleased that the appearance of the helicopters had changed minds.

A few hours later, Doug woke up with a start and sat back against the stone wall. He struggled to sleep outdoors when it was dark and did what he always did. He took out a crumpled photograph of his wife and young daughter and stared at it. This would continue for hours, as long as it took for Doug to fall asleep. His slight movements were enough to startle Mortimer, who lay close by. He had not slept at all.

"They still around?"

"Nah. Kate and Max never made it home. They were killed in the air raids. That's what I was told, but it was a Shield missile that hit them, I reckon. But no bodies were ever found. Maybe Kate just had enough and thought that was best for Max."

Even if Mortimer had been wide awake, he knew there was nothing to add. The silence was broken by the disrespectful snoring of Tennant, curled up foetus-like on Doug's other side. He looked over at her.

"But it's all different now—" pause. "she's a cold bitch. Y'know, the younger you go, the worse it gets. They've seen it all. Terrible things. Humanity's dying out."

Mortimer pulled himself up, pulled out an apple from his pocket and started to peel it with his penknife.

"That's the way it is now," was all Mortimer could say.

"Bullshit, I just won't suck your dick." Without opening an eyelid, Tennant replied to Doug's theory.

Doug then moved out of philosopher mode into something more typical.

"You're a fucking dyke... slag..."

"Night-night," continued Tennant.

"Dyke..." Doug did not take his eyes off the photo of his

wife and son.

It occurred to Mortimer that Doug did not really care any more. He knew it would not be long; the quicker the better. He had probably volunteered to come out here.

This realisation was disturbed by a heavy crunching noise from the path. It was a column of boots that shuffled along the path they had crossed earlier to find the ruins. Then, cursing and angry voices were audible. Mortimer threw the apple away and pressed himself into the ground.

Four ragged adult men, bent forward and stumbling, pulled a metal trailer along the path with a young woman perched in the back with a baby wrapped in her arms: a Madonna and child for the dark ages. It was the sort of single-axle aluminium trailer that might have been used to transport garden waste in more civilised times. The handlebar at the front allowed the adults to be tethered by ropes tightened around their shoulders in a two-by-two formation. Surrounding the trailer team on all sides were ten or eleven men, mainly bearded, in dirty black-brown stained trousers and oily jumpers and heavy padded coats, some overlaid with plastic sheeting splattered in blood. They looked like men who made their living in an abattoir.

The oldest of the four slaves in the back row had collapsed to the ground, weak and exhausted. This dragged the front two backwards, killing the momentum of the cart.

"You lazy cunt. Get up."

The nearest bearded guard threw out his arm, instantly unravelling the electric cable wrapped around his fist like a whip extension to his hand. The flying flex slashed the old man across his eyes, the splayed wiring scratching his left-hand cornea. He let out a horrible high-pitched shriek that you would not think possible from a man in his early sixties, followed by a spluttering

189

whimper that you would think perfectly possible from a man broken by pain and fear.

"Move, you fucking pieces of meat," continued the whip-hand.

The two younger men in front bent low to the ground and managed to strain the cart forward along the muddy floor. This and the other rear slave created enough momentum to haul the cart and the broken trestle table of a man.

The girl and child in the back remained silent. The cart creaked forward again.

"Hey, Joe, you've been practising your aim. I can see that." Another bearded man, closest to the attacker, approved of Joe's accuracy.

"Sure have." Joe smiled and raised his fist with the wire flex re-wrapped tightly around his fist.

"Shut the fuck up, ladies, keep moving." The only man without a beard but also without hair stomped over to the cart from the flank.

"We're all hungry and we need to get back soon."

Then in a softer, sarcastic tone. "Please do not hurt this man... we need him alive."

"But we don't eat the eyes."

The other beards came alive and their mouths opened in a low rumble of laughter.

Chapter 23

Doug wandered over to the far end of the ruined cottage, where there was a door-shaped opening in the gable wall.

"Get down," Tennant hissed at Doug as loud as she could without being heard by the cannibals. Mortimer raised his head over the side wall to look in the direction of the now empty, silent path. The misery train had now wended its way out of sight. It occurred to Mortimer that the histrionics on the path had probably spared them the curiosity of the cannibal gang. But then a splintering crack of sticks from the undergrowth spun his head around. It came from beyond the far end of the cottage.

"Doug…" The hiss had turned into a muffled shout.

"Hey, Miss Fucking Tight Arse. They don't exist. Heh." Doug turned from the far end of the cottage, arms outstretched and shaking in anger mixed with a heavy dose of fear.

Tennant leapt to her feet. "Doug. Get down."

Mortimer turned back to the path that was still empty. He pulled the pistol out of his pocket. "Tennant, get your gun."

"See the fucking walking menu, man. I'm off."

Doug then headed through the door slot in the wall.

"It's all clear, man. It's… shit, a spear." He did not make it through the entrance before a wooden pole with a sharpened end, possibly a broom or garden rake handle in more civilised times, pierced his chest. His knees collapsed to the ground and his head fell forward, driving the lance right though his torso and out the other side. Two bearded men stormed through the doorway, clutching their homemade spears. Mortimer and Tennant went into auto-pilot and drew their pistols and cut down each invader with a single bullet. The silencers might give them a minute or so if they were lucky, enough time for Mortimer to assemble his automatic weapon from his rucksack. Even though he should have done it before he fell asleep.

"Shit…" He tipped the contents of his bag out.

The gun came in three parts: the upper receiver and barrel, the lower receiver with trigger and the magazine.

Tennant ran over to Doug's body. Knees together and head bowed, he was curled on the ground like a punctured foetus, leaking blood.

"Tennant… get back. He's dead."

"Doug… you fool."

It was a generous epitaph for Doug but Tennant did not do herself any favours. From the other side of the ruined wall, a rope lasso spiralled through the air and caught her around the waist. It was jerked tight, pulling her to the ground. Two bearded men jumped over the wall; one clasped the end of the rope. Another marauder burst through the open doorway.

Mortimer raised his now assembled weapon but hesitated to fire. One of the marauders held Tennant down by her shoulders as the other yanked a net over her head. Her torso spun and writhed and her legs kicked out, as if she were wired to the grid. It made it hard for Mortimer to miss her.

Mortimer did not see the younger cannibal behind him jab his gun arm with a broom handle spear. The shot of pain made him drop his machine gun to the ground. Rather than run him through, the young man wanted the gun to impress the older beards. He lunged for it but at a height perfect for Mortimer to swing his knee into the side of his skull. The attacker hit the ground and without looking down Mortimer picked up his weapon then unloaded two bullets into the head of the incorrect-decision-maker.

"Kill me. Shoot me," Tennant screamed at the top of her voice.

Her legs were now bound, and her three assailants started to pull the rope, dragging the frenzied and terrified Tennant towards the doorway. She thrashed and rolled like a trout on a river-bank.

"Kill me." Again she screamed at Mortimer.

One of the cannibals had had enough of her resistance and drew a long steel blade. It was the short, hairless and beardless leader of the band. He dropped to his knees behind her head, knife at the ready, as if he were going to scalp her.

Mortimer set himself and sprayed fire towards the open doorway, killing the bunched captors and captive. It only took a second or so for the commotion to end and for everyone to die. Mortimer waited for a minute but there were no more savages. The silence of the wood returned again, but this time it seemed louder after all the mayhem.

Two bullets, one in the head, the other in the chest, meant a quick death for Tennant. Mortimer untied the ropes and hauled her body into the back of the ruined barn where they had slept earlier. He then pulled the spear out of Doug's blood-soaked body and dragged him over to the same spot. He spotted a shallow trench in the grounds of the derelict cottage long enough for both bodies that would not take too long to deepen. As he scooped out the soft, rooty earth using the small spade from Tennant's pack, he pondered why she had tried to help Doug. Why had she selflessly given her last moments for Doug, a man who probably would not have done the same for her? Maybe humanity was not dying out.

After fifteen minutes or so, he decided he had done enough. He pulled in the dead body of Doug first then slid Tennant on top. He covered the bodies with branches, twigs and leaves before sprinkling the spare soil on top.

He then examined the contents of Tennant's pack and found what he was looking for. The US military compass equipped with GPS, topographic imagery display, human body heat sensors within a two mile radius that she had not switched on and the anti-drone mask. All in all, an inferior gadget to the German-manufactured Shield-issue compass, but it contained his route to Reservation Twenty-seven. Mortimer recorded the position of the graves on the device to help Harper locate the bodies of Tennant and Doug if he wanted to. He guessed Harper probably would, being a sentimental man who loved his children.

Hanging low in the sky, the sun's rays pressed Mortimer's On button. Was it just past dawn or late afternoon, early evening? How long had he been asleep? Of course, the compass would tell him immediately, but he wanted to be the machine, albeit a much slower version. The gable wall end opposite Mortimer was almost completely absorbed in shadow. He stared at the shadow. His hand twitched for the tech in his pocket but he forced his palms into the earth. The path from where they found the ruined cottage ran south to north, so the shadow must be falling from east to west, which meant the sun was in the west. It would soon be dark. But he needed the machines to agree. He reached for his pocket and a second later received verification.

Mortimer celebrated on Doug's composite food bars, a strange mixture of sweetened meat granules and fruit that could only be created in the USA. He was also pleased that he had nearly slept a whole day without any sleep medication. Maybe the frequent heavy dosage at the front had re-wired his brain to know when sleep was needed in combat conditions. Anyway, he did not have time to pen a thank you letter to the pharmacology section of the Shield Security Service; the entire gable wall was in shadow, and Mortimer could get going again. He pressed the flat button on the side of the compass to activate the anti-drone mask then put it in his right-thigh pocket.

The drones were not reliable at night, especially up against the anti-drone mask. It could intercept the image as it was being captured by a drone camera up to two miles and scrub any human projection. Unfortunately, depending upon the model, it sometimes left a blur or scrambled image that could alert the drone monitor to a possible hack from the ground.

Mortimer re-joined the path moving north and within the hour left the forest and dropped down into a vale. On his own, he felt more confident leaving the cover of the canopy. He moved at a rapid walk-march typical of someone with military training. Out into open land, he clung to the hedgerows between fields. The twilight was disappearing as fast as Mortimer jogged down to the river at the bottom of the valley. Once he reached the first clump of willows and alders stationed at the riverbank, he stopped and checked the compass. He had to follow the river westwards for another few hours. Ahead of him ran an uneven and in places collapsed mud path that rose and dipped between the trees. It would be easy to slip or stumble in the darkness, leading to an unscheduled night-time swim. So he started along the path at a spirited amble with his eyes fixed on the ground ahead.

It was not yet midnight when he reached the bridge, a centuries-old stone humpback bridge that carried a main road into a village. Mortimer clambered up the bank onto the brow of the bridge and on the other side, a terrace of nineteenth-century farming cottages, re-plastered in the twentieth century but still thatched and tatty, ran up to a bend in the road. No streetlights nor any house lights; Mortimer felt confident to enter the village along the main road. Around the corner, the cottages were replaced by modern brick boxes crowded along the curb, occasionally broken up by road entrances to drab cul-de-sacs. The lack of artificial light did the place a favour.

Mortimer reached the Norman square tower church at the crossroads. He turned up the stone path towards the doorway then pushed the arch door with his good shoulder. It fell open easily, pulling Mortimer inside. Nothing hung on the walls except the odd ivory plaque to the local nobility long passed away. Rows of empty wooden pews lined the interior with an uncovered communion table at the far end, bare of crosses or any relics of religious observance. Unlocked and unloved, the night-time gloom seemed to brighten the place. But it could still provide sanctuary. Mortimer made for the tower at the other end and turned the iron ring handle to open the tower door. Inside, he twisted and turned up the narrow steps with his semi-automatic bagged up over his shoulder, passed the large, empty space where the bell and bell ropes used to hang then a few more steps before he walked out onto the stone roof. Although it was very dark, he still crouched down, not wanting to draw attention to himself up there. He shuffled over to one of the battlements and lay down and peered out, waiting for the light.

Chapter 24

Just after dawn broke, a flat-bed lorry pulled up, carrying sacks and cardboard boxes, in front of the church. The sound of the engine alerted the villagers, who then streamed out from their houses. It struck Mortimer as he watched from his perch in the tower that old people tend to get up earlier than everyone else. No-one looked under fifty, sixty years old. The slow, the shuffling, the assisted and the reasonably fit but still grey or no-haired all moved towards the lorry. Stood on the bed, the driver doled out sacks of foodstuffs and open boxes of tins to the locals. As expected, the old men and women formed a queue, following their programming from more orderly times.

After about twenty minutes, there was no more food left on the back of the lorry. Those with rations had disappeared back into their homes. Those without hung around, staring at the lorry now driving back towards the bridge. Given the age of the locals, Mortimer felt it was safe enough to go back into the open. He left the tower, walked out of the church and turned northwards, uphill further into the village. He kept his line in the middle of the road, unbothered by watching eyes. Over the top of the hill, Mortimer caught sight of a pub sign hanging from a large brick barn. The Red Lion was wide enough to force the road to dogleg around it to the right. Like the church, it was probably unused these days, but Mortimer felt a deep urge to go inside.

He must have only been a few steps from the double doors when the first explosion boomed from the graveyard of the

Norman church. A second explosion let rip in a cul-de-sac opposite the church and another tore a hole in the main road on the hill. Mortars fired from the humpback bridge announced the arrival of the Shield Special Patrol Group. The next explosion hit the church, right up its nave, laying waste to a nine-hundred-year-old gathering place for the misguided and the foolish. This was enough for Mortimer to charge through the entrance doors into the haven of the saloon bar. Empty, chair-less and table-less, there was nowhere to sit.

The explosions stopped and the engines of the Aardvarks roared over the humpback and up the main road into the village. Mortimer knew what was about to happen. He reckoned they would use the church or the pub. The Red Lion was perfect for a few hundred or so standing, especially given the lack of furniture, and able to fit a lot more civilians than the pew-blocked inside of the church. Anyway, Mortimer was in the only place where the Shield would not enter. He did not bother checking the lounge bar: service would be the same as the saloon.

The oblong metal cellar cover stared up at Mortimer from the stone floor at the side of the bar. The stone floor was exactly what Mortimer needed; not a wooden floorboard in sight. He lifted the cover up to ninety degrees and slipped through the gap onto the rotten wooden steps. Once under the floor, he locked the cover from inside and clattered down into the sodden cavern. A burst water pipe that ran along the wall had flooded the floor no more than calf-deep but enough for Mortimer to feel the cold dankness hanging in the air. The whitewashed brick walls were mottled with dark, damp spores. Moss forced itself into the cracks and chipped openings where it could. But this foetid realm gave him a chance. The sounds from outside above ground broke his lingering in the cold and made him cross towards the only opening in the wall that once housed a ventilator grill. The gap gave Mortimer a reasonably safe view from the front of the pub, looking out down the road. A concrete ledge protruded over the top of the opening, protecting Mortimer from any observant militia man without blocking his vision. He saw nothing but could hear the shouting of burly, angry men down the hill; the clearance operation had started.

Shield militiamen were beating down front doors nearest to the bridge and church, haranguing the occupants to join the line of locals at the church gate. Armed groups sprinted down the backstreets and closes to unload their inhabitants. A black-uniformed officer sat at a fold-up metal desk against the church gate. He got himself in place very quickly and was in a hurry. No chit-chat, charm or explanation given to anyone; head up, name and age and identity number then head down as the official keyed into his tablet. Once processed, the civilian was ushered politely up the hill towards The Red Lion. Some militiamen even lowered their guns and bothered to smile to relax the villagers or offered an arm to help the infirm up the hill.

The residents nearest to the pub now emerged from their houses to watch the stumbling shambling line pass by. The militia shouted and waved at them to go down to the church, which most did without question. The few foolish enough to go back inside soon faced the angry uniforms at their doors. Mortimer could now see the procession. There were even some that looked fit and heathy in their forties but still mostly elderly or late-middle-aged.

Where had all the young men and women gone? No children at all. The militiamen now closed in around the pub entrance, some close enough for Mortimer to make out their faces. No lack of young men here. Two guards at the front came forward and kicked open each entrance door in unison. One of them lost his footing on his balancing leg and fell face-down over the threshold, much to the hilarity of his comrades. For a moment, Mortimer thought he could smell alcohol on the militiamen's laughter. He instinctively pulled away from the grill, not just to avoid detection but because he knew exactly what was going to play out. He had seen this before and he did not need to see the faces of more civilians. Better that way.

The open doors prompted the militiamen to corral the first batch of about fifty villagers inside. Some fell into the saloon bar; others turned into the lounge bar.

Then a roar of engines from the roadside next to the pub; more Aardvarks rumbled around the corner. Militiamen hung from the side or sat on top; some swigged from bottles and laughed as if they were at a party; others looked sullen and downbeat, as if they had not been invited to the party.

Mortimer sighed and looked down at the slimy black floor. There was nothing he could do. The Aardvarks halted outside the now empty houses on each side of the street, leaving the middle of the road clear. Then the music started. The first few bars of a bass-heavy synth-metal version of *Jerusalem* blasted out from one of the Aardvarks. The Special Patrol militiamen slid off their vehicles and made their way to the empty ground in front of the pub entrance.

The second group of locals entered keenly enough, but the third group hesitated outside. The saloon bar and the lounge bar were full, more than they had ever been.

The militiamen, especially the drunk ones, stepped forward and offered more than a helping hand, more a helping shoulder, elbow or fist. A man of eighty or so collapsed from exhaustion in the doorway, jamming the passageway. Two thugs stormed through the melee, picked up the unfortunate geriatric and hurled him head-first through the window. Sacks of rubbish found their way into bins with greater care and attention. The crowd inside gasped; a middle-aged woman at the front screamed as her face took the full force of the human projectile. Another woman burst into tears and an elderly man started to groan loudly. Outside, the last and largest group of civilians were being kicked, punched, cajoled and jeered towards their final destination.

As more villagers crammed through the doors, those inside groaned louder like a herd of panicked and confused cattle. The music now got louder to drown out the choir of misery inside. The militia grew more impatient. The black crescent enclosed the last group and pummelled and funnelled them into the pub. Once all the two hundred or so inhabitants of the village were inside The Red Lion, a few of the more sober militiamen carried concrete blocks from one of the personnel carriers up to the entrance doors and stacked them in front of the double doors to prevent escape. Then, four militiamen jogged forward together and threw hand grenades through the saloon bar and lounge bar windows. The explosions inside caused carnage, the low moaning now became screaming, the throat-shredding, shrieking of pain and fear mixed with the expectation that it would only get worse.

More black uniforms charged the hostelry to propel grenades through the smashed windows, sending the screams of the victims louder and higher. It was now difficult to tell whether it was animal or human, inside or outside. Those militiamen who were spectators to the slaughter cheered and raised their arms to applaud, as if they were standing on a football terrace. But an older man at the front covered his eyes with both hands, head nodding in distress. He was crying. There was always one or maybe two or three who had not lost everything.

Mortimer now decided to retreat to the back of the cellar where the wall had lost almost all its whitewash and was turned sodden brown. It was the coldest and dampest area of the cellar, which was where anyone hiding in that building needed to be.

Four more men stepped forward with cylindrical petrol tanks on their backs, eyes wrapped under goggles, flamethrowers to hand. The music was turned up, the bass increased, the bow of burning gold, the arrows of desire drowning out the agonies of The Red Lion.

Mortimer sank to his knees and started to splash the filthy black water over his shoulders and back like an excited Labrador in a pond.

The first and seconds bursts from each flamethrower spluttered without reaching the building, blackening only the tarmac area before the entrance. But the third attempt spat huge jets of flame that scorched the red-brick wall and set the roof alight. The recoil threw the handlers stumbling backwards. The chariots of fire were now released in their full hellish glory, blasting through the windows, door and roof. A family of dragons after a late-night feed at the local petrol station would have struggled to reproduce such a display.

Mortimer pulled on his balaclava, soaked tight to his head. He wished he had done it earlier to drown out the sound of wailing from above. But this now started to die down. Flames sucked and rushed the air and tore through the captives, as if they were papier mâché mannequins. The blaze on the roof ripped through the ceiling, setting the struts and upper beams alight. Some had lain there for over a hundred years, according to the tourist sign outside, but it only took seconds for them to split and fall, crushing anyone underneath. The only sound from above now was the creaking of the floor from the stress of the heat and fire. The cellar was warming up quickly, but the concrete ceiling held firm.

Outside, the four flamethrowers of the apocalypse stood down, their job done. Larger numbers of militiamen now stepped forward, weapons at the ready and unloaded fire into the burning pub. Others swigged from their bottles of Shield-issue Victory Square lager of 5.5 per cent volume. Some men cried and a few stood around staring blankly with nothing to say. Black smoke now billowed upwards from the hole where the roof had been.

After a few minutes, the officer who had administered the last rites earlier at the fold-up table stationed himself directly behind the militiamen firing into the flames. Legs apart, tablet under his armpit, he raised his hand to his mouth, that now held a whistle, and blew hard. The high-pitch shrill stopped the firing straight away, and the executioners, without a pause or lingering glance at their handiwork, strolled back to the Aardvarks. The other warriors watching from the sides dropped their bottles, wiped their tears away and headed back to their vehicles. The Aardvark engines roared to summon their passengers. Shield procedure dictated that Special Patrol units must leave the scene of any massacre within five minutes, to ensure that the men did not dwell or reflect on their butchery but got a move on, got out of town and away from the smell of burning flesh.

Through the grill, the warm but damp Mortimer watched the personnel carriers trundle away down the hill back to the bridge. For a moment, he pondered the strange procedure that attended the massacre of civilians. Somebody who had obviously never killed another human being in his life was concerned that murderers should not hang around afterwards, savour the atmosphere of their acts, because it might psychologically damage them. It might even make it hard for these men to live in a country where exterminating your fellow human beings was no longer acceptable. There were actually people in the Shield who cared about such things, but he had never met one.

No smoke had entered the cellar, but the odour of burning body fat filled the room. That and the sulphurous stench of the hair moved his mind away from the correct procedure to follow when burning your fellow man. He did not know how long the ceiling would hold, so he had to get out now. In the back of the cellar where he had stood, there was a larger trap door above, the barrel delivery point. He had used the trap door in the middle to enter the cellar, so this one should get him out to what remained of the pub garden.

He raised his arms, slipped the latch and pushed the still intact wooden door up. It flipped open easily to reveal a smoking, acrid daylight. The stench claimed the back of his throat and almost made him retch. To think, old people had enough hair to turn his stomach like this, thought Mortimer. He then fumbled at the other side of the hatch for the pull-down wooden ramp used to roll the barrels in. The end of the barrel ramp dropped to the cellar floor, just missing Mortimer's feet. He hauled himself up the slats into the backyard just beyond the back wall of the pub. The wall still held but the blaze had brought down the entire roof into the burning bars and bodies below.

Mortimer ran through the back door, across the garden area and onto a narrow road that took him away from the charnel house. He did not look back; he did not need to. Mortimer had not just seen it all before or even smelt it all before; he had been one of the drunken rabble spraying at the weak, the helpless and the innocent. He might have been forced to commit these atrocities; war was like that, but he still did it.

But he did always ask himself if all those victims were

innocent. Surely, if one hundred civilians were burnt alive, a few of them deserved it based on their past behaviour. Based on his own experience of his fellow man and woman and everything in between, Mortimer had created his own rule for the human condition which, when applied, he found to be seldom wrong. The sixty-thirty-ten rule: sixty per cent of people were passable, you just pass them by without noticing; thirty per cent were decent, a few may even be worth knowing, leaving the bottom ten per cent who made everyone else's life a misery and they knew it. From abusing kids, probably their own kids, down to doing nothing illegal but day after day of tyrannising over their families or employees. Plenty of the ninety per cent undeservedly get a painful death for their efforts so good riddance to the ten per cent, they deserved to burn. This sense of anonymous but righteous revenge helped him justify cold-blooded murder. So, pass another bottle of Victory Square.

Chapter 25

Dr Franshell smiled at the sleeping man in her bed; a few years younger but not a boy, dark hair and olive skin, from France, even if a little ruined by too many rune tattoos across his back. She had chosen him from the list of available Shield fighters: disease-free and no record of any sexual crimes. If this was what a civilisation unfettered by notions of sexual repression had to offer, then what took her so long to get here?

Unwound and drained in mind and body, she felt like a sated empress as she rose from her bed and paraded naked to the screen on the wall. Even if her room was uncannily like the spartan grey-washed cubicle she had had in Scotland. Anyone would think the US military and the Shield were using the same interior designers. Catherine the Great reached down and pulled on the robe strung over the chair. She was fairly sure someone or some device was watching her from the other end of the screen. They had already got their money's worth.

She switched on the electronic tablet in the robe pocket and opened the screen with her index finger. Still logged onto the Shield stud catalogue, she felt greedy and could not resist clicking on the Viking helmet icon under the banner heading "Battlefield Lover". An explosion of graphical flames consumed the screen before a thick-set man with a wide shaven head and a trimmed red beard appeared, holding a heavy machine gun across his chest. The flames disappeared to reveal the warrior standing in front of a tank, the 65mm cannon protruding over his shoulder hard and erect.

Then in a heavy Eastern-Europeanised English accent, the warrior pitched:

"Over one hundred kills in frontline. Three Oak Crosses. Two Raven Wings. You want Volkic, all the way from Serbia, with a great sense of humour."

His right arm swung upwards, holding a severed head in an American helmet.

"Ha-ha," said the comedian.

Then the screen froze before a new image appeared of Volkic holding a baby in his broad arms next to the crying mother. He turned to the camera and eyed Franshell with low, sad eyes. She surmised that he may well have killed the defenders of the community to which the unfortunate woman belonged.

Franshell pressed the off button.

"Moron. Thank god when I can build my own."

She threw the tablet onto the chair and turned back to the bed. Jean Paul, or was it Jean Jacques, was lying on his front, still out for the count, the single sheet pulled only halfway up his bare buttocks.

As she wondered when he would wake up, there was a hard rap on the door. It swung open and Hendrick walked in without a by-your-leave. "Ah, Martha…"

Martha swung around, as did her right breast, falling out of the V-necked slit in her robe. But Hendrick's eyes caught the young flesh lying on the bed. She shuffled everything back and stared at Hendrick, who lingered over the semi-naked male form. His cheeks were redder than usual; the eyes bulged; he had been drinking. And he seemed rather too interested in the Frenchman in her bed. Martha smiled slyly at the quickly dawning realisation that Hendrick would probably never be a sexual threat to her.

"Can I help?" She thought she should start.

"Oh… yes. Indeed, excellent taste. The Latin physique is also my preferred choice…"

Hendrick smiled, with the leer still alive in his eyes.

"I am glad to see you are enjoying the benefits of a non-Judeo-Christian civilisation, even out in here in Reservation Twenty-seven. And you have certainly not been brainwashed by weird notions of guilt about physical pleasure, like so many US citizens," Hendrick continued.

Franshell felt her cheeks slowly redden at such a direct approval of her personal morality. She looked away at the still-asleep Jean Jacques.

Hendrick could not help himself after an evening with his favourite cognac so continued to open his mind.

"But then, nor are your leaders, according to our intelligence. And so much worse when it is children, don't you think? Now I know why the Christian church loves children so much."

"You have not used that in your propaganda." Franshell was not surprised at this news.

"No-one would believe us… They would say it was fake black propaganda. Even though the Christian church and sexual perversion have always made easy bedfellows."

Hendrick shrugged his shoulders. Of course, Franshell understood very well why people in power rarely besmirched the personalities of other powerful people, even when they were their enemies. Because they were all cut from the same cloth, and US intelligence probably had the same details on the private perversions of the Shield leadership.

"We in Europe see religion as backward. We are trying to find a primitive spirit in man, a more honest view of our humanity, unfettered by suspicion or denial of our humanity."

Franshell knew she was listening to a true believer; she knew how a true believer spoke.

"You mean the Vikings: the runes on all your soldiers' backs," Franshell interjected.

Hendrick could not help himself and continued to stare at the now snoring soldier.

"Symbols are important in European culture. And these symbols convey meaning for many. You know the Norse were never conquered by the Romans. And it was the Roman Empire which was ultimately responsible for spreading Christianity." He paused.

"After the economic collapse and then the war, we had to look deep inside our culture and our genes... our heritage, you understand, to find the real truth."

Franshell crossed her arms and pondered whether Hendrick really did believe in what he had just said. She often had the same problem back home listening to the preachers, but at least Hendrick had been drinking.

"And those people on the road. How do they fit into all this?"

"Thanks to the US forces of Christian love, they have no homes any more. Many of the cities and towns of the Midlands were devastated in the war. So we are returning them to a more natural existence in the country."

Hendrick smiled at Franshell and tried to concentrate on her.

"Anyway, I did not come here to lecture you. I have news. Do you want to go to Paris?"

Franshell raised her eyebrows and smiled.

"I'd love to. I've always wanted to go to France."

She knew that a woman showing gratitude always disarmed a man and lowered any suspicion. But maybe not a gay man.

Hendrick turned back to the sleeping Jean Jacques. "I bet you would.

"Your scientific skills could be very useful to us, in the development of weaponry… but there is one small thing."

Hendrick took a breath.

"I need to be sure that you are loyal to the Shield movement. Fucking one of our young bucks is a start, but before we can move you to our R&D facility, we must be absolutely sure. I am sure you understand."

"I have downloaded everything I know about the US genetic weapons program. Please remember, sir, I was a scientist, not military. I was tortured and abused by my government, so I have no loyalty to the United States of America."

"Glad to hear it." Hendrick smiled, the eyes bulging less now.

Hendrick thought she was relaxed now, maybe too relaxed so wanted to keep her on edge. An extreme opponent of a dictatorship could develop undesirable behaviours and attitudes, like independent critical thought, that do not disappear easily, even if they are welcomed and nurtured in the enemy camp.

"You will be meeting Grand Commissioner Erasmus from the bio-technical division. He is very senior in the Movement and is travelling from Brussels specifically to meet you."

"The Shield has a bio-technical division."

She sounded like an expectant seven-year-old at Christmas.

"Its goals and objectives are utterly core to the Shield vision for the future of this island and Europe, which is why we are so pleased to have you here. We do sometimes take off our horned helmets. Ha-ha." Hendrick laughed and Franshell smiled very politely.

"Now I must leave you."

"Oh, by the way, what catalogue number is he?" Hendrick nodded towards the bed.

"Um, I forgot. Can I message it to you?"

"Of course. Good, I think you will adore France."

Hendrick turned around and clicked out of the cubicle. Franshell wandered back to the slumbering Jean Jacques, still face-down and spread-eagled over the small-sized double bed and wondered if it was normal for Shield fighters to be shared by both sexes. Maybe she should check next time. Her Christian culture had programmed her with assumptions not really relevant to mid-twenty-first-century Europe.

Chapter 26

Reservation Twenty-seven had replaced the town of Leominster on the Welsh side of the A49. It had been close to the western frontline and had suffered huge physical damage from unsuccessful attempts by the US army to smash through to Birmingham and encircle the Homeland forces defending the north country. In order to provide a strong defensive line along the March, the civilian population of the town were forcibly evacuated into the countryside. Unable to return to their devastated homes, the civilians became refugees, wandering the countryside, a pattern repeated throughout the conflict areas in the Midlands and the north.

Mortimer had spent the previous night tramping through the woodland of Dinmore Hill, following the A49 at a distance northwards past what remained of Hereford. When the woods ran out, he was forced into the open fields. He tucked in close to the hedgerows to give himself the requisite cover. Thankfully it was spring and the hedges were tall, dense and green with life. He avoided the lower ground near the roadside, even if the hedges looked thick enough to provide cover. Heavy camouflaged lorries with the silver Shield emblem on their canopies rumbled along the A49 night and day, carrying god knows what.

Occasionally, he caught a red-pinkish spot hovering above in the night sky that signified a Shield drone. Out in the open, he stopped and stretched himself flat on the ground like a Dover sole on the seabed. The point was to hide your shape and stop moving and with the help of technology to make yourself invisible on the ground. Even with the Drone shield switched on, his days on the frontline had made him as sceptical about military technology as he was about military officers. Experience had taught him to never rely completely on any complex technology that carried the promise of an easier life. You had to always take personal responsibility to maximise your chances of survival and hope that that policy, ably assisted by a half-baked piece of kit, did the trick.

It was mid-afternoon now and grey clouds started to move in overhead. Mortimer could not be bothered to check his tracking device but he felt he had covered nearly ten miles so far that day. But he was following a hedge which meandered onto lower ground away from the ridge towards a main road. He could see that the clumps of trees at the top were now becoming more frequent and would give him a view of his destination as well as the requisite cover. An opening in the hedge led into a muddy footpath between his field and the next, both sides overrun with thorny bushes and elders. He took the narrow path up the hill through a copse at the top of the ridge until he reached the edge of the treeline on the other side. From here he got a good view of the A49 winding its way through the valley. He reckoned Reservation Twenty-seven was only about five, six miles away from here. In the distance, Mortimer could see a patchwork of copses and empty fields curving northwards. As he got closer, there would be more evidence of the local security forces, which might mean foot patrols. He would use the woods as giant stepping stones to navigate him through the open country to the reservation.

After the compass agreed with him, he dropped out of the

trees and jogged downhill towards the gloomy embrace of a coniferous plantation which stretched long-ways in the right direction. He crashed through the ferns at the edge, which soon gave way to a boggy, brown humus floor empty of vegetation except for the pines that reached for the sky. The soft, bouncy ground gave Mortimer the impetus to pick up his stiff legs to continue at a decent pace.

After a few hundred metres or so, he caught sight of what looked like red material hanging from the top branches of a tree in the near distance. He accelerated towards the flag and it soon became clear that this tree was different to the others. Like the conifers, man-planted, but unlike the conifers, the top branch was dead. Mortimer had never seen or taken part in this type of atrocity at the front. But he knew it could only be the Shield. Their civilisation must be close now. Arms stretched out and palms nailed to the crossbeam at the top of the pole was the mutilated body of a dead man of indeterminate age. Mortimer could now see another telephone pole in the ground that faced the man. The body of a woman hung here, the cross set at an angle that allowed her and him to watch each other's last moments. They seemed young and were probably somewhere between twenty and forty. The woman was a woman, on account of her breasts, that had now fallen out of her torn and shredded shirt that was once white.

The crosses were not proper crosses but a crude T-frame with another telegraph pole bound horizontally slightly below the top of the vertical with just enough left to support the head. Only the US forces had real crosses and they would consider this action a blasphemy of the highest order. This fact probably explained why the Shield committed such barbarity. But the fact it was perpetrated so deep in woodland that only a rambler or a fugitive could find it showed that this method of execution might even be beyond the pale of the shield or most of them. Executions were usually conducted in the open, in full view, in order to teach and terrorise the local population.

Streaked with black-red lines of congealed blood, both faces had been torn and punctured by the local birdlife. Mortimer was relieved to spot a clean-cut hole in each forehead, clearly made by a bullet. He began to ponder when this atrocity took place and why. Were they a couple? Did they know each other, or were they two unfortunates who only came together in death? At least the red anorak on the male victim seemed the appropriate dress code.

A rather self-satisfied crow was perched on the head of the eyeless male corpse. It eyed Mortimer confidently, as if there were a possibility of another fresh meal. Mortimer felt its gaze, as if it were a new type of drone monitoring his movements. For a split second, he wondered if the crow was real. He reached down and grabbed a solid branch, curved at one end like a boomerang, and hurled it at the curious bird. The crow sensed the incoming missile and opened its wings and escaped to the higher branches of the surrounding pine trees. There it hopped and cawed angrily at Mortimer, head and neck jabbing forward and back mechanically like someone was pulling a string from behind. Mortimer ignored the angry crow and noticed tyre tracks indented in the mud next to the telegraph pole that held the woman. These led back towards a bridle path, wide enough to accommodate a vehicle, that probably ran towards the reservation, or so Mortimer thought.

He followed the path for another mile or so until the trees started to thin and the ridge started to drop away into the vale below. A three-way signpost emerged at the end of the trees. "Hope Under Dinmore" appeared on the arm pointing to the

215

west. Mortimer thought that the Shield Reservations committee had surely missed a propaganda trick in not naming Reservation Twenty-seven after the village. Before he entered the field, he checked his left wrist, and the blue light of the drone shield still flickered.

An undisturbed hour or so later, Mortimer reached Brierley Wood, a thin strip of woodland that had been the furthest point on the horizon from the ridge. The compass agreed that the reservation was close, no more than a mile away. The sky was getting darker as late afternoon passed into evening and his knees were begging him to stop. Yomping up and down the rolling landscape all day long had turned his thighs to bars of lead and the knees had had enough. It was a good time to rest and re-energise from his fruit bars.

Mortimer dropped his weapon and pack and slumped down against an ash tree and pulled out a Blueberry Strike from his breast pocket, a concentrated mixture of blueberries, brown rice syrup, nuts and seeds, lashings of sugar as well as a small dose of Modafinil to help keep you wide awake. It was always blueberries with the Yanks. Three bars a day and you would be up all night. But as soon as you stopped the continuous ingestion you would sleep for a day. A thirty-bar packet was fixed into the lining of his pack, but he always kept a spare one in his pocket handy. So before he ate the Blueberry Strike from his pocket, he slipped the catch on his pack and thrust his hand inside to retrieve the replacement.

The Shield always preferred more oat-based protein-rich supplements, the point of which was also to keep you awake for days on end. You had to take a downer to break the cycle and get a few hours' shuteye. But you never knew if you really slept or just lay in darkness, gently humming like an electronic gadget on standby. If you did not take a downer, the stress on your nerve endings could turn you into a maniac. Mortimer remembered the young French fighter who had kept awake for two weeks without sleep, so the rumour went. He was eventually put to sleep permanently by men from his own squad who survived his gun rampage.

His thoughtful silence was broken by the crack of a rocket exploding in the sky. Not the sort of rocket used by the military but the sort that used to be let off by families on Bonfire Night the length and breadth of the country to commemorate the survival of the United Kingdom as a Protestant country. As Mortimer looked up, another crack and falling blue-and-purple stars lit up the murky sky. He shoved the unopened energy bar back into his top pocket, shot to his feet and ran towards the sound and light in the sky. Another explosion overhead in blue and red this time. The falling stars were lighting his path out of Brierley Wood. As the trees started to thin, he made out the field below, full of silent, slow-moving people. He dropped to his knees behind a wide-trunked oak tree that guarded the treeline before the descent into the field.

Long rows of men and women, young and old, bent double or squatting on the ground, were pulling what seemed to be potatoes out of the ground. Some started to stand up and stared at the sky. Another rocket exploded and this time a shower of red stars. There were at least a hundred peasants in the field below Mortimer, and a similar number in the field next door and in the fields beyond. Another loud crack in the sky and another volley of red stars. By now, nearly everyone in the field was upright. Some clasped their stiff backs and twisted their necks around to relieve the stiffness from a hard day's work. The younger ones moved more easily and started to trudge along the muddy lanes between each line of potatoes. Each person dragged a brown sack bulging with potatoes. The older ones were happy to follow the younger ones. Once they reached the gate at the far end, each worker emptied their sack into a farm trailer quickly and without fuss. All the other fields were also closing for the day.

No-one seemed to talk or communicate with their fellow serfs. Too bored and too exhausted to bother, just as Mortimer used to feel after a hard day in the field. It was the sullen silence of serfs who knew they would be back again tomorrow and the next day. Mortimer raised his binoculars: there were no Shield uniforms, no shouting, haranguing, armed guards. And no-one looked back at Brierley Wood up on the hill. More rockets exploded, with red stars lighting up the sky. This time, no-one looked up but traipsed after the herd spilling out from the neighbouring fields onto the muddy track back to the reservation.

Mortimer ripped a few days' worth of energy bars out of his rucksack and shoved them into his top pocket, patted his pistol already in his side pocket and stroked his deep trouser pocket to check his Shield dagger. He hid the rucksack and rifle under a clump of ferns behind the oak tree. He dashed out of the trees, down the hill and jumped over a sty at the bottom into the potato field. In long loping strides he moved from one soft bank of plants to another bestriding the lanes in between and stayed on his feet. He careered through the gate, past the overflowing farm trailer in the direction of the now disappearing peasant column. A minute or so later, he rounded the bend and then another before the track ran out of earth and the grass took over. But Mortimer never noticed. The beam of bright white light seemed to be pointed right into his eyes. He jammed his legs into the ground and raised his arm to cover his eyes. About twenty yards in front of him, the scruffy phalanx stood, heads bowed, with gazes fixed to the ground, a familiar daily routine to protect their eyes. It was the same blazing white light, the same burning ache in his retina that Mortimer had felt on his first day in the Shield.

Once a pretty market town, Leominster had suffered from the harried and hurried retreat of US forces from the Midlands to their haven in Wales. And far enough from London and what passed for civilisation to allow the Shield to bring back the eleventh century for those unfortunates trapped in the DMZ. The rubble had been cleared and the town was now encircled by a twenty-foot barbed-wire electric fence powered by the sun. Guard towers stood at regular intervals along the wire, the closest two bookending the main gate. A twenty-five-foot sheet of steel swung open at seven a.m. to let the peasants out and then twelve hours later to let them back in. All other roads in and out were for Shield personnel only. Three searchlights stood atop the main gate, the largest cylinder standing in the middle raised higher than the other two with a beam of light strong enough to land an airliner at midnight.

Armed Shield militia fanned out in a crescent either side of the gate. Each wore a dark protective visor over their eyes.

"Please walk towards the beam. Keep within the beam of white light at all times," said the warm, soothing, female voice.

It was that same voice that had serenaded him into the bright white light all those years ago in London. Or what seemed like years ago. A cross between a maternal aunt and a dominatrix, the perfect fantasy combination for many Englishmen of any age.

"For your own safety and security, please keep within the beam of light."

The white glare disorientated and slowed the advancing column, as was the intention. The returning field workers stumbled and scuffed themselves into the beam as best they

219

could. Mortimer used this opportunity to fall in unseen at the rear. No-one pushed past the man, woman or child in front but kept a safe distance. Like everyone else, Mortimer instinctively stared at the ground and raised his forearm across his brow to protect his eyes and slowed to a shuffle. One old man near the front wavered from side to side, about to topple over like he had spent all day in the pub. Eventually, gravity took over and down he went. His followers politely curved around him, oblivious to whether he would stand up again. The guards showed as much interest in his fate as everyone else.

Once inside the gate, the light disappeared as fast as the lines of peasants. There was no street level or overhead luminescence in the reservation. But this did not prevent the ranks of serfs from atomising quickly down the roads and alleys to find their homes. Out of the light, they really did scurry back to their burrows. Mortimer could not help but stop and stare. He then realised two things. Firstly, he did not know how he was to make contact with the US spy in the reservation. There was no-one waiting for him with his name written in large letters on a piece of cardboard. Secondly, he was the only one who had ground to a halt, looking around confused. He decided to walk urgently, straight ahead, even though he did not know where he was going. The white light had done exactly what it was designed to do: distract and discombobulate.

Chapter 27

Mortimer kept going straight on, as he always did if unsure of the direction. He avoided the streets and avenues that led into the residential areas and found the centre of the town formerly known as Leominster. The narrow high street was absent of any people or, it seemed, any human use whatsoever. What had been shops once were empty shopfronts with heavily smashed windows separated by doorless doorways like a line of gouged eyes and broken teeth. The authorities did not even bother boarding them up any more.

Mortimer figured that the chaotic scene at the gate must be a reaction to the inevitable night-time curfew. This meant that the Shield patrols would be out combing the streets soon. The darkness and the emptiness gave him cover, but it was also a risk. He could be boxed in easily by a patrol with nowhere to escape. And how was he going to make contact here? Mortimer wished he was out in the countryside again; the two, three-storey buildings were a poor substitute for a canopy of branches and leaves.

Mortimer started down the left-hand pavement, keeping as tight against the wall as possible. Each second step seemed to find a crack or deep rut in the tarmac that had collapsed ages ago, along with the council responsible for it. But it was better than the road dotted with potholes of varying depth and hazard. A twisted ankle would be of no use if he had to break into a run. And inevitably, about halfway down, as he considered the need to run, the silence was broken by the growl of a chugging Aardvark. The vehicle was about a street away, further down, and Mortimer reckoned the high street was on the itinerary.

He sensed someone standing behind him. He swung his head round but there was nothing there except a smell of alcohol. And not stale either.

"Follow me." The smell spoke as well from somewhere near the ground. The beam of light from the Aardvark slowly slid around the corner and lit up the far end of the high street.

"Here," the low voice continued.

Before he could locate the source of the voice, two short, muscular arms locked round his thighs and dragged the confused Mortimer sideways through a broken doorway into an old shop. The only indicator of its past usage was the shop name that hung in large, dirty pink plastic letters above the glassless front. More dark and dank these days, "Bright & Shiny Things" had closed a long time ago when the bright and shiny things ran out. Once inside the shop, Mortimer was released and his saviour stood in front of him, a man no more than four feet tall and quite powerfully built, despite his obvious disadvantage.

The Aardvark wound its way slowly down the high street, the bright beam of the flashlight found the wall opposite "Bright & Shiny Things".

"Come on," the short man hissed before he shot off into the corridor at the side.

Mortimer stood up and followed into the dark alley that led to the back of the shop. This must be the contact, and he was effective. Thankfully, the floorboards were still firm and in better condition than the high street pavement. Ahead in the gloom, he nearly caught up with his guide, who suddenly seemed to get shorter as he entered the back room. Unlike him, Mortimer missed the double-step drop at the entrance. He stumbled and careered against the back wall and groaned as his sore shoulder felt the impact of his collision. The beam of the Aardvark now fully illuminated the shop front and fell into the corridor. Mortimer dropped to the floor, even though the back room remained dark.

The growl of the Aardvark engine became throatier as it reached the shop. Red laser beams from the rifles of the policemen perched on the side of the vehicle pierced the empty entrance. Mortimer listened hard for boots in the street or in the house. He reckoned there would be at least eight militia men in the patrol. But there was nothing. The vehicle did not stop and no-one got out. The Aardvark rumbled on ignoring Bright & Shiny Things, just like everyone else.

"It's gone ." His short friend stood over him. "We're safe now. Surprising really. What with you hanging around for a lift."

Mortimer ignored him and started to rotate his weak shoulder clockwise as best he could. He screwed his face up in pain as the joint made it clear it did not want to be touched.

"Come on, you need a drink." The man held out a small unlabelled clear glass bottle that contained a cheap Irish whisky.

"Who are you, a fucking waiter?"

"I'm Alex. You should have met me up at the crossroads before the high street. But you were obviously confused."

"I can smell you from here." Mortimer liked a drink but not from a drunk. He eyed the stocky frame and reckoned Alex was younger than him, somewhere in his thirties.

"Like a very slow Labrador."

"Got a smoke?"

"Nah, I don't believe in animal experiments."

Mortimer thought he would settle this without saying a

thing. He stood up slowly and towered over Alex. But this did not stop Alex.

"I saw you at the gate. You didn't know where you were going."

"Well, if you're that good, perhaps you know where the Shield keep their scientists."

"The castle. The Yanks told me your target."

Mortimer nodded. He was now making progress.

"Peasants working in the fields and now a castle. I really am back in the Middle Ages."

"It's what everyone calls it here. And you can't get in unless you're Shield or one of their domestics."

"At least we've still got Belgian TV in London." Pause.

"For now," Alex clarified.

"So, you work for the Yanks."

"I do my best. Someone has to." Pause. "You see, I was one of the lucky ones. An alcoholic dwarf whose poisoned blood ruined their experiments, so the pharmaceutical company, Swiss or something, wouldn't pay for me any more. Most people are not happy with parents strung out on booze and drugs all day. But seeing how it all turned out, it was like being born with a silver spoon in my mouth. Or a whisky bottle instead." Alex laughed at his own joke.

Mortimer was now getting tired. Nothingness swam through his head. He never did open that energy bar. He dropped to his ankles and sat back against the wall.

"Excuse me. I need to sleep."

Alex carried on.

"You see, us dwarves and midgets, like all the other raspberries, were brought here for research just before the war. Mum and Dad went up the chimney in the first few weeks. The tests killed them quickly. But I stayed alive, cos I was younger. But then when they found the shit inside me, I was deemed unfit for their Genetic... Heritage... program." Alex spat out the words.

"So one night, they took me and others down to the tunnel to be shot. But I survived. Just as the firing started, a US missile hit next door. And I've been grateful to the Yanks ever since."

Mortimer was now snoring loudly, mouth agape, head rocked back against the wall. Alex smiled, sat down cross-legged facing Mortimer and took a sip of the amber-brown liquid.

About three hours later, Mortimer's shoulder abruptly woke him on the hard floor. He had rolled over onto his left side and a bolt of pain shot through his arm and up into his neck. He groaned and gripped his shoulder and pulled himself upright back against the wall. Alex still sat cross-legged a few feet away, still swigging from the same bottle. A few inches of erect red wax and a bright white-yellow flame separated them.

"Is that a good idea?" Mortimer broke the silence.

"Candles are a great idea these days. Think I might open a shop." Alex nodded.

"Such enlightened times." Mortimer smiled.

"Exactly. Come on. You need to see the sights." Alex swigged again and stood up.

"What about the Aardvark?"

"Where we're going security is light. No-one lives there except the Shield."

After the guided tour of the alleyways, ginnels and cut-throughs of east Leominster that only someone who needed to know could ever know, they reached a large gaping brick-lined hole set back in a grassy earth bank. The overcast, moonless night meant they could comfortably operate in the open. They both stood on the single tarmac track that entered the ex-railway tunnel.

"Welcome to the castle." Alex nodded at the black hole.

"It's a tunnel." Mortimer was confused.

"That's why it is called the castle," Alex clarified.

Mortimer looked around and saw nothing and heard nothing. No guards, no fences, no spotlights.

"There must be cameras here?" Mortimer enquired.

"Nah. This is where they dump the bodies. The last thing they want is evidence," Alex replied.

"I didn't think they cared."

Mortimer looked down at Alex and nodded in gratitude. He had made it a lot easier for him. He was close to his target now and he had been given a way in as well as a way out.

"Happy?" Alex asked.

"I'm just surprised the Yanks found someone like you. It is my lucky day."

"Yep, no one takes a drunken dwarf seriously except US military intelligence."

Alex walked over to the right-hand side of the tunnel entrance. "This is where we were shot. Everyone panicked when the missile hit nearby; the guards lost control and opened fire. I spent the night under a pile of bodies."

Mortimer did not know what to say and thought better of proving it. Alex advanced into the murk of the tunnel and he followed a few feet behind in silence.

Once inside, the walls seemed to narrow and the space above shrank. The darkness dropped like a huge blackbird engulfing them with its wings. Since London, the night was always a comfort to Mortimer, a safe haven, something that concealed him from his enemies. But this was different: he felt like he was being

226

watched. There were eyes in the dark and he wanted to get out of there. Maybe it was the ghosts of all the dead victims of the Shield staring reproachfully at a former colleague of their murderers. Or maybe the problem was his dependency on someone else in the lair of the enemy.

"Hey…" Mortimer growled.

"Yep… just keep walking straight ahead."

Alex was just a voice hovering a few feet off the ground, without body or form, somewhere in front of Mortimer. He sounded close enough, but it was times and places like this when questions of trust arose in Mortimer's mind.

"Just keep talking. Like earlier."

"You getting lost again? Ha… just follow my laughter."

In about another twenty metres, the laughter stopped.

"Okay, stop a few feet ahead. I am at the door."

Mortimer followed the instructions to the letter, clattering into Alex, who fell into the arched opening in the wall. He pushed his arms out to protect his face from the heavy wooden door just in time.

"Thank you… idiot," Alex hissed.

"Sorry…" mumbled Mortimer, who straightened himself up.

Alex pulled a piece of coiled wire and a very small torch, no wider or longer than a cigarette, from his pocket. He switched on the torch and placed the unlit end between his teeth, head perpendicular to the lock with the light lasered into the lock.

Then he uncoiled the wire, inserted one end through the keyhole and turned slowly clockwise then pushed it deep into the barrel.

"Done."

Alex then switched off the torch and pushed his right shoulder into the middle of the door, forcing it to edge open an inch or so. He then crouched lower and peered into the shaft of light falling through the gap. Beyond the door was a long corridor encased in concrete, lit by a flickering strip light that ran along the length of the ceiling without interruption. The passageway was drab, basic and uncared for, unmistakeably a government design that could have been built any time in the last one hundred years. Green-brown smears of encroaching damp disfigured the walls.

Alex looked at his watch. "They will be asleep."

"We could have used the torch earlier." Mortimer was a little annoyed that the torch was not used earlier.

"It was the darkness that saved me. Gotta respect it."

Alex nailed it again and Mortimer could not disagree. He pushed the door open and set off down the corridor at a rapid jog. Mortimer caught up with his guide and kept a respectful distance. He could watch his feet this time to avoid any clumsy collision. They came to a halt at the first corner.

"What is this place?" muttered Mortimer.

"A nuclear bunker. Goes back to the middle of the last century."

Alex twisted his head around the corner. After a few seconds, he pulled back.

"As expected, the guards are out on Dexydrone. So we can just walk around them. No histrionics, please." Even though he was relieved, he still spoke in a loud whisper.

Around the corner, the corridor ran into a dimly lit circular concourse that intersected with two other corridors. Four Shield guards lay stretched out, side by side, slumbering in the middle of the circle.

At the edge of the concourse, Alex jabbed his finger straight ahead towards the tunnel running directly opposite. He then

228

pressed himself against the wall of the perimeter to keep as far away as possible from the guards.

"Quite sweet, really," whispered Mortimer from behind. Alex spun around and put his index finger to his mouth like a parent to a small child. He slowed his movement, holding his weight between each stride to reduce the sound of his boot on the concrete floor. Mortimer did likewise, exaggerating the rise and fall of his knee to slow himself and not fall over Alex. The pair of them moved almost stealthily, like comedy burglars creeping past sleeping policemen. They completed the semi-circle and entered the tunnel with the number two painted in large black letters in a circle on the wall.

Alex and Mortimer ran towards the next corner and stopped in front of the fire escape stairs. Mortimer stared up at the ceiling but saw no evidence of any surveillance equipment.

"Down and follow the corridor along to the next fire escape then down again to the fourth floor. That's where the scientists are. You need room Four Zero Six."

"Four Zero Six... you sure about that?"

"Oh yeah. My contact in Ventilation told me. You're here to kill the Yank scientist, I guess."

"Yeah, I guess I am."

"I'm off. Good luck." He smiled at Mortimer then slapped the side of his waist affectionately.

"Back out through the tunnel then." Mortimer raised his eyebrows.

"Yep, same way out." Alex turned and sauntered back down the corridor.

"Thank you... Alex."

Mortimer hissed his gratitude, not wishing his sound to travel into the concourse to waken the guards. Alex did not hear him but raised his arm behind his back. Mortimer watched his guide until he turned into the concourse. Then he waited to hear whether the guards were awake. Still silence. About thirty seconds later, Mortimer took to the stairs.

Chapter 28

"The purpose of the Newbold Project was to identify whether deviant, anti-social and criminal behaviour could be explained by a common genetic makeup in males... stop. This project was never completed due to the Blasphemy Ordinance. All scientists engaged in the project were either exiled internally at re-education camps or terminated, depending upon the strengths of their own beliefs. But I was fortunate... stop. I was due to be terminated... stop. And... I was saved by the Shield... stop. New paragraph... The deployment of violent criminals into frontline Shield forces and their success in counter-offensive combat operations against US military forces in central England forced the US into a truce... stop. Due to the high numbers of casualties, the US army engaged me to support a secret program to devise and weaponise a pathogen that on release into the air would attack the central nervous system of any battlefield combatant with the genetic makeup of a criminal..."

Dr Franshell stood in front of the flat screen on the wall, speaking quietly, louder than a mumble but not loud enough for anyone else except for the most intimate bystander. As she spoke, the words appeared a few seconds later in large black letters on the white screen like a karaoke machine in reverse. She was concentrating too hard to hear him push open the unlocked door and enter her quarters. Anyway, the flat screen in her office area was set in an alcove where the partition wall blocked her view of the door.

Mortimer moved behind the alcove and strained to listen to her dictation. The fact he could not make out her words clearly but could hear her voice made him curious about her. It occurred to him that a strange congruity lay between them. Like him, she found herself working for the enemy for what seemed to be the same reason: survival. He had rejected the Shield altogether and to all intents and purposes could be called a traitor for the task he had agreed to undertake. But the fact Colquoun wanted Dr Franshell dead and not even brought back alive to continue her work made Mortimer think there may be a gap in the story. And he wanted to know her story. If Colquoun and his religious maniacs wanted her dead, she must have something interesting to say. They could go fuck themselves. He would not kill her in cold blood.

His thoughts were loud enough now, so he stepped out from behind the partition like an actor appearing from behind the curtain.

"Uggh... who are you?" Franshell spun round, startled.

She felt him behind her immediately.

"We're going home."

"Oh, my saviour. Did they send you to rescue me?"

"The Yanks... who else?"

Franshell got up and lunged athletically out of the alcove towards the door. Mortimer caught her by the waist with his right arm before she could make it and swung her onto her bed against the wall.

"What's the fucking problem?"

"You are the fucking problem... Assassin..."

"I'm here to get you out." Mortimer lowered and slowed his voice.

"Another fucking idiot... you're nearly as stupid as the

lumps of meat you can shag here."

Franshell sprung up from her bed but not before Mortimer loosed the pistol from his belt and pushed the barrel into her flat midriff.

"It has a silencer," Mortimer muttered.

Franshell sighed and sat down on the end of the bed and looked up at Mortimer.

"What's your fucking problem?" Mortimer hissed.

"I was not brought here under duress. I am here because I want to be."

She paused to let it sink in.

"I fled US territory and volunteered my services to the Shield because the regime wants me dead. And you are working for them. That makes you my assassin." Franshell nodded at Mortimer.

Mortimer looked away and let his pistol arm drop to the side.

"This is bullshit." Mortimer knew she was right.

"No, you're confused. But you're not a bad man, else I'd be dead by now. I bet you're the listening type."

"Well, go on, make me listen."

"I am a microbiologist, who helped the underground birth-screening movement. Abortion and birth screening are both capital offences in the land of the free. The army got me out of prison because they wanted my expertise in DNA research to build a new type of biological weapon. I was transferred to a secret scientific site in Scotland. But then the CIA fundamentalists came for me, so I made my excuses and left..."

"So, you defected..."

"Let me guess: you were a policeman once."

"I can see why you pissed them off. So, the army won't protect you any more?"

"No chance. The religious nutters are purging officers not loyal to the regime. And I don't trust them. Once I finished giving the army what they wanted, I'd be finished."

"And now you are here. "

"I go where I am appreciated. And the Shield are interested in technology without any superstitious mumbo jumbo."

"I am your assassin. But you reckon you will get better treatment here?"

Franshell stared through Mortimer as she suddenly realised she must get her door lock fixed. The voice rose up from the now wide-open doorway.

"She will get the best treatment we can offer, Mr Mortimer." It was the voice of the Shield.

Even before he spun around, Mortimer could see the eye patch in his mind's eye. His former master, bedecked in the black dress uniform of a high-ranking member of the Shield elite, stood there with his two bodyguards at either side, the barrels of their pistols trained on Mortimer's forehead. As required, the assassin stretched out his right arm and proffered his pistol.

The bunker had been purpose-built for incarceration. Up to two thousand five hundred inhabitants could live in the underground complex in the event of a nuclear attack that would render the surface uninhabitable. Enough tinned and jarred food could be stored for eighteen months of healthy but plain dining. High-ranking government officials, the military, low-ranking support staff, families, children, pets and of course, if necessary, prisoners, could all be accommodated.

Oblong storage cellars on the lowest floor were used to house prisoners. Prisoner access was strictly through a square hole in the ceiling wide enough to fit a corpulent corporate executive without touching the sides. The drop to the floor was deep enough to guarantee a few broken ankles, especially if the prisoner carried too many pounds.

Unlike at Sheerness, Mortimer offered no resistance. Without any fuss he sat at the edge of the hatch, legs dangling down, before he dropped into the dim light of the cell. A single orange bulb protected by a metal grill glowed from the centre of the far-end wall.

His knees folded gently on impact with the ground, absorbing the nine-to-ten-feet-fall for the rest of his body. The grey-uniformed guard shut the hatch after him. Here he was again, under the lock and key of the Shield. And this time, there was no chance of a reprieve. Oh, the circularity of fate, ha-ha. The joke was on Mortimer, and he knew it. But all he wanted to do, all he could do, was sleep.

Chapter 29

Commissioner Hendrick had always enjoyed fire from a young age. Aged eight, at the behest of the eleven-year-old boy next door, he took a box of matches from the kitchen drawer and lit them behind the wooden shed at the bottom of the garden, where no adult could see them. But the adults did see the shed blazing brightly in the evening sunshine. Even though Father Hendrick took a stick to his son later that evening, young Hendrick never lost the pleasure of fire and never forgot the meaning of the stick. Fire had consequences, just like our own actions.

And tonight, the flames were good, flickering from orange to yellow then receding then rising again, looking for attention from the one-eyed leader. Only one eye but with the power to stare of two eyes, Hendrick sat bolt upright in his tall-backed imitation seventeenth-century oak chair that he always said he had inherited. It was a special occasion this evening, so Hendrick wrapped himself in the garb exclusive to a high-ranking Shield official. Over his black dress uniform, he wore a black velvet cloak that extended from his neck to his knees with a silver braid shield stitched on each shoulder but with the hood furled down. Commissioners were the lowest rank given the cloak, but he was not going to miss this opportunity to show his equality with the upper echelons of the Movement. Hendrick was a lord of war in a time of fire and blood, and the time for people like him had come round again.

Opposite him was the shorter, greyer, fatter Erasmus. He

slouched to his left, uncloaked and top buttons undone, legs splayed out a few feet away. His right hand nursed a glass of red wine. It had been a very long and very tiring day for Grand Commissioner Erasmus. He had flown from Brussels to London at dawn then driven under armed escort across the DMZ for hours to meet Hendrick. The Homeland government in Brussels regarded Hendrick as one of their most effective enforcers, their eyes and ears in a regime that was unreliable and vacuous to its masters in Europe. The British ruling elite knew their time had gone; the country had gone.

Personal financial gain and family or factional enrichment at the expense of what was left of the public realm was the order of the day in Westminster. They gave oligarchy a bad name. Not even a functioning monarchy any more to pretend great dignity and timeless virtues in the hallowed chambers of state. A tragic poisoning, quite possibly the doing of the CIA according to official sources, a lonely suicide and mid-life insanity had put paid to that. Erasmus did not bother with the past; he only wanted to meet the future. And he was very comfortable and relaxed now, slouching in Hendrick's other inherited imitation seventeenth-century tall-backed oak chair.

"The Truce gives us time to purge London of the undecided and malcontents," Erasmus started.

"A number of government figures outside the Movement have been dismissed for corruption and profiteering from bad defence contracts which undermined the war effort. It's very popular," Hendrick chipped in.

"I agree. Corruption charges are always guaranteed to get the masses on our side. But we have to be vigilant within the Movement as well. Some are too close to the banks, you know, and not just in London."

"But the banks provide us with valuable investment and funding here. We need them to fight the Americans. Conspiracy theories only undermine our war effort," Hendrick explained.

"Well, there is a view... that they are not entirely loyal." Erasmus spoke slowly and quietly to make the point. Pause.

"Maybe we should be deporting the bankers over here as well. Ha."

Erasmus was on the radical wing of the Movement, which harboured a number of conspiracy theories about bankers and inevitably, the Jews. Hendrick did not agree with the zealots, not out of a strange belief in racial equality but because he considered that racist ideology missed the point and in practice was a dreadful waste of economic resources. If the Germans had not been so obsessed with exterminating the Jews, they could have conquered the Soviet Union in the Second World War. Hendrick stopped this train of thought, as it was going nowhere useful and was certainly not going to press the point further. Erasmus had been number two in the Political Security Division in Brussels, and his move to the bio-weapons outfit demonstrated his reach and authority.

"Brussels is very impressed with progress. The mass deportation of criminals to E111 has helped to restore order and security in the Homeland. And of course, it has helped the war effort no end." Erasmus smiled at Hendrick.

He liked Hendrick, an early street fighter in the Movement who possessed greater intelligence and organisational ability than most of the British contingent. He was not from a wealthy elite family connected to the Establishment or even privately educated and certainly not held back by a deluded view of his island's history like so many of the servant classes. He saw the island for what it was: tired, decadent, hollowed out by a lazy deference to a failed elite who were only ever in it for the cash and the comfort. Men like Hendrick were different.

"E111… doesn't sound like a country any more," thought Hendrick aloud.

"The island has found its destiny. A prison colony where the prisoners are the guards." Erasmus smiled at his own insight and wit. " Don't you think…"

Hendrick noticed the flames slowing and stuttering lower in the hearth.

"Well, not quite the guards, but I see your point, Grand Commissioner."

A gentle knock at the door took Hendrick away from the flames and the conversation. He stood up and turned to face the figure standing at the open door.

"Ah, Martha. My door is always open. Come in." Hendrick loudly requested her presence.

She moved into the room and curved around the men in black to stand respectfully to the side of the fireplace. Erasmus did what most men do when they see an attractive woman for the first time: he stared and said nothing.

"I must congratulate you, Dr Franshell, for bringing in that criminal renegade earlier. The terrorist Mortimer has caused me a lot of problems," Hendrick continued.

"He wanted to kill me, Commissioner. What else could I do?"

"Ah, self-interest or loyalty. One is naturally suspicious of a turncoat, a traitor to their own."

"They're not my own. Never were," bristled Franshell.

"Please…" Erasmus raised his hand to Hendrick. "You really are too suspicious sometimes."

"You can sit, Martha."

Hendrick pointed to a rudimentary plastic chair against the side wall. She pulled it over and made herself as comfortable as she could in front of these two men.

"Dr Franshell, I am very pleased to meet you. Your arrival has stirred much positive interest in the Homeland. I am Grand Commissioner Erasmus and welcome you to the Shield Movement."

"I am here to serve." She smiled weakly. From her days back in the USA, Franshell knew what middle-aged men liked to hear.

"Indeed, your expertise changes everything. Commissioner Hendrick tells me you were developing a pathogen that could attack the DNA of convicted criminals. Is this true?"

"US military intelligence discovered that criminals and anti-social elements were being conscripted by the Shield into the European military... I mean, the Homeland forces. They proved to be effective frontline soldiers. And you had a large ever-expanding population of conscriptees," Franshell explained.

"The Shield is not a gang of uniformed thugs you know... It has a core philosophy to rebuild European civilisation from its oldest foundations. This begins with the individual and their willingness or unwillingness to accept order and the natural human hierarchy."

Grand Commissioner Erasmus then pulled his chair around to face Franshell.

"You are a clever, resourceful woman, or you wouldn't be here, an intellectual equal and I can respect that. Now, let me tell you what we are about."

The leader paused take a gulp of wine from his glass.

"In the past, what passed for government was obsessed with pandering to the masses and their eternal consumer greed, giving them choice in everything. Did it make them happy or healthy?

Not really; they wanted more and more and in the end the economy collapsed because everyone was in debt and who did people blame? Their governments, who they voted for, the people who fed them their material lifestyle fantasies for decades. So, Europe required renewal, and men like Hendrick and myself and hundreds of others stood up in the chaos to build a new way or bring back a very, very old way, the values of a pre-Christian order of land, community and family. But this system requires living space to prosper... there are simply too many people in Europe to feed. And this causes anti-social and criminal elements to grow."

Franshell interrupted.

"But what will you do with the convicts and criminals once you have defeated the US? Send them back to prison? It'll be very hard to get men trained to kill back into prisons."

"Why would we when we have a perfectly good colony for them on the edge of the Homeland? E111 is a natural barrier between the Homeland and the Atlantic, like an aircraft carrier for all the rejects of our civilisation to guard the northern border." Pause.

"But you do have a point ... which is where you come in, Dr Franshell."

"I come in..." Franshell repeated blankly.

"Firstly, we need to know if you can develop a vaccine to protect our forces. Is this pathogen ready for reproduction?" Erasmus continued.

"You have the genetic DNA on tap for me to build it but testing is the issue. But I can develop the antidote in a few months ."

"Good. We need to. The Truce gives us time."

Hendrick spoke up. "You will have a large test population at your disposal."

"That does help. The army scientists in Scotland have to transport criminals from US prisons and the costs are a nightmare, given that the private prison companies want a cut."

"Do you know their progress?" Erasmus piped up.

"Pretty slow I reckon." Franshell was not absolutely sure but continued anyway to make the point.

"Of course, a pathogen designed to attack the DNA is very complex, and testing requires time for peer review before it can be deployed successfully. It may not actually work, or not work as intended. And there is the issue of genetic mutation, the impact of which needs to be assessed before we can move towards implementation and manufacture."

Franshell's speech quickened as the scientific reservations exploded in her mind. Unfortunately, these home truths conflicted with her human reservation about dying, so waffle and obfuscation had to be the order of the day. What she could not say was that the application of gene technology to building sophisticated battlefield weapons was all theory and completely unproven.

"But if we don't do it, the enemy will," interrupted Hendrick.

"What you can give us changes everything, Dr Franshell. Both sides have large nuclear arsenals, unused due to the inevitable devastation. Even crude biological and chemical weapons leave an area uninhabitable. But a weapon that attacks the central nervous system of the target population and leaves the landscape untouched is invaluable to us... but firstly, we must have a vaccine."

"It's all part of the development procedure. Any manufactured pathogen for use as a battlefield weapon must have an antidote, a vaccine. Or else it would obviously infect your own troops," Franshell clarified. It occurred to her that developing a vaccine for a non-existent pathogen would give her valuable time.

"We can then reverse the original pathogen to develop a weapon that attacks only those without the DNA of a criminal. Tell me, is it true that the US marines and other elite regiments over here are handpicked men of Christian virtue?" Erasmus started to stampede ahead of scientific reality.

"Officially, only men deemed to have lived by the Ten Commandments without any criminal or anti-social acts on their records are allowed in," Franshell clarified.

"And how do the US authorities know? Do they screen their genes?" Erasmus enquired.

"It's all a lie. They just force all conscripts to convert to Christian fundamentalism to get an army of the righteous and virtuous. Great propaganda," Franshell admitted.

"Oh, I am shocked," Hendrick added sarcastically.

"Indeed… but your expertise could also help to eradicate the problem of anti-social behaviour and criminality in the Homeland. All our current remedies are far too costly in money and resources. This opportunity really could change everything."

Erasmus was a man whose intelligence always ran a close second to his ambition.

"A solution to your internal social problems. You mean, kill millions."

"A small price to pay for a cleansed future," Erasmus clarified.

"Your death would be a tragedy, Dr Franshell. But a few million deaths are just a statistic, as the saying goes," Hendrick interjected.

"Let's not be so rude to our guest." Erasmus frowned at

243

Hendrick.

"We will need to move you to Brittany, Dr Franshell, as soon as we can, to advise our research team there. You know, there are lovely beaches in Brittany and beautiful countryside. A lot more pleasant than this rainy old rock." Erasmus sounded upbeat.

"My apologies, Martha. Your final destination will be a far more comfortable place to live than you've been so recently accustomed to." Hendrick always found it easy to switch from malevolent threat to mild reassurance.

But Franshell was not reassured at all. She only heard the word "final". But she nodded and smiled weakly and said nothing.

"Tell me, do you think it is possible to identify religious tendencies in an individual's DNA?"

Franshell could not believe her own ears. She replayed the question back in her mind. Erasmus was as much a zealot and lunatic as found back home in Vice and Virtue. So the answer was simple.

"The propensity to hold a deeply held belief without any evidence, a tendency to the irrational and emotional, is identifiable within the human genome."

Not for the first time, she realised that the time had come when your health and happiness utterly depended on you telling those who might end it exactly what they wanted to hear. Not the truth, not reality, not something complex and nuanced but a simple statement to stimulate their innate desire for opportunity, power and future reward. And fuck me, yes, the irrational and stupid is buried deep in the human genome. She was not lying at all, in fact.

Erasmus smiled warmly at Franshell.

"Brussels will be impressed, sir." Hendrick spoke up.

"It's too late now for a report. I will go back tomorrow and save the good news for my return." Erasmus finished his glass of wine.

"More wine, sir?" Hendrick reached for the bottle and filled up his glass.

Franshell returned to her grey-washed pod and lay down on the bed. Her mind was still buzzing; she was not going to sleep soon. It still amazed her when those in power wanted to use ideas and technology they simply did not understand, even on the simplest, most generalised level. The application of gene theory could never be predictable: given the variables of the environment and the criminal thesis, it was at best an exaggeration of biological facts and at worst, simply not true. But they really wanted to believe it was true, like a religion.

As well as the phrase "final destination", the words "renegade" and "traitor" also lingered in her mind like a cryptic clue to the game called "What the hell do I do now?" Mortimer had a genuine English accent, so he must have been turned for some reason. He had evaded the guards to get close to her, so he must have been trained somewhere, but he did not behave like a zealot or a hired killer in her room. He even seemed to be in two minds about whether to kill her. And Hendrick seemed to have a personal problem with him.

It did not take Franshell much longer to work out that her assassin was probably on the run for a good reason; a man who seemed to have come to the same conclusion as her.

Chapter 30

Time can mean very little if you are stuck underground, but if you are incarcerated as well, then time really is meaningless. It might have been thirty minutes; it might have been thirty hours, but eventually the alarm went off in his shoulder and Mortimer jolted awake. He was still there, lying on the thin, firm mattress that covered his metal-framed bed. So was the hard concrete floor, the four brick walls and the eternal orange glow on the wall. Above him, the other side of the trap door was quiet and no light filtered through at the edges. At least he had slept well, probably because it was the same type of bed as the one in his cell in Sheerness. The mind and body never easily forgets minimalist luxury like that. Mortimer looked around at the four walls and felt a strange reassurance. He then told himself that he had always lived inside his own prison. There was someone else's world out there, a reality created by others, and then there was his reality and his soul inside here and in between, a six-foot-wide concrete wall lined with lead and topped off with razor-edged barbed wire. And nothing could break this wall down.

His back and legs still felt tight from his walking tour of the English-Welsh border country. He needed to loosen up and do whatever stretching he could. First, he needed to get his bad shoulder working again. He started off by rotating his left arm forwards then backwards. After a few minutes, the shoulder loosened and the pain reduced to a more acceptable level of discomfort. He then dropped to the floor to stretch his back and aching sides. From here, he made out a cell door at floor level in the un-lit end of the cellar. He reckoned it would be pointless to try to open or force it. A bucket of water and a pile of ragged towels lay in the corner opposite the door. He had not seen the door or the bucket and towels before.

Maybe it was their presence on the other side that alerted Mortimer to the cell door, but it swung open and banged against the wall as two uniformed Shield pushed their way in.

It was Downton, the intelligence officer from London, with his much larger assistant, Kovacs.

"Mr Mortimer, it's such a shame we have to meet again in these circumstances." Downton sparked up.

Mortimer did not recognise Downton at first, but that smug grin slowly brought him back like a bad smell. He ignored the grey-uniformed Kovacs, as he knew exactly why Downton had brought him along. It was the red plastic cable wrapped tightly around his clenched right fist that gave it away. He rose to his feet anyway.

"Not at all. Always a pleasure."

"You have not changed. Well, Mr Kovacs and I would like to ask a few questions. About how you got here... hheeghhichheehghhic..."

Downton broke off and raised a splayed hand to his coughing mouth.

"Must be damp down here... My apologies."

Kovacs's huge face cracked into a large smirk, his mouth wide enough to comfortably fit three or four compact discs. At this point, Mortimer could not help noticing that Downton wore a uniform that was too big for him whilst the uniform worn by Kovacs was too small for its oversized occupant.

"He ain't no traitor... Bill Mortimer isn't it," Kovacs piped up.

Mortimer found the face of Kovacs in his memory bank. It was the football stadium at Derby, Pride Park, home of the Rams. The US attack had surrounded them on all sides, driving them back into the stadium. The Slovak was part of his group that had fought their way out through the main supplier's entrance by the car park. He had proved himself that day in close hand-to-hand combat. Hence his promotion to the intelligence unit.

"Juri Kovacs, the Third Fairfax Battle Group," smiled Mortimer.

Kovacs recognised Mortimer instantly but could not help twitching in a double-take to make sure. He was confused to see his former colleague here.

"It is you… This man's a fucking hero as well as a sarcastic cunt."

"You're not wrong there." Mortimer smiled.

He felt pleased to see a fellow comrade, a survivor of the siege of Derby, another ex-convict who did what was expected of him and more. Unfortunately, Kovacs was a borderline psychopath who had killed for the mafia in Holland and Germany prior to his employment in the ranks of the Shield. And therefore, he was an ideal interrogator.

"You've bettered yourself, I see." Mortimer nodded in appreciation.

This was all enough to rile Downton.

"I'm sorry to break up the regimental reunion, but you are not a hero; you are a traitor. And you need to answer some questions."

"And Corporal Kovacs… you do have a job to do."

Kovacs stepped forward, inches from Mortimer's face, and hissed, "Go down," at a pitch inaudible to Downton. Before

Mortimer could move, he felt the force of Kovacs's cabled fist in his stomach. But curiously, it did not hurt as much as he would have expected. He buckled his legs but did not collapse to the ground. Kovacs stepped back.

Downton regained his poise now.

"Who sent you here to kill Dr Franshell?"

"Donald Duck…" Mortimer answered in a split-second.

"Ah, an American." Pause. "Mr Kovacs."

Kovacs lurched forward into the face of Mortimer again, who did not move a muscle. He hissed, "This time…" through clenched teeth and threw his cabled fist into Mortimer's stomach with exaggerated intent. Once more, he pulled his punch, but this time Mortimer slumped to his knees. Kovacs then followed up with his weaker left across Mortimer's jaw. Mortimer winced and threw his head back. Blood streamed from his mouth. Even when Kovacs pulled a punch, a man would still feel it. Kovacs stepped back and glanced away sheepishly from Mortimer, who rubbed the blood from his cut lip with the back of his hand. Mortimer rose to his feet and so did his temper.

"Yes, I was picked up by the Yanks, and they offered me a three-week holiday in Florida if I killed Franshell. If I killed Franshell. So, there you are… fucking obvious, really," Mortimer spat out.

"Who ordered you to kill Franshell? CIA or US military?" Downton continued.

"Oh, you two would get on really well. Another fucking arsehole… Colquoun is his name."

"Ah, US army then. And you made contact with those fundamentalist terrorists operating in the DMZ."

"They aren't fucking Christians."

"I need information on this UKP group; the name of the

commander who delivered you to Colquoun."

Downton walked towards Mortimer and circled away from the side where Kovacs stood. And again Mortimer could not help noticing how his uniform was too wide across the shoulders and sagged around his waist and drooped over his backside. Baggy and puffed up, like the wearer's lifelong sense of entitlement. Mortimer could accept the bearing and manner of Downton, as the oligarchy had spawned these buffoons ten-a-penny for centuries in England, but it was the fact he had no frontline combat battle experience that annoyed him. He had never had to put his life on the line for anything.

"You need some medals for that swelling chest." Mortimer smirked.

Downton stopped in his tracks. Kovacs spluttered a cough to hide his rising snigger.

"On your knees," Downton snarled.

Kovacs clasped Mortimer's nearest shoulder with the palm of his huge hand, thankfully for him the uninjured one, and plunged him down to the floor. Mortimer let his legs go to make it easy.

That day in Derby, Mortimer had disobeyed orders to lead them out of the football stadium. Fortunately, the commanding officer who gave the orders to fight to the last man had been killed by a drone missile whilst beating a rapid retreat south in his staff transport. Shield propaganda could never admit to the failed offensive, so Mortimer's actions were heralded in the media as a heroic defence. Dunkirk spirit and all that.

"Kick him hard. The filthy cur is down," Downton spat out. Kovacs swung his weaker left foot into Mortimer's ribcage. But the boot slid across the side of his trunk, avoiding any lasting damage to the thorax. By now, Mortimer knew the script. He clutched his side and toppled sideways.

"Uggh... you bastard." Not a lie in the case of Kovacs, who could not resist the interrogator's follow-through into the pit of the stomach.

"Hhhhnnngghh." Mortimer exhaled loudly and curled up on the floor.

From ground level, Mortimer noticed that Downton's grey trousers were empty of anything that resembled a fully formed rear. Flat and deflated, it was an apology of an arse, unlike the pair of taut bulging cushions squeezed into Kovacs's britches. This really was a humiliation too far. A cretin without any redeeming physical qualities, who could not even dress himself properly, was playing a starring role in what may be his final hours. This was hardly the required termination ritual for a warrior to enter the halls of Valhalla.

"I will ask you again... Who is the commander of the partisan unit?"

Mortimer, not so reeling from the softened blows, hauled himself onto his feet. He clutched his midriff, exaggerating the minimal pain he felt.

"A better man than you."

The now puce facial features of Downton tightened and stretched. The slightly hooked nose became a beak, the cheeks puffed out and the eyes bulged. In concert with the too large flappy uniform, the DMZ regional security head looked like a bilious chaffinch.

"I will be present at your death... Mr Mortimer." The words twisted and turned slowly out of the interrogator's mouth.

"Wish I could return the favour."

Downton shook his head in disgust and stomped out of the cell, slamming the door behind him.

Mortimer looked at Kovacs. "You better go as well."

"You know, cunts like that always have the last laugh." Kovacs stared at the cell door.

"Maybe… but thank you, Kove. Good to see you're getting on in the world."

"What else is there?" Kovacs shrugged and looked at Mortimer.

"If it weren't for you at the football stadium, I'd be dead."

Mortimer laughed then coughed to clear his throat and then laughed even louder. Kovacs turned and left the cell, more quietly than his new boss.

Chapter 31

Franshell slept in late the next morning after a restless night: too much to think about and too many questions to answer. Hendrick was not convinced by her, and Erasmus would surely throw her away like a soiled sample once the DNA of their chosen target had been sequenced and the pathogen developed. She would then be killed after she had ably assisted the killing of millions. Maybe she was being too hard on herself and she was only going to accelerate a process already in hand. And even if she was unsuccessful in identifying the DNA of a religious fanatic or any social group deemed to be the enemy, her fate would probably be the same.

As she stood at the basin in her underwear, she stared at her reflection in the portrait-sized mirror that hung on the grey wall. Her Choctaw complexion seemed to look darker than normal. This was strange, given the local weather and the fact she had been stuck underground for days. Her high cheekbones and black hair still stood strong. The only softness in her face lay in her deep brown eyes. Uncle Luther always said he loved her eyes more than her breasts or her pussy. They teased him, implored him to touch her, to love her. Good old Uncle Luther, he may have been a child rapist but he was also a teacher. His actions had taught her, however trapped, however hopeless you felt, there was always a way out. His abuse had toughened her up for the journey ahead, she reckoned. He had prepared her for a world where the abuser, the bully, the un-human, were in charge. And frankly, how many girls from a trailer park in Louisiana became a gene scientist and got to travel the world?

Franshell never regretted her decision to burn Uncle Luther to death in his trailer or ever remotely considered his pain and suffering at her hands. It was a logical and righteous act that removed the weak, cruel and ignorant from civilisation. It is a medical fact that we are all going to die some time, but some, through their actions, deserve to go sooner rather than later. She knew it was morally wrong to kill another human being, but however hard she tried she could never feel that this act carried any wrong. Because survival with her dignity intact was her settlement with the world she found herself in, a place without morality or goodness, only the rules of science.

She moved away from the mirror and stepped into the prescribed garb of a light-grey jumpsuit adorned with a palm-sized black shield emblem on her right breast and the number 171717 printed above. Since she had arrived at the base, Franshell had given her new masters a full download of her time at South Uist, including a detailed breakdown of her own scientific work, such as the DNA composition of the viral pathogen intended to infect carriers of the criminal gene, the possibility of viral mutation in the pathogen as well as the names of other scientists, details of their research and test results, the role and responsibilities of the military and the CIA in the program, the current level of project progress, timelines and plans, the technology and software used to develop the pathogen and everything she could remember about the location, layout and security. Some top-secret stuff, some stuff not even known to the US military, that could only be understood by a scientist and the sort of stuff that Shield intelligence may already know.

As much what, how, who and where that she could

remember. A bit of embroidery here and a key omission there would only increase her value to the Shield, especially if she frightened them with the progress of the US military. Even if the pathogen had not yet beta tested successfully and was in fact many months, possibly years away from being weaponised in the field, if at all. It did not matter. Fear and paranoia always overcame calm, rational reason in the minds of powerful men like Erasmus: one third ideological zealot, two thirds power-hungry opportunist. Just tell the man what they wanted to hear.

But that morning, 171717 needed to get some exercise and clear her mind after the previous night's haphazard sleep. She had clearly miscalculated the Shield. They may detest the Christian fundamentalist regime, but they still carried the same messianic mania for killing. And Brittany was where her journey would end.

The door clicked open and Franshell entered the empty corridor, not knowing where she was headed. The door fell shut and automatically locked itself behind her. She made for the lifts at the end of the corridor: one went up, the other went down. A Shield man dozed against the wall next to the down lift with a rubbery green tropical plant stood in a pot the other side of him. The uniform woke up and straightened himself out when he saw Franshell stood in front of the up lift. She nodded at him and pressed the call button at the side. The steel industrial doors opened and inside she pressed the letter D on the side panel. Numbered floors indicated the underground section of the castle whilst letters indicated the overground floors. The lift immediately rattled into action, the letters flashed on the side panel and she soon arrived.

The doors opened automatically, and she stepped out into bright sunlight that streamed through the window opposite and covered the hall. Franshell felt even more in need of fresh air and decided to go outside into the courtyard. She looked out of the window at the blue cloudless sky and then down to the courtyard four floors below her. The white concrete floor below sucked up the morning sunlight and threw it back against the surrounding walls.

Like the corridors, it seemed empty of any life. She lifted the handle on the tall side window and pushed it open and leant out as far as she could. Franshell looked down and spotted a human figure splayed diagonally against the wall, a few feet off the ground like St Andrew on the cross.

Franshell hurried back to the lift and took the down lift to the ground floor. There was no slumbering Shield guard at the lift. She turned left and made for the door wedged inside the wall further down the corridor. She pushed down on the long metal bar handle to open the door and entered the courtyard. The human saltire was a few steps away from the doorway.

Mortimer had been staked out on the wall three feet above the ground since early morning. His arms and legs were stretched diagonally and tied to the wall with semi-circular metal clasps around his wrists and ankles. Downton did have the last laugh.

With no handle on the outside, Franshell realised the door could slam shut and lock her out. She took out a tablet pen from her pocket and rammed it in the gap in the bottom corner to keep it ajar.

"It's you... the renegade." Franshell moved closer to him. A small pile of bricks that may have been left to assist the more height-restricted guards sat on the ground between Mortimer's legs. Franshell picked up one of the bricks and took it back to the door and replaced the pen with something more substantial.

"Yep." Mortimer coughed to clear his dry throat. "A friend

of mine thought I needed some sun and fresh air."

Mortimer kept his eyes on the ground to avoid the glare of the sun in his eyes.

"Like me, you could probably do with some vitamin D."

"Indeed…" Mortimer sounded hoarse. Forty-eight hours in a dank cell and then exposure to fresh air on a breezy day made his voice struggle to be clear.

"You need some water."

Franshell then glanced around the courtyard. Her eyes darted over the windows looking down on her. She did not want to be seen talking to Mortimer. Or giving him any comfort. She pulled her water flask from her pocket, uncapped it, moved towards Mortimer and held it against his mouth. He tipped his head back to the maximum he could muster and she poured the cold water down the hatch. After a few seconds, she pulled back and capped the flask and quickly slipped it back into the long pocket on her outfit.

"Thanks." Mortimer coughed again but this time he felt his throat loosen.

"All this. Why? What turned you away from the Shield?" Franshell got to the point.

"Yep, I've got the medals." His throat warmed up now. "I just got sick of killing."

"But you were going to kill me."

"Not Yanks… civilians. Proper people…" Mortimer rasped. He then turned his head up to look across at Franshell.

"I could have killed you. But then I didn't. I got confused."

"I wouldn't have…"

"Would you kill an innocent just to… get on?" Mortimer squinted at the sun now getting higher overhead.

"If I had to…" Franshell replied.

"No-one has to do anything. You chose to." Mortimer tried to pull a smirk at Franshell but his mouth was too tired.

The breeze got stronger and started to bang the door against the brick that kept it ajar. The brick was gradually being shunted away from where she had left it. It was like a warning to Franshell to leave now. The door could close any minute.

"Look, I'd better go." She walked towards the door and held onto it.

"Nice talking..." nodded Mortimer. "Maybe again..."

Although the metal clasps rubbed his wrists and ankles holding his weight against the wall and sent a throbbing pain through his arms and legs, Mortimer could not help noticing the attractive, dark features of Franshell. Unfortunately, she quickly disappeared through the exit and pulled the door closed.

It was not just Mortimer who had been looking at Franshell. From a window high up on the tenth floor on the opposite wall, Hendrick had watched the entire conversation. He was neither surprised nor shocked by what he saw, because it entirely justified his suspicions. So Franshell would have to prove her loyalty to him and the Shield.

Chapter 32

Kovacs unlocked the door and clumped loudly into the underground box. He could not see Mortimer anywhere. He had vanished. His old comrade swivelled his head from left to right but saw nothing save an empty cell under a fading orange light. Silence. But at no time did Kovacs look behind the open cell door. Or even think to.

"You again." The voice came from the darkness behind the open cell door. Mortimer was crouched down on his haunches. He always enjoyed the ninja hiding techniques that he had learnt as a youth during his martial arts period. Hiding like a quail: to crouch down and cover your eyes with your hands may have even saved his life once in a close-quarters firefight during the Cannock Chase offensive. Maybe it didn't; maybe the US marines were not concentrating on their task to clear the barn. The secret was to breathe slowly and think of something that was not your hunter or your current circumstances. According to the theory, this meant your mind would not send out the mental airwaves that could alert the hunter to your very close proximity. He would not be able to feel your presence in the shadows. That was part of the legend of the night-time assassins, and Mortimer was prepared to give them the benefit of the doubt after the episode at Cannock Chase.

Kovacs swung around. "Fuck... you're there." He laughed out of relief and a little embarrassment.

"You should have looked."

"Come on. You need to get cleaned up." Kovacs wanted to get on with it.

Mortimer happily followed the order, because Kovacs was right. Even the netted cotton inner lining of his uniform, devised to absorb the sweat and filth of a US soldier in the field, had now given up. The uniform now stuck to his body like the wrapper of a sticky hard-boiled sweet. But unlike his forebears in the last century, the lining contained a chemical that killed lice or any other bugs that might find comfort on his body. He certainly needed a shower and preferably something light and airy to wear, given the warmth of his cell.

After a few corridors, Mortimer found himself in a narrow bathroom. Kovacs smiled and pulled the plastic curtain back to reveal a white shower cubicle.

"There's a uniform on the door. I'll be back in fifteen."

"This... for me?"

Mortimer eyed the dark black tunic and loose trousers of a Shield officer's dress uniform hanging on the back of the bathroom door. Silver shields flashed at both ends of the collar, but no insignia specific to a Shield division decorated the tunic. And neither was it light or airy, but it was clean, which was good enough. It was a uniform with potential.

"Yes, you have an audience..." Kovacs then quickly disappeared from the bathroom.

The shower did what showers are supposed to do, then Mortimer donned the Shield uniform. He was going to the ball. As he pondered whether to fasten the top button, the large frame of Kovacs squeezed through the door.

"Just like the good old days, eh?" Mortimer smiled. "In fact, better, cos we never wore the black, just the battlefield camouflage."

Kovacs frowned.

"I hated it. I just wanted to get out alive… but now I wish I was back there, y'know, the unit, us all together, that spirit… Never had that before. Never have it again."

"Yeah… we had something. If we didn't, we'd all be dead now."

Mortimer forgot about the top button and stared at Kovacs for a moment. Even memories could stop men like Mortimer and Kovacs in their tracks.

"Come on, let's go." Kovacs turned and Mortimer followed. Things had changed now for both men.

The door was open and the only light came from the fiery hearth in the opposite wall. Kovacs stopped at the entrance and stepped back to allow Mortimer to pass. Mortimer caught his eye and nodded a nanosecond before striding through into the lair.

Hendrick stood at the right-hand side of the fireplace, thrusting and turning a metal poker in and out of the burning logs. On this rare occasion, Hendrick was not in uniform but in what he thought was smart evening wear: a baggy grey suit with black shirt and open collar. Even when off duty, the colours of the Shield adorned his six-foot-two-inch frame. The poker was a decent length of rounded metal, headed by a few inches of pure point, sharp enough to give a man a chance in close-quarters combat.

Mortimer stopped in front of the two tall-backed chairs and studied the figure playing with fire. For the first time, he noticed that Hendrick was probably the same height as him. Not that it changed anything.

"My door is always open." Pause. "Isn't that's what they used to say?"

Hendrick continued to prod without looking away.

261

"But I bet you never used to say that."

"Correct. I hated all that corporate "please like me, I am your manager" bullshit."

Hendrick turned around and smiled at Mortimer.

"Take a seat." Mortimer sat down in the nearest chair to the left.

Hendrick remained at the flames.

"Mr Downton said you were very uncooperative. Quite rude, actually."

"Man's a fucking idiot. Is that the best you can do these days?" Mortimer retorted.

"I wanted to see how Downton would do."

"If he's the future of the Shield then you're fucked."

The shower, clean clothes and now a comfortable chair had relaxed Mortimer and he was going to have some fun.

"You're clearly not impressed. And frankly, nor am I."

"Just another mediocre careerist. A fucking weasel. And I thought the Shield was different... this time."

Mortimer's shoulders loosened into the full width of the fine leather chair.

"The problem is that every organisation needs their weasels. Their Downtons... But they can never play a major role." Pause.

"We do need men who set an example for others to follow. Men of strength and proven character."

"You mean like this chair. Very impressive. Any chair is an improvement for me, but this one seems very trusty and sturdy. From a different time, perhaps."

Mortimer clutched both arms of the chair in tandem and squeezed them hard to prove his point.

"Comfortable, then. It's a Great Wainscot chair. Dates from the 1650s, or something."

Hendrick bent down and picked up two dried logs and under-armed them into the centre of the hearth. The flames jumped up and waved in gratitude.

"Men like you is what I mean. You could join my team and shape the future of the Shield. You can have Downton as your first pupil. I would love to see that flaccid schoolboy face crumple… The damaged pride of a man who thought he was born to rule."

"Well, we do have one thing in common. I never did have you down as a chinless."

Mortimer let a faint smile form at the thought.

"I had to prove myself, like you. You proved yourself at the Derby Kessel. You saved your unit and fought your way out after your commanding officer was down. But your career really took off when you disobeyed me in London in front of my men and in front of the cameras and then escaped across the DMZ. You enlist with US forces, to be sent on a mission to assassinate one of their top scientists… Very, very impressive."

"I'm a proper TV star."

"Don't worry. All can be forgotten in a week or so. There will be new TV stars."

"I've never been interviewed in front of a roaring fire before." Mortimer ran his eyes over the rising flames.

"My order to you to execute that young boy was wrong. It had no purpose and no justification on any level. Please forgive me for my lapse of judgement."

That phrase "lapse of judgement" said it all for Mortimer. A hollow phrase used by men in power to excuse their wrongs. But of course, those who choose these words never believed they were actually wrong or had lapsed at all: A mild admission of poor decision-making to wipe away the fact that they had not got away with it. It allowed them to roll back, restart the world, pretend it never happened and move on to the next lapse of judgement to get away with. Again and again.

"Many policemen died entering that building to flush out the gangs, and those locals were assisting them. They had to be taught a lesson." Hendrick continued.

"So there was a reason after all. You're like a seven-year-old tying up his shoe-laces for the first time."

Hendrick's cheeks reddened, riled at the insolence of Mortimer. He was giving the man a chance to save his life and all he could do was make wisecracks.

"Your high-and-mighty attitude is not justified by your own actions. You were part of the slaughter of unarmed US soldiers at Cannock Chase. And civilian operations as well," Hendrick retorted.

"Hypocrisy, Mr Mortimer." Hendrick pulled away from the hearth and stood in front of Mortimer, waiting for him to speak.

"They'd executed our men days before. We found the bodies, a bullet in each neck. An airborne division; you know what they're like. They don't take prisoners. And neither did we. That's the penalty you pay on the battlefield. Yes, I was part of a detachment that executed prisoners of war."

"So there was a reason, a purpose for this act of barbarism. You received the Oak Leaf Second Class medal as a reward, didn't you?"

Hendrick turned back to the fire, took the poker and prodded the flames into action.

"And the collaborationist civilians."

Mortimer had nothing to say.

"Unfortunately, that is the world, isn't it?" Hendrick felt better now. He had made his point.

"You do something that superficially appears to be wrong but then get rewarded for it because it is morally the correct action in that context. The world around us is our context."

"And what does that make me, in your context?"

"A moral example. That's what you are. We are." Hendrick raised the poker from the flames and pointed the end at Mortimer. Mortimer raised his left eyebrow.

"Just Mortimer will do, thank you."

Hendrick returned to the flames, but rather than interfere with them he looked straight ahead, as if a new thought had entered his head. Then he sucked air deep into his lungs and turned back to Mortimer.

"It is our destiny to set the example for others to follow." He exhaled.

"Nature's eternal binary structure: those who lead and those who follow. And those who follow are only entitled to what the leader decides. By dint of their voluntary servility, they have forfeited their right to be independent and free. As we know, most people choose to follow orders, follow someone else's view of the world, even to their own cost. Literally. Remember consumers: they thought consumerism made them free as they worked harder and harder to buy things they did not need and did not really want; it never made them healthier or happier. They did it because large, powerful organisations persuaded them with lies and illusions and the masses said thank you very much. Please can I borrow money that I can never pay back; let me hand over my dignity and security to you, Mr Banker. And what was left?" Pause.

"I am sure you will tell me," Mortimer jumped in.

"Nothing. When it all collapsed, as it inevitably did, they had nothing... inside or out."

Hendrick stopped and stared at the ground. Even he needed to take a breath.

"Let me tell you a story about the consumer and where it all ends. Early on, I led a detachment of the Ragnar division into a village in the county that used to be known as Northamptonshire. I forget the name but one of those large villages, small towns that used to come ten-a-penny in the countryside. Lots of new housing… you remember the sort. It was near the Midland line but avoided the worst, as the American advance had stalled thirty to forty miles north. Anyway, it was a Thursday. At first, we thought the settlement was empty, but then they emerged, the local civilian population, silently and sullenly in front of their houses, not sure what to do. But there was something not right, something missing. Then, a few locals came forward and said they were starving. The town had run out of food. But you know, they did not look hungry; no sunken faces or swollen bellies in their children." Hendrick sighed and waited. His voice dropped lower.

"That was it; there were no children. Very strange. Anyway, I said to them, as country people, had they not lived off the land? Local farms, woods, orchards, their gardens, even. But they said they were too afraid to leave the town." Hendrick inhaled deeply again.

"Do you know how they had fed themselves? They ate their own children. Can you believe that?"

Mortimer leant forward in the Wainscot, taken aback. He wanted the old warlord to get to the point, but this statement stopped his rising impatience. He now knew first-hand there were roving cannibal cults in the DMZ where the civil infrastructure had been wiped out, but he did not expect it in a settled community. Obviously, things had broken down much earlier than he realised. But save for two raised eyebrows, he did not register any further incredulity and remained silent to let Hendrick finish his tale.

"We found teenagers and younger, naked and manacled in a warehouse. Or larder. There were others, clothed and in a better condition, imprisoned in a block of flats... and even fed. The prettier boys and girls. I think you know why." Pause.

"Do you know where they stored the bones of the children they had consumed? The local church. St Marks had stood since Saxon times, a shrine to Christian spiritual values. A very bold attempt to save people from themselves. But now a repository to the worst endeavours of a humanity with no spirit and even less humanity. The vestry was rammed with bones and skulls. The nave and altar littered... That church stood for a dead God and a dead people."

Hendrick's bottom lip trembled at the disgust it brought back to him and the magnitude of the conclusion he had reached that day. He then looked down at the stone floor. His voice softened, almost to a tone of regret and embarrassment.

"I stood there and wept."

There he was again, using those carefully chosen words. "Wept". Leaders of men never cry or blub, they weep: An epithet that serves only to indulge their personal tragedy and heighten its presentation to men like Mortimer. And even now, Hendrick could not help but wipe the side of his one good eye. He then took a step forward and dropped to his haunches in front of Mortimer. His one eye narrowed but the pupil widened, the black ball bulging like the end of an antenna, waiting for Mortimer to react.

"So, I confronted them with the bones, and the locals... the whole village was in on it. Their representatives, dignitaries...

267

They agreed to release the uneaten and abused children as long as we fed them. As long as we gave them our food and then evacuated them to a safer area. My, what a shopping list of demands," Hendrick spat out.

"No remorse or guilt, just a burning sense of entitlement, so very early twenty-first century. Killing and eating your own children... who could blame them? The world was falling apart."

Hendrick shrugged his shoulders indulgently and smirked.

"They told me that the youngsters had been very difficult to control when war broke out; they were a social problem. So how did our consumer civilisation react? By eating their own young." Pause.

"So what did I do?" Hendrick rocked back on his heels and looked up to the ceiling and rubbed his palms together. A few seconds' pause.

"Free counselling and an ice-cream each," Mortimer replied.

"Ha-ha... I wish you had been there with me."

He snorted then regained himself to his feet.

"I set an example. The correct example. We released the children still alive and fed and clothed them, then we hanged every adult in the town. Trees, lamp posts, statues, we even replaced the hanging baskets in front of the council building. I hanged every damn fucking rotten consumer."

"About three, four hundred that day... yeah, close to four hundred." Hendrick nodded to himself.

Mortimer listened hard but ignored the pictures in his mind. This was all a smokescreen, the doing-it-for-the-kids bit. Every liar and hypocrite since time immemorial has done it for the children.

"That's a lot of rope."

"That's a lot of clarity, Mr Mortimer. In war, there is time for compassion and time for ruthlessness. War is the only thing that brings these conflicting ideas together. To know which is right, you need clarity. Moral clarity… and I had total moral clarity in that moment."

Hendrick raised his shoulders and stiffened his back at the end of the epistle.

And what a punchline to end it. Mortimer had expected some self-serving bullshit but not the word "moral" to be involved. Thankfully, the rigid, robust sides of his rather impressive antique chair stopped his sides from splitting all over the floor and him laughing madly like a hyena. He managed to re-route his rising snort into a throat clearance exercise. But the fact remained that only a deluded zealot, a liar, a psychopath or simply a complete cunt, take your pick, would claim to have "moral clarity" in this wasteland. And Mortimer understood exactly what the phrase meant.

Those dead bodies at your feet never left you; their only life was inside you. And the only way you could extinguish the horror was by telling yourself it had to be done. The victims brought it upon themselves by their own actions and got their just desserts. And you were absolutely certain that you were right. Because we have to be, otherwise we have to admit to ourselves we are nothing but monsters, not fit to call ourselves human. We all like a moral justification, like an angel to guide and lead us, but like angels, they disappear into thin air. And all we have left is silence in our heads and nothing in our souls, all humanity sucked out by Moral Clarity.

Mortimer had executed prisoners of war and collaborators, but that was war. In other words, survival. It could easily have been him on the end of an executioner's bullet. But he still rose to the occasion and had felt the bloodlust. It was never a question of morality but of nature. He was doing something timeless that had been done for centuries.

"Sounds to me like you are telling yourself it was the right thing to do... probably again and again."

Mortimer slid forward in his seat. That chair had been keeping important men comfortable for centuries. But Mortimer reckoned the leather upholstery had probably been replaced since the last witch had been burnt at the stake. Hendrick now sat down in his seat for the first time and stared into the middle distance.

"When the money ran out, what was left? Nothing. Those villagers could not handle that wonderful freedom we all professed to love. They had no values. Just like the Roman Empire, no one thought that the West would end, but it did." On he went. "You know, when the Romans left, nothing was built of stone for another four hundred years. Sometimes, we have to go backwards to start again. And start again we will. Find out true nature and old traditions still buried deep within." Silence. Hendrick swivelled his head towards Mortimer.

"Tradition is the transmission of fire. Not the worship of ashes. A very clever man said that."

"I bet no-one disobeyed you that day, did they?" Mortimer enquired.

"Neither would you if you had seen the bones of the children."

It struck Mortimer as ironic that Hendrick had ordered him to kill a child after he had directed an atrocity to save children.

"Yeah, I'd probably have done the same. But where does it all end? With the children." Pause.

Hendrick smiled faintly at the thought that Mortimer may be coming around to him at last.

"But my son was murdered by men like that," Mortimer

suddenly spat out.

"By men like you. You got a taste for it. Let's not forget."

Mortimer could listen to the philosophising and the self-justification, but to be compared to the child murderers who killed his own son after he refused an order to murder a child was too much. He had fought alongside men he would never want to know in better times; he had saved their lives in order to save his and survive the battlefield. And he did survive, but now it was more than about survival for Mortimer.

"Those men who killed your son; I did some research. You'll be pleased to know they both died in a US drone strike near York on their first day of posting…"

"You know I'm not like them. You know." Mortimer's head lurched sideways at Hendrick as he raised his voice for the first time.

"But you are pleased to judge me." Hendrick spoke carefully.

"You are like me. We are similar men. We like to set an example."

Mortimer stared at the fire. A large flame had caught and enveloped the previously smouldering logs.

"You have nothing, absolutely nothing, to offer me." Mortimer angrily raised his voice.

It was his son who had saved him. It took a few years, but eventually Tom blew away that emptiness that had engulfed him in Sheerness and at the front. Mortimer was not hollow any more; he was filled to the brim.

Hendrick sighed theatrically in the way only a man not used to not getting what he wanted could express disappointment.

"What do you think happens if you refuse? There is only one outcome."

Now Hendrick raised his voice. Mortimer said nothing. The flame grew bolder and brighter now, surging around both ends of the logs and all around the hearth, in total control for that moment before it would inevitably fizzle out and die.

"According to Dr Franshell, the criminal gene creates a fearless and irrational self-interest. What is your self-interest, Mr Mortimer?" Hendrick asked.

"I do not compute."

"You make life so hard for yourself."

"Yeah, dying is easy. It's living that's hard."

Thirty minutes later, Mortimer was back in his cell. He was offered an unmarked black boilersuit to replace his black dress tunic and trousers. The thick protective padding around the groin and anal region made it very clear to Mortimer what was coming: Death with dignity. He slept well that night.

Chapter 33

The Shield Movement never underestimated the importance of public entertainment as an opportunity to manipulate the people. So, the tradition of public execution was revived, a clear and transparent example of power at its most brutal. No hidden camps or detention centres where people disappeared. The island was the detention centre; the prison camp and the inmates always knew when someone was going to be punished forever. No-one in the Shield leadership had to lie about their political aims and intentions. It also revealed the truth about how they perceived human nature. Public execution was an instrument of terror on one level, but on another level, it made the people complicit. By watching, cheering, laughing, crying, drinking, celebrating and just attending the bloody act, it bound them to the beliefs and behaviours of the movement. The value of abuse and cruelty as public entertainment had increased significantly during the years of mass private communications and social media before the collapse and war. Easy access to technology had now disappeared for the masses but the need to be stimulated had not.

The arena lay on the outskirts of town at the local football ground, where Hereford FC reserves had occasionally played decades earlier. At the eastern end of the pitch stood a small open stand that used to seat a few hundred supporters. But now it had been hollowed out and reconfigured with a concrete balcony that ran the width of the stand, replacing the seats in the upper tier. A wooden roof covered the balcony. Even if it was raining, the condemned would still have to face the solemn the gaze of the local Shield elite. Directly opposite the football stand at the other end of the football pitch stood the gallows, a raised wooden platform with what ironically looked like an elongated steel goal post that stretched from one end to the other. Enough width for seven, maybe eight bodies to swing freely. A tall wooden fence then ran from each end of the platform all the way to where the corner flag used to be. Tonight, six nooses hung down from the crossbar, three either side of a gap in the centre where you would expect to see the goalkeeper. A wooden stage ran along the length of the goal line up to each goal post. From each corner of the pitch, the floodlights illuminated the patchily grassed rectangle in the evening gloom. The football pitch, no longer maintained by a groundsman, had been worn and cut up by the feet of large cheering crowds.

Numerous wooden trestle tables were parked along the long sides of the pitch. Each table held brown and green bottles: The brown bottles contained cheap, strong lager beer imported from Belgium; the green bottles contained cheap, strong French wine. A limited choice, but the aim was not quality but quantity. If the strength of the alcohol was not enough, some of the wine was infused with narcotics to get the party going.

Execution day always meant an early finish for the serfs. A few hours less in the fields and the prospect of a night of intoxication always accelerated the shuffling phalanx through the main gate.

The warm, sunny and cloudless day brought with it the promise of a beautiful sunset, especially as the gallows stood at the western end of the pitch. Many punters came straight from the gate. Queues formed at the tables as grey-uniformed Shield men and women handed out brown or green bottles to the thirsty throng. Tunics were loosened, top buttons and straps were undone and sleeves were rolled up. This was the only occasion when the Shield provided any kind of service to the inmates without the mediation of a loaded weapon. For one evening only, they were no longer their guardians and overlords.

Children were encouraged to attend and no rules or restrictions applied to their consumption of alcohol or narcotics. Enormous oval-shaped flat television screens were mounted at each end of the gallows, with the silver Shield logo displayed on a black screen like large bug eyes watching over the crowd. Which of course they were. And if you were not standing right at the front, you could always get a close-up view on TV. That old staple of any Shield party, the techno-metal version of *Jerusalem* boomed out. "And was the holy Lamb of God, on England's pleasant pastures seen," sung the breathy female pop voice over the backing racket. It was followed by other throbbing, bouncy pop-manipulated covers of *The Planets* suite by Holst but without accompanying vocals. Jugglers and fire-eaters walked amongst the crowd, doing their best to create the air of a medieval rock concert.

That day, there was no final meal for Mortimer other than his usual breakfast: a jug of cold water, a loaf of black-brown bread, a thick slice of greasy butter and for once, something runny, red and very sweet that might have been jam. By midday, he was falling into sleep but never quite getting there. His eyes could not close properly because they were kept open by the dragons flying overhead. The jam had been laced with some lysergic put-me-down. Mortimer knew straight away he was hallucinating and quickly became bored and annoyed with the electric blue-and-golden then red-and-green-outlined mythical creatures that swept around the cell. After an hour or so of flesh

275

slipping off dead faces and dragon airways overhead, Mortimer thankfully did drop off.

Before the Shield guard could touch him, Mortimer's eyes caught the dark shadow of the man bending over him. He sat up immediately, stopping the guard in his tracks. He blinked his eyes forcefully and ascertained that the dragons had gone now, but the prison cell had not. Mortimer spent a few seconds working out where he was. The hallucinations had emptied his mind and made him feel withdrawn, disengaged from the cell and the men in uniforms. He was certainly not ready for any confrontation.

"Get up." The guard had an English accent.

Mortimer swung his hips round and sat on the edge of the bed, rubbing his eyes again. He saw the other guard stood inside the doorway.

"Come on. We gotta go." The guard at the cell door was in charge and also sounded like he hailed from this island.

Mortimer rose to his feet and slowly walked towards the door and without looking at the guard, sailed serenely out of the cell. After a few paces, he stopped and waited obediently in the corridor. The guard in charge stepped in front of Mortimer.

"Follow me." He sounded a little terse, as people in charge often do.

The other guard brought up the rear.

Eventually, after a few corridors and up a few floors via an old industrial lift, Mortimer felt the late afternoon sunshine in the courtyard. An Aardvark was parked with doors at the back open, beckoning Mortimer to climb aboard. He looked at the senior guard and nodded. And he nodded at the gaping vehicle. Mortimer got in and sat down on the left-hand side, followed by the guards, who sat opposite, facing him.

The Aardvark pulled away from the building and took the exit road towards a checkpoint. Waved through, the vehicle left the grounds of the castle and turned onto the main road into town. Mortimer felt strangely relaxed. He had nothing to say to his escort, no questions to ask. It must have been whatever they put in his breakfast, but his thoughts returned to Sheerness, his fight with the guards en route to the noose and his boiling anger at the fact he was going to die. But things had changed now. Finding Tom's grave, pressganged to fight in a war, seeing all those deaths or maybe simply the fact he had managed to survive this long against all the odds at his age meant he was probably ready now.

He thought of his son, Tom. He realised that the photograph had disappeared when they took his uniform away and he had forgotten to keep it safe. If there was heaven and he met his son again, the first thing he would say was sorry. Sorry for not protecting him and letting him die before him. The death of a son before his father is a terrible tragedy. The fact Mortimer knew he should have prevented his son from dying in the family home only made his guilt worse. But of course, there was no heaven. Nothing. Just an eternal dreamless sleep.

The Aardvark pulled up next to the other personnel carriers, about one hundred metres behind the gallows end of the football stadium. The Aardvarks were deliberately parked in the shape of a crescent to obscure the view of the gibbet.

The guard nearest to the door lifted the handle to thrust the door open. Mortimer jumped out of the back of the Aardvark onto the grass without waiting for the order. In front of him, four armed Shield policemen clustered around six other men also clad in black jumpsuits like Mortimer. The six victims each knelt, heads bowed, in a semi-circle. And unlike Mortimer, they were each handcuffed.

A sun-glassed police officer emerged from behind the middle parked Aardvark and shouted at the six men, "Okay, up you all get."

Each rose and automatically formed a line one behind the other, as if following a script. The officer turned to Mortimer. "You... fall in at the back."

Mortimer did as he was told. For the first time, Mortimer heard the crowd that had gathered at the football pitch. Or more precisely, the usual Shield bombast blasted from the TV screens: Something about a "home in the country for the British people" and the "success of the Reservations" against the sounds of cheering crowds. Mortimer figured that the cheering came from the screens and not the real crowd.

"Curtain up in ten minutes, ladies." The officer smiled.

He then walked breezily over to the last Aardvark on the right-hand edge of the crescent.

"This way to your stage, please." The Shield policemen started to twitch and jiggle their weapons. The man at the front of the line instantly followed the voice. He was taller than the others, including Mortimer, which was probably why he was at the front.

Flanked by the grey-uniformed policemen, the line wound its way past the Aardvarks into an open space of grass behind the gallows. Mortimer's six colleagues to a man bowed their heads and stared at the ground. Only Mortimer craned his head up to see where they were going. He saw the gallows in front of them and the crowd at the side by the tables.

People of all ages queued or milled around, some laughed, the younger ones pushed and shoved, some stood staring blankly at the screen, swigging from a bottle and others just waited with

278

their own thoughts. Those at the tables saw the line of shufflers first. They started to cheer, wave their arms to greet or insult the unfortunates; some jeered and others called out to those in the main throng that the fun was about to start.

About halfway, two parallel lines of razor-edged barbed wire formed a narrow avenue to their destination. The officer led the group to the entrance and stepped to the side.

"Your red carpet, gentlemen."

The officer's humour annoyed Mortimer, all the more so because this was probably the last comedy act he would witness. The other policemen kept outside of the barbed wire as the column filed straight ahead as requested. Once inside the barbed wire, the images and music from the TV screen cut out. The crowd filled the silence with sounds far more base and raw than the theatrical propaganda of the Shield.

Mortimer turned his head to the west and was struck by the colour of the sky. Bright pink filled the horizon down to a layer of amber around an orange sun. Then a loud crack from exploding fireworks overhead; bright white stars fell from the darkening blue. He stared hard at the sky. Definitely no more dragons; the hallucinogens had worn off. This was all real now. The sun was going down, and so was Mortimer.

The tall man at the front of the line paused in front of the ladder that was tied to the side of the wooden platform. The officer approached and waved him upwards. Still head bowed, he proceeded up the eight rungs of the ladder onto the stage, followed by the others. Oblivious to the baying crowd, now fully distracted by the arrival of the condemned and the policemen stood on the platform, he walked to the noose at the far end and steadied himself behind it. The five others followed and took their places under the remaining nooses.

The still sun-glassed officer drew up behind Mortimer as he stepped onto the stage. He hissed into his ear.

"You... arms out."

Then one of the guards at the back grabbed Mortimer's left-hand wrist, slipped a looped cuff around it then pulled his right wrist into the loop before tightening it. Mortimer smiled at sunglasses.

"Fucking teacher's pet," Sunglasses spat out.

"Get in the middle. You're the main act. No noose for you."

Mortimer slowly paced to the centre of the stage, his tied arms extended in front of him, and faced the crowd. There were two rows of barbed-wire fencing between the crowd and the stage. Five policemen with semi-automatic rifles at the ready patrolled the gap between the fence and the stage. The fugitive scanned all around, but there were no escape routes; armed guards at the side and in the front. They would shoot him down in seconds, so as he was on stage, he might as well give them a show.

The din from the crowd rose as Mortimer eyed the front rows, where mostly younger men and women gathered. Angry contorted mouths jeered and screeched and even tried to flob phlegm at the ex-Shield man. Of course, the globules only reached the guards, who responded by jabbing their rifle butts into those closest to the wire. Mortimer stepped as close to the end of the stage as he could without falling off and stared hard into the eyes at the front. This defiance only seemed to make them angrier. Well, they had come for a show. He caught the words "Child Sexer" chanted somewhere back in the melee. He could not help but smirk at the effectiveness of Shield propaganda. The smirk-turned-sneer only increased the hostility of the mob. From about twenty rows back, the crowd surged forward to get closer to the stage. But the front rows, not wanting to be caught on the razor-edged wire, pushed back. Punches flailed, faces were bloodied and for a minute or so, Mortimer was no longer the centre of attention.

Mortimer pondered to himself: Hendrick might be right after all. As he surveyed the human sewage spewing a few yards below him, this realisation hit Mortimer like one of the rockets exploding above. If this is what was left of humanity then why not bottle it up in reservations and destroy it? This was the natural state of man and woman: beasts fully boxed into the moment of pleasure of seeing other humans suffer, maybe out of fear for themselves, but never mind, there was a mob, a crowd full of others like me to hide in. Call it a deep primeval longing that needed to be purged, but it never went away; it was always there, guiding us.

Beyond the crowd, a group of black-uniformed Shield officers watched from the balcony of the football stand. Hendrick sat in the middle, almost, it seemed, directly opposite to Mortimer. Next to him sat Dr Franshell. Mortimer looked around to his fellow condemned.

The tall man was clearly shaking. His tall angular joints twitched and trembled, except for his head, which still remained bowed. The second male in the line stood dead still, open-eyed, staring ahead in a trance. The third male to Mortimer's right and next to him was not a male. She was crying. It was the dark black smudges under her eyes and the untrammelled heaving tears that gave it away. Mortimer thought to say something, but nothing came out. The man on his left was crouched down on his haunches, head wrapped in his hands, but the earth did not swallow him up. The next man stood close to the edge of the stage, cursing and gesticulating as best he could to the crowd.

281

And the oldest man, whom Mortimer had followed in the line, was on his knees, head and fingers pointed upwards in prayer to his God.

The sun-glassed officer hurried to the front of the stage a few yards away from Mortimer and raised his arms. The crowd immediately ceased punching, jostling, screaming and abusing and fixed itself quietly on the Shield officer. The silence made Mortimer pull back a few steps into line with the other victims. Sunglasses started; his voice boomed through the small microphone attached to his chin

"On my left. Number one. Theft of food and refusal to work."

It was the tall man. A Shield policeman pushed the nervous wreck forward and pulled the noose down and made it right around his neck. He took the other end of the rope hanging down and yanked it hard to lift the victim off the ground. The whole body convulsed for a second or so and then in one last shudder it stopped. The head dropped forward for one last bow and the body dangled lifelessly a few feet above the ground. After what seemed a long second of silence, the crowd roared loudly in unison. Sunglasses raised his right arm and the crowd noise dropped quickly in anticipation. They had done this thing before.

"Number two. Moral crimes with violence."

The same process happened again. No resistance from the condemned man, just the urge to get it over with. The crowd roared louder this time as the body twitched and swayed for a minute or so longer. But Sunglasses did not miss a beat as the cries died away.

"Number three. Sex crimes."

It was the crying woman. Mortimer could not watch this one. A bear of a policeman had to lift her into the noose, one arm around her midriff whilst the other arm clasped the end of the rope. She writhed and flailed but then snuffed out. Sunglasses lingered a little longer than before as the crowd enjoyed her death with even more gusto than the previous end.

"Number four. Moral crime in thought and deed."

The man had already placed the noose around his neck. Shorter and not much heavier than the girl, he was the quickest to die. Once the guard pulled the end of the rope, the body went up and the head dropped limp. This was a great disappointment to the crowd, whose cheering subsided into what sounded like a loud sigh.

But Sunglasses got the entertainment back on track, thanks to the still aggressive number five. "Murder with... cannibalism."

Arms firmly tied in front, all he could do was jut out his chin and headbutt the air in between cursing to show the front rows what he would like to do to them. It took two Shield policemen to drag him back and force the noose round his neck. He kicked and swung madly like a man should do in his last breath, much to the pleasure of the mob. They cheered louder for him than for the young woman.

The older man who prayed had now collapsed to the wooden floor. Two policemen crouched down and checked him. After about a minute, one stood up and drew his forefinger across his throat to signify that indeed the man may now be with his maker.

"Number six, dead on arrival." The crowd groaned. You were not supposed to leave the stage until you had entertained the crowd.

Mortimer now started to feel uneasy, standing there in the middle alone, the only man left to die. He had watched the horror unfold around him, forgetting that he was the main act. Two policemen appeared in front of him. One carried a wicker basket that could fit a small dog and the other carried a thick wooden block, about two feet by two feet, with a curved lip cut into one side. The policeman who carried the block bent down and with both arms carefully placed the block a few feet in front of Mortimer. The curved-lip side was turned towards Mortimer. The other policeman then put the basket a few inches in front of the wooden block. Mortimer stared at the space cut for his head and wondered if his neck and head could rest comfortably. It did not seem big enough.

A burst of flames suddenly shot into the air behind Mortimer and spread outwards for almost the full width of the gallows. The blast of heat spun him around. The sun had almost dropped out of the western sky and the clouds were changing to black. The authorities had ignited a trench filled with petrol and dried wood behind the gallows to improve the visibility of the spectacle.

"We have a guest, everyone... Dr Franshell." Sunglasses then respectfully returned to the side of the stage.

Dr Franshell emerged in full black Shield dress uniform onto the platform, joined by the two policemen, and then a third one carried the executioner's axe. The head of the axe was a perfect titanium crescent that measured exactly one foot in length from tip to tip. It was like something you might see in a medieval torture museum, still very popular in major cities of the Homeland. The long, firm rubber handle was indented to aid the grip of the user and coloured black to lend it the authority it deserved. It was designed to look heavy for the benefit of the audience but was actually light enough for any adult to swing around gaily at a head-chopping party.

The mob at the front led the crowd reaction as usual: it clapped, it cheered and it yelped. Real blood would more than make up for the deflation and disappointment of the public suicide. The two policemen advanced on Mortimer, clasped each shoulder and forced him down onto his knees in front of the block. The front row of the crowd jeered wildly again at Mortimer's downfall. And he could see their gloating eyes more closely now. He obliged the policemen by sliding his knees forward and dropping his neck slowly into the curved lip of the block. He knew he had got it right because it fitted comfortably, and his head hung over the other side, bowed to the ground.

The axe-handler handed Franshell the axe. She clasped the bottom of the handle with both hands, approached the bent and fallen Mortimer from the side and readied her grip.

Back in Monroe, Louisiana, Dr Franshell used to chop firewood regularly at her grandmother's house in the woods outside town. She was more than capable of wielding an axe, even an axe that stood up to her waist from the ground. She knew she would have to raise this axe above her head to do the job properly in one blow. As she started the backswing, she remembered the garden, the chopped wood and her granddaddy, Pastor Franshell. He would sing "What a friend we have in Jesus" as she chopped. When she had finished, Granddaddy would gather up the logs in a wheelbarrow then beckon her, bible in hand, to the wood-store in the shady end of the garden. It always took longer than it should have done in the wood-store with Grandaddy. The sinner should always be punished as well as loved.

Franshell nodded at the policeman nearest to Mortimer, who stepped back to give her space. The mob at the front surged forward and bayed for the blood of the terrorist, the child molester, the traitor. "Kill, kill, kill." Beheadings were a rare treat, and they were certainly getting their money's worth. The

285

chant grew louder as it spread through to the back of the throng.

She swung the axe upwards and raised it above her head. Franshell did not hear the dull cacophony from the crowd, only "What a friend we have in Jesus" sang in her head. And then she swung her arms right round in a semi-circle and loosed the axe into the front row of the crowd. An unfortunate man, a little taller than those next to him in the second row, received the edge of the blade clean through his cakehole and out the other side, cleaving his head into two. The already hysterical mass at the front screeched in shock and horror; the back of the crowd wailed in anger at not getting what was promised. The five guards in front of the barbed-wire fence each turned around to look at Franshell.

Sunglasses advanced on her and drew his pistol at her head. But he had nothing to say. His skin had turned a pinkish purple, a bit like the sky about thirty minutes earlier.

Hendrick had been chatting happily to his junior officers only moments earlier. He ignored the hangings; he only really wanted to see the execution of Mortimer and the loyalty of Franshell. The Shield commissioner had only just returned to his seat at the front, away from his colleagues, when the death blow to Mortimer failed. It was not the chill of the evening air that ran down Hendrick's back but the shudder of personal humiliation. He had been defied in public, in front of the reservation and his own men. Hendrick was not the type to explode in anger or make a spectacle of himself. He sat there, away from the others, pale and speechless, as rigid as a block of white-and-black marble.

His subordinates shuffled uncomfortably in their seats and looked around in all directions except at their master's back. No one on the balcony knew what to say. Hendrick had promised them a show of loyalty: A US turncoat, who had willingly joined the Shield, so much that she would kill one of their own traitors in cold blood in front of his officers and the reservation. It was his idea, and it was exactly what the hopeless Mortimer deserved. The execution of Mortimer by Dr Franshell would demonstrate his own instinct for leadership, authority and obedience: Everything that the Shield demanded of him.

Chapter 34

Alex did not work in the fields. He was a software engineer who maintained the systems to control the supply of light and water to the castle. This made him an ideal spy for the US military. But even this privileged role did not allow him to miss the public executions. He always got home from work an hour or so earlier than the peasants. And if there was an execution to attend, he always liked to read beforehand: a poem, instructions on how to grow flowers and shrubs in his small garden, or a chapter from some long-dead novelist; an inoculation of civilisation to counter the evening horror show.

Reading for pleasure had almost died out amongst the inhabitants of the reservation. Only members of the Shield Movement or those with a special licence, such as bounty hunters, were permitted to own an electronic information device. This ruled out any civilian in a reservation, which left only printed books as a source of information and wisdom. Most of the inmates had not opened a book since they were young children, probably at first school if they were lucky. And by then, the education system had devoted their means of learning and scholarly attention to electronic devices, so there was little need for printed text.

The fact that the Shield did not ban books or even advocate their destruction made it pretty clear to Alex that books were no longer read in great numbers. Only older people could be bothered to read words on paper, and they were dying out. Alex salvaged any books that he could find in derelict houses or ruined shops. It was hardly the great library of Alexandria but nonetheless, his collection ably reflected the high, medium and lowbrows of western civilisation over the last two hundred years: Hardy, Conrad, Blake, Dickens, Nietzsche, Larkin, Kafka, Jackie Collins, Angus Wilson, Alan Titchmarsh, Ernest Hemingway, *The Beano*, *Wisden*, Tom Sharp, Michael Palin (humour and travel) and the BBC Wildlife Unit to name but a few. Lines of paperbacks, interspersed with the occasional hardback, spanned the shelves on the side wall of his small lounge that overlooked the garden. Alex did not care for any system of subject order: *Beano* annuals from the late nineteen seventies next to Nietzsche was good enough and provided some humour.

Sat on a loose, fraying purple sofa that had seen better days, Alex took off his reading glasses and folded back the corner of page seventy-six of *Heart of Darkness*. He always left for an execution as late as possible.

Alex locked the front door of his small terraced house in the old part of town and headed off down the alleyway next door that took him into the centre of town, where he joined the main road leading to the arena. Except for a few stragglers like him, the road was empty. There was no gate or entrance to the arena except for a cordon of armed grey uniforms evenly spaced around the perimeter of the old carpark. Alex swanned through them, winking at the nearest Shield guard, who smiled back. Everyone knew Alex in the reservation: guaranteed to drink too much and make a spectacle of himself in public. Exactly how he wanted it.

Alex continued to do what he always did on execution day: Go to the line of tables at the right-hand side serving beer and get sloshed as soon as possible, or make it look like that. He always went to the right because that was the side from where the victims took the stage. One of the benefits of being an alcoholic was that it took a lot of booze to get you under the table. His small physique should count against him, but like his brain, his body could cope with more than many people might expect.

Alex grabbed two brown 500 ml bottles of Belgium's finest and strongest from the trestle table and then marched towards the gathered throng at the front. Neck arched back to form a straight line from mouth to throat, Alex glugged down the beer in his right hand as fast as he could. Invisible to most, he weaved his way around the thicket of increasingly drunk and excited bodies. A close-knit drinking circle of six or seven young men stood in his way so he opted to walk around. Immediately, the shortest man in the group spotted Alex about to pass behind one of the tallest males in the group. He then poked his hand into the chest of his burly mate, who lost balance and toppled backwards, bottle in hand. Alex's foot caught his heel, which sent him sprawling to the ground. Alex stepped aside to avoid the falling man as the group burst into laughter. Alex turned and twirled his wrist as if ostentatiously removing a wide-brimmed hat and gave a deep bow.

Some members of the group applauded but not the fallen giant, who swung his outstretched right leg at Alex's midriff. Alex dodged the leg, dropped the empty bottle and disappeared quickly into the throng. He made for the far right-hand side of the gallows at the edge of the crowd. As Alex took his position, he heard the muffled shouting of orders behind the wooden barrier. The music stopped and then the cheering and clapping began. This was as good as it was going to get if you wanted to attend a rock festival in mid-twenty-first-century Britain. Alex started to drink from the other brown bottle.

Once Mortimer reached the middle of the stage, bolt upright

in defiance in the black issue of the condemned man, Alex felt his heart and chest sink. He ignored the others and only concentrated on Mortimer, hoping for a liberating thunderbolt from the heavens. Unlike most agents sent into the reservation, Mortimer was an Englishman and not a Yank, so Alex had faith in him. But yet again, it was another failed mission by the Yanks. Hopeless, utterly hopeless. When Franshell raised the axe above her head, he put the bottle to his lips and bowed his head. But the squealing from the crowd as she failed to deliver made him look up without even taking a sip.

Shield guards swarmed the platform like professional stage-hands. They grabbed Franshell from behind and muscled her to the right-hand side of the killing stand. Mortimer was dragged feet first along the floor to the same side. In the distracted and broiling crowd, Alex sidled up to the wooden barrier and sunk to his knees to try and obscure himself. No one was interested in the actions of the drunken dwarf who had fallen asleep by the fence. The anger of the crowd then subsided to a grumbling disappointment. The home fans had experienced a rare defeat and there was nothing they could do about it. They started to melt away to the exit.

Through a hole in the fence, Alex caught the figures of Mortimer and Franshell, their upper bodies tightly bound in rope, with two policemen holding each loose end like a dog lead.

Once they had been led away and out of sight, Alex wandered over towards the corner of the fence. He heard the engine of an Aardvark start up then pull away quickly. Mortimer and Franshell were being taken to the old leisure centre building on the outskirts of town. This was where the Shield disposed of their victims that did not merit a public execution.

Chapter 35

The leisure centre had been built in the penultimate decade of the previous century: A two-storey red-brick oblong box topped with a sloping grey slate pyramid-shaped roof surrounded by tarmac on three sides. A now empty twenty-five-metre swimming pool and male – female changing rooms stood on the ground floor, and a sports hall and gym with male – female changing rooms sat on the first floor. Empty swimming pools make a decent holding pen: prisoners in the deep end, guards at the shallow end. It was no longer a leisure centre unless you were a sadist.

Nelson was not a sadist, but he was clearly still pissed. That night, he had been off duty and thought he would enjoy himself at the evening entertainment. He had not forgotten that he was on night call for the leisure centre; he just assumed that the executions would empty the place, and no-one ever came back from the gallows. But that evening, he rushed out of the arena and managed to get a lift back to the barracks from an idle Aardvark parked outside the arena. By the time the order to go to the leisure centre came in, he was back in his police uniform. Anyway, he could take his beer and still perform. By the time Nelson had steamed into the pool area, all red-faced and sweating, ready to go, Mortimer and Franshell were manacled in the deep end.

"Have you attached the prisoners to the wall correctly?"

From the poolside, the four Shield Security men turned around in unison and stared at Nelson. The shortest, and also the officer in charge, walked over to him. Before he reached Nelson, the officer could smell him.

"At last… Do stay awake."

He continued past Nelson and out through the doorway without waiting for a reply. The other three then followed, noses in the air, not even wasting a glance on their inferior comrade. Like many in the police battalions, Nelson hated the black-uniformed goons of Shield Security: arrogant, sly and ruthless, always quick to goad, as if you were no better than civilians. But the sight of two prisoners shackled at his feet did console Nelson. He would be having some fun tonight.

Instead of going home, Alex made his way to the northern end of town. It was dark now and he only had about thirty minutes before the Aardvarks would be out enforcing curfew. He wandered through a residential area of red brick hutches, built around the same time as the leisure centre. There were no lights in the windows but there were still windows. People still lived here but the electricity was always turned off at curfew. Maybe tonight, the anti-climax at the arena had sent everyone to bed early. At the end of the housing estate, he found himself outside the entrance to a warehouse with the sign "Tyres & Exhaust Fitters" hung across the front. He jogged around to the back of the warehouse and stopped at the opening in the fence. The four-foot aluminium railings now only existed to define a border rather than provide a meaningful obstacle for Alex. On a previous visit, he had taken a hacksaw to five bars and carved out an opening wide enough for someone larger than him.

He dropped into a ditch on the other side and scurried up the overgrown grass bank that overlooked the leisure centre. He was there in time to catch the Aardvark carrying the snooty Shield Security men pull away. The beam of its headlights passed over the grass bank opposite, forcing Alex to reverse down the other side out of sight. Once the vehicle had crawled off the exit road and the darkness returned, Alex ran down the bank, crossed the open wasteland and headed into the carpark in front of the red-brick box. He then turned onto the narrow concrete path that wound its way from the entrance around the side until he reached the fire-escape door. Weathered to the point of distress, the wooden door was grey and cracked like the face of an elderly alcoholic. Alex took a screwdriver from his pocket, jammed it into the slit between the door and the wall and jemmied it open.

He stepped into a dark unlit corridor and pulled the door shut behind him. He edged along the wall in the gloom until the wall stopped and he stumbled into the opening of a built-in storage area. Columns of unopened cardboard boxes containing unused cleaning fluids and heavy-duty chemical substances, once required for changing rooms and swimming pools, filled most of the space. But a narrow gap, wide enough for Alex, lay between the nearest stack of boxes and the wall. He squeezed through the opening sideways and reached the corner of the store-room, where he located his weapon. A crossbow: A traditional Recurve with a shorter than normal barrel stood upright on its limb. Six aluminium bolts, each with a feathered shaft, lay on the ground next to it. Relieved to find it still here, Alex raised the device in front of his face and caressed the curved edge of the limb with his palm back and forth. This made his blood pump. He felt the adrenalin start to swell inside, up through his chest and down through his legs.

Both prisoners lay a few feet apart on the hard blue concrete floor in the deep end. Their arms were outstretched behind their heads with their wrists coiled in chains, pulled taut and tightly looped though a semi-circular iron link hammered into the back wall. Likewise, their ankles were chained together and hooked to an iron link in the floor. The chains were of the light, easy-to-use common-or-garden type for connecting a trailer, tying over a cover or wrapping up a body in cloth before you threw it in the river. It was impossible to roll onto your side. But if you lay still on the concrete floor, you only felt a slight discomfort rather than any pain.

Nelson sauntered up from the shallow end and glided over to Franshell with rather too much confidence. Her high cheekbones and dark brown eyes were attractive, but it was the golden-brown skin that really moved Nelsen. She looked foreign and exotic, Asian or maybe from the Mediterranean. He had only ever known girls who were like him: white and pasty, with round faces and a bit unruly. But she lay there, still and silent. Nelson smiled and leant over her slowly, gently swaying but just about staying upright. His right arm lunged towards her hair like a chimpanzee dazzled by a diamond. Franshell smelt what was coming. She whiplashed her head away to one side, covering her face with a swish of unruly dark hair.

"Leave her alone." Mortimer spoke up.

"Oh, I am sorry." Nelson recoiled a few steps backwards. "Am I disturbing the happy couple?"

"Just do your fucking job, man, without any bullshit."

"Oh, what is my job? Perhaps you want to tell me… war hero." Nelson moved closer and stood over Mortimer.

"Well, once upon a time. Now look at you: tied up like a stray dog about to be put down." He sneered.

"Well, you won't be killing me. You know that." Mortimer knew the buttons to press.

"Really? You telling me my job, motherfucker?"

Somewhat peeved, Nelson stormed back to the deep end and

retrieved his semi-automatic weapon.

"I've got the gun. See. And you try anything, I will shoot you down.". Nelson took aim at Mortimer through the sight on his semi-automatic rifle.

"No, you can't." Pause.

"Shield Security will have your balls if anything serious happens to me or Franshell. You can kick, punch, even bruise us a little if we try to wriggle out of these chains. But if things get difficult, you'll need to call the blackshirts back."

Nelson's mouth started to chew manically, as if someone next to him were pulling a wire fixed to his lower jaw. He chewed nothing but a mixture of rising tension and anger and was too wound up to hear Alex enter through the side door into the pool area. The crossbow bolt entered his neck, pierced his throat and poked out the other side.

Nelson started to gurgle as his breathing struggled. He grabbed the end of the bolt and pulled on it, trying to remove it from his neck. The sound from his throat only got worse. He slumped to his knees. Alex sloped over to the dying Nelson, pulled a short, sharp knife from his pocket and slit the base of his throat to finish the job. Blood immediately burst out from the policeman's neck and pooled around his head.

"If I could, I'd give you a round of applause," Mortimer called out.

"You know him?" Franshell turned to Mortimer.

"Oh yeah." Mortimer broke into a wide smile.

Without saying a word, Alex circled around behind Mortimer and Franshell and untied their chains from the iron link in the back wall. Both fugitives pulled the loosened chains over their shoulders and shook their hands free. Alex then loosed the chains that bound their legs to the floor. They slipped themselves free and stood up.

"You've got till dawn. Well, dawn-ish, when he will be relieved." explained Alex.

"Where are we going?" Franshell asked.

"For a country stroll."

Alex returned to the body of the now-deceased Nelson and yanked the crossbow bolt out of this throat. He used Nelson's uniform to clean the blood off the tip like he was wiping a dirty fork.

Their saviour led them out through the fire escape and out onto the main road.

"We're lucky here. No cameras around the leisure centre. Don't want to record their crimes."

Instead of going back into the reservation, they headed in the other direction going out of town. They soon passed a large area of muddy ground, cratered and pockmarked by large earth-moving vehicles. The traces of foundations in the grounds showed it was an unfinished housing development, probably from a decade or so ago but certainly from before the economic collapse.

Then, without a warning, Alex turned off the road onto a dirt vehicle track adjacent to the future archaeology site. The other two followed in silence. The track went on for half a mile or so before it rose uphill into woodland. They maintained a brisk pace and possibly even accelerated up the hill as the security of the canopy layer got closer. The track continued into the woodland. After a few hundred metres, the conifers started to thin out and the group found themselves in a clearing. Alex stopped and faced the other two.

"You gotta go south. To a village called Winterborne Farringdon, where you'll reach the partisans." He took out a hard metal object from his pocket and handed the compass to Mortimer.

"A village… Won't that draw attention?"

"Not a real one. It's deserted. Just the remains of a medieval church," Alex clarified.

Mortimer flicked the compass lid open to reveal a low white light sat inside its housing.

"I will message the UKP on my way back," Alex continued.

"German… fantastic." Mortimer held the compass aloft.

Mortimer extended his hand to thank him but then let it flop awkwardly to his side. He really wanted to get on his knees and thank him properly, but this might seem rather condescending to a man who had probably done this sort of thing lots of times. First Franshell, now Alex. The angels were queuing up.

"Look out for yourself back there. And stay pissed," was the best Mortimer could bring himself to say.

"Thank you. That is my secret." Alex smiled.

"Thank you. You've saved my life," Franshell started.

"Maybe. Good luck." Alex nodded at Franshell.

"One last question… Why do you work for the Yanks?" Mortimer enquired.

"Because I loved watching westerns as a kid… Now fuck off, the pair of you."

Mortimer raised his right hand in a sort of mock salute-cum-wave of gratitude. Alex raised his arm awkwardly and then turned and strode across the clearing, disappearing into the conifers on the other side.

Chapter 36

Ever since they had left the leisure centre, Franshell really wanted to ask where she was going, her final destination. She felt this was a little ungrateful and an unnecessary distraction whilst Alex was taking them to safety, away from the reservation. And she was not completely assured that Mortimer would not kill her, even after she had refused to kill him. Experience had taught Franshell that one good turn did not necessarily lead to another. And this lonely place was as good as any. But out amongst the trees again, her fears started to ebb away and be replaced by the feeling of utter relief at her escape from the Shield. She could have killed Mortimer, and everything would have been a lot easier for her. But of course, it would not be longer term and she would only have to escape again, and that would be a lot harder from Homeland Europe. And the dark silence of the pine copse did bring back that warm feeling of freedom and security she first felt in the woods after the helicopter crash. So a few minutes in limbo, not knowing where she was heading, was fine by her. But she did want to know more about Mortimer.

"So what did they give you… to kill me?" Franshell started.

"Free passage to your country, actually." Mortimer was fiddling with the compass, checking the direction to Winterborne Farringdon on the screen.

"Well, I hope you are a Christian."

"It's my only way off this island." Mortimer looked up at Franshell.

"Problem is, they don't love the sinner any more." Pause. "But prisons are the same there; you should fit in."

"Your science bullshit hasn't got you very far."

"It's not bullshit to the US army or the Shield. They really believe it."

"Believe... how scientific."

"It may all be bullshit but the idea nearly saved my life twice." Franshell smiled.

"Well, don't raise your hopes. Ideas kill." Mortimer smirked.

Franshell smiled at Mortimer and then looked away self-consciously. Maybe it was something in the trees or Mortimer's unspoken gratitude for her saving his life that made her relax with him. He really was not going to kill her, she felt. But it did annoy her that he had not shown any gratitude for earlier.

Mortimer caressed the dial of the compass back and forth to find south.

"Come on, daydreamer. We gotta go."

"Where? The US military...?"

"No. The partisans. The Yanks arm them but don't control them. They can't. They were officially designated as a... terrorist group at the Peace conference."

"In case you forgot, I didn't kill you back there."

"Oh, my apologies, I didn't thank you. But why?" Pause.

"Because you make it hard for yourself. Like me." Mortimer answered his own question. He looked down at the compass again and then marched off towards the far end of the clearing. Franshell kept on his shoulder.

"You really must have pissed off the Shield. What did you do?"

"It's what I didn't do."

Mortimer stopped and faced Franshell.

"Well, Martha, I didn't die in prison as I was supposed to. I didn't fight on the frontline like a hero but as a murderer who killed unarmed US soldiers and civilians. And I didn't obey an order to execute a child and ended up here."

She felt his hard gaze pierce her, even in the dark. Franshell could not help crossing her right hand over her other shoulder and tugging at the skin around her neck in discomfort. She knew she had gone far enough.

"Your first name. You must have one."

"Nope, just Mortimer," who shook his head and set off into the trees, head down, focussed on the compass.

They soon left the wooded hill and entered a field that swept down into a valley. The cloudless night obscured the steep, uneven ground caused by the remains of the medieval strip field once cultivated there. Circular ridges of hard grassed earth protruded at regular intervals from the slope, making it hard for Mortimer and Franshell to stay on their feet.

"You gotta pick your feet up on tricky ground. Don't want to sprain your ankle."

To show her, Mortimer turned sideways on to improve his balance and get a stable foot-hole in the descent. Franshell, however, was not as practised in hiking through the English countryside, so when she tried this method, the distance between her and Mortimer only got wider.

"Come on, we gotta use the night."

"Back to the US zone. Home sweet home," Franshell called out.

"Fuck knows… It's about ten to twelve miles south to the partisans." Mortimer still kept one eye on the compass. The compass was Shield-issue and had been designed for warfare in the British Isles. The bearing did not just overlay the Ordnance

301

Survey map but calculated your best route to follow, highlighting the nearest footpaths, bridleways, byways, tracks, B roads and A roads.

Mortimer waited a minute or so for Franshell to reach the bottom corner of the field before they clambered over a rusty barbed-wire fence and pushed through a gap in the hedgerow.

On the other side lay a single-lane dirt track, which made it easier for Franshell to keep pace with Mortimer. They curved around the bottom of the shallow valley and soon passed a deserted farmyard, made up of a large empty barn opposite a row of cottages. Due to a mixture of fatigue and the comforting silent security of the country night, both said nothing for the next half an hour. As one speeded up, the other automatically accelerated without comment and vice versa. Eventually, after a few miles Mortimer stopped on the track and looked down at his compass and then up at the bridleway sign on his left and back to his compass for a final check.

"This way…" Mortimer nodded to Franshell, who looked at him and said nothing.

"You okay?"

"Yeah… I keep thinking of the dead guard and if they've found him. Or caught Alex…"

"Don't. It's too quiet. Nothing to worry about."

Indeed, there was nothing to worry about. The bridleway took them along a ridge further away from Leominster and the A44 and deep in to the borderlands between US and Shield lines. Neither side patrolled this area of the March.

It was not quite four a.m. when Mortimer and Franshell reached the edge of Chapel Hill coppice, that bordered the rendezvous point with the partisans. Standing lost in the middle of the field were the broken-down side walls and end alter wall of St German church, the remains of Winterborne Farringdon. The village had lost its population at the time of the Great Plague in the seventeenth century and no-one had ever returned.

Mortimer motioned Franshell to crouch down in the ferns at the side of the footpath. They were about one hundred and fifty metres away from the ruins and Mortimer wanted to know if anyone was waiting there. As he pondered what to do next, he did not hear or see the partisan.

When the tall partisan stood up a few metres behind them, the disturbance to the ferns caused both renegades to spin around. Wary of causing alarm, the man pointed his semi-automatic weapon to the ground. In the murk, Mortimer recognised the tiger-striped pattern of the camouflage. Dark-green-and-brown stripes intermittently splashed across a light-green uniform, the standard woodland camouflage of the US army. For a moment, he saw the enemy there, who had to be killed. The hand-to-hand fighting at Cannock Chase flashed in his memory for a nanosecond then disappeared. Pause.

Mortimer smiled. "Pleased to meet you."

"Is she the woman?" The partisan nodded at Franshell, still hunkered down.

"I am." She stood up.

The tall partisan strode past the two of them into the field.

"Let's go... There's someone to see you." He continued on towards the church.

Mortimer turned to Franshell. "Don't worry, there are no Yanks here. They're all locals."

As they approached the church, three dark figures stood up in the church ruins. Two of the shadows stepped over the low-lying wall and fanned out on either side of the third man, who stood on the wall with his arms planted on his hips. He was obviously in charge.

Before they reached the church, the man standing on the wall bellowed.

"Mortimer…" The tone was clipped and annoyed, as if the man had unfinished business with the aforementioned.

Like any ex-schoolteacher who liked an audience, Harper waited for them to reach him. Harper decided to take the camouflage one step further than his men: his face was decorated in stripes of dark green and light green.

"You've got a fucking nerve." The emerald tiger greeted the weary travellers.

Mortimer was relieved to see Harper and not the US military. Like Alex, men like Harper were rare these days, and Mortimer felt nothing but gratitude.

"You look angry." Mortimer said hello.

"You lost two of my men." Harper raised his forefinger at Mortimer.

"One was a woman."

"Donald was a dead man walking but Tennant was good… Very good…" Pause.

The anger had now turned to sadness. He then fiddled in his pocket and raised a hip flask to his lips, as if he were toasting her memory. He then stepped down from the wall.

"You might get a more-than-adequate replacement." Mortimer turned to Franshell.

"Let me introduce you. This is Harper, who leads this rag-tag rebel army."

Then back to Harper. "And this Dr Franshell… a very capable scientist."

"You're supposed to kill her." Harper moved closer.

"Nah… I owe her," Mortimer retorted.

"I don't know what's going on." Harper sighed and shook his head, puzzled.

"Leominster called us out to get you. And that's what I've done. We gotta get going… it'll be light soon."

Harper shrugged his shoulders and took a step past both of them.

"What are you going to do with me?" Franshell spoke to Harper.

"What the fuck…? I thought you were a bit quiet for a Yank." Harper glared back at Franshell and took another swig from his hipflask.

"You might have heard of the phrase "a necessary evil" but that's how I look at your compatriots in my country. Maybe you should be dead by now, maybe not, but I don't really care."

Harper walked away from the remains of Winterborne Farringdon towards the copse at the edge of the field. Mortimer and Franshell followed him, where more partisans were gathered at the six-bar gate but also with two horses tied to each end post.

"We're gonna get you back in style." Harper's mood lightened now that he had had his say.

"Pony-trekking with the partisans, eh…" quipped Mortimer.

"We saved these hunters from slaughter. We got a few back at the ranch."

"Every modern army needs a cavalry unit," continued Mortimer.

"Damn sight quieter than mechanised transport. Also means the women have something to do." Harper nodded and smiled at Franshell.

"I need a weapon." Mortimer turned to Harper.

"Sure, we'll get you one at the farm," Harper replied.

Franshell walked up to the nearest horse and calmly rubbed

her hand up and down her white forehead. The horse sidled up to her and nodded gently in pleasure. The young male partisan who held the reins of the mare smiled at Franshell, impressed with her easy confidence with horses.

"A beautiful creature."

The young warrior was now close enough to Franshell to allow himself to be fully distracted by her high cheekbones and bright, shining eyes.

"Yeah, she is," responded the young man. "Do you ride…?"

The partisans roundabouts started to snigger. The young man blushed.

"I mean…" The sniggers now rose to laughter.

Franshell ignored him and his embarrassment and attended to the horse. She gently rolled her hand up and over her forehead and round her ears and down her mane. Neither the horse nor she wanted their encounter to end. In fact, Franshell did not want the open country or the chilly night to end. Once the sun came up, so would the threats, or if she was lucky, a soothing lie from Mortimer and Harper before they handed her over to their paymasters.

"Tell me, Harper," Mortimer raised his voice, "was there anything left of Tennant?"

"Her head. We only ever found her head." Harper glared at Mortimer; his tone darkened again.

"Interesting…"

Chapter 37

The young partisan enjoyed the ride back with Franshell's arms wrapped around his waist. The journey along bridlepaths and tracks took close to half an hour but seemed like a few minutes to him. The female partisan who carried Mortimer would also have preferred to have given Franshell a ride.

Both horses galloped into the Came Estate farmstead as the morning twilight started to spread across the sky. It was located a few miles into the US military zone, out of harm's way. A long two-storey brick barn with a gaping entrance, easily tall enough and wide enough to fit a combine harvester, dominated the site on one side. Opposite the barn was a line of five terraced cottages, where the farm workers must have lived many years, maybe even centuries, before. A muddy stone track, wide enough for even two combine harvesters to pass, ran between the barn and the cottages. The farm lay at the bottom of a valley, which helped to protect it from prying drones.

On arrival, Mortimer and Franshell were immediately ushered through one of the cottage front doors and into a back room. Two US military-issue metal-framed single beds with a thin mattress on top waited for them.

Mortimer slumped down exhausted onto the bed nearest the window and fell into a deep sleep very quickly. He started to dream. He was back in the office in St James at the bank and Franshell introduced herself as his new boss. She promised to allow him to run with his ideas rather than listening to senior management. She told him it was their secret, their shared truth that the senior managers and the board were utterly clueless and were only there to line their pockets at the expense of the staff, the shareholders and the whole fucking world.

Meanwhile, the partisan who fancied Franshell hung around the entrance door.

"He's sparked out... but you're still going."

"Yeah... what about the guns?"

"Oh... of course."

Without consideration of clearing the request with Harper, the young adorer scuttled outside and entered one of the cottages further down. In a minute or so, he returned with a Russian snub-nosed machine pistol in one hand and a pistol in the other. He eyed Mortimer. As he clutched both weapons, he realised that he would be in trouble if he gave an armed weapon to Franshell.

Mortimer remained comatose as the partisan knelt down and quietly left the machine pistol on the floor on the far side of his bed, next to the wall. The partisan then raised the other pistol in his hand and offered it to Franshell.

"This isn't loaded, so I can give it to you... I'm sorry, I can't..."

"I know... this'll be fine." Franshell smiled and accepted the gift.

"Now I need to sleep."

The young man nodded and back-pedalled to the bedroom door.

"Okay. I'll go..."

He stayed in the doorway long enough for his cheeks to blush again. Franshell smiled and the young warrior disappeared.

Franshell lay back, resting her head on the single flaccid military-issue pillow. She closed her eyes but did not sleep.

Maybe it was the pistol gripped tightly in her right hand that kept her on edge. Or the noise from the partisans outside, roused by the early morning light. This was as good as it was going to get, she thought. Word would get through to the US army of her existence here and the partisans would hand her over. They would have to. They were in the pocket of the US Army. Mortimer was a good man, she could see that, but what could he do, even if he wanted to not send her back? Only the Shield wanted him dead. Both sides wanted her dead and there was not a rock this side of the Atlantic free of the Shield or her previous employers. She was stuck in a long, dark tunnel and all she could see was the train speeding towards her.

Franshell jolted her eyes open and looked across at Mortimer. He had not moved since he fell onto his bed; he still faced the wall in a deep slumber. She sat up and swung her feet to the floor and raised the pistol in her right arm. She leant forward and pushed the end of the barrel into the back of his head.

Mortimer groaned. The barrel was cold and Mortimer's hair was thinner at the back than it used to be. He opened his eyes and rolled his cheeks into the end of the barrel. Franshell withdrew the pistol slightly.

"Made up your mind yet?" Franshell wanted an answer this time.

"I'm sleeping on it. So should you," Mortimer muttered.

In fact, he had been awake since the arrival of the machine pistol.

"If I'm lucky, I may only get thirty years in a labour camp in Dakota." Pause.

"You think I'd tell you, with that pointed at me?"

Mortimer pulled himself up, propping his head up against the damp wall and leant away from the pistol. He let his right arm droop over the other side of the single bed.

"I can still kill you…" Franshell curled her index finger around the trigger.

"And then go where?" Mortimer scoffed.

"You'd have saved yourself a whole lotta trouble if you'd used the axe properly."

"If I'd killed you, I'd end up killing millions, just like a religious maniac…"

"Not even to save yourself. How noble of you."

Mortimer smiled and smiled a bit longer until his right hand located the grip on the machine pistol. Franshell sighed.

"Goodbye…"

Her finger did not move. Instead, she counted to three in her mind to give Mortimer enough time. He duly responded. He swung the machine pistol up from the floor in one action and pointed the barrel into her eyes. In fact, he did it in two.

Franshell pressed the trigger slowly. Click. Mortimer did not respond this time. Pause.

"You're slow. Slow," Franshell hissed in anger and lowered her face in embarrassment.

"You wanted me to shoot you…" Mortimer was confused.

"I'm all out of time…" Franshell forlornly placed the pistol in the middle of her pillow.

For the first time in her life, she felt something she had never felt before. Something she despised in others and had rejected her whole life. Self-pity. That feeling that all the pain in the world was in you, and there was nothing she could do. She was helpless. The soft amber-brown of her irises glistened as the tears started to well up, something else she had not really done before.

She then sniffed and blithely pulled up her black-uniformed sleeve to her elbow to reveal a bandaged forearm. She then pulled

310

a small penknife from her trouser pocket. It carried a delicate oval-shaped blade, the sort any boy scout would treasure. She thrust it into the edge of the material, splitting the covering to unearth a two-to-three-centimetre red scab below the elbow.

Mortimer was even more confused at this performance, and when confused, he always kept his counsel. Franshell pinched the scab open and winced as the red stuff erupted, running down faster than her tears.

"Here you go... they'll want this..."

Franshell then picked the thin black bio-rod from her arm.

"I've already cut it out once... it wasn't too deep." She offered the biochip in the flat of her outstretched hand whilst rivulets of blood criss-crossed her elbow, dripping onto the bed.

"You put the fucking chip back..."

Mortimer stared at her scars, a little stunned but also deeply moved by this ritual of pain and self-laceration.

"Seemed the best place for it..."

She wiped away the moistness from her eyes with her free hand but left the pain untouched.

"I bet you were a self-harmer."

"That does make it easier." Franshell sighed.

"Go on, take it. I feel sorry for you. You really believe this'll make you free..."

Mortimer did not want Franshell to hurt herself any more, so he took the biochip with his weapon-less arm and moved it into his tunic pocket.

"I have made up my mind. You think I dragged your sorry ass over here... as you Yanks would say... to turn you in. After what you did for me." Pause.

Mortimer sighed. "You really do have a low opinion of your fellow man."

At last, Mortimer tossed the machine pistol onto the floor between the beds.

"Did you know... the pistol was not loaded?" Franshell enquired gently.

"Yep. I heard lover boy mumbling his apology."

Chapter 38

Harper and Mortimer walked up the shallow slope in the green pasture towards the burial mound. Like other Bronze Age round barrows, this soft green pyramid was a place to bury the remains of fallen warlords. Tennant had always decorated herself with Celtic jewellery and charms, partly because she believed these symbols would keep her safe. So Harper, being the sort of man who recognised the individuality in his men and women, had taken it upon himself to dig a hole in the nearest ancient tumulus to bury what was left of her after the confrontation with the cannibals. To be able to lie in the same earth as those who had fought and died for their tribe thousands of years ago would have been appreciated by Tennant.

"If Franshell goes back, she'll end up a labour camp in the mid-west for the rest of her life... if she's lucky."

"Yeah, I see all that praying bullshit... It really is a fucking theocracy over there," Harper concurred.

"The Yanks and the Shield are both the same, really. You got to wonder why there is war... Call it quits and get on treating their own people like shit. A hell of a lot cheaper."

"It's Hitler and Stalin, Mr Mortimer, all over again... and we are in the middle, like the fucking Poles."

"Or it's the Baxters and the Rojos... but no dollars for me to make here."

"Ah, a Sergio Leone man; you are a man of culture and taste..." Harper appreciated Mortimer's reference to one of his favourite films.

"Somebody's gotta be making money out of this war," Mortimer continued.

Both men stopped in front of the shallow ditch that circled the round barrow.

Now it was Harper's turn to enlighten Mortimer. "It's the fucking banks… always was, always will be."

Mortimer appreciated this insight, given his previous career.

"Yep, can't argue with that."

Both men now started up the side of the mound.

"So you're not gonna turn her in and escape to the promised land…"

"Nah, I can't. My head would be on the gates of Leominster if it weren't for her. Anyway, I'm not really sure there is a promised land," Mortimer admitted.

"I thought the Yanks said you'd get free passage away from here."

"Would you believe them if your life depended on it?"

"You do have a point."

Harper stopped and turned to Mortimer. "I agree to do this for you and her. But it's still fucking sacrilege."

"And you don't like Yanks either and love to see Colquoun shown up."

Mortimer dug the end of his feet into the ground to push himself upwards as the grass bank steepened.

"True… our enemy's enemy is our friend bullshit and simple practical necessity means we need them; they arm us." Harper stopped to get his breath.

"But I would love to be a fly on the wall in Colquoun's office when he finds out…"

"Once I'm back from Ajax, we'll be away." Mortimer turned

to Harper. "You can tell Colquoun I came in alone and told you Franshell was dead."

"You know somewhere where you can hide from the Yanks and the Shield?"

"We're off to the South West somewhere. It's pretty quiet down there."

Mortimer knew he could trust Harper.

"Well, good luck in Cornwall. You'll probably need it." Pause. "You ever hear of the Invisible Army?"

"They're a myth, aren't they? Nothing but a few cyber jokers making threats. They're nothing to the Shield."

"Maybe. Maybe not," Harper said.

Both men arrived at the pinnacle. It was no more than five feet of rounded earth rather than a real point. Harper moved to the middle, fell to his knees and took out a short-handled garden trowel from his pocket. He stabbed the steel blade into the earth and sliced a chunk of turf out of the ground then thrust deeper. After a few twists and turns, he reached down and pulled a necklace out of the ground. It was a silver collaret, crafted in open Celtic knotwork with each half meeting in the middle around a dark emerald stone. He put it in his trowel pocket and ploughed on, now cutting a wider hole in the earth, around where he found the necklace.

"I can see you were a keen gardener." Mortimer broke the silence.

"You know, people would be disgusted at this. Nothing is too low for a decorated hero of the Shield." Harper looked up at Mortimer.

"That's about right... we always got the job done at the front."

"But you are also a rare man of principle and still alive. And

Tennant's dead."

Harper returned to the hard earth. For the first time, Mortimer wondered whether Harper had ever fought on the Mercian Front against the Shield. Plenty of collaborators had been captured and executed, but these were rarely armed combatants: Mainly PR men, profiteers, local administrators who willingly assisted the US military occupation, who could not prove they had been pressed into service. He considered whether to enquire but thought better of it.

The partisan leader soon dropped the trowel and let his arms loosen at his sides. For a few seconds, he bowed his head over Tennant's grave. He sighed then bent forward and twisted and turned the head out of the ground. He brushed soil off the scalp and sides but avoided touching the face, given what might be lurking in her very open cavities. He then took out the collaret and placed it carefully back in the head-shaped hole.

"Only right that something of hers should stay here…"

With both arms outstretched he then proffered the mud-caked eyeless skull to Mortimer. He grabbed it by the still thick but now very slimy brunette hair in his right hand.

Harper stood up. "You really think that will fool Colquoun."

"They're both brunettes. That's good enough. He's not a detail man, y'know."

Mortimer took a black plastic bag from his pocket, opened it as wide as the opening would allow and shoved the head inside like an unwashed cabbage.

"And Colquoun's usually more interested in his own hair."

Chapter 39

The US soldier smiled and stroked the mane of the horse. The young, dark stallion was roped to a metal fence that ran in front of the officer's bloc.

"Beautiful animal. We have a few back home on the farm," he drawled in an accent somewhere from the mid-west.

Even though the young partisan was standing next to his ally, he still felt uneasy at the Yank's interest in his horse. He knew that they called the shots, and if this soldier liked the horse that much, he could take it.

"Great way to get around out there in the open country…" the US soldier continued.

"It's the only way for us… out here," the young partisan piped up.

Mortimer had asked his driver to remain at Camp Ajax during his meeting with Colquoun and be ready to leave quickly.

"Shame we have not got any stables where he could get fed and watered properly."

The US soldier scanned the camp to see if there were any possible substitute equine facilities.

"That's okay; we aren't staying long…" The young partisan sounded as if he were in a hurry.

The secretary ushered Mortimer into the office. He pulled up in front of Major General Colquoun, who was sat ready and waiting behind his desk, flanked as before by Captain Daines and O'Donald.

"This is a very pleasant surprise. I did not think we'd be…" Colquoun started.

Meanwhile, Mortimer dipped into the black bag and pulled out the head of Tennant by the hair. No effort had been made to remove the dirt or clean the skull except around the eye sockets. The eyeless skull glared at the three Americans.

"Good God, man, you really are a barbarian." O'Donald was shocked.

"What can I say?" Colquoun spoke again.

"What about, thank you." Mortimer then pushed the head back into the bag.

"Daines… take the bag from Mr Mortimer."

Captain Daines got to his feet, reached over and took the bag from Mortimer.

"We will need to verify its identity. And we need the bio-rod," Daines explained.

Colquoun raised his neatly trimmed eyebrows at Mortimer, who had already taken the thin black cylinder from his pocket. This object had been washed since Franshell had cut it out of her forearm. He casually lobbed the identity storage device at Daines's free arm. Daines neatly caught it in one hand.

"Good. All seems to be in order. But why the head? You can take the man out of the Shield but not the Shield out of the man." Colquoun started again.

"Savages," O'Donald followed up.

"We'll send the head to the lab this afternoon. It will be a day or so before we get the results." Daines remained focussed on procedure.

"Now, what about my travel plans?" Mortimer stared at Colquoun.

"We will arrange a plane immediately to fly you to

318

Greenland, the west coast of Greenland to be precise."

"Greenland…" Mortimer sounded confused but underneath was relieved at this news. This meant Colquoun would not be surprised if he did not remain at Ajax after the meeting to wait for his transport to freedom.

"Greenland is the holding centre for immigrants, where everyone is checked prior to entry to the United States of America," Colquoun continued.

"Certain moral tests have to be completed as well to ensure you are fit for US citizenship. You see, we can't just let anyone in," O'Donald interjected.

"Well, you failed my moral test."

Mortimer's voice hardened before his mouth broke into a slow smile.

"But why I am not surprised."

"Of course, your efforts here will be recognised and will accelerate your application. You'll probably be out in three months," Colquoun continued.

"And you did not tell me the truth about Dr Franshell."

Mortimer glared at O'Donald, who remained silent.

"You seem disappointed. I cannot believe you actually trusted us to give a man like you an expenses-free penthouse suite in New York." Pause.

Colquoun then smiled the smile of a man who enjoyed the sound of frustration and anger in his subordinates who did not get the big picture until it was too late. Only he got the big picture, and that was why he was on this side of the desk.

"This isn't a good world any more, Mr Mortimer. That's why you are here." Colquoun let him have it.

"You still talk too much."

Mortimer turned on his heels, strode past the secretary sat

beside the doorway and out of the building and out of Ajax.

It was late afternoon when Mortimer slid his leg over the back of the stallion and landed in the courtyard of the farm. He nodded in gratitude to the young partisan in the saddle. Harper and Franshell walked out of the barn to see Mortimer.

"Do you see it…?"

Harper called out before he reached Mortimer. An Enfield green Land Rover Defender, last used by the British Army at the end of the last century, stood parked outside of the barn.

"It's the best we could do. Checked the engine and filled it up. All working."

"Thanks for your staff car," Mortimer replied.

"It's still light. You ready?" He turned to Franshell, who had now reached him.

"I got some food, clothing and guns in the back. And there's a map," Franshell added.

"It's in good nick. But the clutch is heavy, so keep it smooth," Harper advised.

"Good. Let's be off… we don't have much time."

Mortimer then paused and moved towards the older man, who was saving his life again. He was that rarity, the boss at work you could trust. The wise, experienced man who knew the ropes, knew how the system worked, always on hand to do the right thing. Not a bull-shitter, a show-off or a liar. He would miss this moral and physical bear of a man.

"Oh, I put in the route on the map thing inside. You'll avoid the motorways and stick to the back roads and lanes. You'll be okay then," he continued.

"Thanks for a hell of a lot."

Harper extended his hand to Mortimer, who paused for a

second before he clasped it firmly. He felt like he should give the man a hug at the very least, but he guessed Harper was not a man for such close physical engagement with another man. That was why he was Harper.

"Stay lucky." Harper said goodbye.

"Yeah, and you…"

Mortimer broke away and wandered towards the parked vehicle with Franshell.

"What the fuck did you say to Colquoun?"

"The cunts were going to send me to Greenland," Mortimer answered.

"And the head. He will know soon enough."

"I know. But so will everyone else in Camp Ajax." Mortimer smiled the smile of a man who knows.

"You want to humiliate him?" Franshell asked.

"Don't you?"

Colquoun sneezed and wiped his nose with his US-military-issue green handkerchief. Although the weather was getting warmer, the officer in charge of Ajax could not shake off the head cold that had persisted for months. That morning, he struggled through his daily thirty-minute call to the Mid-Western Zone HQ, but he was still able to confirm the demise of Dr Franshell. This act spoke for itself and could get him a promotion and a comfortable office in Washington. Of course, O'Donald had thrown a bucket of cold water over Colquoun's moment, claiming they still needed lab evidence to confirm her demise. But that was a formality.

Daines pushed through the double-door entrance and called for his commanding officer.

"Sir… sir."

Colquoun pulled away from the mirror in his bathroom and passed through the open doorway back into his office.

"The lab have got back. The head... sir..." Daines stopped. Pause.

"Yes... I'm waiting." Colquoun stood behind the corner of his desk.

Daines shook his head.

"It's not Franshell's head. The test showed it's an unknown female."

"But the biometric data on the rod." The words came out hard and heavily accented in a staccato.

"That is Franshell. That was confirmed."

"Well, what bullshit is Mortimer pulling here?" Colquoun thought aloud.

Daines kept his thoughts to himself. By turning up in person and dropping the head of the wrong female victim on the table, Mortimer was making it very clear who was still alive. If Franshell had sustained a bad injury to her forearm, the bio-rod could have moved to the surface of her skin and could be removed with a bit of DIY surgery. And after what Franshell had been through, it would not be beyond her. And Mortimer made it very clear that he was not going to Greenland.

Colquoun looked down at the floor and started to inhale deep breaths.

"Get me Harper. I gotta call Harper."

Daines pulled the phone from his pocket and tapped in Harper's details and handed it to his boss. Colquoun slammed the phone to his left-hand ear. Harper was expecting the call and picked up straight away.

"Ah, Harper... yes... yes... fine... Well, not exactly... It's Mortimer."

Pause.

"He's not there. Must have left after he got back from Ajax."

"He's that sort of man," Harper responded.

"Tell me, when he arrived, was he alone or with an American female?"

"Yes, with an American female. He got her out of Shield custody to bring her back, as you asked him to… I believe."

Harper knew that Mortimer's story would not fool Colquoun and he would know they were both lying. And there was always a chance that Military Intelligence would intercept a Shield message about a missing American scientist. For a few seconds, a glorious lie flashed across Harper's mind. One of his men had found tyre tracks heading north, and Mortimer had said he was planning to get to the coast and then on a boat to Ireland. But Harper always knew his limits.

"Really. And do you have any idea where they are now?"

Colquoun's speech slowed and his cheeks and mouth tightened as his tone of patient enquiry struggled to contain the seething inside. He never trusted Harper, too flip and too clever for his liking.

"Nope… I presume the woman is with you," Harper replied.

"It was US army business, so I did not enquire. As you've always said, you'd tell me if I needed to know."

O'Donald strode through the double doors, as if it was his office, and stopped next to Daines. The CIA man wore a smart black suit with a slate-grey tie and a crisp white shirt. Even he could not bring himself to wear the black tie. He fixed his gaze on Colquoun and drew the finger of his right arm from one side of his neck to the other. Colquoun withdrew the phone and pressed the off button.

"This is now a CIA matter," O'Donald snapped.

"I need to send a report, then I will be leaving for HQ in Swansea to co-ordinate operations… Goodbye, Captain Daines."

O'Donald then left Colquoun's office with the same indecent haste as he had arrived.

Major General Colquoun stood there with the phone still in hand. He had not sneezed or coughed since he had heard the news.

Chapter 40

Since the disappearance of Martha Franshell, Commissioner Hendrick had retreated to his private quarters within the walls of the castle. No official word of his loss had been communicated to London or Brussels. Hendrick needed to gather his thoughts and plan his next move. His time for invention was limited by the duration of Erasmus's journey back to Brussels. Thankfully, he had left Reservation Twenty-seven on the morning of execution, Thursday, and was currently in transit back to the Homeland. But once he got back to Brussels, the order would be issued to move Franshell.

The best explanation Hendrick could devise was that evidence had arisen showing Franshell to be a spy, who therefore had to be terminated for security reasons. But he knew Grand Commissioner Erasmus would be angry at having to waste his time in E111. This outcome would not reflect well on Hendrick's own ambitions but it was a lot better than the truth. Hendrick guessed that the renegades had made for the US military zone in Wales. It was not far, and the surveillance drones had not spotted anyone or any unofficial vehicle moving northwards, southwards or eastwards in the DMZ.

His private quarters were a large room on a split-level floor about the length and width of a badminton court. The raised section at the windowless end took up about a quarter of the room and contained a double bed laid longways. The chamber was encased on three sides in faux Jacobean wood panelling. A door almost seamlessly cut into the dark wooden squares at the side of the bed led into a private bathroom. Minimal furniture filled the main section of the room: a modest desk and chair, overlooked by a mounted TV screen, were placed against the wall just down from the door; a three-seater Chesterfield spread across the middle of the room facing a double window and a sparsely populated bookcase was fixed to the other wall. The walls were coloured a burnt orange and carried framed prints of some of Hendrick's favourite artworks: gloomy pictures of north-European forests and countryside and coastlines from the eighteenth century. Hendrick liked to think here, and for that he needed empty space. Thinking for him was best done alone in motion and not in stasis. He had lapped his uncluttered quarters hundreds of times since the flight of Franshell and Mortimer.

Hendrick thought he would call Downton to explain his official explanation. But he could not do it quite yet. He still needed more time to accept and accommodate his loss of face. He had chosen Downton as his head of intelligence precisely because of his lack of it; the weed's ambition for power, which he clearly thought was his by familial right and custom, somewhat outweighed his grey matter. Men like that were always useful as long as you kept them guessing and dependent upon your favour. But Downton would now have something on him, as would the rest of the Shield staff who attended the ceremony. For a few seconds, Hendrick then pondered whether he should arrest Downton on trumped up charges of assisting Mortimer. Judging by his performance during the interrogation, he may as well have been working in cahoots with the renegade. But he would have to execute Downton and this would necessitate an enquiry. From London. As Hendrick's mind tried to climb out of the four walls again, there was a hard knock at the door. The door opened.

The adjutant officer apologised straight away.

"Sorry to interrupt, but there's an urgent message from

326

London. It's on your…"

"Just tell me." Hendrick had reached the door.

"Sir, Grand Commissioner Erasmus unfortunately passed away en route to London last night."

"Dead… how?" Hendrick asked.

"He died of a heart attack, sir," the adjutant continued.

Hendrick turned away and walked towards the window to look at the grey, cloudy sky outside. But inside, blue sky was poking through and the sun was shining brightly. Erasmus did drink too much and was not particularly healthy, so a heart attack was not entirely inconceivable. But Hendrick also knew how sudden solitary death events like suicide and heart failure did seem to occasionally afflict men of authority close to or inside the regime. Nothing, of course, could be proven, but these explanations were required for public consumption. The senior government politician who uncovered the Shield "false flag" terrorist attack in London, who strangely died by his own hand in the woods of Oxfordshire, had actually been poisoned by men under Hendrick's command.

He wondered why anyone in the hierarchy wanted Erasmus dead. No one in the regime would have the nerve to assassinate a grand commissioner. It was quite possible that he had been sent to E111 in order to be eliminated. Erasmus was a fanatic, on the radical wing of the movement, and men like that often went too far and offended powerful people. Ideological zealots often had little understanding of the practicalities of policy. Grand ideals and designs without much focus on the detail. And the ability to focus on detail and implementation was what had carried Hendrick into the highest echelons of Shield office. His competence had made him highly trusted. And now the only man of higher rank than him who had witnessed and understood the potential of Dr Franshell was dead.

327

Hendrick smiled and turned to his adjutant.

"Have the media been told yet?"

"Yes. The story will go out tonight," informed the adjutant.

"All very unfortunate for Grand Commissioner Erasmus. A great loss to the cause."

He felt the stress of the last forty-eight hours start to seep away. The problem of Franshell and Mortimer could now be resolved on his terms.

"So we need to find the traitors and this time terminate without public invitation."

"But they could be behind US lines now, sir," the adjutant commented.

Hendrick stepped closer towards his adjutant.

"Maybe. But then Mr Mortimer will have to hand over his saviour for possible execution. Or at best a life in some mid-west labour camp. But he is a man of conscience. He will not hand her over."

The fire was now burning in Hendrick again.

"I also know that he will head south-west. To Cornwall. Unoccupied territory. The moors are open again since the peace treaty. It is the only place where there are no Yanks and no us." Pause.

"We need to double the drones between here and Dartmoor day and night."

"Should I alert the Shield outpost in Bristol?" the adjutant enquired.

"No, that's not necessary. We have enough competence here to handle this."

Chapter 41

It was after midnight when Mortimer and Franshell crossed back into the DMZ. Only the A roads were blocked by US border posts, so as per Harper's instructions in the map tablet on the dashboard, Mortimer followed the minor roads and back roads into the deserted villages of the Wye Valley. Out again in the open under the night sky, Mortimer wanted to relax; it had become his natural habitat recently. But the bends and dips of the carriageway forced Mortimer to stay awake and concentrate more than usual on the road as well as keep one eye on the route. At least if Hendrick was chasing him by road he might find himself in the ditch.

Every few miles, the Land Rover illuminated a barn or a line of houses or even the occasional thousand-year-old church on the roadside before they quickly disappeared again into the darkness. No light or evidence of human habitation shone from inside. These buildings were now monuments to families, communities and beliefs that no longer existed. Thousands of civilians had died from the US bombardment and the brutal fighting that took place along the border. Refugees flooded westwards into the urban areas of the Midlands, where many were then killed in the heavy air attacks on Birmingham, causing panic and flight into the countryside. Here, they struggled to stay alive without supplies of food and water. It was the huge number of refugees, a mass of people on the move with nowhere to settle, that enabled the Shield to create the reservations so easily.

Curled up with her knees pulled up over the lip of the sagging front seat, Franshell slept soundly next to Mortimer. One of the two semi-automatic rifles lay tilted, barrel up, inside the footwell between her and the door. As Mortimer swung and jerked the vehicle, accelerating then decelerating as the tarmac twisted and straightened then twisted again, the thought lurked at the back of his mind that this might all be pointless. In fact, worse than pointless: bloody stupid. Although they both wore anti-personnel drone bracelets on their wrists, the Shield drones still worked at night and this vehicle had no protection of its own.

Maybe the Shield assumed they were still sheltering behind US lines, but it would only be a matter of time. And what if they hit another vehicle coming in the opposite direction, literally, as the single lane gave them nothing. Then they would be walking, if they were lucky. Mortimer realised they had to go as far as they could that night, then stop and rest during the daylight hours. But at least the Land Rover was fitted with a working map tablet on the dashboard. The yellow arrow hovered over the red route on the green screen, lighting the path for him. Harper had selected the tourist setting that gave you the slow, picturesque route running south-east through the Wye Valley towards the M5. Ideal for middle-aged holidaymakers before the war and renegades on the run after the war.

The M5 motorway was still used by the Shield to man and supply the Bristol and Bath Reservation, the last Shield outpost of any substance before the South West. In the weeks leading up to war, much of the civilian population of Cornwall, Devon and Somerset had been evacuated eastwards to prepare for defence from a US invasion that never happened there. Defence lines had been constructed along the River Tamar, Dartmoor and then further east including the Taunton Stop Line, which was originally created during World War Two. But instead of invading the South West, US forces landed on the west coast of Scotland, moving fast to take the whole country before going south to invade northern England and link up with the invasion force in Wales. The British Army, with huge military assistance from the Shield Movement and its masters in Homeland Europe, fought the US forces to a standstill in the North Midlands and along the March. Since the Truce, the security of the South West peninsula was left to the navy and a few coastal military bases. Rather than allowing the forcibly evacuated civilians to return, it was now easier for the Shield to move the refugees into the newly created reservations in the DMZ.

The village sign of Eastington was still intact, as it seemed were some of the inhabitants, or maybe they were refugees who had wandered for days and decided to stop there. Men and women of all ages huddled around bonfires lit on either side of the road. The sound and headlights of the Land Rover crashing through their settlement turned many filthy and scarred faces. Something hit the side of the vehicle, like a stone, then something heavier thumped against the back, followed by a high-pitched screech. A teenage girl had pulled a burning log from her bonfire and thrown it against the rear window. The glass held firm but was singed and smeared with black charcoal from the burnt wood.

Mortimer accelerated. No-one stepped into the road to block the Defender's passage. Franshell still slept. A few miles later and Mortimer eased his speed. According to the map they were now close to the M5 flyover bridge. When he saw the bridge ahead, Mortimer slowed to about twenty miles an hour and turned off the headlights. The motorway was empty of vehicles for as far as the eye could see on both sides. Once they were over and the trees rose along the side of the road, Mortimer switched on the headlights again. The Land Rover now wound its way into the Gloucestershire Cotswolds. Before the war, this area was a popular destination for the well-heeled and prosperous, which probably explained the better condition of the roads. The tarmac seemed to stretch wider into the grass verge and bend less, allowing Mortimer to relax a bit. After nearly an hour they reached the M4 and another flyover without lights. The town of Corsham appeared as the next major destination on the map. Mortimer remembered that the Shield used the old twentieth-century civil defence bunkers in Corsham as a military command centre. And Corsham was on the eastern perimeter of the Bristol and Bath Reservation.

Mortimer pulled over and changed the route to go eastwards around Chippenham then south towards the village of West Ashton. From here, Mortimer headed west towards the Mendip Hills. The on-board map showed another forty to fifty minutes of driving via the tourist route to the Hills. By then it would be close to sunrise, which could leave them stranded on the road, and they were still too close to the Bristol Reservation for comfort. The hills would give them cover for a day.

When the map showed he was ten minutes away from the Mendips, Mortimer stopped at a crossroads. He wound down his window to look at the sky. There was little evidence of the imminent arrival of the sun, so Mortimer pondered whether to keep going to Exmoor. But as his brain ticked over the calculations, he felt his eyelids flickering and he was getting drowsy. Then Franshell's eyes opened as Mortimer's were heading in the other direction.

"Do you want me to drive?" Franshell opened up.

"Never thought you'd ask." Pause. "Nah... we're nearly there."

"Okay... Quiet, isn't it," Franshell continued.

"Let's hope so."

Mortimer turned off into what the dashboard map designated as the "Mendips", and a thick continuous hedgerow rose on either side of the single-lane road. It stood taller than the Land Rover. After what seemed a lot longer than a few miles, this natural tunnel made up Mortimer's mind. As they rose steadily into the hills, a low stone wall replaced the hedgerow. A mile or so further and the road dropped into a valley with trees advancing down the hills on both sides. Mortimer slowed the car to a crawl to not miss any possible shelter off the side of the road. An open gate invited them along a dirt track into a copse that grew wider and thicker as it climbed the side of the valley. As soon as he reckoned they were no longer visible from the road, Mortimer pulled into a flat strip of muddy ground and stopped next to a tree stump. There was enough space around them to park ten to fifteen vehicles before the trees took over. He switched off the car lights and engine.

"We'll stay here for the day. Best not to go wandering off."

Mortimer turned to Franshell, who had stayed awake since their entry into the Mendip Hills. But she was still too dozy to say anything. Her mouth opened into a wide yawn before closing back into a soft, fleshy grin. She then wiped her eyes clean of the night fuzz. Mortimer watched her eyes carefully for a few seconds then flicked his door handle up and climbed out. He immediately opened the passenger door behind the driver and slid back inside the vehicle. "Good morning" were his last words before his eyelids closed.

Franshell was ready for some exercise, whatever Mortimer

had said. Without disturbing Mortimer, she left the Defender and crossed the carpark towards the steep wooded ridge. She found an opening with a path, but this soon disappeared into a thicket of brambles, thorns and smallish ivy-clad trees that blocked her way. So she swerved under the low-hanging branches and escaped through the ferns like an experienced rambler. The thick undergrowth receded to reveal lines of fir and spruce. She weaved her way around the evergreens until she reached a path that wound its way upwards. To warm herself up in the early morning chill, Franshell decided to run up the incline. The birds were waking up noisily in time for the sun. Older trees, like beech and oak, stood at the top of the ridge, and Franshell felt the comfort of the canopy above.

She sat down against an oak tree on the edge of the treeline. The thick trunk gave her cover and protection from behind. Franshell ripped open the Velcro lining of her US-military-issue green tunic and let her chest and midriff breathe. She still felt drowsy after a limited and uncomfortable night's sleep in the Defender. But, she was on her own, without her self-appointed guardian or some fucking cunt in a black uniform: Just her and the sun and a lot of trees that did not know her or care for her sitting there. And it had been a very long time since no-one else knew where she was.

She gazed into the open countryside that lay around her: hedgerowed fields covered the gentle downward slope and stretched all the way to the horizon. Copses and clumps of woodland regularly dotted the undulating fields to show that there was life in this green carpet. The woodland on the ridge curved downwards to her right, thickening out at the bottom before it sprawled further to the south. Directly ahead, the eastern horizon was a layer of violet sky that dropped into a band of bright orange as the sun began its morning ascent. Franshell could not help but feel the timelessness and eternity of what was in front of her. She emptied her mind and let all of this natural sensation wash through her. Half-awake, half in a dream, she even reckoned she could sense the movement of the earth in its endless rotation around the sun.

And the solitude in that place gave her a sense of freedom she had never felt before.

It was not only freedom without but freedom within. It was not just the absence of external coercion and control from others but a feeling inside of herself coming into life. Something was getting released, like a heavy stone was being moved from the door. Franshell was a scientist, a rational thinker, who thought she understood the mechanics of the natural world. She had observed, studied, investigated, constructed and de-constructed the building blocks of life without emotion and with very little empathy. Intellectual and detached was her modus operandi in her work and in life.

But sat under the oak tree, fixed to the land and the sky for the first time ever, Franshell felt science. Of course, this could all be in her genes. Her Native American ancestry recognised the same wild wonder in the old English countryside that it had first seen in the forests and glades of Louisiana. She turned her gaze from the land and the horizon upwards into the branches and leaves of the oak tree. This indeed was a good place to dream.

Chapter 42

It was late afternoon when Franshell returned to the Land Rover. Mortimer was leaning against the bonnet, chewing on an energy bar kindly provided by the US military.

"Full of sugar, your bars... not like the more health-conscious Shield supplies," Mortimer opened up.

"They're weaned on sugar in the States."

"I'm glad you're back. See anything out there...?"

"No... nothing. Really quiet," Franshell replied. "It's a wonderful place to stop, after everything back there."

"And you slept well up there?"

Mortimer swallowed the remains of his over-sugared blueberry, apple, nut and broccoli energy bar.

"I really appreciate the landscape here," Franshell continued. She moved towards Mortimer.

Mortimer could see the smile in her warm, brown eyes as she gently tilted her head to the left and looked up at him. She brushed her fringe over her left eye and made her long hair come alive. He could not help lingering over her eyes, deep brown pupils that locked onto you. She had the eyes that made a man want to look right through them to see what was inside. Franshell was hard, teak hard, and to get this far she knew what men were about and what they liked. But he still wanted to kiss her, and he was fairly sure she wanted him to. But that had to wait. And at that moment, he could see her standing on a beach in Cornwall, eyes glistening and hair blowing in the breeze, both of them alone. That was good enough for now and motivation enough to get moving again.

"I need to check the fuel gauge. We got an extra can in the back."

Mortimer moved around to the driver's side and pulled open the door. It did not creak or make a sound but something triggered a swooshing sound high above in the trees on the slope. The crows and rooks were suddenly evacuating their homes. No longer interested in fuel levels, Mortimer reached down and grabbed the semi-automatic weapons out of the passenger footwell. He managed to throw one to Franshell, who caught it cleanly with both hands. But they were too late. From the trees on the far right came the voice.

"Drop your weapons; you are surrounded."

It was the electronically enhanced voice of Intelligence Officer Downton of the Shield. He sounded stilted and more breathy than usual, like he had been running or was maybe a little nervous.

"Raise your arms and kneel to the ground. Now." The voice sounded more confident now.

Mortimer raised his weapon to his shoulder and slipped off the safety catch. He trained it on the direction of the voice. A bullet whistled over the top of the Land Rover and then another smashed a hole in the side window. Another ricocheted off the ground a few feet in front of Mortimer. He took the hint and threw his weapon to the ground and Franshell dropped hers. Both then complied with the second part of Downton's instructions as requested. Mortimer remained by the side of the Land Rover. Franshell faced him but was exposed, left out in the open. She stared at Mortimer, who felt the fear in her bulging eyeballs. Mortimer emptied his mind and looked away at the trees and concentrated on the source of the gunfire.

Straight ahead of the Land Rover, towards the trees, three Shield soldiers in their distinctive mottled battlefield camouflage moved out of the undergrowth into the open with weapons clasped across their chests. Three more followed from another section of the trees further down. Then, behind them, five grey uniforms of the Shield Police appeared. The lead group slowed to a halt close to Franshell. One of the soldiers turned his head back, as if he were waiting for someone. The other soldiers and policemen took his cue and also stopped and waited. Inside the undergrowth, Downton was struggling along the path that Franshell had taken earlier. To ease his passage through the brambles he swivelled his hips from side to side, like a salsa dancer who had spent the day locked in a freezer. It might have only been a minute or so of standing around, but it seemed a lot longer when the flustered, red-faced intelligence officer made it into the open ground. He took out his pistol with an extravagant sweep of the arm and held it awkwardly at his side. His men moved forward again.

Mortimer recognised the red Vs on the camouflaged collars as men from a grenadier brigade. The grenadiers were one of the elite military formations that had fought with Mortimer at Derby. They were volunteers, zealous supporters of the Shield regime and not the scum of Europe. Even though they were better equipped, the grenadiers had vacated the football stadium as soon as the heavy US bombardment took its toll, leaving Mortimer and the special convict units to cover their retreat. They had been sacrificed in order to preserve the grenadiers for another day. Although he received the Oak Cross for ensuring a successful retreat and getting most of his men out alive, that experience made him realise he was nothing but cannon fodder for the

Shield. And how ironic it was that the grenadiers were back again to try and shorten his life. They might even take some direct responsibility this time.

The burliest grenadier approached the kneeling Franshell and grabbed the end of her hair from behind. She yelped as he yanked her head, toppling her backwards towards him. She then screamed properly as he started to drag her by her hair towards the Defender. Her legs splayed and kicked out in both directions as she struggled against the bully.

"Move yourself, beetch. Over to the other traitor," snarled the grenadier in a heavily accented French version of English.

Franshell got the message. She used her arms and thighs to lever herself over the soft, rooty ground to ease her movement and the pain in her scalp. Mortimer quietly seethed inside but knew he could do nothing,

"It's always the women with you, Joubert. Leave her."

Downton stood there, unimpressed, with his hands on his hips, trying to look like he could command this group of frontline atrocity-hardened veterans. Joubert released Franshell's dark mane and left her next to Mortimer.

"Sir…" He turned and glared at the intelligence officer. Not quite insubordination but a lack of respect that was certainly clear to the intended recipient.

"What is it with you Frenchmen…"

Mortimer thought it was the right time to reminisce.

"Hey… you're a grenadier, aren't you…?" Mortimer spoke up.

"Yes," the Frenchman replied.

"Were you at Derby? Fighting the Yanks… Did well, the grenadiers, that day…"

The other grenadiers now joined the throng. The Frenchman

raised his eyebrows, more than a little taken aback by this strange enquiry.

"I hope you've all been sent new underwear since your famous retreat. Big tough guy, eh, with unarmed women."

Mortimer gave it his all to distract the burly beast. The Frenchman leered at Mortimer and his eyelids flickered in anger. He propelled himself towards the kneeling Mortimer.

"Stop..." But before Downton could squeal any further command, the Frenchman, Mortimer and everyone else there felt a long shadow fall over them from behind the Land Rover. The shadow was dark enough to stop the raging bull in his tracks.

"What is this?" the voice bellowed in contempt. "Fucking amateur dramatics show."

From the other side of the Land Rover, Hendrick sat bolt upright astride a Hunter, with his two bodyguards fixed on equally impressive steads.

"Commissioner, sir... we have captured the renegades... sir." Downton spoke up.

"Yes, that's why I am here." Hendrick sounded tired.

The Shield commander and his two bodyguards had entered the clearing from the road and along the track.

Hendrick was clad in battle-ready camouflage, from shaven head to toe. Unlike the grenadiers, his face was streaked in lines of light-green camo paint underneath brown-and-yellow smudges dotted from his forehead down to his neck. Only his black eye patch was not coloured for combat. He looked like a druid high priest ready to lead a human sacrifice deep inside the forest.

He dismounted and moved into the centre of the gathering, between Downton's group and his captives.

"Usually, we like to bind their wrists in this situation."

"You two, now…" Downton turned to the nearest policemen.

None of the grenadiers moved, but two grey uniforms dashed towards Mortimer and Franshell. Mortimer stretched his arms forward. Franshell immediately followed. This made it easier for the policemen to wrap the thin black plastic straps around their wrists. And as Mortimer had learnt to his cost when taking prisoners who did not resist, this sometimes meant that that the ties were not always applied as rigorously as expected. Two US marines had managed to shoot their guards and escape after supposedly being securely manacled at Derby. Maybe it had been the incompetence of his unit that saved them; the US marines may have reported that they were not worth the cost of the ordnance required to wipe them out in a single strike. Or maybe they thought they had been manacled inexpertly on purpose, to allow them to escape from probable execution later. Whatever, it was no surprise really. Half the unit were stoned and the other half were mentally shredded and might as well have been flying in a haze after the three-day US bombardment in the city centre that had driven them to the outskirts at Pride Park.

Job done quickly, the policemen fell back into line behind Downton.

"Very good… Now, you two."

Hendrick squatted down and faced his prisoners, eye to eye. His slightly oversized green-brown camo tunic rode up and bulged above his waist, and the collar now engulfed his neck. With his painted head he looked like a giant toad inspecting his prey.

"I am taking you two into the woods up there and then allow you to dig your own graves." Hendrick nodded in approval of his own decision.

"Very thoughtful. I always loved gardening."

Mortimer glared into Hendrick's one eye.

Hendrick smiled at the joke. Franshell did not catch it or even hear the bit about digging her grave. Her head was now filled with the dawn sky and the green haven on the ridge; she wanted to go back there. If this was to be her last conscious thought then it seemed right. The realisation of her imminent death tried to burst through her consciousness but the sun was just too bright.

"Up we get." All three stood up together.

The one-eyed overlord, with his acolyte in tow, led the column into the trees and up the slope. Both captives were kept in the middle behind the policemen whilst the grenadiers protected the flanks and rear. One of the bodyguards was left behind to look after the horses. Once they reached the top of the ridge, the execution party continued northwards as the canopy layer thickened. Older trees, like beech, horse chestnut and oak, took over and replaced the conifers.

Hendrick stopped at a junction, where a new path dropped down the other side of the ridge. He silently raised his arm to bring everyone to a halt and took out his compass. After a few seconds, he nodded and veered off onto the new path. For once, he justified himself to Downton.

"We'll do it down here. I can see a glade down there."

"Of course. Done and dusted by nightfall, sir."

Mortimer continued to twist and turn his wrists in the tie, purposefully low in front of his groin, to avoid drawing attention. He had been trying to loosen the ties since they had left the car-park. It also helped that Franshell walked directly behind him rather than one of the guards. But she was nearly stepping on his heels. She had to slow down. He turned his head around and hissed under this breath.

"Slower... slow down."

The presence of Joubert directly behind her motivated Franshell to maintain a decent pace. But she now stopped in her tracks.

"What's up... lady? You've gotta keep moving or you'll miss your death."

Joubbert laughed out loud like an idiot. No-one else joined him.

"It's getting darker and we need it." Mortimer hissed again, not really sure whether Franshell heard him. Franshell cleared her head and slowed down, even though Joubert felt closer.

The daylight was drawing in and the canopy above was changing from dark green to brownish-black, the thick branches increasingly silhouetted against the grey sky.

After another half a mile or so, the trees started to thin and a wide glade opened up in front of them, as Hendrick expected. Soft, rooty soil around the edge gave way to occasional clumps of ferns that had broken out of the trees before a round open space of wild grass. The other side of the glade gently lipped upwards to a mud bank that formed a cliff edge overhanging a steep drop to a tree-filled gorge below.

Chapter 43

Hendrick strode into the middle of the glade, followed by his acolyte. He stopped where he thought the middle was and stamped his heel into the short, spongy grass. He sliced a chunk of it out of the surface with ease.

"Good. Let's do it." He nodded at Downton, who looked up at the sky. It would all be over by nightfall.

"Bring the prisoners forward," Downton shouted to the uniforms at the side, waving his arm towards the centre.

Joubert grabbed Franshell by both her shoulders and drove her into the glade like a farmer rushing a reluctant cow into the abattoir. Franshell relaxed her body, making herself as heavy as possible for the French lout before she was forced inevitably to the ground a few metres in front of the officers.

Mortimer took it upon himself to march into the middle with both arms raised, still clinched together in the tie. The other guards let him enter the ring unmolested. He concentrated on the mud bank beyond Hendrick and Downton and saw the treetops poking up in the distance. He guessed it must be a steep drop, about twenty to thirty metres from the middle, but it was the only chance they had. He stopped next to Franshell, who now raised herself to her feet. Downton moved away, back to the uniforms at the side, and started calling impatiently.

"Spades, get the spades," the intelligence officer shouted to the side.

Two policemen, red-faced and sweaty after their hike in the

woods, ran past the returning Downton, one carrying two lightweight trench spades in each hand. The policeman carrying the spades reached the centre first and dropped a spade at the feet of Mortimer and Franshell. The other uniform slit the ties around their wrists. By now, Hendrick's two bodyguards had appeared at their master's side with their pistols drawn. Without waiting to be told, both policemen ran back to the edge of the glade. Hendrick moved closer to Mortimer and Franshell.

"Both of you were given a chance but you both refused. So pick up your spades and dig your graves," Hendrick commanded in a bored, matter-of-fact tone.

"Always a performance for you. Isn't it. Death," Mortimer started.

"Ending life is not a trivial act. We need to remind ourselves of that."

"Speak for yourself," Franshell piped up.

"The ground is soft. You've got ten minutes each. No more."

Franshell picked up her spade and pressed it hard into the ground with her right foot before easily lifting then scattering a lump of soft black earth away to her side. Head down, she moved the spade a few inches along and repeated the action a little faster. Within a few minutes, she had cut out a crevice about the length of her body. She was digging in a hurry, Franshell wanted it to end soon. A bullet to the neck was quick and a humane way to go. And there were worse places to sleep in the ground than amongst these trees. Unnerved by her haste, Mortimer scratched at the ground with all the vigour of an elderly archaeologist who knew there were extremely precious artefacts inches below the surface.

"I will shoot you anyway, Mr Mortimer. There really is no way out this time."

Hendrick then turned around and sauntered over to join the huddle of grenadiers and policemen at the edge of the grass. Both bodyguards remained with their pistols ready if required.

Mortimer started to use the spade as awkwardly and as inefficiently as he thought he could get away with. He let the earth slide off the spade back into the body-hole area that was forming slowly. He knew this resistance was pointless: Even if he took down the nearest guard with his spade, the other would shoot him dead immediately. And Franshell was certainly not thinking along these lines. Although the light was falling, it was still not dark and the mud cliff edge was too far away. He would be shot down, heavily wounded at best before he could tumble down the other side. And how the hell was he going to bring Franshell with him? It now looked like she had nearly finished the job, which did not help the situation.

All Mortimer could do was look up to the sky and at that moment, the nearest bodyguard fell to the ground with an arrow stuck in the side of his skull. The other guard turned to lean over him and at that moment Mortimer lunged forward with the spade, striking him on the temple. Even Franshell stopped digging when the second guard went down. Mortimer belly-flopped down into his pre-dug grave. For a split-second, he wished he had made a bit more progress, but the arrow told him who had arrived.

"Down… lie down," he hissed at Franshell.

"Hey…" shouted one of the grenadiers.

But it was too late. Two grey uniforms at the side of the huddle took arrows to their heads and chests and instantly collapsed to the ground. Then a grenadier hit the ground, clasping an arrow that had punctured his side. The huddle broke and the grenadiers formed a kneeling semi-circle around Hendrick. But the policemen remained standing and drew their weapons and fired into the trees, at nothing in particular. Then a volley of arrows discharged from both sides of the glade took down most of the grey uniforms. The grenadiers opened up in the direction of the arrows. It was a perfect setting for an ambush. Franshell lay flat in her unfinished grave; fear and utter confusion filled her mind. She pressed her body hard into the ground, imploring the earth to swallow her up forever.

Four long-bearded men armed with axes and spears charged into the glade from near the entrance. But the twenty-first century showed its advanced technology and mowed them down before they could reach Hendrick.

The sound of the marauders raised Mortimer to his feet.

"Get up. Follow me," he shouted at Franshell, still glued to the ground. He pointed at the mud bank in front of them. They had to move now and use the cannibals as well as the gathering gloom as cover. Mortimer sprinted ahead, torso bowed as low as he could whilst lifting his legs as fast as he could. Franshell forgot her fear and scurried after him. As Mortimer closed in on the edge he tripped on a tree root and sprawled into the ground on his injured shoulder. But the momentum bounced him into a desperate crawl, knees and elbows pumping him towards the drop.

Franshell swerved past him but did not realise that the ground would soon become thin air. Mortimer lunged at her ankle with his right arm to slow her down and caught her enough to make her stumble. Although she could now see the ground disappear a few metres ahead, she did not want to stop. But as she readied herself, the soft earth bank gave way before she reached the edge. Feet and legs first, she slid down the bank like a toboggan with broken brakes and broken steering. Mortimer frantically followed a few seconds later, face first and arms flailing like a man trying to swim badly in the air.

The drop over the scarp was probably no more than twenty to thirty feet, enough for you to feel sore but not enough to cripple you significantly, especially if you were being followed by cannibals. Franshell bumped down the mud wall, over broken roots and tree stumps. Her tunic and trousers were shredded, her skin scratched and bruised, her back and sides felt like she had run a gauntlet of ten crowbar-wielding maniacs. But in that moment of pain she knew she wanted to live. She got to her feet and lurched and stumbled as fast as she could into the clump of fir trees ahead. Fortunately, Mortimer missed the broken trees and nosedived into the soft, rooty mud midway down the slope then rolled down to the bottom. The shock of the cold, dank puddle that welcomed his face sparked him back to his feet. He then careened into the trees ahead and tried to follow Franshell.

Hendrick knew their position was lost when another volley of arrows felled most of the grenadiers. Unlike their colleagues in the police, who panicked at the sight of their medieval wounds and stopped using their weapons, the grenadiers who were still alive continued to unload their weapons on the advancing cannibals. With the only two elite soldiers who could still run providing him covering fire in a backwards retreat, Hendrick dashed across the glade into the trees at the side. There he pushed through the undergrowth and slid down a shallower slope than that faced by his captives and sprinted into the woods.

Franshell did not stop and wait for Mortimer but kept on running ahead. Although the woods were getting denser, she slalomed the trees with ease and glided over the fallen branches and broken stumps. You thought you were going to die, you accepted it and even tried to prepare yourself. Not that anyone ever told you how.

But then the fates chickened out and you were back again. All the fear that froze her spirit in the glade and the pain that tore into her back and shoulders on her descent was now blasted away by an energy that made her run. And run without any thought in her head other than the ecstasy of being alive.

This meant she felt very little as the bayonet drawn by Hendrick drove deep into her still smarting side flesh. Crouched low behind an unusually thick-trunked pine tree, Hendrick had taken this position to avoid detection from any possible pursuers. Maybe it was the width of the trunk and the low-hanging branches that gave Franshell a misguided sense of security and drew her towards it. Even though she was moving at speed, Hendrick was good enough with a weapon to easily take her down in a single blow. She yelped and buckled instantly to the ground. Then she wailed, a long, agonised yowl of realisation and of regret.

Mortimer could not keep up with the two-legged doe. He wanted to shout her name but that would only attract unwanted attention. Unlike Franshell, he kept to a narrow path to give him some bearing in the gathering gloom. But then he heard her sound nearby, of a woman in distress. He launched himself off the path into the direction of the lament. There was little undergrowth here, just a mud floor strewn with pine needles and tall coniferous trees.

There in the middle distance he saw a human figure standing over something long that showed a speck of light at one end. Franshell may have had golden-brown skin but her face still lit a pale glow against the dark earth. He guessed that it was Hendrick stood over her, legs stretched wide apart and hands on hips, just like the strutting cock of the Lewisham massacre. Mortimer kept close to the trees, sliding in behind one then sliding out and around to get as close as he could to Hendrick. A pile of whitish flint stones lay by a tree; the larger ones looked like weapons from the Stone Age. Mortimer crouched down and picked up the one that would seem to fit most easily in his hand. Flattish and tear-shaped, it took up most of his palm, with a serrated edge at one end poking out of his grip.

Hendrick wanted to watch her die. No cannibals had ventured down the slope, but if they did then he was armed with a loaded pistol and a reasonable knowledge of hiding techniques learnt during his brief time with Shield Special Forces.

"I would like to make this quick, but the trouble you have caused me and my men..."

The Shield man loomed over Franshell as she held her bleeding side and sucked in long, deep gasps of air.

"He really should be here to save you. But alas, Mortimer has left you on your own. The great survivor does that." Pause.

"And I bet you must now be thinking... why, why did I bother...?"

Franshell's breathing quickened and became harder.

Hendrick thought he heard the low crack of a trampled twig behind him and spun round. But it was too late. Mortimer sank the sharp edge of the flint deep into the side of his throat. Hendrick screamed in agony. The shot of pain made his knees start to give way. Mortimer barged him to the ground and then threw himself at the prone master of war. He landed on top of him, waist against waist and with his outstretched right arm ploughed the sharp edge into his face. Again and again. Hendrick gurgled and snorted hard under the blows. He struggled to even groan under the pain convulsing his body. His right arm raised itself in surrender but then quickly fell limp. He now lost his other eye, followed a moment later by his consciousness. But

Mortimer did not stop. He continued to hammer away at the brittle urn of thick bone stew for a few more seconds. Only when his hands got sticky with the blood and ooze from Hendrick's head did he stop.

He sat up over the dead man's chest and then caught the body of Franshell lying nearby. He scrambled over on his arms and knees, but her eyes had gone, so Mortimer pushed down on her chest with his palms to try and pump life back into her. But nothing twitched and she did not wake up. When he saw the bayonet rammed three quarters deep into her blood-soaked side, he felt his own life drain out of him. She would never survive that wound even if she were not fleeing a gang of savages deep in the woods, miles away from any medical facilities. He pulled the bayonet gently out of Franshell and cast it away. He then stood up and realised that the cannibals might be out there. He scanned all around him and saw nothing and heard nothing. If the savages were able to so skilfully ambush a Shield brigade in the open, they would certainly have made their presence felt by now. He moved towards the thick-trunked pine tree and took cover for a minute or so. He wanted to be sure that he was alone.

In that time, he decided to do the honourable thing, the least a man could do for someone who had saved his life. He would bury Franshell as best he could in the woods. Hendrick would be left as carrion, a fitting end for someone who got so much life out of death.

When he had had enough of the heavy, dank silence, Mortimer decided to return to the glade to get one of the spades. He circled around the bottom of the ridge until he was fairly certain there were no cannibals. He also found a dense patch of trees on the slope that could cover his entrance into the glade. He forced himself through the branches up to the edge of the perimeter. There were no cannibals and no dead soldiers in the glade. Even the twenty-first-century weapons were all gone. The only evidence of any human activity was the two shallow trenches and two spades.

Mortimer now felt it was safe to walk into the middle, but to be sure, he wound his way through the trees until he reached the main path. This was the same path that the execution party had followed an hour or so earlier and from where the cannibals had attacked. Here the surface was disturbed by boot-prints going in both directions, treading on each other but also furrowed by thick waving lines, as if something heavy had been dragged along the ground. Mortimer guessed that the cannibals had tethered and dragged their Shield victims, too dead or too wounded to walk. He stared down the path and into the darkness. Too bad that Hendrick had wanted to kill him here; he had brought this end upon himself and his men. But thank God for human savagery at its worst. Mortimer then wandered into the empty execution ground, reached the shallow graves and picked up one of the spades.

He returned to Franshell. This time, he put his back into it, like a professional gravedigger or even a mechanised digger. Even the machines were getting tired of digging graves these days. But maybe grave-digging might earn a man a decent income again, like spear-making or shoeing horses. Three foot was deep enough. Mortimer dropped the spade and moved towards the dead body of Franshell. He dropped to his knees and looked into her eyes. Even in death, those dark brown eyes still seemed to hold a light. The light of an intelligence that had always defied the cruelty, ignorance and corruption of the world in order to find her own way, her own personal moral code, even if she might die. And she had sacrificed herself for him back on the gallows. Mortimer turned away from her eyes and stared at the earth next to her. He was still alive and she was stone cold dead. And this did not feel right. Then a deep realisation gripped Mortimer: There was now something of her inside him. They had never gotten too close, but who knew if they had made it to Cornwall. But she was the only reason he was still alive so she had the right to a piece of his soul.

He scooped up Franshell in his arms and carried her to the grave. He slowly dropped again to his knees and carefully laid her down in the deep trench. He did not look at her for very long before he started to cover her with the loose earth. When he had finished flattening and patting the soft earth with the back of the spade, Mortimer went back to the tree where he had found the flint stone earlier. He picked up five or six smaller quartz stones. He then brushed off the dirt and placed each one in a line equally spaced along the low-lying mound. He did not fashion a cross from branches, knowing Franshell would not care for such a symbol, given her experience of the Christian faith. And why those timeless stones were lying there under the trees, who knew, but they had helped to save Mortimer's life and there was nothing else to signify Franshell's.

All this time, Mortimer had ignored the dead body of Hendrick. But as he was about to leave, he noticed the rather disrespectful proximity of the fallen criminal to the fallen hero. He also eyed a thicket of brambles about twenty metres away. So he grabbed the carcass by its wrists and hauled his ex-tormentor over the bumpy ground like a heavy sack of rubbish until he reached the thicket. There he hurled the body as best as he could into the bed of thorns.

The compass had provided Mortimer with a record of his route into the glade, so he was able to easily find his way back to the Land Rover. The sensor function also showed that there was no human activity nearby, though a purple luminous blob dilated and contracted spasmodically on the compass screen about one mile away, travelling eastwards into the DMZ. Given that a single person was indicated by a dot, Mortimer reasoned this one-centimetre blob must be the cannibal raiding party with their quarry.

Back at the Land Rover, there was no sign of the lone bodyguard or the horses. The sensor told Mortimer that but so did the silvery light of the full moon cast over the open ground between the wooded ridge and the road. Either the bodyguard had fled the scene or he had entered the woods at some stage to find his master. Mortimer thought about getting a torch and examining the ground for hoofprints, but this was not the time to play Sherlock Holmes. He had to leave.

Mortimer climbed into the Land Rover and found the ignition key under the driver's seat. He switched on the lights' full beam and pulled away slowly towards the open gate before he turned left onto the road. The cool night air and probably the absence of Franshell made him shiver for the first few minutes. He did not think he deserved to put the heating on. Anyway, the cold always helped him concentrate in the driver's seat and this time it was necessary to distract him from his racing thoughts, round and round, back to the start, then another lap.

He should be dead now and Franshell should certainly be alive, if he was still here, hurtling through the night. But this time, the savages saved him. Maybe he should go back and dig up Hendrick's body and take it to the cannibals as a thank you present, wreathed in blackberry brambles to improve the taste when heated over an open fire. And why not? If anyone deserved to be eaten, that one-eyed cunt did. And Mortimer should surrender himself to the savages at the same time, because he really did not deserve to be alive with Franshell lying in the ground. At least she was safe now, her spirit set free in the English woodland.

But it had never been about just desserts. We don't get what we deserve; we get what we can. Gather ye rosebuds whilst ye may, but do try and do the right thing. Rise above the fear gnawing away inside us, dragging us down, put there to frighten us; we all know what is right and wrong. We survive on our own terms but we still choose those terms. Even in a world that is all wrong, we make the decision. In the end, all we can ever be is thankful that we are not in the ground yet. And that's what should make us try to do the right thing.

Chapter 44

It was around dawn when Mortimer reached the house owned by the estate of his ex-brother-in-law, Jerry, in the village of Crackington Haven on the north Cornish coast. Jerry had purchased the bungalow as a holiday let from the proceeds of a successful career in vintage taxidermy and big game antiques. Mortimer and Karen had used it a few times for summer holidays before and after the birth of Tom. Unfortunately, a year or so before the US invasion, whilst on a field trip to purchase potential candidates for not-so-vintage taxidermy from a wildlife park in Derbyshire, Jerry was attacked and killed by a lion. Needless to say, the lion did not return the compliment and leave Jerry in any state to be preserved and stuffed.

Mortimer walked around to the back of the house and pushed through the dilapidated back door that led into the conservatory. Although locked, the wooden doorframe had been rotting for years from the damp sea air and was in no fit state to stand up to Mortimer's right shoulder. Inside, everything was left as it had been since anyone had last stayed there. A faded paperback copy of *Rogue Male* by Geoffrey Household lay closed on one of the armchairs. Mortimer swung past the lounge door and headed for the kitchen, an old kitchen from the late twentieth century with an electric cooker and a pantry in the corner.

Mortimer opened the pantry door and smiled. Stacks of canned food: baked beans, carrots, tomatoes, tuna, ravioli, frankfurter sausages, mixed fruit, rice pudding and even potatoes greeted him. You did not need total social economic collapse and war to prepare for an apocalypse in Cornwall; just live in a village without a shop, many miles from the nearest town. He moved over to the electric cooker and turned the large white dial to "On", in the middle of the control panel that hung over the oven door. And the red light next to the dial switched on. Thankfully, the only concession to twenty-first-century housing fashion, the solar panels on the roof, still functioned, absorbing the abundant sunlight of Cornwall. Mortimer breakfasted well that morning and then fell asleep on the sofa in the lounge. No dreams, no return to the trauma in the woods, just a comfortable nothingness.

A few hours later, he was too far gone to hear or sense the thin man enter the room. Taller and younger than Mortimer, sinewy and shaven-headed and clad in a grey padded jacket decorated with four pockets across his chest and light-green military-issue moleskins, the quiet man sat down in the armchair opposite. After a few minutes, he forced a low cough from his throat. Immediately, Mortimer's head jerked up from the cushion and his eyes burst open.

"Good morning... You really will need to be more aware..."

"Who are you?" Mortimer interrupted before his brain could start to process the man sat opposite him.

"I am surprised you did not hear me come in." Pause.

"I am from the Invisible Army... and I would like to invite you to join us." The thin man's speech was like his movements, quiet and to the point.

Mortimer rubbed the sleep from his eyes and sat up.

"But you don't exist. No one from the Army of the Invisibles was ever picked up."

"We are not invisible and we are not really an army, but I can assure you an organisation exists with the aim to assassinate, eliminate, kill the leaders of the Shield.

"The name is really for the benefit of our enemies. It conjures up images of a ghostly horde marching on the gates of the Shield citadel." The invisible man smiled the thinnest of smiles.

Maybe it was the narrow slits with a pale blue twinkle that served as eyes in his long face, but Mortimer was struck by how nothing warm came from those eyes. At least he looked the part of an assassin.

"And we would like William Alexander Mortimer to join us..." Uttered with all the verve of a man ordering his morning coffee still half-asleep.

"You know, I always thought the Invisible Army, or whatever, was fake, made up by the Shield to cover up their dirty work."

For the first time, the recruiter raised his voice.

"Only a few days ago, we assassinated a Commissioner Erasmus, a Shield ideologue, on his return to Brussels. We are a very small organisation dedicated to physically eradicating the Shield leadership. We are not a political movement or a guerrilla army, like the partisans. The partisans are a welcome distraction for the Shield out in the border areas but are far too reliant on the Americans and will never overthrow the tyranny in London. We are assassins, killers, Mr Mortimer. Our aim is to sever the head of the snake."

"Well, I am no friend of the Shield."

"The Shield movement has gone way beyond the pale of morality and civilisation, as you know personally. If we kill the leaders then the movement will collapse. So, we need good men and women who know how to exercise moral judgement in the most difficult circumstances, who know when it is right to kill. Killing is dirty work best done by decent human beings like you.

358

That is the paradox that creates civilisation, my friend."

"A philosopher. I do like a man who can think," Mortimer continued.

"I am flattered by your offer. I won't ask how you found me, as you seem to know a lot already. But I bet you do know the partisans. And probably a commander called Harper."

"Harper is a good man. We hacked the Land Rover's GPS with his help."

"You're right. He's a damn good man."

And also probably a better employer than the man now sat opposite Mortimer. Mortimer pondered why he didn't stay with the partisans. But truth be told, he had had enough of roughing it outdoors in the eternal damp and cold of the Anglo-Welsh border country. And their days were numbered anyway, at the mercy of both the Yanks and the Shield. Sooner or later, a drone-orchestrated precision strike would take them out of the picture altogether.

"You know, you sound a bit like the last man who offered me a job. I turned it down and it nearly got me killed. S'pose I'd better accept." Pause. "But if I don't…"

"Then I will say goodbye and leave you. Eventually, the Shield will track you down and kill you. It's your choice." The quiet assassin got quieter again.

"An offer I cannot refuse."

Mortimer beamed a smile at the quiet man.

"We could sit around and chat, look out and admire the view. But you're probably right: the Shield will find me… But one thing: do you have a name?"

The quiet man shook his head slowly.

"That will come later. Just think of me as your guardian angel."

Mortimer and his guardian angel then left the house via the broken back door, went round to the front and climbed into the Land Rover. This time, Mortimer was the passenger as he was driven away from the coast along empty country roads into central Cornwall. Being an angel, his driver knew the way and did not need to use the satellite navigation system. And Mortimer did not feel the need to ask any more questions so fell back into a doze.

About thirty minutes later, the Land Rover turned onto a muddy track that led to a cluster of roofless but walled buildings, disused since the local tin mine closed in the last century. From there, Mortimer was led to the local operational base of the Invisible Army, an underground tunnel system originally dug from a mineshaft by the local auxiliary unit during World War Two. These were the stay-behinds, the secret cells who would have continued the fight against the Nazis in the event of a successful invasion in 1940. Nearly one hundred years later, the same base was being used by a new underground army resisting a tyranny that came from within the British Isles. And Mortimer would become a part of that struggle.

The End